Charles Lever, Hablot Knight Browne

The novels of Charles Lever

Charles Lever, Hablot Knight Browne

The novels of Charles Lever

ISBN/EAN: 9783337046170

Printed in Europe, USA, Canada, Australia, Japan

Cover: Foto ©Andreas Hilbeck / pixelio.de

More available books at **www.hansebooks.com**

THE CONFESSIONS OF HARRY LORREQUER

Vol. I

BOSTON,
LITTLE, BROWN, and COMPANY.

THE NOVELS OF CHARLES LEVER.

With an Introduction by Andrew Lang.

HARRY LORREQUER.

WITH ILLUSTRATIONS BY PHIZ.

IN TWO VOLUMES.

VOL. I.

BOSTON:
LITTLE, BROWN, AND COMPANY.
1894.

OF·THE·LIMITED·EDITION·OF
·CHARLES·LEVER'S·NOVELS·
·TWELVE·HVNDRED·AND·FIFTY·
·SETS·HAVE·BEEN·PRINTED·FOR
·AMERICA·

NVMBER·

THE NOVELS OF CHARLES LEVER.

THERE are two kinds of literary immortality; authors, dead and gone, as far as the life of earth is concerned, may inhabit either the Paradise or the Limbo of men of letters. The works of the fortunate dwellers in the former region are read by later generations, as Fitzgerald said, "for human pleasure." It does not follow, of course, that even they are very widely read in proportion to the number of people who now have the art of reading thrust on them. No sanguine anticipation of reformers has been more sadly disappointed than the hope that a vast increase in the numbers of people who can read, would mean a large increase in the numbers of people who can read good books; perhaps even the opposite result has followed compulsory education. While the multitude study cheap journals of politics, gossip, scraps, and sport, the more highly educated minority perhaps read literature less than they have done since the invention of printing. Thus even the dead authors who dwell in the Paradise of their class, and who are actually "read for human pleasure," are not very widely read after all.

Year by year we see the numbers of the more fortunate immortals diminishing. Reputation after reputation grows dim and distant; author after author
slips from among those who are read for pleasure, and
declines on the estate of those who are perused only by
the curious, the professional book-worm, or are valued
for their scanty nuggets of historical information.
Even the most popular and amusing writers of the
past endure this change. Among poets of old times,
Shakspeare is almost alone in the Paradise of Poets.
They who read Marlowe, "The Faery Queen," "Paradise
Lost," the plays of Jonson, of Webster, of Ford, or even
the "Canterbury Pilgrims," are the few, the remnant of a
remnant, the minority of a minority. The general world
of readers is ignorant of Richardson, is unfamiliar, to
say the least, with Fielding. These authors hover on the
limits of the Limbo and the Paradise, but they tend
towards the Limbo. Scholars, inquirers, students, know
them; the world knows them not. Of the older novelists, Miss Austen and Scott alone keep their place in
the general affections; Miss Ferrier, Miss Burney, Miss
Edgeworth, are among things "half remembered and
half forgot." Among great writers of the early Vic-
torian period, Dickens has apparently lost his vogue
rather among the "cultured" than among the mass of
readers. Thackeray was never really popular; he still
has, he will always have, his circle of adorers. Trollope
is nearly forgotten; the vogue of George Eliot is
diminishing.

How fares it then, we may ask, with an author once
so popular as Lever, whose collected novels are here

again offered to the public? In one respect Lever is lucky; like Dorat of old, *il se sauve sur les planches.* The illustrations of Lever's early editions, the designs of Hablot Browne, are valued by amateurs, and these editions are assiduously collected. Yet we can by no means say, as was said of Rogers's "Italy" with the engravings after Turner, that Lever "would be dished, but for his plates." In his earlier manner, in his romances of war and sport, Lever was really writing for two very loyal audiences, for sportsmen and for boys,—we may add, for all men who have some smack of their youth, and a friendly recollection of their non-age; these were true to him, and these will remain true. In this respect Lever's fortunes are like those of a writer more careful, more genuine, more robust, the admirable Captain Marryat.

Time, with the changes which it brings, must always diminish the obvious attractions, and lower the sympathetic powers of every author not on the level of Homer, Shakspeare, Scott, and Molière. Manners and ideas and forms of expression change. New writers, who possess the new ideas, who deal with the new manners, who are masters of the modern touch, will always have the most potent claim on all who live in the day and for the day. To very many critics, as well as to most readers, their own day is everything; all the past is a blank: "the dark ages" come down to about 1870. The central and essential things in human nature seem insignificant compared with the latest notions, manners, and mannerisms. The more the ancient classics are neglected; the more a set of half-educated critics arises, clever, but imperfectly instructed, — the more must novelty seem to be three fourths at least of merit. To critics of this kind "style" (and they will talk much about style) means only the latest experiments in the *précieux*. Now nothing is really so fugitive as "preciosity," yet older writers who were plain and straightforward in manner will be despised, contemned for their very virtues, — contemned in the name of "Art." Few considerable writers deal less in self-conscious word-picking, in research of epithets, in queer inversions, than Lever; hence, in an age when these defects are valued, Lever is likely to be no special favorite of persons who lay claim to "culture." He has his own faults, — the fault of carelessness, of inadvertent repetition. The blemishes which attend all who write from hand to mouth undeniably spot Lever's work, especially when Lever was young, was most truly himself, and was revelling in the genius of high spirits. "Charles O'Malley" was like champagne when it first foamed from Lever's mind; but if the champagne has lost its sparkle? — well, it can never cease to sparkle for those who were lucky enough to make acquaintance with Micky Free and Frank Webber and Major Monsoon, — delightful Major, — while they were young. We have drunk of the King of Spain's sherry, and are neither unmindful nor ungrateful. *Qui a bu boira*, and I still prefer the Major's company, and that of honest Jack Falstaff, to the society of all the prigs, all the pessimists, all the philanthropists, who prose through the new fiction dear to persons of culture. As Tennyson says of "the greater Ape," "I was born for other things," —

not that the Laureate's remark shows an intelligent view of evolution!

Lever, we said, had the genius of high spirits, and high spirits are dead and gone ; it is no wonder! Lever represents the world before the Revolution, before education, refinement, birth, respect for things old, were swamped in democracy. Now there is nothing to be said here, or elsewhere, by me against democracy when once it is settled and clarified. That all men should have their part in whatever is best, that is a noble conception. When it is fulfilled in fact, the New Jerusalem will have come down to men like a Bride. But when the historical process has only reached the point of taking away their share (their exorbitant share) of what is best from those who had it, without conferring it, or anything but discontent, on those who have it not, then the world is in an ill way, and high spirits are scarcely within reach of the reflective man, — of anybody who has lived beyond his boyhood. It is rather an age for Pessimism, and as Pessimism is in vogue, and peasant girls (in fiction) call this world " a withered planet," Lever cannot be in tune with these ideas; we really cannot decorously request the Ibsenite to share our pleasure in Lever. An old fellow reading him again, remembers his early youth, when the Great Duke was his hero, when Charles O'Malley was his love, when, being a very idle little boy, he read Scott, Thackeray, Harry Lorrequer, Dickens, Marryat, Captain Mayne Reid, indiscriminately and assiduously, neglecting Cæsar's valuable commentaries " De Bello Gallico." We were not critical then, and we enjoyed a romance in the "London Journal"—a romance about the wicked Muscovites and the cruel Duke Constantine—almost as much as "Old Mortality." These uncritical days do not return, but time cannot shake our affection for Lever. As it was then, so it is yet with boys, one presumes. On these, I think, the enterprising publisher may confidently rely, on these, and on the generation which read Lever when, like Polixenes they were

> "Lads that thought there was no more behind,
>   But such a day to-morrow as to-day,
>   And to be boy eternal."

If all the world has altered, no region has changed more than Ireland. Poor, miserable in worldly wealth, rack-rented, the people were; but they had mirth, they had wit, they had even a mild kind of content. They took their share of such crumbs of sport as fell from the richer table; they loved a horse and a hound, a lass, a glass, and a song; their Celtic loyalty to birth and blood were not yet wholly ruined, not soured to hatred and envy and longing for revenge. These blessings have now been for long enjoyed in Ireland. Hounds have been poisoned; peasant families have been murdered in bed; "Boycotting" has been invented; and the Interdict revived. These may be inevitable steps in the progress of democracy, but that the Irish peasant was *happier* without them than he is in the day of discontent can scarcely be denied. What he shall be, we know not; what he was, or rather what he seemed to Lever to be, we know with pity and admiration, with melancholy and mirth. This is not a political treatise; but it is evident that the feudal world everywhere, despite its injustice, was a world not widowed of content, was a merrier world than this chaos of Industrialism. Centuries will probably pass before the world settles down to any social steadiness; Lever began to write while it still had a waning semblance of its old organization. He came too late for the mutual massacres of '98; his later works are overshadowed by the nascent Revolution, which it is pretty plain that he cordially detested. The melancholy which Thackeray recognized as the *fond* of the Irish character, and humor are always present in him, despite his rollicking mirth. However, this historical position of his (and this is our point) would give him a place among authors, read not " for human pleasure," but for information about the past, the old reckless and ruinous days of drinking, of duels, of hard living, and hard riding, of ancient loyalty to the clan and the chief. It was all going; it has all gone; it was not a society to admire, or to regret. Whatever happens, it can never return, unless the world goes back to barbaric conditions, and emerges from these on the old lines, as for all we know or can guess the world yet may do. The ruin of Roman civilization by the Northern hordes produced barbarism and then feudalism. Any other ruin of a civilization by other forces, by internal forces, may have analogous results. However, we have strayed far enough from Lever's words, written in an age when Irish society was passing from one form of ruin to another, of which the end is not yet.

Among the lives of authors, Lever's is hardly, to literary readers, one of the most sympathetic; he was so much of a man, so little of a literary man. His character, and the circumstances and accidents of his career account for the qualities of his books; so much reason as that we have for being interested in his Biography.[1]

Indeed, the well-known method of Sainte Beuve, which studies a writer's work in the light of his personality, his adventures, the conditions of his time, has in the case of Lever a very easy and congenial topic. Heredity, climate, environment, early youth, adventures, character, later life, are all very much what we might naturally have expected them to be. It is almost as easy to construct his career out of his novels, as to show that his novels are the natural, inevitable fruit of his character and career. His tales are autobiographical, and are revelations of himself.

Neither career nor character, as we said, is in all points entirely sympathetic. As we study them, in spite of many endearing and admirable qualities in Lever's nature, qualities reflected in his books, we do not invariably feel inclined to admire and applaud. There is an untidiness, so to speak, in his life, and a love of display, which is not congenial either to an Englishman or a Scot. In the eyes of the graver nations which make the but slackly United Kingdom, the character of Lever is typified in his habit of wearing long ringlets! Disraeli also was a ringletted young Hebrew Adonis; Charles Dickens, in his youth, was an Absalom. But we cannot fancy Thackeray or Wordsworth or Scott

____

[1] *The Life of Charles Lever.* Chapman and Hall. London, 1879. By W. J. Fitzpatrick, LL.D.

rejoicing in long love-locks; in that respect the sheriff
of the Forest was no true Cavalier. The impression
of blonde curls, monumental breastpins, cascades of
silk cravat, or white steppes of shirt-front is left by the
descriptions of Lever in his youth. In later life we
hear of him riding about Carlsruhe and Florence, at
high speed, surrounded by his girls with thick chestnut
manes,— a brilliant spectacle indeed, but one which made
strangers at Florence mistake Lever for a circus master!
This enjoyment of display is so un-English that perhaps,
if we would be in the scientific fashion, we may account
for it by heredity and climate. On neither side was
Lever of pure Irish blood; but his mother's family had
long been settled in Ireland. By the same influences
if we please, we may explain the moral purity, as far as
the passion of love is concerned, which marks the novels
of Lever. By the confession of all, the Irish are con-
spicuous for a virtue which is rather deficient north of
the Tweed. Lever himself married the love of his boyhood,— the girl to whom he had carried flowers before
he left school. To her he was all through life devotedly
attached; she was his best critic, and to please her he
is said to have made many an excision in his novels.
Of women (except of a few garrison hacks and matrimonial adventuresses) he speaks always with respectful
and admiring chivalry; his Baby Blake is as innocent
as she is charmingly gay. In the quality of domestic
affection, Lever's life is worthy of all admiration. His
novels, at least his early novels, are full of hard convivial drinking, such as was common in his time; but
there is more of high spirits than of claret or whiskey in

his revels. He thought that his artist, Hablot Browne, exaggerated the uproarious element in his romances. According to his biographer, Lever was almost as fond as Dr. Johnson of the beverage dear to Cowper. But when Phiz stayed with Lever in Brussels, on one occasion, the novelist avers that nine dozen of champagne were drunk in sixteen days. No doubt he was keeping open house; but even before he began to be a novelist he had suffered terribly from gout, and it was with champagne that this misguided physician attempted to heal himself. The Faculty is always changing its mind about gout; but champagne, one believes, is not recognized as " the sovranest thing an earth " for that malady. Among other needless diversions, Lever was at one time devoted to cards. He was a great whist player, like a delightful novelist of our own time, who probably never (as is told of Lever) won £200 at whist in a single evening. The imaginative attractions of *Trente-et-Quarante* and *Roulette* were also strong for Lever; like other people he began by winning, and ended by losing heavily. He was fond of dining well, and would correct at breakfast the *menu* for dinner. All this, and his passion, derided by Poe, for devilled kidneys, we might gather from his novels as readily as from his biography. He lived in an age when it was fashionable for literary men to " rollick ;" the example set by Wilson and the Shepherd in " Noctes Ambrosianæ " was dear to Lever. Now, as Mr. Payes says, " novelists live like other men, but more purely." The rollicking humor is out of fashion ; we wonder at rather than envy these nights and suppers of the gods. In this, as in other things, manners have greatly changed, and we are no longer at the point of view of Irish society about 1840, nor even of English society. In Dickens's novels also there is far more of milk-punch and frolic than a modern taste can applaud; we are obliged to take the milk-punch and the occasional excesses of Mr. Pickwick as historical affairs, like Falstaff's intolerable deal of sack. Our faults are different, and perhaps are less genial than those of our hard drinking, merry ancestors.

In one other respect, besides these matters of incongruous display and exorbitant revelry, Lever fails to win our sympathy. It is the fault of the prig in letters to take himself and his "Art" too seriously. Lever, we think, did not take his art quite seriously enough. It is perfectly right and wise in a novelist to feel that his business is by no means one of the gravest things in the world. In reality it may be regarded as a contribution to play, to pleasure, to intellectual luxury. Fielding, we may be sure, looked on his duty as a magistrate as his main affair; Scott repeatedly avows his preference for the life of action; Thackeray constantly insists that literature is by no means the momentous business which many men of letters more or less consciously take it to be. The wide world wags along with scant regard for letters; even had there been no Shakspeare, the "great cosmic movement" would have been unaffected. Men of letters are scarce higher than parasites at the table of the great toiling world; they are at most like the Homeric minstrel singing in halls of wars and loves that have been. They are worthy of their slice of the beef, and their cup of the wine, and the compliments about the inspiring Muse. But that is all, and it becomes them to be modest about their gift of tale and song. All this we admit, and of the two prefer Lever's negligence, to the conceit of those who are ever prating, like Andrea Fick, of their "h'art." But Lever carried indifference, at least in his early days, beyond the limits laid down by self-respect. "You pay your money and you take your choice," he wrote to his publisher on a question about the whole conduct of a story. He never in these days would take any care; he would alter with the utmost readiness, merely to please a publisher, or to catch the market. For this reason Lever preferred the form of publication in monthly numbers; he had his rose-colored covers, as Thackeray had yellow, and Dickens green. He could ramble at will and alter at pleasure in tales written from month to month, giving prominence to a character, or making it subordinate, as he found that public taste approved or was indifferent. This is fatal to plot and plan. "Pendennis" and "David Copperfield" would have been shorter, better, more concentrated and artistic, had the author not written month by month, always only a month in advance of the press. A wise novelist writes all his book before he hands it to a serial. His amiable easiness Lever carried far beyond the limits of Scott, himself too easily moved by the remonstrances of James Ballantyne. It is difficult always to believe in stories in which the author himself believed so little.

In another way he showed his want of respect for his

own work; he introduced real characters almost without scruple. We are often told that Harry Foker was an actual person, with some others, among Thackeray's people; but we all love Harry Foker, and the original, if he can look down on us now, finds nothing to regret. Dickens, by some deplorable lack of tact, caricatured Leigh Hunt in Harold Skimpole. But Lever seriously annoyed one or two Catholic priests by his exaggerated portraits of them, innocently meant, but disagreeable in their consequences. As to the original of Monsoon, he bought that worthy's consent, and they signed a solemn treaty. But Monsoon's son wanted to challenge Lever to the duel! The novelist even, like other novelists, deliberately introduced people who had offended him as disagreeable persons in his tales. This is not a manly revenge, as the aggrieved ones have no kind of remedy, and not being novelists, cannot retaliate.

These blemishes have to be recognized by any critic of Lever's ways, in life and in art. The good and the bad in his earlier and more popular tales alike spring from his natural high spirits, his Irish recklessness, which has its defects as well as its qualities. His education, his temperament, the company that he kept, all combined to make him what he was, the Harry Lorrequer who lives in his writings.

Charles Lever was born at Dublin, on August 31, 1806. His father, Mr. James Lever, was an Englishman of a Lancashire stock; the family was ancient, but had fallen on evil days. The elder Lever was a carpenter and builder who had emigrated to Ireland, and there, under powerful patronage, had flourished and thriven. Mrs. Lever was a daughter of a Cromwellian family; her people had lived long enough in Ireland to become Irish in many respects, like her son. Charles was a very handsome and lively boy, whose early education was promiscuous. He passed from one flogging schoolmaster to another, distinguishing himself by his practical jokes, and, like Scott, by story telling to his comrades. Like Scott, in the affair of Green Breeks, he was a leader in the wars of school-boys, and was present at a great fight in which the enemy's position was mined by a boyish engineer. Nobody was much hurt, but the police interfered. The persuasive eloquence of young Lever caused the magistrate to take a lenient view of these excesses. A boy named Ottiwell is said to have been the original of Frank Webber; but there are other claimants, and the real Webber was probably Lever himself. He had already fallen in love with his future wife, Miss Kate Baker, lamented in the dedication to his last novel, "Lord Kilgobbin." At the age of seventeen he entered Trinity College, Dublin, where he distinguished himself by practical jokes, ballad singing in the streets (like Fergusson the Scotch poet), and by many of the adventures recorded in "Charles O'Malley." "He drove and rode much," and read very little. He was already fond of horses; and his love of horses was one of the chief causes of rather reckless, but perfectly honest, extravagance in later days. He began to write an occasional paper in Irish magazines as early as his twentieth year.[1] In this casual way, like Scott in Liddesdale, he "was making himself," collect-

---

[1] In *Bolster's Quarterly Magazine.* Cork, 1826.

ing anecdotes, acting adventures to be later described, living with soldiers, barristers, students, studying the lively ragged people of the streets. In 1829, after some slight medical training, he went to Canada as surgeon of an emigrant ship. He wandered west till he joined, and was affiliated to, a tribe (what tribe we are not told) of Red Indians. It was as difficult to leave them as it was in the last century to leave the Gypsies; but by the aid of a friendly squaw Lever managed to give his tribesmen the slip, and to regain civilization, bringing his scalp with him. Traces of these voyages and adventures appear in "Harry Lorrequer," but are more freely used in "Con Cregan; The Irish Gil Blas." In "Arthur O'Leary," too, he draws on this fund of early experience, and in "Roland Cashel." He returned to Dublin, visited Germany, enjoyed student life at Göttingen, saw Weimar and Goethe, and coming back to Dublin, resumed his medical studies and his practical jokes, while he established a kind of Burschenschaft Club. When cholera broke out, and all the misery commemorated in his "St. Patrick's Eve," he went on a medical mission to Clare, thence to Derry, and later to Port Stewart. In all these places he was collecting anecdotes, and studying original characters, who did not always like their portraits. While a country doctor at Port Stewart, he married his boyish love, Miss Baker. But Nature had not fitted him for the part of a rural surgeon, a Gideon Gray. He won admiration, as "the Mad Doctor," by jumping his horse over a turf cart; but he was inattentive at his Dispensary, and finally, he threw up his appointment in a moment of disgust.

He went to Brussels, where he was very unofficially attached to the English Mission. The "Dublin University Magazine" had been started, as a rival to "Blackwood" and "Fraser's," in 1833. It was now in the hands of publishers named Curry and McGlashan, and from Port Stewart Lever had contributed a few articles. He sent the earlier "Confessions of Harry Lorrequer," which began to appear in 1837; his Port Stewart experiences are recorded in "One of them." The "Confessions" were continued from Brussels (1837), and suffered much from delayed "proofs" and lost copy. Lever had really no chance of writing carefully at this time, even had he been so inclined, which, by his own admission, he was not. "Harry Lorrequer," by an accident to his despatch, had two distinct conclusions. Mr. Hablot K. Browne was already illustrating his works, though they had not yet met in the flesh.

Mr. Browne's etchings were not without influence on the popularity of Lever's works. Our ideas of Micky Free, Father Tom, Corney Delany, and the other heroes are inseparably associated with Mr. Browne's designs. They almost out-rollic the rollicking text, as Lever declared; but when more seriously romantic matter was in hand, Mr. Browne could illustrate it with spirit and effect. His horses especially are just the spirited animals in which Lever and his characters rejoice. Mr. Browne was nine years younger than Lever, in 1839 he was but twenty-four. It was in 1836 that he began to draw for Dickens, in his rare tract, "Sunday under Three Heads." His horses he had studied from his boyhood, with the Surrey hounds. In vivacity, rapidity, exuberance, grace, and occasional gloom, as in "The Cholera Hut" in "St. Patrick's Eve," he was very much akin to Lever, and admirably fitted to be his artist. From 1839 to 1863, he illustrated fifteen of Lever's novels, from "Harry Lorrequer" to "Luttrell of Arran."

"Harry Lorrequer" is little more than a humorous note-book; the author, like Malory's Knights, "rides at adventure" through his reminiscences. The public enjoyed it; the critics held aloof or sneered. Lever was always very easily elated by kindly criticism; as for that which is unkindly, he begged his publisher to send him none of it. Assuredly the critics did not make his reputation. Maginis at first attacked him for inaccuracy; later he changed his note. Lever's was not the talent most congenial to Poe. More different minds and tastes there could not be, and Poe criticised him severely. Thackeray was doubtless Lever's most careful and candid judge; and Thackeray, as we shall see, appears to have been of influence in his change of style.

"I wrote as I felt," says Lever, — "sometimes in good spirits, sometimes in bad; always carelessly, for God help me, I can do no better." A greater genius has made a similar confession.

"Charles O'Malley" was written at Brussels, when Lever, as he said much later, was "as I have ever been, very low in fortune. The success of a new venture was pretty much as eventful to me as the turn of the right color at *rouge-et-noir*. At the same time I had then an amount of spring in my temperament and a power of enjoying life which I can honestly say

I never found surpassed." Thackeray is said to have remonstrated with him on his unthrift, but in vain.

This unusual gift, the exuberant enjoyment of life, makes the charm of Lever's early works. He enjoyed life in very mixed society at Brussels: there was a military English colony; there was Sir Hamilton Seymour, to whom Lever owed much in the way of anecdote and pleasant society; there were reckless fugitives from England; there were noble persons on their travels. One of these Lever elaborately entertained; how he was repaid we may read in " The Book of Snobs."

Careless as it is, containing many repetitions, " Charles O'Malley " remains Lever's masterpiece. It is no mere budget of anecdotes; it is a historical picture of the old, gallant, drinking and duelling Ireland, between '98 and Waterloo. The mirth, the wretchedness, the loyalty, the high spirit, the gay audacity in peace and war, are not exaggerated. The characters live and endure. Considine, O'Shaughnessy, Micky Free, Frank Webber, Baby Blake, Power, they are all our friends immortal. The heroine is not much more interesting or memorable than most other heroines; the men, with their songs, dances, and duels seem imperishable, enrolled among the deathless creations of romance. The campaign is as brilliantly and perhaps as accurately described as if Marbot had held the pen. The Duke himself wondered how Lever got his information: much of it he got from Monsoon, whom the Duke had so nearly hanged. Lord Londonderry also contributed an account of the battle of the Douro. Yet " Charles O'Malley " was almost unnoticed by the reviewers, though the historian of the

Peninsular War, Sir William Napier, was among Lever's most grateful admirers.

"Jack Hinton" followed,— an attempt to show how Englishmen misunderstand Ireland; largely by reason of the Irish love of *blague*, of hoaxing, and through the indomitably dramatic character of the Irish. Being cast, as it were for a part, they play it with a vigor of conviction which may almost deceive themselves, and often does deceive the Saxon. When Thackeray was in Ireland, shortly after this date, people said that he seemed reserved and on his guard as it were. For this caution only Irishmen can blame him. They confess that they delight to mystify; they condemn us for our gullibility, and again for not being gullible. They are difficult people to please.

Father Tom, in "Jack Hinton," is understood to be a portrait, or caricature, of Father Michael Comyns, whom Lever had known in Clare; Paul Rooney was also a portrait; and to the pathetic figure of Tipperary Joe, Lever lent most of the pathos. The real Tipperary Joe asked to be paid as a model, and we trust that Lever was generous.

Some hopes of political patronage brought Lever to Dublin in 1842. He was disappointed, gave up his profession, and for a few years edited the "University Magazine." His house at Templeogue, near Dublin, was as hospitably noisy for some time as if Dumas had been the occupant. Lever was not a good editor, probably he lost manuscripts; he could not endure the endless attempts of the impossible and unabashed amateur. 'Volunteered contributions were seldom, or never, of any value; there was constant trouble with their authors. That wandering hero, Arthur O'Leary, now occupied Lever with his adventures and reflections; "Tom Burke" was begun, and Thackeray made Lever's acquaintance at Dublin.

He found him unpopular with the Nationalists. Their contention was that Lever gave a false impression of Irish character: the Irish were an oppressed people of serfs panting for freedom; Lever made them light-hearted like himself. It is really the old story of the two sides of the shield. The Nationalist, the dark side, has been presented to the world for long, and long enough; it was the other side that Lever drew, till his memories of the Cholera year, his pity, his indignation, were expressed in "St. Patrick's Eve." Perhaps the best illustrations of Irish character are to be found in Miss Edgeworth's novels (she lived to applaud and encourage Lever as her example had stimulated Scott) and in "Barry Lyndon." But "a stranger intermeddleth not," to the satisfaction of the natives, with Irish character, with the character of any sensitive people. In England we do not care much what our own or foreign authors say about us. "In the bowels of Christ believe that you may possibly be mistaken," said Cromwell, with much humor, to certain religious politicians. We believe that we may be very much mistaken, and that if mistakes are made about us, it is natural and not very important. In Ireland, and indeed elsewhere, he who tries to sketch national traits is less leniently judged.

In 1844 Thackeray wrote on Lever's novels in "Fraser's Magazine." He averred that melancholy was the basis of the humor, as surely it always is. "From ' Castle Rackrent' downwards, every Hibernian tale that I have read is sure to leave a sort of woeful, tender impression." "I have always been surprised, while the universal English critic has been laughing over the stirring stories of Harry Lorrequer, that he has not recognized the fund of sadness beneath .... He *will* have the sham Irishman in preference to the real one," — this is just what Lever's Irish opponents were saying. His gayety, like all Pantagruelism, is " gay in despite of Fortune," as Rabelais declares ; but how else can mortals be gay ? *Sursum corda* is not the least manly of mottoes.

In Ireland, we are among a fitful people, — a people never fortunate, never at peace. O'Connell had been thundering at Lever in his speeches ; " from the 'Nation' you would fancy," says Thackeray, " that the man is a stark traitor." Envy, no doubt, as Thackeray said, inspired some of the critics ; no one fell foul of Lever till the publisher sold twenty thousand of his books. The enemy even objected to his military chapters as if *they* had never glorified " the Irish at Waterloo, the Irish at Fontenoy, the Irish at Seringapatam, and the Irish at Timbuctoo."

For the rest, Thackeray found that Lever's tales " show no art of construction ;" that his heroes are like Irish copies of Scott's heroes (no one knew better than Sir Walter that his heroes were not his strong point) ; that Lever shows " an almost womanlike delicacy, and amidst all the wild scenes through which he carries his characters, and with all his outbreaks of spirit and fun, he never writes a sentence that is not entirely pure." As for Hablot Browne, while praising his horses, land-scapes, and girls, Thackeray avers far too roundly, that "his humor is stark naught; ay, worse." What took Thackeray most in "Tom Burke" was the desolation of the old country-house near Athlone. He blamed Lever for calling his villain (by a pure accident of ignorance) Amédée Pichot. Monsieur Pichot was the author of a "Life of Prince Charles Stuart," which Thackeray calls "excellent" (I have never succeeded in seeing it), and had been a friend of Scott, as he was a friend of England. "It is a sin and a shame that Harry Lorrequer should have slaughtered Amédée Pichot in this wanton and cruel manner." Many such unlucky uses of real names befell Lever. M. Pichot made the most urbane remonstrance, remarking that he was a peaceful man of the pen.

"St. Patrick's Eve" was one of Lever's next tales. It shows, as his biographer says, that his early Conservatism was waning. "He was as sick of the ignorant stupidity of the high Tory, as he was disgusted with the sordid conduct of the Repealer. His health was bad, his high spirits were dying out, he was attacked by both political parties, and he gave up his magazine and retired to the Continent. Here he wandered about, he lived in eccentric display, he lost money at the Baden tables, he visited many cities. As to his adventures at the tables, we may regard them in the light of what he says more than once about gambling, — not avarice, but the pleasure of backing his luck was his motive. Then he settled at Florence, where he lived during the revolutionary year of 1848. He obtained a practical sinecure with a small salary, the English consulship at Spezzia, and he boated much in the beautiful bay.   He had grown very corpulent, but was an admirable swimmer.   He had a favorite story of an upset of his boat; an Italian officer praised the vivacity of his fancy, for though he often told the tale, he always told it with new incidents.   Though Consul at Spezzia, he usually resided at Florence in a very varied society, — political, diplomatic, and pleasure-loving.   Here his style entirely altered.   The change is sometimes attributed to Thackeray's famous parody in "Novels by Eminent Hands."   It is not easy to believe that even the sensitive Lever took that amusing burlesque seriously to heart; he laughed at and enjoyed Mr. Bret Harte's brilliant parody in later years.   More probably he merely yielded to the natural promptings of age and reflection.   Young in mind, in wit, in habit of life, he remained almost to the last; but it was not desirable that he should always be Lorrequer. "Con Cregan" he wrote anonymously, almost in the old vein, while he was publishing "The Daltons" with his signature.   He felt jealous of the praises which "Con-Cregan" won; it was preferred to its more reflective and mature companion.   This verdict really reflected the popular opinion that Lever was far more successful as a romancer than as a *psychologue*, more fitted to paint incident than to analyze character.   This is an opinion which one must confess that one shares: the old heroes live in our memory; the later heroes are comparatively less easily distinguished from the crowd of fictitious personages.   But a critic must be wary in this matter.   We all naturally remember best the characters who delighted us when we were young. The Dodds and Daltons, Tony Butler and Lord Kilgobbin came later, to tastes more staled, and to memories less retentive of impressions.

"A Day's Ride, or Life's Romance," written for Mr. Dickens's periodical, did not increase its popularity; Dickens announced the date of its conclusion before-hand, and the public seems to have shared the editor's impatience. The later novels are those of a wearied, though not sated, man who has seen a great deal of life, has known men and cities; who is not soured exactly, but who is a little disappointed. In 1867 the Conservative Government gave Lever the consulship at Trieste, with a better salary; but his life was now cast in uncongenial society, in a place for which he did not care. He lost his son, a young officer whose high spirits emulated, with expensive results, the frolics of O'Malley. Memories of this lad inspire "Barrington." Lever revisited Ireland, and was gay enough; but his old friends were passing away. The loss of his wife, the love of his youth, was the final blow : —

> "He a little tried
> To live without her, liked it not, and died."

He became drowsy, his rest was near. He passed away in his sleep; and in him died the last voice of the Ireland before the Deluge. He had been a kind of Irish Odysseus, — a man of many wanderings; he had seen much, learned much of men, and had greatly enjoyed. Among Irish novelists, as Miss Edgeworth is too much neglected; as Sheridan Le Fanu never won due recognition; as Maxwell, Banim, and Carleton, and Lover are little read, — he is far the most popular. He has an exotic quality, a cosmopolitan touch, in spite of his sincere attachment to his native land. The melancholy which Thackeray was alone in detecting became very marked in his later works. His favorite character is a wanderer, — one who has known many climes and races. His people we may almost call homeless; they are "evicted" as it were by circumstances, by poverty, or by preference. Like Lever himself, they do not stay in their own place, their own country. No novelist of the kingdom has cast his plots so much in alien lands; the Irish element, the Irish inspiration is always there, but the perpetual voyaging and change of scene in the end produce an effect of restlessness. Military adventure takes the earlier personages abroad; the later are diplomatists, personal economists, or adventurers, always nomads.

One element, concerning which it may be argued whether it contributes to permanence or not, is conspicuously wanting in Lever's fiction. He is a novelist who knows men and life solely by personal contact and experience, not by books. He was never studious, never a haunter of libraries; here he differs from Scott, Fielding, and Thackeray. Widely as Sir Walter knew his countrymen in his own time, he knew them, if possible, still better in their historic past. His mind, like his remarkable library, was a treasure of things old; his books are filled with references to all poetic and dramatic literature; and in these references the literary reader finds an undying charm. Thackeray again, in an early letter, tells his correspondent how much he likes to be occupied with history, — "it is such gentlemanly work." In a book on "The Reign of Queen Anne," which he seems to have contemplated, he would have been far better engaged than on his "Philip," perhaps than on his "Virginians." His Lectures on the Georges, his Lectures on the English Humorists, hardly give a full idea of what it was in his power to do for social, literary, and political history. He who drew James III. in "Esmond" might have given us an invaluable study of that singular, that unfortunate, and finally that resigned and sympathetic prince. Few things in history are more touching than his later letters, — his "ingeminating Peace, Peace," to his brawling adherents; his letters of hopeless wisdom and tenderness to his "dearest Carluccio," the wayward Charles. Here, in a world he knew so well, was matter for Thackeray. Even in his lightest work his knowledge of the great literatures animates the whole; he is an admirable critic as well as a creative and analytic genius. He seems to have wrought with most pleasure and satisfaction when his novels brought him into the neighborhood of his favorite history, his favorite writers in the past. He has a fragrance of scholarship; in his company we are constantly charmed by an ingenious illustration or allusion. The same remarks apply to Fielding. Deeply versed in life, both as a man and a magistrate, he is no less versed in letters, classical and modern. His introductory chapters, though they do not speed on his novel, and so far may be called inartistic excrescences, are rich in criticism of life, of philosophy, of

letters ; and his classical studies declare themselves
freely even in the body of his fictions, in the course of
his narrative.　Lever, on the other hand, lives in the
present, or, as far as Ireland is concerned, in what was
then the very recent past, familiar through vivid tradition.　His attention to politics was keen; he had reflected on them seriously, as may be learned both from
his later stories, and from his collected notes in " Cornelius O'Dowd."　At one time it was intended, by the
Conservative party, to offer him a post as editor of an
important newspaper.　His purpose, as he told Lord
Lyndhurst, was to introduce " as much sense as the
party would stand."　But, as a writer, he lived by
constant immersion in the current of actual life, diplomatic, political, social, in Ireland or in Italy.　We find
scarcely any evidence of interest in the great literatures
of the world.　His mental retrospect is very limited.
Had he been more of a student, one can fancy the
admirable Irish historical novels which he might have
written, illuminating events full of interest, and in
England very little known.　This would have been a
salutary change from the earlier novels, whereof the
vein was obviously in danger of being overworked.
But Lever, so industrious as a writer, was indolent as
a reader.　He had a passion for living, whether in the
various societies which his wit illuminated and glad-
dened, or simply as one who basks in the sun, and con-
templates the beauty of the bay of Spezzia, in his time
unspoiled by the arsenal of the Italian navy.　He was
one of the least bookish of men, though he had done
much modern reviewing for the " Dublin University

Magazine," and had even discussed a writer so alien to his early taste as the *psychologue* Stendhal. For these reasons, which gave Lever much of his brilliance and vivacity, he lacks the reflective and, we may say, the scholarly charm of some other great novelists. His style, admirable in rapid narrative, has no marked attraction of its own, as have the styles of Thackeray, of Fielding, and in our own time of Mr. Stevenson. If he equals Dumas on occasion in clearness and speed, he has none of Dumas's colossal, if not always accurate, knowledge. In short, he writes as a man of the world, rather than as a man of letters ; and this may rank either among his defects or his qualities.

" For sixty odd years he lived in the thick of it,"

he wrote, in a curious quatrain, composed just before his death. He had, indeed, lived in " the thick " of life, always preferring the current where it was swiftest, deepest, and most broken. His voice comes to us cheery and confident, or hollow and mournful, from the stream of waters that have long passed under the bridges of this world, and reached their rest in the sea.

The moral "tendency" and influence of Lever's novels it is hardly necessary to discuss. There is a well-known anecdote of a boy, naturally timid, the son of a widow, who became brave and a good officer in consequence of reading Lever. But he himself knew that he was writing for a class, — for officers, not for the rank and file. He does not pretend to know and love the private soldier, as Mr. Kipling, for example, does. As to his examples of revelry and recklessness, considered as examples, they are out of date, and can harm no man, while they entertain thousands. Nobody thinks of imitating Harry Lorrequer, any more than he thinks of fighting duels. Nothing is left but pure diversion, amusement, and amazement. Healthier novels, of a fancy more delicate, chivalrous, and pure, there cannot be. The later tales, if not exactly buoyant and hopeful, hold by the old virtues, — courage, manliness, kindness, purity of heart. " In every page I have written, in every line, I have ever had before me an ardent desire . . . to serve that cause of truth and morals which can be benefited by the efforts of one even weak and humble as myself," Lever says in an *envoy* to one of his novels. He is not a didactic novelist, does not preach; but actions, in his tales, have their destined moral consequences.

The chief critical point in a discussion of Lever is one which the present writer has an unmanly desire to shirk. I do not, I confess, like to face the question, Is Lever as good in his later as in his earlier style ? Throughout this attempt at an estimate of Lever, I have been avoiding this problem. It is better, perhaps, to be honest, and to say that, as far as one's own taste is concerned, Lever was best at the start. After all, it could hardly be otherwise; youth was his inspiration, youth and gayety. The middle-aged and the old may attempt to deceive themselves; but, in verity, youth is the age for creative and imaginative writing. Fitzgerald thought that nothing of Tennyson's was so good as the poems before 1842. Fitzgerald's own zest for poetry was keenest before 1842; but, even discounting that, Fitzgerald was right. " The first sprightly runnings " are ever the best. Lever himself spoke of " shaking the cask " in his maturity, as George Whyte Melville, talking of his own later tales, said that " the tea was very weak." There are exceptions to the rule that youth is the age of literary creative genius. Scott was a middle-aged man when he published " Waverley," in 1814; but then he had not written novels before: heavy crops, as he said, he had taken off his intellectual soil, but not that particular crop. In Lever's case the crop was always that of prose fiction. It is probable that if Sir Walter had possessed iron health, and had been untroubled by his affairs, he might have gone on delighting the world for ten or fifteen years longer. But Lever's health and Lever's affairs have also to be reckoned with. His fortunes were always hazardous, his health had been undermined for more than twenty years before his death. No one can say that " The Virginians " is as good as " Barry Lyndon," or " Philip " as good as " Vanity Fair ; " " Little Dorrit," and " Our Mutual Friend " and " Dombey " are shakings of the cask, in Lever's phrase, — the runnings are no longer sprightly. We must all grow old, and age must tell ; nor could even Lever's youth of heart inspire him in 1862, or in 1852, as in 1842. It is melancholy to see how his artist ages with him, and to compare the Hablot Browne of " Barrington " with the Hablot Browne of " Charles O'Malley."

Lever's change of style, after all, is less than he supposed it was. His early tales deal with reckless young Irishmen amusing themselves ; his later, with sad old Irishmen who are reaping the fruit of their amusement.

One character Lever drew with much sympathy and repeatedly, — that of the ruined Irish squire.   The hounds
have been given up, the estate is in decay, the manor
house is ruinous, the claret is drunk out, but the wild,
foolish, generous heart is unchanged.   Geoffrey O'Malley,
in the early tale, is more closely studied in Barrington and Peter Dalton.   "They went to the war, but they
always fell;" they set themselves against the constitution of things, and it was revenged on them.   In a novel
far from the foremost rank of Lever's, Barrington, in
his way, is a figure almost as touching as Colonel New-
come.   One result of Lever's continental life is unfortu-
tunate : he saw much of a society, idle, second-rate,
selfish, and ignoble, and he set himself to satirize it.
But his nature was not adapted for satire; he had not the
steady view of the relations of things, real and unreal,
which marks Thackeray.   Thus (to my taste) Lever's
satires of Florentine Society are only too like Scott's
satire of watering-place society, in "St. Ronan's Well."
To Scott, as he knew, satire did not come naturally ; he
had not the right touch, and he was far more prone to
forgive than to be indignant.   So it is, too, with Lever
in "The Daltons," for example.   People may have bad
taste, bad manners, bad tempers, but somehow Lever does
not catch the right tone.   His butts in "The Daltons"
are burlesqued and caricatured.   We decline to accept
Lord Norwood and Haggerstone, and Miss Barrington,
as veracious studies.   Zoe and her brother are overdone,
like Sir Bingo Binks; the very manners are out of
drawing.   Men do not address another man as "my
lord," though he is a peer, or the son of a duke, or what

not. Though Lever fancied he was working a new vein in "The Daltons," an old one in "Con Cregan," "The Daltons" are really of the old vintage. We have duels, war, adventure, gambling; but, alas, the cask has to be shaken, the wine is not clear, the plot is as plotless as ever it had been of old. The best character is still the old character, — Peter Dalton, witty, puzzle-reader, incapable of a sum in simple addition, and with the most remarkable inconsistencies in his social ideas. Yet even about Peter we ask whether an Irish gentleman, however run to seed, really used the idioms which Irish novelists generally reserve for their peasantry. Probably Lever would not have tolerated this license in another, and possibly his own recollections of Ireland may have been growing dim.

It would be a mistake to think that Lever was "written out." His latest novel, "Lord Kilgobbin," of which he pathetically says that he hopes it may be his "last," is by no means the work of a weakened and exhausted brain. There is no touch of "Castle Dangerous" in it, nor of the unpublished "Siege of Malta." The wit, the intelligence, the half melancholy, half mirthful view of the Irish chaos, the intellectual audacity of the past, are all present in "Lord Kilgobbin." The tone is less melodramatic, more plausible, than in some tales ten, or even twenty, years earlier. With "Tony Butler," the novel shows Lever advanced in his art beyond some efforts of what may be called his middle period. But, after all, modern politics and modern diplomacy cannot inspire a romance as it is inspired by Waterloo, or the Douro; and as to politics, "Lord Kilgobbin," is already ancient history. "The Whigs," as they were called in 1872, have quite come up to Lever's expectations.

No student of Lever can afford to neglect the three volumes of his "Cornelius O'Dowd upon Men and Women." These brief essays, which he contributed to "Blackwood's Magazine," in the years about 1862–1865, are, in his work, what the "Roundabout Papers" are in Thackeray's. They are rambling discourses in which he pours out his ideas on things in general. It is noteworthy that they scarcely ever touch on literature. Politics and life are what concern Lever; he speaks very strongly in favor of that most depressing literature, the newspapers. A single number of "The Times" is much more to him than what Mr. Cobden called "all the works of Thucydides." Concerning the life of English exiles on the Continent, Lever had much to say. In England our effort is to do a great many things at the smallest possible cost, and abroad to do without half of them. He did not love the Americans, whose presence made continental life more expensive, — they having money, and "the heart for to spend it," like Larry O'Toole. To quote his remarks would not add to his popularity in the United States. "There is a rough unvarnished Yankee that I like much," he is kind enough to say. "I like his self-reliance, his vigor, his daring earnestness; and I don't dislike his intense acuteness, and I forgive his ill-humor with England." About the Americans whom he did *not* like, such as "the literary gentleman from Boston," he says, "These people are not the nation, they are not even like it." From these considerations he passes to *Parsonitis*, the clerical sore-throat, and vows that it comes from preaching in an assumed voice. One never hears of *Parsonitis*, somehow among Dissenters, or among the Catholic clergy. As a fat man, he detested Mr. Banting, who tried to teach fat men how to become slim. There is only too much slimness, he said; and he denounced all hypochondriacs in a very healthy and energetic way. He praises "tuft-hunters," and prefers the jackal to his lordly lion. He praised duelling as a check on bad manners; it is a common argument, and probably a fallacy. The manners of a bully who could shoot, like Fighting Fitzgerald, were the worst in the world. But Lever is right on one point: one objection to duelling is like our Free Trade,—if all the world were free-traders, it would be very well; if all Europe forswore the duello, it would be excellent. But an Englishman in a quarrel abroad is certainly in an ill position. A year or two ago there were some duels between Englishmen and foreigners; our side did not show the worse shooting. For want of being "ready with the pistol," England, he said, was' in a constant state of national humiliation. Oh the mud-pies we have made and eaten! oh the shameful concessions and withdrawals! But we are an industrial democracy, and must take the consequences of the situation. The days of Pitt and Wellington cannot return, though perhaps we might have found many matters not to our liking in the days of Pitt and Wellington. "Have we anything, have we anybody, to be proud of?" Lever asked himself, and found no satisfactory answer. He had outlived the world he liked. He vowed that England wanted "to be wicked at small cost." He liked to recall old Florentine days, when

Louise of Stolberg (the wife of an English King out of place) lived with Alfieri, and was adored by society. Then people were wicked it seems, at a lordly rate, and Louise of Stolberg, with the Royal arms of England on her plate, "received all that was great and noble and brilliant or, better still, beautiful." I confess that I cannot share Lever's admiration of the Countess of Albany. He found a good word to say even for the Davenport Brothers; if any one remembers who they were, he will find in this a rather extreme instance of Lever's paradox. His general and ruling idea was that the world was becoming very intolerable for himself and his class; that it should be made more convenient for a gentleman. This is a very natural idea, which all of us who are fairly comfortable share more or less consciously; but our poor little protests are not listened to in a friendly spirit by the nature of things and the constitution of the Universe. Lever's protests, at least, were made with wit, with good-humor, probably with some degree of irony; they are still very readable, though in form, and often in matter apparently so ephemeral. Of course Irish affairs are constantly introduced with an odd mingling of prejudices and a genial disregard of inconsistencies and contradictions.

Lever was not a philosopher with a system, any more than he was a man of study and of books. The characters which he knew well, and with which he was in sympathy, he could design admirably. At his lowest point he has energy; he is a born teller of tales, regardless of art, and incapable of penning considerations on "style" and descriptions of his own "method." It is undeniable that a more refined and self-conscious manner has arisen in fiction ; and it is pretty certain that Lever is not at present widely read by men professionally engaged in literature. But the mere aspect of his books in a library shows that they have been well and duly thumbed by that large majority of readers who " read for human pleasure," and like a story for the story's sake. He aimed at no higher or more distant goal, and what he aimed at he attained. He was sensitive, but he was not vain ; and as to his achievements, he had not an atom of conceit or self-consciousness. To be the most popular romancer of his country, beyond all question the most widely read, sufficed for Charles Lever. In literature, as in life, he was an unsophisticated example of the natural man; and while we cannot place him among the six or seven great novelists of the world, — with Cervantes, Lesage, Fielding, Scott, Dumas, Thackeray, Tolstoi, — we owe him a great deal of gratitude and liking.

ANDREW LANG.

PREFACE.

THAT some thirty years after the sketches which form this volume were written I should be called on to revise and re-edit them, is strange enough to me, well remembering, as I do, with what little hope of permanence they were penned, how lightly they were undertaken, and how carelessly thrown together. But there is something still stranger in the retrospect, and that is that these same papers — for originally they were contributed as articles to the "Dublin University Magazine" — should mainly have directed the course of my future life and decided my entire career.

I may quote from a former preface that I was living in a very secluded spot when I formed the idea of jotting down these stories, many of them heard in boyhood, others constructed out of real incidents that had occurred to my friends in travel, and some, again, — as the adventures of Trevanion and the French duellist, for instance, — actual facts well known to many who had formed part of the army of occupation in France.

To give what consistency I might to a mass of incongruous adventure, to such a variety of strange situations befalling one individual, I was obliged to imagine a character which probably my experiences (and they were not very mature at the time) assured me as being perfectly possible, — one of a strong will and a certain energy, rarely persistent in purpose, and perpetually the sport of accident, with a hearty enjoyment of the pleasure of the hour and a very reckless indifference as to the price to be paid for it. If I looked out on my acquaintances, I believed I saw many of the traits I was bent on depicting, and for others I am half afraid I had only to take a peep into myself. If it is an error, then, to believe that in these "Confessions" I have ever recorded any incidents of my own life, there is no mistake in supposing that — without being in the least aware of it — in sketching Harry Lorrequer I was in a great measure depicting myself, and becoming, allegorically, an autobiographist.

Here is a confession which, if thirty odd years had not rolled over, I might be indisposed to make; but time has enabled me to look back on my work, and even on myself as I wrote it, with a certain degree of impartiality, and to feel, as regards both, as the great Paley said a man feels after he has finished his dinner, "that he might have done better."

It is perfectly unnecessary that I should say when and where I wrote these sketches; no thought of future authorship of any kind occurred to me, far less did I dream of abandoning my profession as a physician for the precarious livelihood of the pen. Indeed, their success, such as it was, only became known to me after I had left Ireland and gone to live abroad; and it was there — at Brussels — my publishers wrote to me to request a continuance of my "Confessions," with the assurance they had found favor with the world and flattering notice from the Press. Though I have been what the sarcastic French moralist called " blessed with a bad memory" all my life, I can still recall the delight — I cannot call it less — with which I heard my attempt at authorship was successful. I did not awake, indeed, " to find myself famous," but I well remember the thrill of triumphant joy with which I read the letter that said " Go on," and the entrancing ecstasy I felt at the bare possibility of my one day becoming known as a writer. I have had, since then, some moments in which a partial success has made me very happy and very grateful ; but I do not believe that all these put together, or indeed any possible favor the world might mete to me, would impart a tithe of the enjoyment I felt on hearing that Harry Lorrequer had been liked by the public, and that they had asked for more of him.

" If this sort of thing amuses them," thought I " I can go on forever ; " and believing this to be true, I launched forth with all that prodigal waste of material which, if it forms one of the reasons of the success, is, strictly speaking, one among the many demerits of this story. That I neither husbanded my resources nor imagined that they ever could fail me, were not my only mistakes; and I am tempted to show how little I understood of the responsibilities of authorship by repeating, what I have told elsewhere, an incident of the last number of " Harry Lorrequer." The MSS. which contained the conclusion of the story had been sent through the Foreign Office bag from Brussels, and possibly had been mistaken for a despatch. At all events, like King Theodore's letter, it had been thrown to one side and forgotten. In this strait my publishers wrote to me in a strain that the trade alone knows how to employ towards an unknown author.

Stung by the reproaches — and they were not mild — of my correspondent, I wrote back, enclosing another conclusion, and telling him to print either, or both, as he pleased. Years after, I saw the first-sent MSS., which came to hand at last, bound in my publisher's library, and lettered, " Another ending to H. L."

When the great master of fiction condescended to inform the world on what small fragments of tradition or local anecdote the Waverley Novels were founded, he best exalted the marvellous skill of his own handiwork in showing how genius could develop the veriest incident of a life into a story of surpassing power and interest. I have no such secrets to reveal, nor have I the faintest pretension to suppose the public would care to hear about the sources from which I drew either my characters or my incidents. I have seen, however, such references to supposed portraiture of individuals in this story that I am forced to declare that there is but one character in the book of which the orginal had any existence, and to which I contributed nothing of exaggeration. This is Father Malachi Brennan. The pleasant priest was alive when I wrote the tale, and saw himself in print, and — worse still — in picture, — not, I believe, without a certain mock indignation, for he was too racy a humorist and too genuine a lover of fun to be really angry at this caricature of him.

The amusing author of the " The Wild Sports of the

West," Hamilton Maxwell, was my neighbor in the little watering-place where I was living, and our intimacy was not the less close from the graver character of the society around us. We often exchanged our experiences of Irish character and life, and in our gossipings, stories were told, added to, and amplified in such a way between us that I believe neither of us could have pronounced at last who gave the initiative of an incident, or on which side lay the authorship of any particular event.

It would have been well had our intercourse stopped with these confidences ; but unfortunately it did not. We often indulged in little practical jokes on our more well-conducted neighbors, and I remember that the old soldier from whom I drew some of the features I have given to Colonel Kamworth was especially the mark of these harmless pleasantries. Our colonel was an excellent fellow, kind-hearted and hospitable, but so infatuated with a propensity to meddle with every one, and to be a partner in the joys, the afflictions, the failures, or the successes of all around him, that, with the best possible intentions and the most sincere desire to be useful to his neighbors, he became the cause of daily misconceptions and mistakes, sowed discord where he meant unity, and, in fact, originated more trouble and more distrust than the most malevolent mischief-maker of the whole country side.

I am forced to own that the small persecutions with which my friend Maxwell and myself followed the worthy colonel, the wrong intelligence with which we supplied him, particularly as regarded the rank and station of the various visitors who came down during the bathing season, the false scents on which we sent him, and the absurd enterprises on which we embarked him, even to the extent of a mock address which induced him to stand for the " borough " (the address to the constituency being our joint production), — all these follies, I say, more less disposed me, I feel sure, to that incessant flow of absurd incident which runs through this volume, and which, after all, was really little other than the reflex of our daily plottings and contrivings.

I believe my old friend the colonel is still living; if he be, and if he should read these lines, let him also read that I have other memories of him than those of mere jest and pleasantry, — memories of his cordial hospitality and genial good-nature, — and that there are few things I would like better than to meet and talk with him over bygones, knowing no one more likely to relish a pleasant reminiscence than himself, nor more certain to forgive a long-past liberty taken with him.

If there are many faults and blunders in this tale which I would willingly correct, if there be much that I would curtail or cut out altogether, and if there be also occasionally incidents of which I could improve the telling, I am held back from any attempts of this kind by the thought that it was by these sketches, such as they are, I first won that hearing from the public which for more than thirty years has never deserted me, and that the favor which has given the chief pride and interest to my life dates from the day I was known as Harry Lorrequer. Having given up the profession for which, I believe, I had some aptitude, to follow the precarious life of a writer, I suppose I am only admitting what many others under like circumstances might declare, that I have had my moments, and more than mere moments, of doubt and misgiving that I made the wiser choice; and bating the intense pleasure an occasional success has afforded, I have been led to think that the career I had abandoned would have been more rewarding, more safe from reverses, and less exposed to those variations of public taste which are the terrors of all who live on the world's favor.

Strangely enough, it is only my old doctorial instinct which should suggest the consolation to this passing regret. The life of the physician has nothing so thoroughly regarding, nothing so cheering, so full of hearty encouragement, as in the occasional friendships to which it opens the way. The doctor attains to a degree of intimacy and stands on a footing of confidence so totally exceptional that if personal qualities lend aid to the position, his intercourse becomes friendship. Whether, therefore, my old career gave me any assistance in new roads, whether it imparted to me any habits of investigation as applicable to the full in morals as to matter, it certainly imparted to me the happy accident of standing on good terms with — I was going to say — my patient, — and perhaps no better word could be found for him who has heard me so long, trusted me so much, given me so large a share of his favor, and come to look on me with such friendliness. It would be the worst of ingratitude in me if I did not own that I owe to my books, not only the pleasant intimacies of my life, but some of my closest friendships. A chance expression, a fairly shadowed thought, a mere chord struck at random by a passing hand, as it were, has now and then placed me, as mesmerists call it, *en rapport* with some one who may have thought long and deeply on what I had but skimmed over; and straightway there was a bond between us.

No small satisfaction has it been to me occasionally to hear that out of the over-abundance of my own buoyancy and light-heartedness — and I had a great deal of both long ago — I have been able to share with my neighbor and given him part of my sunshine, and only felt the warmer myself. A great writer — one of the most eloquent historians who ever illustrated the military achievements of his country — once told me that as he lay sick and care-worn after a fever, it was in my reckless stories of soldier life he found the cheeriest moments of his solitude ; and now let me hasten to say that I tell this in no spirit of boastfulness, but with the heartfelt gratitude of one who gained more by hearing that confession than Harry Lorrequer ever acquired by all his own.

One word now as regards the task I am immediately engaged in, and I have done.

My publishers propose to bring out in this edition a carefully revised version of all my books, in the order in which they were written, each story to be accompanied by some brief notice explaining the circumstances under which it was written, and to what extent fact or fiction had their share in the construction.

If such notices may occasionally be but leaves of an autobiography, I must ask my reader to pardon me, and to believe that I shall not impose my egotism upon him when it be possible to avoid it, while at the same time he shall know all that I myself know of the history of these volumes.

If to go over again the pages I wrote so many years ago is in a measure to revisit in age the loved scenes of boyhood, and to ponder over passages the very spirit of whose dictation is dead and gone, — if all this has its sadness, I am cheered by remembering that I am still addressing many old and dear friends, and have also for my audience the sons and grandsons, and, what I like better, the daughters and granddaughters, of those who once listened to Harry Lorrequer.

CHARLES LEVER.

Trieste, 1872.

CONTENTS.

1 CONTENTS.

ILLUSTRATIONS BY PHIZ IN VOL. I.

Etchings.

Illustrations in the Text.

HARRY LORREQUER.

CHAPTER I.

ARRIVAL IN CORK. — CIVIC FESTIVITIES. — PRIVATE THEATRICALS.

It was on a splendid morning in the autumn of the year 181— that the "Howard" transport, with four hundred of his Majesty's 4—th Regiment, dropped anchor in the picturesque harbor of Cove. The sea shone under the purple light of the rising sun with a rich rosy hue, beautifully in contrast with the different tints of the foliage of the deep woods already tinged with the brown of autumn. Spike Island lay "sleeping upon its broad shadow," and the large ensign which crowns the battery was wrapped around the flagstaff, there not being even air enough to stir it. It was still so early that but few persons were abroad; and as we leaned over the bulwarks, and looked now, for the first time for eight long years, upon British ground, many an eye filled, and many a heaving breast told how full of recollections that short moment was, and how different our feelings from the gay buoyancy with which we had sailed from that same harbor for the Peninsula. Many of our best and bravest had we left behind us, and more than one native to the land we were approaching had found his last rest in the soil of the stranger. It was, then, with a mingled sense of pain and pleasure we gazed upon that peaceful little village, whose white cottages lay dotted along the edge of the harbor. The moody silence our thoughts had shed over us was soon broken; the preparations for disembarking had begun, and I recollect well to this hour how, shaking off the load that oppressed my heart, I descended the gangway, humming poor Wolfe's well-known song, —

> " Why, soldiers, why
> Should we be melancholy, boys ? "

And to this elasticity of spirits, whether the result of my profession, or the gift of God — as Dogberry has it — I know not, I owe the greater portion of the happiness I have enjoyed in a life whose changes and vicissitudes have equalled most men's.

Drawn up in a line along the shore, I could scarce refrain from a smile at our appearance. Four weeks on board a transport will certainly not contribute much to the *personnel* of any unfortunate therein confined; but when, in addition to this, you take into account that we had not received new clothes for three years, — if I except caps for our grenadiers, originally intended for a Scotch regiment, but found to be all too small for the long-headed generation. Many a patch of brown and gray variegated the faded scarlet of our uniform, and scarcely a pair of knees in the entire regiment did not confess their obligations to a blanket. But with all this, we showed a stout, weather-beaten front, that, disposed as the passer-by might feel to laugh at our expense, very little caution would teach him it were fully as safe to indulge it in his sleeve.

The bells from every steeple and tower rang gayly out a peal of welcome as we marched into "that beautiful city called Cork," our band playing "Garryowen," — for we had been originally raised in Ireland, and still among our officers maintained a strong majority for that land of punch, priests, and potatoes, — the tattered flag of the regiment proudly waving over our heads, and not a man among us whose warm heart did not bound behind a Waterloo medal. Well, well! I am now — alas that I should say it! — somewhat in the "sere and yellow;" and I confess, after the experience of some moments of high, triumphant feeling, that I never before felt within me the same animating, spirit-filling glow of delight as rose within my heart that day as I marched at the head of my company down George's Street.

We were soon settled in barracks; and then began a series of entertainments on the side of the civic dignities of Cork which led most of us to believe that we had only escaped shot and shell to fall less gloriously beneath champagne and claret. I do not believe there is a coroner in the island who would have pronounced but the one verdict over the regiment, "Killed by the mayor and corporation," had we so fallen.

First of all, we were dined by the citizens of Cork; and to do them justice, a harder-drinking set of gentlemen no city need boast. Then we were feasted by the corporation; then by the sheriffs; then came the mayor, solus; then an address, with a cold collation, that left eight of us on the sick-list for a fortnight. But the climax of all was a grand entertainment given in the Mansion House, and to which upwards of two thousand were invited. It was a species of fancy ball, beginning by a *déjeûner* at three o'clock in the afternoon, and ending — I never yet met the man who could tell when it ended! As for myself, my *finale* partook a little of the adventurous, and I may as well relate it.

After waltzing for about an hour with one of the prettiest girls I ever set eyes upon, and getting a tender squeeze of the hand as I restored her to a most affable-looking old lady in a blue turban and a red velvet gown, who smiled benignly at me and called me "*Meejor*," I retired, to recruit for a new attack, to a small table where three of ours were quaffing *ponche à la Romaine*, with a crowd of Corkagians about them eagerly inquiring after some heroes of their own city whose deeds of arms they were surprised did not obtain special mention from "the Duke." I soon ingratiated myself into this well-occupied clique, and dosed them with glory to their hearts' content. I resolved at once to enter into their humor; and as the "ponche" mounted up to my brain, I gradually found my acquaintanceship extend to every family and connection in the country.

"Did ye know Phil Beamish, of the 3—th, sir ?" said a tall, red-faced, red-whiskered, well-looking gentleman, who bore no slight resemblance to Feargus O'Connor.

"Phil Beamish!" said I. "Indeed I did, sir, and do still; and there is not a man in the British army I am prouder of knowing." Here, by the way, I may mention that I never heard the name till that moment.

"You don't say so, sir ?" said Feargus, for so I must call him, for shortness' sake. "Has he any chance of the company yet, sir ? "

"Company!" said I, in astonishment. "He obtained his majority three months since. You cannot possibly have heard from him lately, or you would have known that ? "

"That's true, sir. I never heard since he quitted the 3—th to go to Versailles, I think they call it, for his health. But how did he get the step, sir ? "

"Why, as to the company, that was remarkable enough !" said I, quaffing off a tumbler of champagne to assist my invention. "You know it was about four o'clock in the afternoon of the 18th that Napoleon ordered Grouchy to advance with the first and second brigade of the Old Guard and two regiments of chasseurs and attack the position occupied by Picton and the regiments under his command. Well, sir, on they came, masked by the smoke of a terrific discharge of artillery, stationed on a small eminence to our left, and which did tremendous execution among our poor fellows; on they came, sir, and as the smoke cleared partially away, we got a glimpse of them, and a more dangerous-looking set I should not desire to see, — grizzly-bearded, hard-featured, bronzed fellows, about five and thirty or forty years of age; their beauty not a whit improved by the red glare thrown upon their faces and along the whole line by each flash of the long twenty-fours that were playing away to the right. Just at this moment Picton rode down the line with his staff, and stopping within a few paces of me, said, 'They're coming up! Steady, boys; steady now! We shall have something to do soon!' And then turning sharply round, he looked in the direction of the French battery, that was thundering away again in full force. 'Ah! that must be silenced,' said he. 'Where's Beamish?'"

"Says Picton!" interrupted Feargus, his eyes starting from their sockets, and his mouth growing wider every moment, as he listened with the most intense interest.

"Yes," said I, slowly. And then, with all the provoking nonchalance of an Italian improvisatore, who always halts at the most exciting point of his narrative, I begged a listener near me to fill my glass from the iced punch beside him. Not a sound was heard as I lifted the bumper to my lips; all were breathless in their wound-up anxiety to hear of their countryman who had been selected by Picton — for what, too, they knew not yet, and, indeed, at that instant I did not know myself, and nearly laughed outright, for the two of ours who had remained at the table had so well employed their interval of ease as to become very pleasantly drunk, and were listening to my confounded story with all the gravity and seriousness in the world. "'Where's Beamish?' said Picton. 'Here, sir,' said Phil, stepping out from the line, and touching his cap to the general, who, taking him apart for a few minutes, spoke to him with great animation. We did not know what he said; but before five minutes were over, there was Phil with three companies of light-bobs drawn up at our left; their muskets at the charge, they set off at a round trot down the little steep which closed our flank. We had not much time to follow their movements, for our own amusement began soon; but I well remember, after repelling the French attack and standing in square against two heavy charges of cuirassiers, the first thing I saw, where the French battery had-stood, was Phil Beamish and about a handful of brave fellows, all that remained from the skirmish. He captured two of the enemy's field-pieces, and was 'Captain Beamish' on the day after.

"Long life to him!" said at least a dozen voices behind and about me, while a general clinking of decanters and smacking of lips betokened that Phil's health, with all the honors, was being celebrated. For myself, I was really so engrossed by my narrative, and so excited by the "ponche," that I saw or heard very little of what was passing around, and have only a kind of dim recollection of being seized by the hand by "Feargus," who was Beamish's brother, and who, in the fulness of his heart, would have hugged me to his breast, if I had not opportunely been so over-powered as to fall senseless under the table.

When I first returned to consciousness, I found myself lying exactly where I had fallen. Around me lay heaps of slain, the two of "ours" among the number. One of them —I remember he was the Adjutant—held in his hand a wax candle (two to the pound). Whether he had himself seized it in the enthusiasm of my narrative of flood and field, or it had been put there by another, I know not; but he certainly cut a droll figure. The room we were in was a small one off the great saloon, and through the half-open folding-door I could clearly perceive that the festivities were still continued. The crash of fiddles and French horns and the tramp of feet, which had lost much of their elasticity since the entertainment began, rang through my ears, mingled with the sounds, "Down the middle," "Hands across," "Here's your partner, captain." What hour of the night or morning it then was, I could not guess; but certainly the vigor of the party seemed little abated, if I might judge from the specimen before me, and the testimony of a short, plethoric gentleman who stood wiping his bald head, after conducting his partner down twenty-eight couple, and who, turning to his friend, said, "Oh, the distance is nothing; but it is the pace that kills!"

The first evidence I showed of any return to reason was a strong anxiety to be at my quarters; but how to get there I knew not. The faint glimmering of sense I possessed told me that "to stand was to fall," and I was ashamed to go on all-fours, which prudence suggested.

At this moment I remembered I had brought with me
my cane, which, from a perhaps pardonable vanity, I was
fond of parading. It was a present from the officers of
my regiment (many of them, alas! since dead), and had a
most splendid gold head, with a stag at the top, — the arms
of the regiment. This I would not have lost for any consideration I can mention; and this now was gone! I looked
around me on every side; I groped beneath the table; I
turned the sleeping sots who lay about me in no very gentle
fashion: but, alas! it was gone. I sprang to my feet, and
only then remembered how unfit I was to follow up the
search, as tables, chairs, lights, and people seemed all
rocking and waving before me. However, I succeeded in
making my way through one room into another, sometimes
guiding my steps along the walls; and once, as I recollect,
striking the diagonal of a room, I bisected a quadrille with
such ill-directed speed as to run foul of a Cork dandy and
his partner who were just performing the *en avant;* but
though I saw them lie tumbled in the dust by the shock
of my encounter, — for I had upset them, — I still held on
the even tenor of my way. In fact, I had feeling for but
one loss; and, still in pursuit of my cane, I reached the
hall-door. Now, be it known that the architecture of the
Cork Mansion House has but one fault; but that fault is a
grand one, and a strong evidence of how unsuited English
architects are to provide buildings for a people whose
tastes and habits they but imperfectly understand. Be
it known, then, that the descent from the hall-door to the
street was by a flight of twelve stone steps. How I should
ever get down these was now my difficulty. If Falstaff
deplored "eight yards of uneven ground as being three
score and ten miles a foot," with equal truth did I feel
that these twelve awful steps were worse to me than would
be M'Gillicuddy's Reeks in the daylight and with a head
clear from champagne.

While I yet hesitated, the problem resolved itself; for
gazing down upon the bright gravel, brilliantly lighted by
the surrounding lamps, I lost my balance and came tum-

bling and rolling from top to bottom, where I fell upon a
large mass of some soft substance to which, in all proba-
bility, I owe my life.   In a few seconds I recovered my
senses; and what was my surprise to find that the downy
cushion beneath snored most audibly!   I moved a little to
one side, and then discovered that in reality it was nothing
less than an alderman of Cork, who, from his position, I
concluded had shared the same fate with myself.   There
he lay, "like a warrior taking his rest," but not with his
"martial cloak around him," but a much more comfortable
and far more costly robe, — a scarlet gown of office, — with
huge velvet cuffs and a great cape of the same material.
True courage consists in presence of mind; and here mine
came to my aid at once.   Recollecting the loss I had just
sustained, and perceiving that all was still about me, with
that right Peninsular maxim that reprisals are fair in an
enemy's camp, I proceeded to strip the slain; and with
some little difficulty, — partly, indeed, owing to my own
unsteadiness on my legs, — I succeeded in denuding the
worthy alderman, who gave no other sign of life during the
operation than an abortive effort to "*hip, hip, hurrah,*" in
which I left him, having put on the spoil, and set out on
my way to the barrack with as much dignity of manner as
I could assume in honor of my costume.   And here I may
mention (in a parenthesis) that a more comfortable morn-
ing-gown no man ever posssessed, and in its wide, luxuriant
folds I revel while I write these lines.

When I awoke on the following day I had considerable
difficulty in tracing the events of the past evening.   The
great scarlet cloak, however, unravelled much of the mystery, and gradually the whole of my career became clear
before me, with the single exception of the episode of Phil
Beamish, about which my memory was subsequently re-
freshed.   But I anticipate.   Only five appeared that day
at mess; and, Lord! what spectres they were! — yellow
as guineas.   They called for soda-water without ceasing,
and scarcely spoke a word to each other.   It was plain that
the corporation of Cork was committing more havoc among

us than Corunna or Waterloo, and that if we did not change our quarters, there would be quick promotion in the corps for such as were "seasoned gentlemen." After a day or two we met again together, and then, what adventures were told! — each man had his own story to narrate; and from the occurrences detailed, one would have supposed years had been passing instead of the short hours of an evening party. Mine were, indeed, among the least remarkable; but I confess that the air of *vraisemblance* produced by my production of the aldermanic gown gave me the palm above all competitors.

Such was our life in Cork, — dining, drinking, dancing, riding, steeple-chasing, pigeon-shooting, and tandem-driving, filling up any little interval that was found to exist between a late breakfast and the time to dress for dinner; and here I hope I shall not be accused of a tendency to boasting while I add that among all ranks and degrees of men, and women too, there never was a regiment more highly in estimation than the 4—th. We felt the full value of all the attentions we were receiving, and we endeavored, as best we might, to repay them. We got up Garrison Balls and Garrison Plays, and usually performed once or twice a week during the winter. Here I shone conspicuously. In the morning I was employed painting scenery and arranging the properties; as it grew later, I regulated the lamps and looked after the footlights, mediating occasionally between angry litigants, whose jealousies abound to the full as much in private theatricals as in the regular *corps dramatique.* Then I was also leader in the orchestra, and had scarcely given the last scrape in the overture before I was obliged to appear to speak the prologue. Such are the cares of greatness. To do myself justice, I did not dislike them; though, to be sure, my taste for the drama did cost me a little dear, as will be seen in the sequel.

We were then in the full career of popularity, — our balls pronounced the very pleasantest, our plays far superior to any regular corps that had ever honored Cork with their talents,—when an event occurred which threw a gloom over all our proceedings, and finally put a stop to every project for amusement we had so completely given ourselves up to. This was no less than the removal of our Lieutenant-Colonel. After thirty years of active service in the regiment he then commanded, his age and infirmities, increased by some severe wounds, demanded ease and repose; he retired from us bearing along with him the love and regard of every man in the regiment. To the old officers he was endeared by long companionship and undeviating friendship; to the young, he was in every respect as a father, assisting by his advice and guiding by his counsel; while to the men, the best estimate of his worth appeared in the fact that corporal punishment was unknown in the corps. Such was the man we lost; and it may well be supposed that his successor, who or whatever he might be, came under circumstances of no common difficulty amongst us: but when I tell that our new Lieutenant-Colonel was in every respect his opposite, it may be believed how little cordiality he met with.

Lieutenant-Colonel Carden—for so I shall call him, although not his real name—had not been a month at quarters when he proved himself a regular martinet. Everlasting drills, continual reports, fatigue parties, and ball practice, and Heaven knows what besides, superseded our former morning's occupation; and at the end of the time I have mentioned, we, who had fought our way from Albuera to Waterloo, under some of the severest generals of division, were pronounced a most disorderly and ill-disciplined regiment by a colonel who had never seen a shot fired but at a review at Hounslow, or a sham battle in the Fifteen Acres. The winter was now drawing to a close—already some little touch of spring was appearing—as our last play for the season was announced, and every effort to close with some little additional *éclat* was made; and each performer in the expected piece was nerving himself for an effort beyond his wont. The Colonel had most unequivocally condemned these plays; but that mattered not, they came not within his jurisdiction, and we took no notice of his displeasure further than sending him tickets, which were as immediately returned as received. From being the chief offender, I had become particularly obnoxious, and he had upon more than one occasion expressed his desire for an opportunity to visit me with his vengeance; but being aware of his kind intentions towards me. I took particular care to let no such opportunity occur.

On the morning in question, then, I had scarcely left my quarters when one of my brother officers informed me that the Colonel had made a great uproar, that one of the bills of the play had been put up on his door, which, with his avowed dislike to such representations, he considered as intended to insult him: he added, too, that the Colonel attributed it to me. In this, however, he was wrong; and to this hour I never knew who did it. I had little time, and still less inclination, to meditate upon the Colonel's wrath, — the theatre had all my thoughts; and indeed it was a day of no common exertion, for our amusements were to conclude with a grand supper on the stage, to which all the *élite* of Cork were invited. Wherever I went through the city, — and many were my peregrinations, — the great placard of the play stared me in the face; and every gate and shuttered window in Cork proclaimed "THE PART OF OTHELLO BY MR. LORREQUER."

As evening drew near, my cares and occupations were redoubled. My Iago I had fears for; 'tis true he was an admirable Lord Grizzle in "Tom Thumb" — but then — then I had to paint the whole company, and bear all their abuse besides, for not making some of the most ill-looking wretches perfect Apollos; but, last of all, I was sent for, at a quarter to seven, to lace Desdemona's stays. Start not, gentle reader, my fair Desdemona — she "who might lie by an emperor's side and command him tasks" — was no other than the senior lieutenant of the regiment, and who was as great a votary of the jolly god as honest Cassio himself. But I must hasten on; I cannot delay to recount our successes in detail. Let it suffice to say, that, by universal consent, I was preferred to Kean; and the only fault the most critical observer could find to the representative of Desdemona was a rather unladylike fondness for snuff. But whatever little demerits our acting might have displayed, were speedily forgotten in a champagne supper. There I took the head of the table; and in the costume of the noble Moor toasted, made speeches, returned thanks, and sang songs, till I might have exclaimed with Othello himself, "Chaos is come again;" and I believe I owe my ever reaching the barrack that night to the kind offices of Desdemona, who carried me the greater part of the way on her back.

The first waking thoughts of him who has indulged overnight are not among the most blissful of existence; and certainly the pleasure is not increased by the consciousness that he is called on to the discharge of duties to which a fevered pulse and throbbing temples are but ill suited. My sleep was suddenly broken in upon the morning after the play by a "row-dow-dow" beat beneath my window. I jumped hastily from my bed and looked out, and there, to my horror, perceived the regiment under arms. It was one of our confounded Colonel's morning drills; and there he stood himself, with the poor Adjutant, who had been up all night, shivering beside him. Some two or three of the officers had descended; and the drum was now summoning the others as it beat round the barrack-square. I saw there was not a moment to lose, and proceeded to dress with all despatch; but, to my misery, I discovered everywhere nothing but theatrical robes and decorations. There lay a splendid turban; here a pair of buskins. A spangled jacket glittered on one table, and a jewelled scimitar on the other. At last I detected my "regimental small-clothes," most ignominiously thrust into a corner in my ardor for my Moorish robes the preceding evening.

I dressed myself with the speed of lightning; but as I proceeded in my occupation, guess my annoyance to find that the toilet-table and glass, ay, and even the basin-stand, had been removed to the dressing-room of the theatre. And my servant, I suppose, following his master's example, was too tipsy to remember to bring them back, so that I was unable to procure the luxury of cold water; for now not a moment more remained, the drum had ceased, and the men had all fallen in. Hastily drawing on my coat, I put on my shako, and buckling on my belt as dandy-like as might be, hurried down, the stairs to the barrack-yard. By the time I got down, the men were all drawn up in line along the square, while the Adjutant was proceeding to examine their accoutrements as he passed down. The Colonel and the officers were standing in a group, but not conversing. The anger of the commanding officer appeared still to continue, and there was a dead silence maintained on both sides. To reach the spot where they stood, I had to pass along part of the line. In doing so, how shall I convey my amazement at the faces that met me, — a general titter ran along the entire rank, which not even their fears for consequences seemed able to repress; for an effort on the part of many to stifle the laugh only ended in a still louder burst of merriment. I looked to the far side of the yard for an explanation, but there was nothing there to account for it. I now crossed over to where the officers were standing, determining in my own mind to investigate the occurrence thoroughly when free from the presence of the Colonel, to whom any representation of ill conduct always brought a punishment far exceeding the merits of the case.

Scarcely had I formed this resolve, when I reached the group of officers; but the moment I came near, one general roar of laughter saluted me, the like of which I never before heard. I looked down at my costume, expecting to discover that in my hurry to dress I had put on some of the garments of Othello. No, all was perfectly correct. I waited for a moment till, the first burst of their merriment over, I should obtain a clew to the jest. But there seemed no prospect of this, for as I stood patiently before them, their mirth appeared to increase. Indeed, poor G——, the senior major, one of the gravest men in Europe, laughed till the tears ran down his cheeks; and such was the effect upon me that I was induced to laugh too, — as men will sometimes, from the infectious nature of that strange emotion; but no sooner did I do this, than their fun knew no bounds, and some almost screamed aloud in the excess of their merriment. Just at this instant the Colonel, who had been examining some of the men, approached our group, advancing with an air of evident displeasure, as the shouts of laughter continued. As he came up, I turned hastily round, and touching my cap, wished him good morning. Never shall I forget the look he gave me. If a glance could have annihilated any man, his would have finished me. For a moment his face became purple with rage, his eye was almost hid beneath his bent brow, and he absolutely shook with passion.

"Go, sir," said he at length, as soon as he was able to find utterance for his words, "go, sir, to your quarters; and before you leave them a court-martial shall decide if such continued insult to your commanding officer warrants your name being in the Army List."

"What the devil can all this mean?" I said, in a half-whisper, turning to the others. But there they stood, their handkerchiefs to their mouths, and evidently choking with suppressed laughter.

"May I beg, Colonel Carden," said I —

"To your quarters, sir," roared the little man in the voice of a lion; and with a haughty wave of his hand, prevented all further attempt on my part to seek explanation.

"They're all mad, every man of them," I muttered, as I betook myself slowly back to my rooms, amid the same evidences of mirth my first appearance had excited, which even the Colonel's presence, feared as he was, could not entirely subdue.

With the air of a martyr I trod heavily up the stairs and entered my quarters, meditating within myself awful schemes for vengeance on the now open tyranny of my Colonel, upon whom I, too, in my honest rectitude of

"Errors upon Parade?"

heart, vowed to have a "court-martial." I threw myself
upon a chair, and endeavored to recollect what circumstances of the past evening could have possibly suggested
all the mirth in which both officers and men seemed to par-
ticipate equally; but nothing could I remember capable of
solving the mystery. Surely the cruel wrongs of the manly
Othello were no laughter-moving subject.

I rang the bell hastily for my servant. The door
opened.

"Stubbes," said I, "are you aware — "

I had only got so far in my question when my servant,
one of the most discreet of men, put on a broad grin, and
turned away towards the door to hide his face.

" What the devil does this mean?" said I, stamping with
passion; "he is as bad as the rest. Stubbes" — and this
I spoke with the most grave and severe tone — "what is
the meaning of this insolence?"

"Oh, sir," said the man, "oh, sir, surely you did not
appear on parade with that face?" And then he burst into
a fit of the most uncontrollable laughter.

Like lightning a horrid doubt shot across my mind. I
sprang over to the dressing-glass, which had been replaced,
and oh, horror of horrors! there I stood as black as the
king of Ashantee. The cursed dye which I had put on for
Othello, I had never washed off; and there, with a huge
bearskin shako and a pair of dark bushy whiskers, shone
my huge, black, and polished visage, glowering at itself in
the looking-glass.

My first impulse, after amazement had a little subsided,
was to laugh immoderately; in this I was joined by
Stubbes, who, feeling that his mirth was participated in,
gave full vent to his risibility. And, indeed, as I stood
before the glass, grinning from ear to ear, I felt very little
surprise that my joining in the laughter of my brother officers a short time before, had caused an increase of their
merriment. I threw myself upon a sofa, and absolutely
laughed till my sides ached, when, the door opening, the
Adjutant made his appearance. He looked for a moment

at me, then at Stubbes, and then burst out himself as loud as either of us. When he had at length recovered himself, he wiped his face with his handkerchief, and said, with a tone of much gravity, —

"But, my dear Lorrequer, this will be a serious, a devil-ish serious affair. You know what kind of man Colonel Carden is; and you are aware, too, you are not one of his prime favorites. He is firmly persuaded that you in-tended to insult him, and nothing will convince him to the contrary. We told him how it must have occurred, but he will listen to no explanation."

I thought for one second before I replied. My mind, with the practised rapidity of an old campaigner, took in all the *pros* and *cons* of the case; I saw at a glance it were better to brave the anger of the Colonel, come in what shape it might, than be the laughing-stock of the mess for life, and with a face of the greatest gravity and self-posses-sion, said, —

"Well, Adjutant, the Colonel is right. It was no mis-take. You know I sent him tickets yesterday for the theatre. Well, he returned them; this did not annoy me, but on one account: I had made a wager with Alderman Gullable that the Colonel should see me in Othello. What was to be done? Don't you see, now, there was only one course, and I took it, old boy, and have won my bet!"

"And lost your commission for a dozen of champagne, I suppose," said the Adjutant.

"Never mind, my dear fellow," I replied; "I shall get out of this scrape, as I have done many others."

"But what do you intend doing?"

"Oh! as to that," said I, "I shall, of course, wait on the Colonel immediately; pretend to him that it was a mere blunder from the inattention of my servant, hand over Stubbes to the powers that punish" (here the poor fellow winced a little), "and make my peace as well as I can. But, Adjutant, mind," said I, "and give the real version to all our fellows, and tell them to make it public as much as they please."

"Never fear," said he, as he left the room still laughing, "they shall all know the true story; but I wish with all my heart you were well out of it."

I now lost no time in making my toilet, and presented myself at the Colonel's quarters. It is no pleasure for me to recount these passages in my life in which I have had to bear the "proud man's contumely." I shall therefore merely observe that after a very long interview the Colonel accepted my apologies and we parted.

Before a week elapsed, the story had gone far and near; every dinner-table in Cork had laughed at it. As for me, I attained immortal honor for my tact and courage. Poor Gullable readily agreed to favor the story, and gave us a dinner as the lost wager; and the Colonel was so unmercifully quizzed on the subject, and such broad allusions to his being humbugged were given in the Cork papers, that he was obliged to negotiate a change of quarters with another regiment, to get out of the continual jesting; and in less than a month we marched to Limerick, to relieve, as it was reported, the 9th, ordered for foreign service, but in reality only to relieve Lieutenant-Colonel Carden, quizzed beyond endurance.

However, if the Colonel had seemed to forgive, he did not forget; for the very second week after our arrival in Limerick, I received one morning at my breakfast-table the following brief note from our Adjutant: —

My dear Lorrequer, — The Colonel has received orders to despatch two companies to some remote part of the County Clare ; and as you have "done the state some service," you are selected for the beautiful town of Kilrush, where, to use the eulogistic language of the geography books, "there is a good harbor and a market plentifully supplied with fish." I have just heard of the kind intention in store for you, and lose no time in letting you know.

God give you a good deliverance from the *garçons blancs*, as the "Moniteur" calls the Whiteboys, and believe me ever yours,

CHARLES CURZON.

I had scarcely twice read over the Adjutant's epistle, when I received an official notification from the Colonel

directing me to proceed to Kilrush, then and there to afford
all aid and assistance in suppressing illicit distillation,
when called on for that purpose; and other similar duties
too agreeable to recapitulate. Alas! alas! "Othello's occupation" was indeed gone! The next morning at sunrise
saw me on my march, with what appearance of gayety I
could muster, but in reality very much chapfallen at my
banishment, and invoking sundry things upon the devoted
head of the Colonel which he would by no means consider
as "blessings."

How short-sighted are we mortals, whether enjoying all
the pomp and state of royalty, or marching, like myself, at
the head of a detachment of his Majesty's 4—th.

Little, indeed, did I anticipate that the Siberia to which
I fancied I was condemned should turn out the happiest
quarters my fate ever threw me into. But this, including
as it does one of the most important events of my life, I
reserve for another chapter.

"What is that place called, Sergeant?"

"Bunratty Castle, sir."

"Where do we breakfast?"

"At Clare Island, sir."

"March away, boys!"

CHAPTER II.

For a week after my arrival at Kilrush, my life was one of the most dreary monotony. The rain, which had begun to fall as I left Limerick, continued to descend in torrents, and I found myself a close prisoner in the sanded parlor of "mine inn." At no time would such "durance vile" have been agreeable; but now, when I contrasted it with all I had left behind at headquarters, it was absolutely maddening. The pleasant lounge in the morning, the social mess, and the agreeable evening party were all exchanged for a short promenade of fourteen feet in one direction, and twelve in the other, such being the accurate measurement of my *salle à manger;* a chicken, with legs as blue as a Highlander's in winter for my dinner; and the hours that all Christian mankind were devoting to pleasant intercourse and agreeable chit-chat, spent in beating that dead-march to time, "the Devil's Tattoo," upon my rickety table; and forming, between whiles, sundry valorous resolutions to reform my life and "eschew sack and loose company."

My front window looked out upon a long, straggling, ill-paved street, with its due proportion of mud-heaps and duck-pools; the houses on either side were for the most part dingy-looking edifices with half-doors and such pretension to being shops as a quart of meal or salt displayed in the window confers; or sometimes two tobacco-pipes, placed "saltier-wise," would appear the only vendible article in the establishment. A more wretched, gloomy-looking picture of woe-begone poverty I never beheld.

If I turned for consolation to the back of the house, my eyes fell upon the dirty yard of a dirty inn, — the half-thatched cow-shed, where two famished animals mourned their hard fate, "chewing the cud of sweet and bitter fancy;" the chaise, the yellow post-chaise, once the pride and glory of the establishment, now stood reduced from its wheels, and ignominiously degraded to a hen-house. On the grass-grown roof a cock had taken his stand, with an air of protective patronage to the feathered inhabitants beneath, —

"To what base uses must we come at last!"

That chaise, which once had conveyed the blooming bride, all blushes and tenderness, and the happy groom on their honeymoon visit to Ballybunnion and its romantic caves or to the gigantic cliffs and sea-girt shores of Moher, or, with more steady pace and becoming gravity, had borne along the "going judge of assize," was now become a lying-in hospital for fowls and a nursery for chickens. Fallen as I was from my high estate, it afforded me a species of malicious satisfaction to contemplate these' sad reverses of fortune; and I verily believe — for on such slight foundation our greatest resolves are built — that if the rain had continued a week longer, I should have become a misanthropist for life. I made many inquiries from my landlady as to the society of the place, but the answers I received only led to greater despondence. My predecessor here, it seemed, had been an officer of a veteran battalion, with a wife and that amount of children which is algebraically expressed by an x, — meaning an unknown quantity. He, good man, in his two years' sojourn here had been much more solicitous about his own affairs than making acquaintance with his neighbors; and at last the few persons who had been in the habit of calling on "the officer" gave up the practice; and as there were no young ladies to refresh Pa's memory on the matter, they soon forgot completely that such a person existed. And to this happy oblivion I, Harry Lorrequer, succeeded, and was thus left, without benefit of clergy, to the tender mercies of Mrs. Healy, of the Burton Arms.

As during the inundation which deluged the whole country around I was unable to stir from the house, I enjoyed abundant opportunity of cultivating the acquaintance of my hostess; and it is but fair that my reader, who has journeyed so far with me, should have an introduction.

Mrs. Healy, the sole proprietor of the Burton Arms, was of some five-and-fifty — "or, by 'r lady," threescore — years, of a rubicund and hale complexion; and though her short neck and corpulent figure might have set her down as "doubly hazardous," she looked a good life for many years to come. In height and breadth she most nearly resembled a sugar-hogshead, whose rolling, pitching motion, when trundled along on edge, she emulated in her gait. To the ungainliness of her figure her mode of dressing not a little contributed. She usually wore a thick linsey-wolsey gown, with enormous pockets on either side, and, like Nora Creina's, it certainly inflicted no undue restriction upon her charms, but left

> "Every beauty free,
> To sink or swell as Heaven pleases," ·

Her feet — ye gods! such feet — were apparelled in listing slippers, over which the upholstery of her ankles descended, and completely relieved the mind of the spectator as to the superincumbent weight being disproportioned to the support. I remember well my first impression on seeing those feet and ankles reposing upon a straw footstool, while she took her afternoon doze, and I wondered within myself if elephants were liable to the gout. There are few countenances in the world that, if wishing to convey an idea of, we cannot refer to some well-known standard, and thus nothing is more common than to hear comparisons with "Vulcan, Venus, Nicodemus," and the like; but in the present case I am totally at a loss for anything resembling the face of the worthy Mrs. Healy, except it be, perhaps, that most ancient and sour visage we used to see upon old circular iron rappers formerly, — they make none of them now, — the only difference being that Mrs. Healy's nose had no ring through it; I am almost tempted to add, "more's the pity."

Such was she in "the flesh;" would that I could say she was more fascinating in the "spirit!" But, alas! truth, from which I never may depart in these my "Confessions," constrains me to acknowledge the reverse. Most persons, in this miserable world of ours, have some prevailing, predominating characteristic, which usually gives the tone and color to all their thoughts and actions, forming what we denominate temperament; this we see actuating them, now more, now less. But rarely, however, is this great spring of action without its moments of repose. Not so with her of whom I have been speaking. She had but one passion, —but, like Aaron's rod, it had a most consuming tendency, —and that was to scold and abuse all whom hard fate had brought within the unfortunate limits of her tyranny. The English language, comprehensive as it is, afforded no epithets strong enough for her wrath, and she sought among the more classic beauties of her native Irish such additional ones as served her need; and with this holy alliance of tongues she had been for years long, the dread and terror of the entire village.

"The dawning of morn, the daylight sinking,"

ay, and even the "night's dull hours," it was said, too, found her laboring in her congenial occupation; and while thus she continued to "scold and grow fat," her inn, once a popular and frequented one, became gradually less and less frequented, and the dragon of the Rhine-fells did not more effectually lay waste the territory about him than did the evil influence of her tongue spread desolation and ruin around her. Her inn, at the time of my visit, had not been troubled with even a passing traveller for many months; and, indeed, had I had any, even the least, foreknowledge of the character of my hostess, its privacy should have still remained uninvaded for some time longer.

I had not been many hours installed, when I got a specimen of her powers; and before the first week was over, so

constant and unremitting were her labors in this way that
I have, upon the occasion of a slight lull in the storm,
occasioned by her falling asleep, actually left my room to
inquire if anything had gone wrong, in the same way as
the miller is said to awake when the mill stops. I trust I
have said enough to move the reader's, pity and compassion
for my situation; one more miserable it is difficult to conceive. It may be thought that much might be done by
management, and that a slight exercise of the favorite
Whig plan might avail. Nothing of the kind. She was
proof against all such arts; and what was still worse, there
was no subject, no possible circumstance, no matter, past,
present, or to come, that she could not wind, by her diabolical ingenuity, into some cause of offence; and then
came the quick transition to instant punishment. Thus,
my apparently harmless inquiry as to the society of the
neighborhood suggested to her — a wish on my part to
make acquaintance; therefore to dine out; therefore not to
dine at home; consequently to escape paying half-a-crown
and devouring a chicken; therefore to defraud her, and
behave, as she would herself observe, "like a beggarly
scullion, with his four shillings a day, setting up for a
gentleman," etc.

By a quiet and Job-like endurance of all manner of
taunting suspicions and unmerited sarcasms, to which I
daily became more reconciled, I absolutely rose into something like favor; and before the first month of my banishment expired, had got the length of an invitation to tea in
her own snuggery, — an honor never known to be bestowed on any before, with the exception of Father
Malachi Brennan, her ghostly adviser; and even he, it
is said, never ventured on such an approximation to intimacy until he was, in Kilrush phrase, "half screwed,"
thereby meaning more than half tipsy. From time to
time, thus, I learned from my hostess such particulars of
the country and its inhabitants as I was desirous of hearing; and among other matters, she gave me an account of
the great landed proprietor himself, Lord Callonby, who

was daily expected at his seat within some miles of Kilrush, at the same time assuring me that I need not be looking so "pleased and curling out my whiskers; that they'd never take the trouble of asking even the name of me." This, though neither very courteous, nor altogether flattering to listen to, was no more than I had already learned from some brother officers who knew this quarter, and who informed me that the Earl of Callonby, though only visiting his Irish estates every three or four years, never took the slightest notice of any of the military in his neighborhood; nor, indeed, did he mix with the country gentry, confining himself to his own family or the guests who usually accompanied him from England and remained during his few weeks' stay. My impression of his lordship was therefore not calculated to cheer my solitude by any prospect of his rendering it lighter.

The Earl's family consisted of her ladyship, an only son, nearly of age, and two daughters, — the eldest, Lady Jane, had the reputation of being extremely beautiful; and I remembered when she came out in London, only the year before, hearing nothing but praises of the grace and elegance of her manner, united to the most classic beauty of her face and figure. The second daughter was some years younger, and said to be also very handsome; but as yet she had not been brought into society. Of the son, Lord Kilkee, I only heard that he had been a very gay fellow at Oxford, where he was much liked, and although not particularly studious, had given evidence of talent.

Such were the few particulars I obtained of my neighbors, and thus little did I know of those who were so soon to exercise a most important influence upon my future life.

After some weeks' close confinement, which, judging from my feelings alone, I should have counted as many years, I eagerly seized the opportunity of the first glimpse of sunshine to make a short excursion along the coast; I started early in the morning, and after a long stroll along the bold headlands of Kilkee, was returning late in the evening to my lodgings. My path lay across a wild, bleak moor, dotted with low clumps of furze, and not presenting on any side the least trace of habitation. In wading through the tangled bushes, my dog Mouche started a hare; and after a run "sharp, short, and decisive," killed her at the bottom of a little glen some hundred yards off.

I was just patting my dog and examining the prize, when I heard a crackling among the low bushes near me, and on looking up, perceived, about twenty paces distant, a short, thickset man, whose fustian jacket and leathern gaiters at once pronounced him the gamekeeper; he stood leaning upon his gun, quietly awaiting, as it seemed, for any movement on my part, before he interfered. With one glance I detected how matters stood, and immediately adopting my usual policy of "taking the bull by the horns," called out, in a tone of very sufficient authority, —

"I say, my man, are you his lordship's gamekeeper?"

Taking off his hat, the man approached me, and very respectfully informed me that he was.

"Well, then," said I, "present this hare to his lordship with my respects, — here is my card, — and say I shall be most happy to wait on him in the morning and explain the circumstance."

The man took the card, and seemed for some moments undecided how to act; he seemed to think that probably he might be ill-treating a friend of his lordship's if he refused, and on the other hand might be merely "jockeyed" by some bold-faced poacher. Meanwhile I whistled my dog close up, and humming an air, with great appearance of indifference stepped out homeward. By this piece of presence of mind I saved poor Mouche; for I saw at a glance that, with true gamekeeper's law, he had been destined to death the moment he had committed the offence.

The following morning, as I sat at breakfast meditating upon the events of the preceding day, and not exactly determined how to act, whether to write to his lordship explaining how the matter occurred, or call personally, a loud rattling on the pavement drew me to the window. As the house stood at the end of a street, I could not see in the direction the noise came; but as I listened, a very handsome tandem turned the corner of the narrow street, and came along towards the hotel at a long sling trot; the horses were dark chestnuts, well matched, and showing a deal of blood. The carriage was a dark drab, with black wheels, the harness all of the same color. The whole turn-out — and I was an amateur of that sort of thing — was perfect; the driver — for I come to him last, as he was the last I looked at — was a fashionable-looking young fellow, plainly but knowingly dressed, and evidently handling the "ribbons" like an experienced whip.

After bringing his nags up to the inn-door in very pretty style, he gave the reins to his servant and got down. Before I was well aware of it, the door of my room opened, and the gentleman entered with a certain easy air of good-breeding, and saying, —

"Mr. Lorrequer, I presume," introduced himself as Lord Kilkee.

I immediately opened the conversation by an apology for my dog's misconduct on the day before, and assured his lordship that I knew the value of a hare in a hunting country, and was really sorry for the circumstance.

"Then I must say," replied his lordship, "Mr. Lorrequer is the only person who regrets the matter; for had it not been for this, it is more than probable we should never have known we were so near neighbors, — in fact, nothing could equal our amazement at hearing *you* were playing the Solitaire down here. You must have found it dreadfully heavy, ' and have thought us downright savages.' But then I must explain to you that my father has made some ' rule absolute ' about visiting when down here; and though I know you 'll not consider it a compliment, yet I can assure you there is not another man I know of he would pay attention to but yourself. He made two efforts to get here this morning, but the gout ' would not be denied,' and so he deputed a most inferior ' diplomate; ' and now will you let me return with some character from my first mission, and inform my friends that you will dine with us to-day at seven, — a mere family party; but make your arrangements to stop all night and to-morrow. We shall find some work for my friend there on the hearth, — what do you call him, Mr. Lorrequer?"

' Mouche. Come here, Mouche."

' Ah ! Mouche, come here, my fine fellow. A splendid dog indeed; very tall for a thoroughbred. And now you 'll not forget, — seven, *temps militaire;* and, so *sans adieu.*"

And with these words his lordship shook me heartily by the hand; and before two minutes had elapsed had wrapped his box-coat once more across him, and was round the corner.

I looked for a few moments on the again silent street, and was almost tempted to believe I was in a dream, so rapidly had the preceding moments passed over, and so surprised was I to find that the proud Earl of Callonby, who never did the "civil thing" anywhere, should think proper to pay attention to a poor sub in a marching regiment, whose only claim on his acquaintance was the suspicion of poaching on his manor. I repeated over and over all his lordship's most polite speeches, trying to solve the mystery of them, but in vain; a thousand explanations occurred, but none of them I felt at all satisfactory. That there was some mystery somewhere I had no doubt; for I remarked all through that Lord Kilkee laid some stress upon my identity, and even seemed surprised at *my* being in such banishment. "Oh !" thought I at last, "his lordship is about to get up private theatricals, and has seen my Captain Absolute, or perhaps my Hamlet," — I could not say "Othello" even to myself, — "and is anxious to get ' such unrivalled talent' even ' for one night only.'"

After many guesses this seemed the nearest I could think of; and by the time I had finished my dressing for dinner, it was quite clear to me I had solved all the secret of his lordship's attentions.

The road to "Callonby" was beautiful beyond anything I

had ever seen in Ireland. For upwards of two miles it led along the margin of some lofty cliffs, now jutting out into bold promontories, and again retreating and forming small bays and mimic harbors, into which the heavy swell of the broad Atlantic was rolling its deep blue tide. The evening was perfectly calm, and at a little distance from the shore the surface of the sea was without a ripple. The only sound breaking the solemn stillness of the hour was the heavy plash of the waves as in minute peals they rolled in upon the pebbly beach and brought back with them, at each retreat, some of the larger and smoother stones, whose noise, as they fell back into old Ocean's bed, mingled with the din of the breaking surf. In one of the many little bays I passed, lay three or four fishing-smacks. The sails were drying, and flapped lazily against the mast. I could see the figures of the men as they passed backwards and forwards upon the decks, and although the height was nearly eight hundred feet, could hear their voices quite distinctly. Upon the golden strand, which was still marked with a deeper tint, where the tide had washed, stood a little white cottage of some fishermen, — at least so the net before the door bespoke it. Around it stood some children, whose merry voices and laughing tones sometimes reached me where I was standing. I could not but think, as I looked down from my lofty eyrie upon that little group of boats and that lone hut, how much of the "world," to the humble dwellers beneath, lay in that secluded and narrow bay. There the deep sea, where their days were passed in "storm or sunshine;" there the humble home where at night they rested, and around whose hearth lay all their cares and all their joys. How far, how very far removed from the busy haunts of men and all the struggles and contentions of the ambitious world; and yet, how short-sighted to suppose that even they had not their griefs and sorrows, and that their humble lot was devoid of the inheritance of those woes which all are heirs to!

I turned reluctantly from the sea-shore to enter the gate of the park, and my path in a few moments was as completely screened from all prospect of the sea as though it had lain miles inland. An avenue of tall and ancient lime-trees, so dense in their shadows as nearly to conceal the road beneath, led for above a mile through a beautiful lawn, whose surface, gently undulating, and studded with young clumps, was dotted over with sheep. At length, descending by a very steep road, I reached a beautiful little stream, over which a rustic bridge was thrown. As I looked down upon the rippling stream beneath, on the surface of which the dusky evening flies were dipping, I made a resolve, if I prospered in his lordship's good graces, to devote a day to the "angle" there before I left the country. It was now growing late; and remembering Lord Kilkee's intimation of "sharp seven," I threw my reins over my cob Sir Roger's neck (for I had hitherto been walking), and cantered up the steep hill before me. When I reached the top, I found myself upon a broad tableland encircled by old and well-grown timber, and at a distance, most tastefully half concealed by ornamental planting, I could catch some glimpse of Callonby. Before, however, I had time to look about me, I heard the tramp of horses' feet behind, and in another moment two ladies dashed up the steep behind, and came towards me at a smart gallop, followed by a groom, who, neither himself nor his horse, seemed to relish the pace of his fair mistresses. I moved off the road into the grass to permit them to pass; but no sooner had they got abreast of me than Sir Roger, anxious for a fair start, flung up both heels at once, pricked up his ears, and with a plunge that very nearly threw me from the saddle, set off at top speed. My first thought was for the ladies beside me, and to my utter horror, I now saw them coming along in full gallop; their horses had got off the road, and were, to my thinking, become quite unmanageable. I endeavored to pull up, but all in vain. Sir Roger had got the bit between his teeth, — a favorite trick of his, — and I was perfectly powerless to hold him. By this time they, being mounted on thoroughbreds, got a full neck before me, and the pace was now tremendous. On we all came, each horse at his utmost stretch. They were evidently gaining, from the better stride of their cattle; and will it be believed, or shall I venture to acknowledge it in these my Confessions, that I, who a moment before would have given my best chance of promotion to be able to pull in my horse, would now have "pledged my dukedom" to be able to give Sir Roger one cut of the whip unobserved? I leave it to the wise to decipher the *rationale*, but such is the fact. It was complete steeple-chasing, and my blood was up.

On we came, and I now perceived that about two hundred yards before me stood an iron gate and piers, without any hedge or wall on either side. Before I could conjecture the meaning of so strange a thing in the midst of a large lawn, I saw the foremost horse, now two or three lengths before the other, still in advance of me, take two or three short strides, and fly about eight feet over a sunk fence; the second followed in the same style, the riders sitting as steadily as in the gallop. It was now my turn, and I confess as I neared the dike I heartily wished myself well over it, for the very possibility of a "mistake" was maddening. Sir Roger came on at a slapping pace, and when within two yards of the brink, rose to it, and cleared it like a deer. By the time I had accomplished this feat, not the less to my satisfaction that both ladies had turned in their saddles to watch me, they were already far in advance. They held on still at the same pace, round a small copse which concealed them an instant from my view, and which when I passed, I perceived that they had just reached the hall door, and were dismounting.

On the steps stood a tall, elderly-looking, gentlemanlike person, who I rightly conjectured was his lordship. I heard him laughing heartily as I came up. I at last succeeded in getting Sir Roger to a canter; and when a few yards from where the group were standing, sprang off, and hastened up to make my apologies as I best might for my unfortunate runaway. I was luckily spared the awkwardness of an explanation, for his lordship, approaching me with his hand extended, said, —

"Mr. Lorrequer is most welcome at Callonby. I cannot be mistaken, I am sure; I have the pleasure of addressing the nephew of my old friend Sir Guy Lorrequer, of Elton. I am indeed most happy to see you, and not the less so that you are safe and sound, which, five minutes since, I assure you I had my fears for."

Before I could assure his lordship that my fears were all for my competitors in the race, — for such in reality they were, — he introduced me to the two ladies, who were still standing beside him: "Lady Jane Callonby, Mr. Lorrequer; Lady Catherine."

"Which of you young ladies, may I ask, planned this 'escapade;' for I see by your looks it was no accident?"

"I think, papa," said Lady Jane, "you must question Mr. Lorrequer on that head; he certainly started first."

"I confess, indeed," said I, "such was the case."

"Well, you must confess, too, you were distanced," said Lady Jane.

His lordship laughed heartily, and I joined in his mirth, feeling at the same time most terribly provoked to be quizzed on such a matter: that I, a steeple-chase horseman of the first water, should be twitted by a couple of young ladies on the score of a most manly exercise! "But come," said his lordship, "the first bell has rung long since, and I am longing to ask Mr. Lorrequer all about my old college friend of forty years ago. So, ladies, hasten your toilet, I beseech you."

With these words, his lordship, taking my arm, led me into the drawing-room, where we had not been many minutes till we were joined by her ladyship, a tall, stately, handsome woman of a certain age, resolutely bent upon being both young and beautiful, in spite of time and wrinkles Her reception of me, though not possessing the frankness of his lordship, was still very polite, and intended to be even gracious. I now found, by the reiterated inquiries for my old uncle, Sir Guy, that he it was, and not Hamlet, to whom I owed my present notice; and I must include it among my Confessions that it was about the first advantage I ever derived from the relationship. After half an hour's agreeable chatting, the ladies entered· and then I had time to remark the extreme beauty of their appearance. They were both wonderfully like; and except that Lady Jane was taller and more womanly, it would have been almost impossible to discriminate between them.

Lady Jane Callonby was then about twenty years of age, rather above the middle size, and slightly disposed towards *embonpoint ;* her eye was of the deepest and most liquid blue, and rendered apparently darker by long lashes of the blackest jet, — for such was the color of her hair; her nose slightly, but slightly, deviated from the straightness of the Greek, and her upper lip was faultless, as were her mouth and chin. The whole lower part of the face, from the perfect repose and from the carriage of her head, had certainly a great air of hauteur; but the extreme melting softness of her eyes took from this, and when she spoke, there was a quiet earnestness in her mild and musical voice that disarmed you at once of connecting the idea of self with the speaker. The word "fascinating," more than any other I know of, conveys the effect of her appearance; and to produce it, she had, more than any other woman I ever met, that wonderful gift, *l'art de plaire.*

I was roused from my perhaps too earnest, because unconscious, gaze at the lovely figure before me by his lordship saying, "Mr. Lorrequer, her ladyship is waiting for you." I accordingly bowed, and offering my arm, led her into the dinner-room. And here I draw rein for the present, reserving for my next chapter my adventures at Callonby.

CHAPTER III.

My first evening at Callonby passed off as nearly all first
evenings do everywhere.   His lordship was most agreeable;
talked much of my uncle, Sir Guy, whose fag he had been
at Eton half a century before, promised me some capital
shooting in his preserves, discussed the state of politics,
and as the second decanter of port "waned apace," grew
wondrous confidential, and told me of his intention to start
his son for the county at the next general election, such
being the object which had now conferred the honor of his
presence on his Irish estates.

Her ladyship was most condescendingly civil; vouchsafed
much tender commiseration for my "exile," as she termed
my quarters in Kilrush; wondered how I could possibly
exist in a marching regiment (who had never been in the
cavalry in my life!); spoke quite feelingly of my *kindness*
in joining their stupid family party, for they were living,
to use her own phrase, "like hermits;" and wound up all
by a playful assurance that as she perceived, from all my
answers, that I was bent on preserving a strict incognito,
she would tell no tales about me on her return to "town."
Now, it may readily be believed that all this and many
more of her ladyship's allusions were a "Chaldee manu-
script" to me.   That she knew certain facts of my family
and relations was certain, but that she had interwoven in
the humble web of my history a very pretty embroidery of
fiction was equally so; and while she thus ran on, with
innumerable allusions to Lady Marys and Lord Johns, who
she pretended to suppose were dying to hear from me, I
could not help muttering to myself, with good Christopher

Sly, "An all this be true, then Lord be thanked for my good amends;" for up to that moment I was an ungrateful man for all such high and noble solicitude. One dark doubt shot for an instant across my brain. Mayhap her ladyship had "registered a vow" never to syllable a name unchronicled by Debrett, or was actually only mystifying me for mere amusement. A minute's consideration dispelled this fear; for I found myself treated *en seigneur* by the whole family. As for the daughters of the house, nothing could possibly be more engaging than their manner. The eldest, Lady Jane, was pleased, from my near relationship to her father's oldest friend, to receive me "from the first" on the most friendly footing, while with the younger, Lady Catherine, from her being less reserved than her sister, my progress was even greater; and thus, before we separated for the night, I contrived to "take up my position" in such a fashion as to be already looked upon as one of the family party, — to which object Lord, and indeed Lady Callonby seemed most willing to contribute, and made me promise to spend the entire of the following day at Callonby, and as many of the succeeding ones as my military duties would permit.

As his lordship was wishing me good-night at the door of the drawing-room, he said, in a half-whisper, —

"We were ignorant yesterday, Mr. Lorrequer, how soon we should have the pleasure of seeing you here; and you are therefore condemned to a small room off the library, it being the only one we can insure you as being well aired. I must therefore apprise you that you are not to be shocked at finding yourself surrounded by every member of my family hung up in frames around you. But as the room is usually my own snuggery, I have resigned it without any alteration whatever."

The apartment for which his lordship had so strongly apologized stood in very pleasing contrast to my late one in Kilrush. The soft Persian carpet, on which one's feet sank to the very ankles; the brightly polished dogs, upon which a blazing wood-fire burned; the well-upholstered

fauteuils which seemed to invite sleep without the trouble
of lying down for it; and, last of all, the ample and luxurious bed, upon whose rich purple hangings the ruddy glare
of the fire threw a most mellow light, — were all a pleasing
exchange for the *garniture* of the "Hotel Healy."

' Certes, Harry Lorrequer," said I, as I threw myself
upon a small ottoman before the fire, in all the slippered
ease and *abandon* of a man who has changed a dress-coat
for a morning gown, — "certes, thou art destined for great
things; even here, where fate had seemed ' to do its worst '
to thee, a little paradise opens, and what to ordinary mortals had proved but a ' flat, stale, and most unprofitable '
quarter, presents to thee all the accumulated delight of an
hospitable mansion, a kind, almost friendly host, a conde-
scending Madame Mère, and daughers too! ah, ye gods! —
But what is this? " And here for the first time lifting up
my eyes, I perceived a beautiful water-color drawing in the
style of "Chalon," which was placed above the chimney-
piece. I rose at once, and taking a candle proceeded to
examine it more minutely. It was a portrait of Lady Jane,
a full-length too, and wonderfully like; there was more
complexion, and perhaps more roundness of the figure than
her present appearance would justify; but if anything was
gained in brilliancy, it was certainly lost in point of expression, and I infinitely preferred her pale but beautifully
fair countenance to the rosy cheek of the picture. The
figure was faultless; the same easy grace, the result of perfect symmetry and refinement together, which only one in
a thousand of handsome girls possess, was portrayed to the
life. The more I looked, the more I felt charmed with it.
Never had I seen anything so truly characteristic as this
sketch, for it was scarcely more. It was after nearly an
hour's quiet contemplation that I began to remember the
lateness of the night, — an hour in which my thoughts had
rambled from the lovely object before me to wonder at the
situation in which I found myself placed; for there was so
much of "attention" towards me, in the manner of every
member of the family, coupled with certain mistakes as to

my habits and acquaintances, as left me perfectly unable to unravel the mystery which so evidently surrounded me. "Perhaps," thought I, "Sir Guy has written in my behalf to his lordship. Oh! he would never do anything half so civil. Well, to be sure, I shall astonish them at head-quarters: they'll not believe this. I wonder if Lady Jane saw my Hamlet; for they landed in Cork from Bristol about that time. She is indeed a most beautiful girl. I wish I were a marquis, if it were only for *her* sake. Well, my Lord Callonby, you may be a very wise man in the House of Lords; but I would just ask, is it exactly prudent to introduce into your family, on terms of such perfect inti-macy, a young, fascinating, well-looking fellow of four-and-twenty, albeit only a subaltern, with two such daughters as you have? *Peut-être!* One thing is certain — *I* have no cause of complaint; and so good-night, Lady Jane." And with these words I fell asleep, to dream of the deepest blue eyes and the most melting tones that ever reduced a poor lieutenant in a marching regiment to curse his fate that he could not call the Commander of the Forces his father.

When I descended to the breakfast-room, I found the whole family assembled in a group around Lord Kilkee, who had just returned from a distant part of the county, where he had been canvassing the electors and spouting patriotism the day before. He was giving an account of his progress with much spirit and humor as I entered; but on seeing me, immediately came forward and shook hands with me like an old acquaintance. By Lord Callonby and the ladies I was welcomed also with much courtesy and kindness, and some slight *badinage* passed upon my sleep-ing in what Lord Kilkee called the "Picture Gallery," which, for all I knew to the contrary, contained but one fair portrait. I am not a believer in Mesmer; but certainly there must have been some influence at work very like what we hear of in magnetism, for before the breakfast was con-cluded there seemed at once to spring up a perfect under-standing between this family and myself, which made me feel as much *chez moi* as I had ever done in my life; and from that hour I may date an intimacy which every succeeding day but served to increase.

After breakfast Lord Callonby consigned me to the guidance of his son, and we sallied forth to deal destruction amongst the pheasants, with which the preserves were stocked; and here I may observe, *en passant*, that with the single exception of fox-hunting, which was ever a passion with me, I never could understand that inveterate pursuit of game to which some men devote themselves. Thus, grouse-shooting and its attendant pleasures of stumping over a boggy mountain from daylight till dark, never had much attraction for me; and as to the delights of widgeon and wild-duck shooting, when purchased by sitting up all night in a barrel with your eye to the bung, I'll none of it. No, no! give me shooting or angling merely as a *divertimento*, a pleasant interlude between breakfast and luncheon-time, when, consigning your Manton to a corner and the gamekeeper "to the dogs," you once more humanize your costume to take a canter with the daughters of the house, or, if the day look loweringly, a match of billiards with the men.

I have ever found that the happiest portions of existence are the most difficult to chronicle. We may — nay, we must — impart our miseries and annoyances to our many "dear friends" whose *forte* is sympathy or consolation; and all men are eloquent on the subject of their woes, — not so with their joys. Some have a miser-like pleasure in hoarding them up for their own private gratification; others — and they are prudent — feel that the narrative is scarcely agreeable even to their best friends; and a few — of whom I confess myself one — are content to be happy without knowing why, and to have pleasant souvenirs without being able to explain them.

Such must be my apology for not more minutely entering upon an account of my life at Callonby. A fortnight had now seen me *enfoncé*, the daily companion of two beautiful girls in all their walks and rides through a romantic, unfrequented country, seeing but little of the other members of the family; the gentlemen being entirely occupied with their election tactics, and Lady Callonby, being a late riser, seldom appearing before the dinner hour. There was not a cliff on the bold and rocky coast we did not climb, not a cave upon the pebbly beach unvisited. Sometimes my fair companions would bring a volume of Metastasio down to the little river where I used to angle, and the "gentle craft" was often abandoned for the heart-thrilling verses of that delightful poet. Yes, many years have passed over, and these scenes are still as fresh in my memory as though they had been of yesterday. In *my* memory, I say, "as for thee, —

> "Chi sa se mai
> Ti sovverrai di me?"

At the end of three weeks the house became full of company, from the garret to the cellar. Country gentlemen and their wives and daughters came pouring in on every species of conveyance known since the Flood; family coaches, which but for their yellow panels might have been mistaken for hearses, and high barouches, the ascent to which was accomplished by a step-ladder, followed each other in what appeared a never-ending succession. And here I may note an instance of the anomalous character of the conveyances, from an incident to which I was a witness at the time.

Among the visitors on the second day came a maiden lady from the neighborhood of Ennistimon, Miss Elizabeth O'Dowd, the last of a very old and highly respectable family in the county, and whose extensive property, thickly studded with freeholders, was a strong reason for her being paid every attention in Lord Callonby's power to bestow. Miss Betty O'Dowd — for so she was popularly styled — was the very personification of an old maid; stiff as a ramrod, and so rigid in observance of the proprieties of female conduct that in the estimation of the Clare gentry Diana was a hoyden compared to her.

Miss Betty lived, as I have said, near Ennistimon, and

the road from thence to Callonby at the time I speak of —
it was before Mr. Nimmo — was as like the bed of a mountain torrent as a respectable highway. There were holes
that would have made a grave for any maiden lady within
fifty miles, and rocks thickly scattered enough to prove
fatal to the strongest wheels that ever issued from "Hut-
ton's." Miss O'Dowd knew this well; she had upon one
occasion been upset in travelling it, and a slate-colored
silk dress bore the dye of every species of mud and mire to
be found there, for many a year after, to remind her of her
misfortune and keep open the wound of her sorrow. When,
therefore, the invitation to Callonby arrived, a grave coun-
cil of war was summoned to deliberate upon the mode of
transit, for the honor could not be declined, *coûte qu'il
coûte*. The chariot was out of the question, — Nicholas
declared it would never reach the "Moraan Beg," as the
first precipice was called; the inside car was long since
pronounced unfit for hazardous enterprise; and the only
resource left was what is called in Hibernian parlance a
"low-backed car," that is, a car without any back whatever, it being neither more nor less than the common
agricultural conveyance of the country, upon which, a
feather-bed being laid, the farmers' wives and daughters
are generally conveyed to fairs, wakes, and stations, etc.
Putting her dignity, if not in her pocket, at least wherever
it could be most easily accommodated, Miss O'Dowd placed
her fair self, in all the plenitude of her charms and the
grandeur of a "bran-new green silk," a "little off the grass,
and on the bottle" (I love to be particular), upon this humble conveyance, and set out on her way, if not "rejoicing,"
at least consoled by Nicholas that "It 'id be black dark
when they reached the house, and the devil a one 'id be the
wiser than if she came in a coach and four." Nicholas was
right; it was perfectly dark on their arrival at Callonby,
and Miss O'Dowd, having dismounted and shaken her plum-
age, a little crumpled by her half-recumbent position for
eight miles, appeared in the drawing-room to receive the
most courteous attentions from Lady Callonby, and from

his lordship the most flattering speeches for her kindness in risking herself and bringing "her horses" on such a dreadful road, and assured her of his getting a presentment the very next assizes to repair it. "For we intend, Miss O'Dowd," said he, "to be most troublesome neighbors to you in future."

The evening passed off most happily. Miss O'Dowd was delighted with her hosts, whose character she resolved to uphold in spite of their reputation for pride and haughtiness. Lady Jane sang an Irish melody for her, Lady Callonby gave her slips of a rose geranium she got from the Princess Augusta, and Lord Kilkee won her heart by the performance of that most graceful step yclept "cover the buckle," in an Irish jig. But alas! how short-lived is human bliss; for while this estimable lady revelled in the full enjoyment of the hour, the sword of Damocles hung suspended above her head. In plain English, she had on arriving at Callonby, to prevent any unnecessary scrutiny into the nature of her conveyance, ordered Nicholas to be at the door punctually at eleven, and then to take an opportunity of quietly slipping open the drawing-room door and giving her an intimation of it, that she might take her leave at once. Nicholas was up to time; and having disposed the conveyance under the shadow of the porch, made his way to the door of the drawing-room unseen and unobserved. He opened it gently and noiselessly, merely sufficient to take a survey of the apartment, in which, from the glare of the lights and the busy hum of voices, he was so bewildered that it was some minutes before he recognized his mistress. At last he perceived her: she was seated at a card-table, playing whist with Lord Callonby for her partner. Who the other players were, he knew not. A proud man was Nicholas as he saw his mistress thus placed, actually sitting, as he afterwards expressed it, "forenint the lord;" but his thoughts were bent on other matters, and it was no time to indulge his vauntings.

He strove for some time patiently to catch her eye, — for she was so situated as to permit of this, — but without success. He then made a slight attempt to attract her attention by beckoning with his finger. —all in vain. "Oh, murther!" said he, "what is this for? I'll have to spake afther all."

"Four by honors," said his lordship, "and the odd trick. Another double. I believe, Miss O'Dowd."

Miss O'Dowd nodded a graceful assent, while a sharp-looking old dowager at the side of the table called out. "A rubber of four only, my lord;" and now began an explanation from the whole party at once. Nicholas saw this was his time, and thought that in the *mélée* his hint might reach his mistress unobserved by the remainder of the company. He accordingly protruded his head into the room, and placing his finger on the side of his nose and shutting one eye knowingly, with an air of great secrecy, whispered out, "Miss Betty —Miss Betty, alanah!" For some minutes the hum of the voices drowned his admonitions; but as by degrees waxing warmer in the cause, he called out more loudly, every eye was turned to the spot from whence these extraordinary sounds proceeded; and certainly the appearance of Nicholas at the moment was well calculated to astonish the company of a drawing-room. With his one eye fixed eagerly in the direction of his mistress, his red scratch wig pushed back off his forehead, in the eagerness of his endeavor to be heard, there he stood, perfectly unmindful of all around, save Miss O'Dowd herself. It may well be believed that such an apparition could not be witnessed with gravity, and, accordingly, a general titter ran through the room, the whist party, still contending about odd tricks and honors, being the only persons insensible to the mirth around them. "Miss Betty, arrah, Miss Betty!" said Nicholas, with a sigh that converted the subdued laughter of the guests into a perfect burst of mirth.

"Eh," said his lordship, turning round, "what is this? We are losing something excellent, I fear."

At this moment he caught a glimpse of Nicholas, and throwing himself back in his chair, laughed immoderately. It was now Miss Betty's turn; she was about to rise from the table, when the well-known accents of Nicholas fell upon her ear. She fell back in her seat, — there he was; the messenger of the foul fiend himself would have been more welcome at that moment. Her blood rushed to her face and temples, her hands tingled, she closed her eyes; and when she opened them, there stood the accursed Nicholas glowering at her still.

"Man — man!" said she at length, "what do you mean? What do you want here?"

Poor Nicholas, little guessing that the question was intended to throw a doubt upon her acquaintance with him, and conceiving that the hour for the announcement had come, hesitated for an instant how he should designate the conveyance. He could not call it a coach; it certainly was not a buggy, neither was it a jaunting car: what should he say? He looked earnestly, and even imploringly, at his mistress, as if to convey some sense of his difficulty, and then, as it were catching a sudden inspiration, winked once more, as he said, —

"Miss Betty — the — the — the — " — and here he looked indescribably droll — "the thing, *you know*, is at the door."

All his lordship's politeness was too little for the occasion, and Miss O'Dowd's tenantry were lost to the Callonby interest forever.

CHAPTER IV.

"The carriage is at the door, my lord," said a servant, entering the luncheon-room where we were all assembled.

"Now then, Mr. Lorrequer," said Lord Callonby, "*allons*, take another glass of wine, and let us away.   I expect you to make a most brilliant speech, remember!"

His lordship here alluded to our intention of visiting a remote barony, where a meeting of the freeholders was that day to be held, and at which I was pledged for a "neat and appropriate" oration in abuse of the Corn-laws and the Holy Alliance.

"I beg pardon, my lord," said her ladyship, in a most languishing tone, "but Mr. Lorrequer is pre-engaged.   He has for the last week been promising and deferring his visit to the new conservatory with me, where he is to find out four or five of the Swiss shrubs that Collins cannot make out, and which I am dying to know all about."

"Mr. Lorrequer is a false man, then," said Lady Catherine; "for he said at breakfast that we should devote this afternoon to the chalk caves, as the tide will be so far out that we can see them all perfectly."

"And I," said Lord Kilkee, "must put in my plea that the aforesaid Mr. Lorrequer is booked for a coursing-match —'Mouche *versus* Jessie.'   Guilty, or not guilty?"

Lady Jane alone of all said not a word.

"Guilty on every count of the indictment," said I; "I throw myself on the mercy of the court."

"Let his sentence then be banishment," said Lady Catherine, with affected anger, "and let him go with papa."

"I rather think," said Lord Kilkee, "the better plan is to let him visit the conservatory; for I'd wager a fifty he finds it more difficult to invent botany than canvass freeholders, eh?"

"I am sure," said Lady Jane, for the first time breaking silence, "that mamma is infinitely flattered by the proposal that Mr. Lorrequer's company is to be conferred upon her for her sins."

"I am not to be affronted nor quizzed out of my chaperon. Here, Mr. Lorrequer," said Lady Callonby, rising, "get Smith's book there, and let me have your arm; and now, young ladies, come along, and learn something, if you can."

"An admirable proviso," said Lord Kilkee, laughing, "if his botany be only as authentic as the autographs he gave Mrs. MacDermot, and all of which he wrote himself, in my dressing-room, in half an hour. Napoleon was the only difficult one in the number."

Most fortunately this unfair disclosure did not reach her ladyship's ears, as she was busily engaged putting on her bonnet, and I was yet unassailed in reputation to her.

"Good-by, then," said Lord Callonby; "we meet at seven." And in a few moments the little party were scattered to their several destinations.

"How very hot you have this place, Collins," said Lady Callonby, as we entered the conservatory.

"Only seventy-five, my lady, and the magnolias require heat."

I here dropped a little behind, as if to examine a plant, and in a half-whisper said to Lady Jane, —

"How came it that you alone, Lady Jane, should forget that I had made another appointment? I thought you wished to make a sketch of Craigmoran Abbey. Did you forget that we were to ride there to-day?"

Before she could reply, Lady Callonby called out: "Oh! here it is, Mr. Lorrequer. Is this a heath? that is the question."

Here her ladyship pointed to a little scrubby thing that

looked very like a birch rod. I proceeded to examine it most minutely, while Collins waited with all the intense anxiety of a man whose character depended on the sentence.

"Collins will have it a jungermania," said she.

"And Collins is right," said I, not trusting myself with the pronunciation of the awful word her ladyship uttered.

Collins looked ridiculously happy.

"Now that is so delightful," said Lady Callonby, as she stopped to look for another puzzle.

"What a wretch it is," said Lady Catherine, covering her face with a handkerchief.

"What a beautiful little flower," said Lady Jane, lifting up the bell of a lobelia splendens.

"You know, of course," said I, "what they call that flower in France, — *L'amour tendre.*"

"Indeed!"

"True, I assure you. May I present you with this sprig of it?" cutting off a small twig, and presenting it at the same instant unseen by the others.

She hesitated for an instant, and then extending her fair and taper hand, took it. I dared not look at her as she did so, but a proud, swelling triumph at my heart nearly choked me.

"Now, Collins," said Lady Callonby, "I cannot find the Alpen-tree I brought from the Gründenwald."

Collins hurried forward to her ladyship's side.

Lady Catherine was also called to assist in the search.

I was alone with Lady Jane.

"Now or never," thought I. I hesitated — I stammered; my voice faltered. She saw my agitation; she participated in and increased it. At last I summoned up courage to touch her hand; she gently withdrew it, but so gently, it was not a repulse.

"If, Lady Jane," said I at length, "if the devoted — "

"Holloa, there!" said a deep voice without, "is Mr. Lorrequer there?"

It was Lord Kilkee, returned from his coursing-match.

None but he who has felt such an interruption can feel for me. I shame to say that his brotherhood to her for whom I would have perilled my life, restrained me not from something very like a hearty commendation of him to the powers that burn.

"Down, dogs! there, down!" continued he; and in a moment after entered the conservatory, flushed and heated with the chase.

'Mouche is the winner, — two to one; and so, Master Shallow, I owe you a thousand pounds."

Would to Heaven that I had lost the wager, had it only taken a little longer to decide it! I of course appeared overjoyed at my dog's success, and listened with great pretense of interest to the narrative of the "run," — the more so because, that though perhaps more my friend than the older members of the family, Lord Kilkee evidently liked less than they my growing intimacy with his sister; and I was anxious to blind him on the present occasion, when, but for his recent excitement, very little penetration would have enabled him to detect that something unusual had taken place.

It was now so nearly dark that her ladyship's further search for the alpine treasure became impossible, and so we turned our steps towards the garden, where we continued to walk till joined by Lord Callonby. And now began a most active discussion upon agriculture, rents, tithes, and Toryism, in which the ladies took but little part; and I had the mortification to perceive that Lady Jane was excessively bored, and seized the first opportunity to leave the party and return to the house, — while her sister gave me from time to time certain knowing glances, as if intimating that my knowledge of farming and political economy were pretty much on a par with my proficiency in botany.

"One has discovered me, at least," thought I; but the bell had rung to dress for dinner, and I hastened to my room to think over future plans, and once more wonder at the singular position into which fate and the "rules of the service" had thrown me.

CHAPTER V.

"Any letters?" said her ladyship to a servant as she crossed the hall.

"Only one, my lady, — for Mr. Lorrequer, I believe."

"For me!" thought I; "how is this?" My letters had been hitherto always left in Kilrush. Why was this forwarded here? I hurried to the drawing-room, where I found a double letter awaiting me. The writing was Curzon's, and contained the words, "To be forwarded with haste," on the direction. I opened and read as follows:

DEAR LORREQUER, — Have you any recollection, among your numerous "escapades" at Cork, of having grievously insulted a certain Mr. Giles Beamish in thought, word, or deed? If you have, I say, let me know with all convenient despatch whether the offence be one admitting of apology; for if not, the Lord have mercy on your soul! a more wrothy gentleman than the aforesaid it having rarely been my evil fortune to foregather with. He called here yesterday to inquire your address, and at my suggestion wrote a note which I now enclose. I write in great haste, and am ever yours faithfully,

C. CURZON.

N. B. — I have not seen his note, so explain all and everything.

The enclosed ran thus: —

SIR, — It can scarcely have escaped your memory, though now nearly two months since, that at the Mayor's *déjeûner* in Cork, you were pleased to make merry at my expense, and expose me and my family for your amusement. This is to demand an immediate apology, or that satisfaction which, as an officer, you will not refuse your most obedient servant,

GILES BEAMISH.

Swinburne's Hotel.

"Giles Beamish! Giles Beamish!" said I, repeating the name in every variety of emphasis, hoping to obtain some clew to the writer. Had I been appointed the umpire between Dr. Wall and his reviewers, in the late controversy about "Phonetic signs," I could not have been more completely puzzled than by the contents of this note. "Make merry at his expense!" a great offence truly, — I suppose I have laughed at better men than ever he was; and I can only say of such innocent amusement, as Falstaff did of sack and sugar, if such be a sin, "then Heaven help the wicked!" But I wish I knew who he is, or what he alludes to, provided he is not mad, which I begin to think not improbable. "By the by, my lord, do you know any such person in the South as a Mr. Beamish, — Giles Beamish?"

"To be sure," said Lord Callonby, looking up from his newspaper; "there are several of the name, of the highest respectability. One is an alderman of Cork, — a very rich man too; but I don't remember his Christian name."

"An alderman, did you say?"

"Yes, Alderman Beamish is very well known. I have seen him frequently, — a short, florid little man."

"Oh! it must be he," said I, musingly; "it must have been this worthy alderman from whose worshipful person I tore the robe of office on the night of the fête. But what does he mean by 'my exposing him and his family'? Why, zounds, his wife and children were not with him on the pavement! Oh! I see it; it is the Mansion House school of eloquence: did not Sir William Curtis apologize for not appearing at court from having lost an eye, which he designated as an awful 'domestic calamity'?"

It being now settled to my satisfaction that Mr. Beamish and the great uncloaked were "convertible terms," I set about making the *amende* in the most handsome manner possible. I wrote to the alderman a most pacific epistle, regretting that my departure from Cork deprived me of making reparation before, and expressing a most anxious hope that "he caught no cold," and a fervent wish that "he would live many years to grace and ornament the dignity of which his becoming costume was the emblem." This I enclosed in a note to Curzon, telling him how the matter occurred, and requesting that he would send it by his servant, together with the scarlet vestment, which he would find in my dressing-room. Having folded and sealed this despatch, I turned to give Lord Callonby an acount of the business, and showed him Beamish's note, at which he was greatly amused; and, indeed, it furnished food for mirth for the whole party during the evening. The next morning I set out with Lord Callonby on the long-threatened canvassing expedition, with the details of which I need not burden my "Confessions." Suffice it to say that when Lord Kilkee was advocating Toryism in the West, I, his accredited ambassador, was devoting to the infernal gods the prelacy, the peerage, and the pension list, — a mode of canvass well worthy of imitation in these troublesome times; for, not to speak of the great prospect of success from having friends on both sides of the question, the principal can always divest himself of any unpleasant consequences as regards inconsistency by throwing the blame on his friend, "who went too far," as the appropriate phrase is.

Nothing could be more successful than our mission. Lord Callonby was delighted beyond bounds with the prospect, and so completely carried away by high spirits, and so perfectly assured that much of it was owing to my exertions, that on the second morning of our tour — for we proceeded through the country for three days — he came laughing into my dressing-room with a newspaper in his hand.

"Here, Lorrequer," said he, "here's news for you. You certainly must read this." And he handed me a copy of the "Clare Herald," with an account of our meeting the evening before.

After glancing my eye rapidly over the routine usual in such cases, — "Humph, ha — nearly two hundred people — most respectable farmers — room appropriately decorated — 'Callonby Arms' — 'after the usual loyal toasts, the chairman rose' — Well, no matter. Ah! here it is: 'Mr.

Lorrequer here addressed the meeting with a flow of eloquence it has rarely, if ever, been our privilege to hear
equalled. He began by ' — humph — "

' Ah! " said his lordship, impatiently, "you will never
find it out. Look here: ' Mr. Lorrequer, whom we have
mentioned as having made the highly exciting speech, to
be found on our first page, is, we understand, the son of Sir
Guy Lorrequer, of Elton, in Shropshire, one of the wealthi-
est baronets in England. If rumor speaks truly, there is a
very near prospect of an alliance between this talented and
promising young gentleman and the beautiful and accomplished daughter of a certain noble earl with whom he has
been for some time domesticated.' "

"Eh, what think you? Son of Sir Guy Lorrequer. I
always thought my old friend a bachelor; but you see the
' Clare Herald ' knows better. Not to speak of the last
piece of intelligence, it is very good, is it not? "

"Capital indeed," said I, trying to laugh, and at the
same time blushing confoundedly, and looking as ridiculous as needs be.

It now struck me forcibly that there was something
extremely odd in his lordship's mention of this paragraph,
particularly when coupled with his and Lady Callonby's
manner to me for the last two months. They knew enough
of my family, evidently, to be aware of my station and
prospects, — or rather my want of both, — and yet in the
face of this they not only encouraged me to prolong a most
delightful visit, but by a thousand daily and dangerous
opportunities absolutely threw me in the way of one of
the loveliest of her sex, seemingly without fear on their
parts. "Well! " thought I, with my old philosophy, " Time,
that ' pregnant old gentleman,' will disclose all, and so let
us be patient! "

My reveries on my good and evil fortune were suddenly
interrupted by a letter which reached me that evening,
having been forwarded from Callonby by a special messenger "What! another epistle from Curzon," said I, as my
eye caught the address; and wondering not a little what

pressing emergency had called forth the words on the cover, — "To be forwarded with haste," — I eagerly broke the seal and read the following: —

My dear Harry, — I received yours on the 11th, and immediately despatched your note and the raiment to Mr. Beamish. He was from home at the time, but at eight o'clock I was sent for from the mess to see two gentlemen on most pressing business. I hurried to my quarters, and there found the aforesaid Mr. B., accompanied by a friend, whom he introduced as Dr. de Courcy Finucane, of the North Cork Militia, — as warlike-looking a gentleman, of his inches, some five feet three, as you would wish to see. The moment I appeared, both rose, and commenced a narrative, for such I judge it to be, but so energetically and so completely together that I could only bow politely, and at last request that one or the other would inform me of the object of their visit. Here began the tug of war, the doctor saying, "Arrah, now, Giles ;" Mr. Beamish interrupting by "Whisht, I tell ye, — now, can't you let *me ?* Ye see, Mr. Curzoin," — for so they both agreed to designate me. At last, completely worn out, I said, "Perhaps you have not received my friend's note?" At this Mr. Beamish reddened to the eyes, and with the greatest volubility poured forth a flood of indignant eloquence that I thought it necessary to check; but in this I failed, for after informing me pretty clearly that he knew nothing of your story of the alderman or his cloak, added that he firmly believed your pretended reparation was only a renewed insult, and that — But, in a word, he used such language that I was compelled to take him short ; and the *finale* is, that I agreed you should meet him, though still ignorant of what he calls the "original offence." But Heaven knows, his conduct here last night demands a reprimand, and I hope you may give it ; and if you shoot him, we may worm out the secret from his executors. Nothing could exceed the politeness of the parties on my consenting to this arrangement. Dr. Finucane proposed Carrigaholt as the rendezvous, — about twelve miles, I believe, from Kilrush, — and Tuesday evening, at six, as the time, which will be the very earliest moment we can arrive there. So pray be up to time, and believe me yours,

C. Curzon.

Saturday Evening.

It was late on Monday evening when this letter reached me, and there was no time to be lost, as I was then about forty Irish miles from the place mentioned by Curzon; so, after briefly acquainting Lord Callonby that I was called off by duty, I hurried to my room to pack my clothes and again read over this extraordinary epistle.

I confess it did appear something droll, how completely Curzon seemed to imbibe the passion for fighting from these "bloodthirsty Irishmen;" for by his own showing he was utterly ignorant of my ever having offended this Mr. Beamish, of whom I recollected nothing whatever. Yet when that gentleman waxes wrothy, rather than inconvenience him, or perhaps anxious to get back to the mess, he coolly says, "Oh! my friend shall meet you," and then his present jest, "find out the cause of quarrel from his executors"!

"Truly," thought I, "there is no equanimity like his who acts as your second in a duel. The gentlemanlike urbanity with which he waits on the opposite friend; the conciliating tone with which he proffers implacable enmity; the killing kindness with which he refuses all accommodation; the Talleyrand air of his short notes, dated from the Travellers, or Brookes, with the words 'three o'clock' or 'five o'clock' on the cover, — all indicative of the friendly precipitancy of the negotiation. Then, when all is settled, the social style with which he asks you to take a 'cutlet' with him at the Clarendon, 'not to go home,' is only to be equalled by the admirable tact on the ground, — the studiously elegant salute to the adverse party, half *à la Napoléon*, and half Beau Brummell; the politely offered snuff-box, the coquetting raillery about ten paces or twelve, are certainly the *beau idéal* of the stoicism which preludes sending your friend out of the world like a gentleman."

How very often is the face of external nature at variance with the thoughts and actions, "the sayings and doings," we may be most intent upon at the moment! How many a gay and brilliant bridal party has wended its way to St. George's, Hanover Square, amid a downpour of rain one would suppose sufficient to quench the torch of Hymen, though it burned as brightly as Captain Drummond's oxygen light; and, on the other hand, how frequently are the bluest azure of heaven and the most balmy airs shed upon the heart bursting with affliction or the head bowed with grief; and without any desire to impugn, as a much higher authority has done, the moral character of the moon, how many a scene of blood and rapine has its mild radiance illumined! Such reflections as these came thronging to my mind as on the afternoon of Tuesday I neared the little village of our rendezvous. The scene, which in all its peaceful beauty lay before me, was truly a strong contrast to the occasion that led me thither. I stood upon a little peninsula which separates the Shannon from the wide Atlantic. On one side the placid river flowed on its course between fields of waving corn or rich pasturage, — the beautiful island of Scattery, with its picturesque ruins reflected in the unrippled tide; the cheerful voices of the reapers and the merry laugh of the children were mingled with the seaman's cry of the sailors, who were "heaving short" on their anchor, to take the evening tide. The village, which consisted merely of a few small cabins, was still, from its situation, a pleasing object in the picture, and the blue smoke that rose in slender columns from the humble dwellings took from the scene its character of loneliness, and suggested feelings of home and homely enjoyments, which human habitations, however lowly, never fail to do.

"At any other time," thought I, "how I could have enjoyed all this; but now — And, ha! I find it is already past five o'clock, and if I am rightly informed I am still above a mile from 'Carrigaholt,' where we were to meet."

I had dismissed my conveyance when nearing the village, to avoid observation, and now took a footpath over the hills. Before I had proceeded half a mile the scene changed completely. I found myself traversing a small glen, grown over with a low oak shrub, and not presenting on any side the slightest trace of habitation. I saw that the ground had been selected by an adept. The glen, which grew narrow as I advanced, suddenly disclosed to my view a glimpse of the Atlantic, upon which the declining sun was pouring a flood of purple glory. I had scarcely turned from the contemplation of this beautiful object when a long low whistle attracted my attention. I looked in the direction from whence it proceeded, and discovered at some distance from me three figures standing beside the ruin of an old abbey, which I now for the first time perceived.

If I had entertained any doubt as to who they were, it had been speedily resolved, for I now saw one of the party waving his hat to me, whom I soon recognized to be Curzon. He came forward to meet me; and in the few hundred yards that intervened before our reaching the others, told me as much as he knew of the opposite party, which, after all, was but little. Mr. Beamish, my adversary, he described as a morose, fire-eating Southern, that evidently longed for an "affair" with a military man, — then considered a circumstance of some *éclat* in the South; his second, the doctor, on the contrary, was by far "the best of the cut-throats," a most amusing little personage, full of his own importance, and profuse in his legends of his own doings in love and war, and evidently disposed to take the pleasing side of every occurrence in life. They both agreed in but one point, — a firm and fixed resolve to give no explanation of the quarrel with me. "So then," said I, as Curzon hurried over the preceding account, "you absolutely know nothing whatever of the reason for which I am about to give this man a meeting?"

"No more than you," said Curzon, with imperturbable gravity; "but one thing I am certain of. Had I not at once promised him such, he would have posted you in Limerick the next morning; and as you know our mess-rule in the 4—th, I thought it best — "

"Oh! certainly, quite right; but now are you quite certain I am the man who offended him? For I solemnly assure you I have not the most remote recollection of having ever heard of him."

"That point," said Curzon, "there can be no doubt of; for he not only designated you as Mr. Harry Lorrequer, but the gentleman that made all Cork laugh so heartily by his representation of Othello."

"Stop!" said I; "not a word more. I 'm his man."

By this time we had reached the ruins, and turning a corner came in full contact with the enemy. They had been resting themselves on a tombstone, and rose as we approached.

"Allow me," said Curzon, stepping a little in advance of me, "allow me to introduce my friend Mr. Lorrequer, Dr. Finicane: Dr. Finicane, Mr. Lorrequer."

"Fin*u*cane, if quite agreeable to you, — Fin*u*cane," said the little gentleman, as he lifted his hat straight off his head, and replaced it most accurately, by way of salute. "Mr. Lorrequer, it is with sincere pleasure I make your acquaintance." Here Mr. Beamish bowed stiffly, in return to my salutation; and at the instant a kind of vague sensation crossed my mind that those red whiskers and that fiery face were not seen for the first time, — but the thumb-screws of the Holy Office would have been powerless to refresh my memory as to when.

"Captain," said the doctor, "may I request the favor of your company this way one minute?" They both walked aside; the only words which reached me as I moved off to permit their conference, being an assurance on the part of the doctor "that it was a sweet spot he picked out, for, by having them placed north and south, neither need have a patch of sky behind him." Very few minutes sufficed for preliminaries, and they both advanced, smirking and smiling as if they had just arranged a new plan for the amelioration of the poor or the benefit of the manu-facturing classes, instead of making preparations for send-ing a fellow-creature out of the world.

"Then, if I understand you, Captain," said the doctor, "you step the distance, and I give the word."

"Exactly," said Curzon.

After a joking allusion to my friend's length of limb, at which we all laughed heartily, we were placed, Curzon and the doctor standing and breaking the line between us. The pistols were then put into our hands, the doctor saying, "Now, gentlemen, I 'll just retire six paces, and turn round, which will be quite time enough to prepare, and at the word 'Fire!' ye 'll blaze away; mind now." With a knowing wink, the doctor delivered this direction, and immediately moved off. The word "Fire!" followed, and both pistols went off together. My hat was struck near the top, and as the smoke cleared away, I perceived that my ball had taken effect upon my adversary; he was wounded a little below the knee, and appeared to steady himself with the greatest difficulty. "Your friend is hit," said Curzon to the doctor, who now came forward with another pistol. "Your friend is hit."

"So I perceive," said he, placing his finger on the spot; "but it is no harm in life; so we proceed, if you please."

"You don't mean to demand another shot?" said Curzon.

"Faith do I," said the doctor, coolly.

"Then," said Curzon, "I must tell you most unequivocally I refuse, and shall now withdraw my friend; and had it not been for a regulation peculiar to our regiment, but never intended to include cases of this nature, we had not been here now, for up to this hour, my principal and myself are in utter ignorance of any cause of offence ever having been offered by him to Mr. Beamish."

"Giles, do you hear this?" said the doctor.

But Giles did not hear it; for the rapid loss of blood from his wound had so weakened him that he had fainted, and lay peaceably on the grass. Etiquette was now at an end, and we all ran forward to assist the wounded man. For some minutes he lay apparently quite senseless, and when he at last rallied and looked wildly about him, it appeared to be with difficulty that he recalled any recollection of the place and the people around him. For a few seconds he fixed his eyes steadily upon the doctor, and with a lip pale and bloodless and a voice quivering from weakness, said:

"Fin! didn't I tell ye that pistol always threw high? Oh!"—and this he said with a sigh that nearly overpowered him—"oh, Fin, if you had only given me the saw-handled one, that *I am used to* — But it is no good talking now."

In my inmost heart I was grateful to the little doctor for his mistake; for I plainly perceived what "the saw-handled one he was used to" might have done for me, and could not help muttering to myself with good Sir Andrew, — "If I had known he was so cunning of fence, I 'd have seen him damned before that I fought with him."

Our first duty was now to remove the wounded man to the high road, about which both he himself and his second seemed disposed to make some difficulty. They spoke together for a few moments in a low tone of voice, and then the doctor addressed us: "We feel, gentlemen, this is not a time for any concealment; but the truth is, we have need of great circumspection here, for I must inform you we are both of us bound over in heavy recognizances to keep the peace."

"Bound over to keep the peace!" said Curzon and myself together.

"Nothing less; and although there is nobody hereabout would tell, yet if the affair got into the papers by any means, why there are some people in Cork would like to press my friend there, for he is a very neat shot when he has the saw-handle." And here the doctor winked.

We had little time permitted us to think upon the oddity of meeting a man in such circumstances, for we were now obliged to contribute our aid in conveying him to the road, where some means might be procured for his transfer to Kilrush or some other town in the neighborhood, for he was by this time totally unable to walk.

After half an hour's toiling we at last did reach the highway, by which time I had ample opportunity, short as the space was, to see something of the character of our two opponents. It appeared that the doctor exercised the most absolute control over his large friend, dictating and commanding in a tone which the other never ventured to resist. For a moment or two Mr. Beamish expressed a great desire to be conveyed by night to Kilrush, where he might find means to cross the Shannon into Kerry. This, however, the doctor opposed strenuously, from the risk of publicity, and finally settled that we should all go in a body to his friend Father Malachi Brennan's house, only two miles off, where the sick man would have the most tender care, and, what the doctor considered equally indispensable, we ourselves a most excellent supper and a hearty welcome.

"You know Father Malachi, of course, Mr. Lorrequer?"

"I am ashamed to say I do not."

"Not know Malachi Brennan, and live in Clare! Well, well, that is strange! Sure he is the priest of this country for twelve miles in every direction of you, and a better man and a pleasanter there does not live in the diocese, though I 'm his cousin that says it."

After professing all the possible pleasure it would afford my friend and myself to make the acquaintance of Father Malachi, we proceeded to place Mr. Beamish in a car that was passing at the time, and started for the residence of the good priest. The whole of the way thither I was occupied but by one thought, — a burning anxiety to know the cause of our quarrel; and I longed for the moment when I might get the doctor apart from his friend to make the inquiry.

"There! look down to your left, where you see the lights shining so brightly, — that is Father Malachi's house; as sure as my name is De Courcy Finucane, there 's fun going on there this night."

"Why, there certainly does seem a great illumination in the valley there," said I.

"May I never," said the doctor, "if it is n't a station —"

"A station! — pray may I ask —"

"You need not ask a word on the subject; for if I am a true prophet, you 'll know what it means before morning."

A little more chatting together brought us to a narrow road, flanked on either side by high hedges of hawthorn, and in a few minutes more we stood before the priest's residence, — a long, whitewashed, thatched house, having great appearance of comfort and convenience. Arrived here, the doctor seemed at once to take on him the arrangement of the whole party; for after raising the latch and entering the house, he returned to us in a few minutes, and said, —

"Wait a while, now; we 'll not go in to Father Malachi till we 've put Giles to bed."

We accordingly lifted him from the car and assisted him into the house; and following Finucane down a narrow passage, at last reached a most comfortable little chamber, with a neat bed. Here we placed him, while the doctor gave some directions to a bare-headed, red-legged hussy, without shoes or stockings, and himself proceeded to examine the wound, which was a more serious one than it at first appeared.

After half an hour thus occupied, during which time roars of merriment and hearty peals of laughter burst upon us every time the door opened, from a distant part of the house, where his Reverence was entertaining his friends, and which, as often as they were heard by the doctor, seemed to produce in him sensations not unlike those that afflicted the "wedding guest" in the "Ancient Mariner" when he heard the "loud bassoon," and as certainly imparted an equally longing desire to be a partaker in the mirth, we arranged everything satisfactorily for Mr. Beamish's comfort, and with a large basin of vinegar and water to keep his knee cool, and a strong tumbler of hot punch to keep his heart warm, — homœopathic medicine is not half so new as Dr. Hahnemann would make us believe, — we left Mr. Beamish to his own meditations and doubtless regrets that he did not get the "saw-handled one he was used to," while we proceeded to make our bows to Father Malachi Brennan.

But as I have no intention to treat the good priest with ingratitude, I shall not present him to my readers at the tail of a chapter.

CHAPTER VI.

At the conclusion of our last chapter we left our quondam antagonist, Mr. Beamish, stretched at full length upon a bed practising homœopathy, by administering hot punch to his fever, while we followed our chaperon, Dr. Finucane, into the presence of the Reverend Father Brennan.

The company into which we now, without any ceremony on our parts, introduced ourselves consisted of from five and twenty to thirty persons, seated around a large oak table plentifully provided with materials for drinking, and cups, goblets, and glasses of every shape and form. The moment we entered, the doctor stepped forward, and touching Father Malachi on the shoulder, — for so I rightly guessed him to be, — presented himself to his relative, by whom he was welcomed with every demonstration of joy. While their recognitions were exchanged, and while the doctor explained the reasons of our visit, I was enabled, undisturbed and unnoticed, to take a brief survey of the party.

Father Malachi Brennan, P. P. of Carrigaholt, was what I had often pictured to myself as the *beau idéal* of his caste. His figure was short, fleshy, and enormously muscular, and displayed proportions which wanted but height to constitute a perfect Hercules; his legs, so thick in the calf, so taper in the ankle, looked like nothing I know, except, perhaps, the metal balustrades of Carlisle Bridge; his face was large and rosy, and the general expression a mixture of unbounded good-humor and inexhaustible drollery, to which the restless activity of his black and arched eyebrows greatly contributed; and his mouth, were it not for a character of sensuality and voluptuousness about the nether lip, had been actually handsome; his head was bald, except a narrow circle close above the ears, which was marked by a ring of curly dark hair, — sadly insufficient, however, to conceal a development behind that, if there be truth in phrenology, boded but little happiness to the disciples of Miss Martineau.

Add to these external signs a voice rich, fluent, and racy, with the mellow "doric" of his country, and you have some faint resemblance of one "every inch a priest." The very antipodes to the *bonhomie* of this figure confronted him as croupier at the foot of the table. This, as I afterwards learned, was no less a person than Mister Donovan, the coadjutor, or "curate." He was a tall, spare, ungainly looking man of about five and thirty, with a pale, ascetic countenance, the only readable expression of which vibrated between low suspicion and intense vulgarity; over his low, projecting forehead hung down a mass of straight red hair, — indeed (for Nature is not a politician), it almost approached an orange hue. This was cut close to the head all round, and displayed in their full proportions a pair of enormous ears, which stood out in "relief" like turrets from a watch-tower, and with pretty much the same object; his skin was of that peculiar color and texture to which not all "the water in great Neptune's ocean" could impart a look of cleanliness, while his very voice, hard, harsh, and inflexible, was unprepossessing and unpleasant. And yet, strange as it may seem, he, too, was a correct type of his order; the only difference being that Father Malachi was an older coinage, with the impress of Douai or St. Omer, whereas Mister Donovan was the shining metal, fresh stamped from the mint of Maynooth.

While thus occupied in my surveillance of the scene before me, I was roused by the priest saying, —

"Ah, Fin, my darling, you need n't deny it, you 're at the old game as sure as my name is Malachi, and ye 'll never be easy nor quiet till ye 're sent beyond the sea, or maybe have a record of your virtues on half a ton of marble in the churchyard yonder."

' Upon my honor, upon the sacred honor of a De Courcy — "

' Well, well, never mind it now; ye see ye 're just keeping your friends cooling themselves there in the corner. Introduce me at once."

"Mr. Lorrequer, I 'm sure — "

"My name is Curzon," said the Adjutant, bowing.

"A mighty pretty name, though a little profane. Well, Mr. Curseon," for so he pronounced it, "ye 're as welcome as the flowers in May; and it 's mighty proud I am to see ye here."

"Mr. Lorrequer, allow me to shake your hand; I 've heard of ye before."

There seemed nothing very strange in that; for go where I would through this county, I seemed as generally known as ever was Brummell in Bond Street.

"Fin tells me," continued Father Malachi, "that ye 'd rather not be known down here, in regard of a reason; " and here he winked. "Make yourselves quite easy; the king's writ was never but once in these parts, and the ' original and true copy' went back to Limerick in the stomach of the server. They made him eat it, Mr. Lorrequer! But it 's as well to be cautious, for there are a good number here. A little dinner, a little quarterly dinner we have among us, Mr. Curseon, to be social together, and raise a ' thrifle' for the Irish college at Rome, where we have a probationer or two ourselves."

"As good as a station, and more drink," whispered Fin into my ear.

"And now," continued the priest, "ye must just permit me to re-christen ye both, and the contribution will not be the less for what I 'm going to do; and I 'm certain you 'll not be the worse for the change, Mr. Curseon, — though 't is only for a few hours ye 'll have a dacent name."

As I could see no possible objection to this proposal, nor did Curzon either, our only desire being to maintain the

secrecy necessary for our antagonist's safety, we at once
assented; when Father Malachi took me by the hand, but
with such a total change in his whole air and deportment
that I was completely puzzled by it. He led me forward
to the company with a good deal of that ceremonious
reverence I have often admired in Sir Charles Vernon
when conducting some full-blown dowager through the
mazes of a Castle minuet. The desire to laugh outright
was almost irresistible as the Rev. Father stood at arm's
length from me, still holding my hand, and bowing to the
company pretty much in the style of a manager introducing
a blushing *débutante* to an audience. A moment more, and
I must have inevitably given way to a burst of laughter,
when what was my horror to hear the priest present me to
the company as their "excellent, worthy, generous, and
patriotic young landlord, Lord Kilkee. Cheer, every
mother's son of ye; cheer, I say!" and certainly precept
was never more strenuously backed by example, for he
huzzaed till I thought he would burst a blood-vessel. May
I add, I almost wished it, such was the insufferable annoyance, the chagrin, this announcement gave me; and I
waited with eager impatience for the din and clamor to
subside, to disclaim every syllable of the priest's announcement, and take the consequences of my baptismal epithet,
cost what it might. To this I was impelled by many and
important reasons. Situated as I was with respect to the
Callonby family, my assumption of their name at such a
moment might get abroad, and the consequences to me be
inevitable ruin; and independent of my natural repugnance
to such sailing under false colors, I saw Curzon laughing
almost to suffocation at my wretched predicament, and (so
strong within me was the dread of ridicule) I thought,
"What a pretty narrative he is concocting for the mess
this minute!" I rose to reply; and whether Father Malachi, with his intuitive quickness, guessed my purpose or
not, I cannot say, but he certainly resolved to out-manœuvre
me, and he succeeded. While with one hand he motioned
to the party to keep silence, with the other he took hold of

Curzon, but with no peculiar or very measured respect, and introduced him as Mr. M'Neesh, the new Scotch steward and improver, — a character at that time whose popularity might compete with a tithe proctor or an exciseman. So completely did this tactic turn the tables upon the poor Adjutant, who the moment before was exulting over me, that I utterly forgot my own woes, and sat down convulsed with mirth at his situation, — an emotion certainly not lessened as I saw Curzon passed from one to the other at table "like a pauper to his parish," till he found an asylum at the very foot, in juxta with the engaging Mr. Donovan, — a propinquity, if I might judge from their countenances, uncoveted by either party.

While this was performing, Dr. Finucane was making his recognitions with several of the company, to whom he had been long known during his visits to the neighborhood. I now resumed my place on the right of "the father," abandoning for the present all intention of disclaiming my rank, and the campaign was opened. The priest now exerted himself to the utmost to recall conversation into the original channels, and if possible to draw off attention from me, which he still feared might perhaps elicit some unlucky announcement on my part. Failing in his endeavors to bring matters to their former footing, he turned the whole brunt of his attentions to the worthy doctor, who sat on his left.

"How goes on the law," said he, "Fin? Any new proofs, as they call them, forthcoming?"

What Fin replied I could not hear; but the allusion to the "suit" was explained by Father Malachi informing us that the only impediment between his cousin and the title of Kinsale lay in the unfortunate fact that his grandmother, "rest her sowl," was not a man.

Dr. Finucane winced a little under the manner in which this was spoken, but returned the fire by asking if the bishop was down lately in that quarter? The evasive way in which "the father" replied having stimulated my curiosity as to the reason, little entreaty was necessary to persuade the doctor to relate the following anecdote, which was not relished the less by his superior that it told somewhat heavily on Mr. Donovan.

"It is about four years ago," said the doctor, "since the bishop, Dr. Plunkett, took it into his head that he 'd make a general inspection, ' a reconnoissance,' as we 'd call it, Mr. Lor — that is, my lord! — through the whole diocese, and leave no part, far or near, without poking his nose in it and seeing how matters were doing. He heard very queer stories about his reverence here, and so down he came one morning in the month of July, riding upon an old gray hack, looking just for all the world like any other elderly gentleman in very rusty black. When he got near the village he picked up a little boy to show him the short cut across the fields to the house here; and as his lordship was a ' sharp man and a shrewd,' he kept his eye on everything as he went along, remarking this, and noting down that.

"' Are ye regular in your duties, my son?' said he to the child.

"' I never miss a Sunday,' said the gossoon; ' for it 's always walking his reverence's horse I am the whole time av prayers.'

"His lordship said no more for a little while, when he muttered between his teeth, 'Ah! it 's just slander; nothing but slander and lying tongues.' This soliloquy was caused by his remarking that on every gate he passed, or from every cabin, two or three urchins would come out half naked, but all with the finest heads of red hair he ever saw in his life.

"' How is it, my son,' said he at length, ' they tell very strange stories about Father Malachi, and I see so many of these children with red hair, eh? Now, Father Malachi 's a dark man.'

"' True for ye,' said the boy, ' true for ye, Father Malachi 's dark; but the coadjutor,—the coadjutor 's as red as a fox.' "

When the laugh this story caused had a little subsided, Father Malachi called out, "Mickey Oulahan! Mickey, I say, hand his lordship over 'the groceries,'"—thus he designated a square decanter containing about two quarts of whiskey and a bowl heaped high with sugar. "A dacent boy is Mickey, my lord, and I'm happy to be the means of making him known to you." I bowed with condescension, while Mr. Oulahan's eyes sparkled like diamonds at the recognition.

"He has only two years of the lease to run, and a 'long charge'" (*anglicè*, a large family), continued the priest.

"I'll not forget him, you may depend upon it," said I.

"Do you hear that?" said Father Malachi, casting a glance of triumph round the table, while a general buzz of commendation on priest and patron went round, with many such phrases as "Och, thin," "it's his riv'rance *can* do it," "na bocklish," "and why not," etc. As for me, I have already "confessed" to my crying sin, — a fatal, irresistible inclination to follow the humor of the moment wherever it led me; and now I found myself as active a partisan in quizzing Mickey Oulahan as though I was not myself a party included in the jest. I was thus fairly launched into my inveterate habit, and nothing could arrest my progress.

One by one the different individuals round the table were presented to me and made known their various wants, with an implicit confidence in my power of relieving them which I with equal readiness ministered to. I lowered the rent of every man at table. I made a general jail-delivery, — an act of grace, I blush to say, which seemed to be peculiarly interesting to the present company. I abolished all arrears, made a new line of road through an impassable bog and over an inaccessible mountain, and conducted water to a mill which (I learned in the morning) was always worked by wind. The decanter had scarcely completed its third circuit of the board when I bid fair to be the most popular specimen of the peerage that ever visited the "Far West." In the midst of my career of universal benevolence, I was interrupted by Father Malachi, whom I found on his legs pronouncing a glowing eulogium on his cousin's late regiment, the famous North Cork.

"That was the corps!" said he.   "Bid them do a thing, and they'd never leave off; and so, when they got orders to retire from Wexford, it's little they cared for the comforts of baggage, like many another regiment, for they threw away everything but their canteens, and never stopped till they ran to Ross, fifteen miles farther than the enemy followed them.   And when they were all in bed the same night, fatigued and tired with their exertions, as ye may suppose, a drummer-boy called out in his sleep, ' Here they are — they're coming!' they all jumped up and set off in their shirts, and got two miles out of town before they discovered it was a false alarm."

Peal after peal of laughter followed the priest's encomium on the doctor's regiment; and, indeed, he himself joined most heartily in the mirth, as he might well afford to do, seeing that a braver or better corps than the North Cork, Ireland did not possess.

"Well," said Fin, "it's easy to see ye never can forget what they did at Maynooth."

Father Malachi disclaimed all personal feeling on the subject, and I was at last gratified by the following narrative, which I regret deeply I am not enabled to give in the doctor's own words; but writing as I do from memory, in most instances, I can only convey the substance.

It was towards the latter end of the year '98 — the year of the troubles — that the North Cork was ordered, "for their sins," I believe, to march from their snug quarters in Fermoy and take up a position in the town of Maynooth, — a very considerable reverse of fortune to a set of gentlemen extremely addicted to dining out and living at large upon a very pleasant neighborhood.   Fermoy abounded in gentry; Maynooth, at that time, had few, if any, excepting his Grace of Leinster, and he lived very privately and saw no company.   Maynooth was stupid and dull, — there were neither belles nor balls; Fermoy (to use the doctor's well-remembered words) had "great feeding" and "very genteel young ladies, that carried their handkerchiefs in bags, and danced with the officers."

They had not been many weeks in their new quarters when they began to pine over their altered fortunes, and it was with a sense of delight, which a few months before would have been incomprehensible to them, they discovered that one of their officers had a brother, a young priest in the college; he introduced him to some of his confrères, and the natural result followed. A visiting acquaintance began between the regiment and such of the members of the college as had liberty to leave the precincts, who, as time ripened the acquaintance into intimacy, very naturally preferred the mess of the North Cork to the meagre fare of "the refectory." At last, seldom a day went by without one or two of their reverences finding themselves guests at the mess. The North Corkians were of a most hospitable turn, and the fathers were determined the virtue should not rust for want of being exercised; they would just drop in to say a word to "Captain O'Flaherty about leave to shoot in the demesne," as Carton was styled; or they had a "frank from the Duke for the Colonel," or some other equally pressing reason; and they would contrive to be caught in the middle of a very droll story just as the "roast beef" was playing. Very little entreaty then sufficed, — a short apology for the "derangements" of dress, and a few minutes more found them seated at table without further ceremony on either side.

Among the favorite guests from the college, two were peculiarly in estimation, — "the Professor of the Humanities," Father Luke Mocney, and the Abbé d'Array, "the Lecturer on Moral Philosophy and Belles-Lettres;" and certain it is, pleasanter fellows, or more gifted with the "convivial bump," there never existed. He of the Humanities was a droll dog, — a member of the Curran Club, the "monks of the screw," — told an excellent story, and sang the "Cruiskeen Lawn" better than did any before or since him; the moral philosopher, though of a different *genre*, was also a most agreeable companion, — an Irishman transplanted in his youth to St. Omer, and who had grafted upon his native humor a considerable share of French smartness and repartee. Such were the two who ruled supreme in all the festive arrangements of this jovial regiment, and were at last as regular at table as the adjutant and the paymaster, and so might they have continued, had not prosperity, that in its blighting influence upon the heart spares neither priests nor laymen, and is equally severe upon mice (see Æsop's fable) and moral philosophers, actually deprived them, for the "nonce," of reason, and tempted them to their ruin. You naturally ask, what did they do? Did they venture upon allusions to the retreat upon Ross? Nothing of the kind. Did they, in that vanity which wine inspires, refer by word, act, or inuendo, to the well-known order of their colonel when reviewing his regiment in "the Phœnix," to "advance two steps backwards, and dress by the gutter"? Far be it from them, — though indeed either of these had been esteemed light in the balance with their real crime. "Then what was their failing? Come, tell it, and burn ye!" They actually — I dread to say it — quizzed the Major *coram* the whole mess! Now, Major John Jones had only lately exchanged into the North Cork from the "Darry Ragement," as he called it. He was a red-hot Orangeman, a deputy-grand something, and vice-chairman of the "'Prentice Boys" besides. He broke his leg when a schoolboy by a fall incurred in tying an orange handkerchief around King William's august neck in College Green on one 12th of July, and three several times had closed the gates of Derry with his own loyal hands on the famed anniversary, — in a word, he was one that, if his Church had enjoined penance as an expiation for sin, would have looked upon a trip to Jerusalem on his bare knees as a very light punishment for the crime on his conscience that he sat at table with two buck priests from Maynooth, and carved for them, like the rest of the company!

Poor Major Jones, however, had no such solace, and the cankerworm ate daily deeper and deeper into his pining heart. During the three or four weeks of their intimacy with his regiment, his martyrdom was awful. His figure wasted, and his color became a deeper tinge of orange, and all around averred that there would soon be a "move up" in the corps, for the Major had evidently "got his notice to quit" this world and its pomps and vanities. He felt "that he was dying," to use Haynes Bayley's beautiful and apposite words, and meditated an exchange; but that, from circumstances, was out of the question. At last, subdued by grief, and probably his spirit having chafed itself smooth by such constant attrition, he became to all seeming calmer; but it was only the calm of a broken and weary heart. Such was Major Jones at the time when, *suadente diabolo*, it seemed meet to Fathers Mooney and D'Array to make him the butt of their raillery. At first he could not believe it, — the thing was incredible, impossible; but when he looked around the table, when he heard the roars of laughter, long, loud, and vociferous; when he heard his name bandied from one to the other across the table, with some vile jest tacked to it "like a tin kettle to a dog's tail," he awoke to the full measure of his misery, — the cup was full. Fate had done her worst, and he might have exclaimed with Lear, "Spit, fire — spout, rain," there was nothing in store for him of further misfortune.

A drum-head court-martial, a hint "to sell out," ay, a sentence of "dismissed the service," had been mortal calamities, and, like a man, he would have borne them; but that he, Major John Jones, D.G.S.C.P.B., etc., who had drunk the "pious, glorious, and immortal," sitting astride of "the great gun of Athlone," should come to this! Alas and alas He retired that night to his chamber a "sadder, if not a wiser man;" he dreamed that the "statue" had given place to the unshapely figure of Leo X., and that "Lundy now stood where Walker stood before." He jumped from his bed in a moment of enthusiasm, he vowed his revenge, and he kept his vow.

That day the Major was "acting field-officer." The various patrols, sentries, pickets, and outposts were all under his especial control, and it was remarked that he took peculiar pains in selecting the men for night duty, which, in the prevailing quietness and peace of that time, seemed scarcely warrantable.

Evening drew near, and Major Jones, summoned by the "oft-heard beat," wended his way to the mess. The officers were dropping in, and true as "the needle to the pole," came Father Mooney and the Abbé. They were welcomed with the usual warmth, and, strange to say, by none more than the Major himself, whose hilarity knew no bounds.

How the evening passed, I shall not stop to relate; suffice it to say that a more brilliant feast of wit and jollification not even the North Cork ever enjoyed. Father Luke's drollest stories, his very quaintest humor, shone forth, and the Abbé sang a new *chanson à boire* that Béranger might have envied.

"What are you about, my dear Father d'Array?" said the Colonel. "You are surely not rising yet? Here's a fresh cooper of port just come in; sit down, I entreat."

"I say it with grief, my dear Colonel, we must away; the half-hour has just chimed, and we must be within 'the gates' before twelve. The truth is, the superior has been making himself very troublesome about our 'carnal amusements,' as he calls our innocent mirth, and we must therefore be upon our guard."

"Well, if it must be so, we shall not risk losing your society altogether for an hour or so now; so, one bumper to our next meeting, — to-morrow, mind; and now, *Monsieur l'Abbé, au revoir.*"

The worthy fathers finished their glasses, and taking a most affectionate leave of their kind entertainers, sallied forth under the guidance of Major Jones, who insisted upon accompanying them part of the way, as, "from information he had received, the sentries were doubled in some places, and the usual precautions against surprise all taken." Much as this polite attention surprised the objects of it. his brother officers wondered still more, and no sooner did they perceive the Major and his companions issue forth than they set out in a body to watch where this most novel and unexpected complaisance would terminate.

When the priests reached the door of the barrack-yard, they again turned to utter their thanks to the Major, and entreat him once more "not to come a step farther. There now, Major, we know the path well, so just give us the pass, and don't stay out in the night air."

"*Ah, oui, Monsieur Jones,*" said the Abbé, "*retournez, je vous prie. We are, I may say, chez nous. Ces braves gens, les* North Cork, know us by this time."

The Major smiled, while he still pressed his services to see them past the pickets; but they were resolved, and would not be denied.

"With the word for the night we want nothing more," said Father Luke.

"Well, then," said the Major, in the gravest tone, — and he was naturally grave, — "you shall have your way; but remember to call out loud, for the first sentry is a little deaf, and a very passionate, ill-tempered fellow to boot."

"Never fear," said Father Mooney, laughing; "I'll go bail he'll hear me."

"Well, the word for the night is, 'Bloody end to the Pope,' — don't forget, now, 'Bloody end to the Pope.'" And with these words he banged the door between him and the unfortunate priests; and as bolt was fastened after bolt, they heard him laughing to himself like a fiend over his vengeance.

"And big bad luck to ye, Major Jones, for the same, every day ye see a paving-stone," was the faint, sub-audible ejaculation of Father Luke, when he was recovered enough to speak.

"*Sacristi! que nous sommes attrapés,*" said the Abbé, scarcely able to avoid laughing at the situation in which they were placed.

"Well, there's the quarter chiming now; we've no time to lose. Major Jones! Major darling! don't now, ah, don't! sure ye know we'll be ruined entirely. There now, just change it, like a dacent fellow! The devil's luck to him, he's gone! Well, we can't stay here in the rain all night, and be expelled in the morning afterwards, so come along."

They jogged along for a few minutes in silence, till they came to that part of the "Duke's" demesne wall where the first sentry was stationed. By this time the officers, headed by the Major, had quietly slipped out of the gate, and were following their steps at a convenient distance.

The fathers had stopped to consult together what they should do in this trying emergency, when, their whisper being overheard, the sentinel called out gruffly, in the genuine dialect of his country, "Who goes *that?*"

"Father Luke Mooney and the Abbé d'Array," said the former, in his most bland and insinuating tone of voice, — a quality he most eminently possessed.

"Stand, and give the countersign."

"We are coming from the mess, and going home to the college," said Father Mooney, evading the question, and gradually advancing as he spoke.

"Stand, or I 'll *shot* ye," said the North Corkian.

Father Luke halted, while a muttered "Blessed Virgin!" announced his state of fear and trepidation.

"D'Array, I say, what are we to do?"

"The countersign," said the sentry, whose figure they could perceive in the dim distance of about thirty yards.

"Sure ye 'll let us pass, my good lad, and ye 'll have a friend in Father Luke the longest day ye live; and ye might have a worse in time of need, — ye understand."

Whether he did understand or not, he certainly did not heed, for his only reply was the short click of a gun-lock, that bespeaks a preparation to fire.

"There 's no help now," said Father Luke; "I see he 's a haythen; and bad luck to the Major, I say again." And this, in the fulness of his heart, he uttered aloud.

"'That 's not the countersign," said the inexorable sentry, striking the butt-end of his musket on the ground with a crash that smote terror into the hearts of the priests.

Mumble — mumble — "to the Pope," said Father Luke, pronouncing the last words distinctly, after the approved practice of a Dublin watchman on being awoke from his dreams of row and riot by the last toll of the Post-office,

and not knowing whether it has struck "twelve" or "three," sings out the word "o'clock" in a long, sonorous drawl, that wakes every sleeping citizen, and yet tells nothing how "Time speeds on his flight."

"Louder," said the sentry, in a voice of impatience.

"— to the Pope."

"I don't hear the first part."

"Oh, then," said the priest, with a sigh that might have melted the heart of anything but a sentry, "Bloody end to the Pope; and may the saints in heaven forgive me for saying it!"

"Again," called out the soldier, "and no muttering."

"Bloody end to the Pope," cried Father Luke, in bitter desperation.

"Bloody end to the Pope," echoed the Abbé.

"Pass, Bloody end to the Pope, and good-night," said the sentry, resuming his rounds ; while a loud and uproarious peal of laughter behind told the unlucky priests they were overheard by others, and that the story would be over the whole town in the morning.

Whether it was that the penance for their heresy took long in accomplishing, or that they never could summon courage sufficient to face their persecutor, certain it is the North Cork saw them no more, nor were they ever observed to pass the precincts of the college while that regiment occupied Maynooth.

Major Jones himself and his confederates could not have more heartily relished this story than did the party to whom the doctor related it. Much, if not all, the amusement it afforded, however, resulted from his inimitable mode of telling, and the power of mimicry with which he conveyed the dialogue with the sentry; and this, alas! must be lost to my readers, — at least to that portion of them not fortunate enough to possess Dr. Finucane's acquaintance.

"Fin! Fin! your long story has nearly famished me," said the *padre*, as the laugh subsided; "and there you sit now with the jug at your elbow this half-hour; I never

thought you would forget our old friend Martin Hanegan's
aunt."

"Here's to her health," said Fin; "and your reverence
will give us the chant."

"Agreed," said Father Malachi, finishing a bumper; and
after giving a few preparatory hems, he sang the following
"singularly wild and beautiful poem," as some one calls
"Christabel:"—

> "Here's a health to Martin Hanegan's aunt
> And I 'll tell ye the reason why!
> She eats bekase she is hungry,
> And drinks bekase she is dry.
>
> "And if ever a man
> Stopped the course of a can,
> Martin Hanegan's aunt would cry, —
> 'Arrah, fill up your glass,
> And let the jug pass ;
> How d 'ye know but your neighbor 's dhry ?'

"Come, my lord and gentlemen, *da capo*, if ye please —
'Fill up your glass,'" etc.; and the *chanson* was chorused
with a strength and vigor that would have astonished the
Philharmonic.

The mirth and fun now grew "fast and furious;" and
Father Malachi, rising with the occasion, flung his reckless
drollery and fun on every side, sparing none, from his
cousin to the coadjutor. It was now that peculiar period
in the evening's enjoyment when an expert and practical
chairman gives up all interference or management, and
leaves everything to take its course; this, then, was the
happy moment selected by Father Malachi to propose the
little "conthribution." He brought a plate from a side-
table, and placing it before him, addressed the company in
a very brief but sensible speech, detailing the object of the
institution he was advocating, and concluding with the following words: "And now ye 'll just give whatever ye like,
according to your means in life and what ye can spare."

The admonition, like the "morale" of an income tax, had

the immediate effect of pitting each man against his neighbor, and suggested to their already excited spirits all the ardor of gambling, without, however, the prospect of gain. The plate was first handed to me, in honor of my "rank;" and having deposited upon it a handful of small silver, the priest ran his fingers through the coin, and called out, —

"Five pounds at least, — not a farthing less, as I am a sinner. Look, then, — see, now; they tell ye the gentlemen don't care for the like of ye! but see for yourselves. May I trouble y'r lordship to pass the plate to Mr. Mahony, — he's impatient, I see."

 Mr. Mahony, about whom I perceived very little of the impatience alluded to, was a grim-looking old Christian in a rabbit-skin waistcoat with long flaps, who fumbled in the recesses of his breeches-pocket for five minutes, and then drew forth three shillings, which he laid upon the plate with what I fancied very much resembled a sigh.

"Six and sixpence, is it, or five shillings? All the same, Mr. Mahony; and I'll not forget the thrifle you were speaking about this morning, any way." And here he leaned over, as interceding with me for him, but in reality to whisper into my ear, "The greatest miser from this to Castlebar."

"Who's that put down the half guinea in goold?" (and this time he spoke truth) — "who's that, I say?"

"Tim Kennedy, your reverence," said Tim, stroking his hair down with one hand, and looking proud and modest at the same moment.

"Tim, ye're a credit to us any day, and I always said so. It's a gauger he'd like to be, my lord," said he, turning to me in a kind of stage whisper. I nodded, and muttered something, when he thanked me most profoundly, as if his suit had prospered.

"Mickey Oulahan, the Lord's looking at ye, Mickey." This was said *pianissimo* across the table, and had the effect of increasing Mr. Oulahan's donation from five shillings to seven, — the last two being pitched in very much in the style of a gambler making his final *coup*, and crying, " *Va, banque!*" "The Oulahans were always dacent people, — dacent people, my lord."

"Be gorra, the Oulahans was niver dacenter nor the Molowneys, anyhow," said a tall, athletic young fellow as he threw down three crown-pieces with an energy that made every coin leap from the plate.

"They 'll do now," said Father Brennan; "I 'll leave them to themselves." And truly the eagerness to get the plate and put down the subscription fully equalled the rapacious anxiety I have witnessed in an old maid at loo to get possession of a thirty-shilling pool, be the same more or less, which lingered on its way to her in the hands of many a fair competitor.

"Mr. M'Neesh" — Curzon had hitherto escaped all notice — "Mr. M'Neesh, to your good health," cried Father Brennan. "It 's many a secret they 'll be getting out o' ye down there about the Scotch husbandry."

Whatever poor Curzon knew of "drills," certainly did not extend to them when occupied by turnips. This allusion of the priest's being caught up by the party at the foot of the table, they commenced a series of inquiries into different Scotch plans of tillage, — his brief and unsatisfactory answers to which, they felt sure, were given in order to evade imparting information. By degrees, as they continued to press him with questions, his replies grew more short, and a general feeling of dislike on both sides was not very long in following.

The father saw this, and determining, with his usual tact, to repress it, called on the Adjutant for a song. Now, whether he had but one in the world, or whether he took this mode of retaliating for the annoyances he had suffered, I know not; but true it is, he finished his tumbler at a draught, and with a voice of no very peculiar sweetness, though abundantly loud, began "The Boyne Water."

He had just reached the word "battle," in the second line, upon which he was bestowing what he meant to be a shake, when, as if the word suggested it, it seemed the signal for a general engagement. Decanters, glasses, jugs, candlesticks, — ay, and the money-dish, — flew right and left, all originally intended, it is true, for the head of the luckless Adjutant, but as they now and then missed their aim, and came in contact with the "wrong man," invariably provoked retaliation, and in a very few minutes the battle became general.

What may have been the doctor's political sentiments on this occasion, I cannot even guess; but he seemed bent upon performing the part of a "convivial Lord Stanley," and maintaining a dignified neutrality. With this apparent object, he mounted upon the table, — to raise himself, I suppose, above the din and commotion of party clamor, — and brandishing a jug of scalding water, bestowed it with perfect impartiality on the combatants on either side. This Whig plan of conciliation, however well intended, seemed not to prosper with either party; and many were the missiles directed at the ill-starred doctor. Meanwhile Father Malachi, whether following the pacific instinct of his order, in seeking an asylum in troublesome times, or equally moved by old habit to gather coin in low places (much of the money having fallen), was industriously endeavoring to insert himself beneath the table. In this, with one vigorous push, he at last succeeded; but in so doing lifted it from its legs, and thus destroying poor "Fin's" gravity, precipitated him, jug and all, into the thickest of the fray, where he met with that kind reception such a benefactor ever receives at the hand of a grateful public. I meanwhile hurried to rescue poor Curzon, who, having fallen to the ground, was getting a cast of his features taken in pewter, for such seemed the operation a stout farmer was performing on the Adjutant's face with a quart. With considerable difficulty, notwithstanding my supposed "lordship," I succeeded in freeing him from his present position; and he concluding, probably, that enough had been done for one "sitting," most willingly permitted me to lead him from the room. I was soon joined by the doctor, who assisted me in getting my poor friend to bed; which being done, he most eagerly entreated me to join the company. This, however, I firmly but mildly declined, very much to his surprise; for, as he remarked, "They'll all be like lambs now, for they don't believe there's a whole bone in his body."

Expressing my deep sense of the Christian-like forbearance of the party, I pleaded fatigue, and bidding him goodnight, adjourned to my bedroom; and here, although the arrangements fell somewhat short of the luxurious ones appertaining to my late apartment at Callonby, they were most grateful at the moment; and having "addressed myself to slumber," fell fast asleep, and only awoke late on the following morning to wonder where I was; from any doubts as to which I was speedily relieved by the entrance of the priest's bare-footed "colleen," to deposit on my table a bottle of soda-water, and announce breakfast, with his reverence's compliments.

Having made a hasty toilet, I proceeded to the parlor, which, however late events might have impressed upon my memory, I could scarcely recognize. Instead of the long oak table and the wassail-bowl, there stood near the fire a small round table covered with a snow-white cloth, upon which shone in unrivalled brightness a very handsome tea-equipage. The hissing kettle on one hob was balanced by a gridiron with three newly taken trout frying under the reverential care of Father Malachi himself; a heap of eggs, ranged like shot in an ordnance yard, stood in the middle of the table, while a formidable pile of buttered toast browned before the grate; the morning papers were airing upon the hearth, — everything bespoke that attention to comfort and enjoyment one likes to discover in the house where chance may have domesticated him for a day or two.

"Good-morning, Mr. Lorrequer. I trust you have rested well," said Father Malachi, as I entered.

"Never better; but where are our friends?"

"I have been visiting and comforting them in their affliction, and I may with truth assert it is not often my fortune to have three as sickly looking guests. That was a most unlucky affair last night, and I must apologize — "

"Don't say a word, I entreat; I saw how it all occurred, and am quite sure if it had not been for poor Curzon's ill-timed melody —"

"You are quite right," said the father, interrupting me. "Your friend's taste for music — bad luck to it! — was the *teterrima causa belli*."

"And the subscription," said I, — "how did it succeed?"

"Oh! the money went in the commotion; and although I have got some seven pounds odd shillings of it, the war was a most expensive one to me. I caught old Mahony very busy under the table during the fray — But let us say no more about it now; draw over your chair. Tea or coffee? There's the rum, if you like it in French fashion."

I immediately obeyed the injunction, and commenced a vigorous assault upon the trout, — caught, as he informed me, "within twenty perches of the house."

"Your poor friend's nose is scarcely regimental," said he, "this morning; and as for Fin, he was never remarkable for beauty, so, though they might cut and hack, they could scarcely disfigure him. As Juvenal says — is n't it Juvenal? —

"' Cantabit vacuus coram latrone viator ; '

or, in the vernacular, —

"' The empty traveller may whistle
Before the robber and his pistil' [pistol].

There's the Chili vinegar, — another morsel of the trout?"

"I thank you. What excellent coffee, Father Malachi!"

"A secret I learned at St. Omer's some thirty years since. Any letters, Bridget?" — to a damsel that entered with a packet in her hand.

"A gossoon from Kilrush, y'r reverence, with a bit of a note for the gentleman there."

"For me? Ah, true enough! 'Harry Lorrequer, Esq., Kilrush. — Try Carrigaholt.'" So ran the superscription, — the first part being in a lady's handwriting; the latter very like the "rustic paling" of the worthy Mrs. Healy's style. The seal was a large one, bearing a coronet at top;

and the motto, in old Norman-French, told me it came from
Callonby.

With what a trembling hand and beating heart I broke it
open, and yet feared to read it, — so much of my destiny
might be in that simple page! For once in my life my sanguine spirit failed me; my mind could take in but one casu-'
alty, that Lady Jane had divulged to her family the nature
of my attentions, and that in the letter before me lay a cold
mandate of dismissal from her presence forever.

At last I summoned courage to read it; but having scrupled to present to my readers the Reverend Father Brennan
at the end of a chapter, let me be not less punctilious in
the introduction of her ladyship's billet.

CHAPTER VII.

HER ladyship's letter ran thus: —

CALLONBY, Tuesday morning.

MY DEAR MR. LORREQUER, — My lord has deputed me to convey to you our adieus, and at the same time express our very great regret that we should not have seen you before our departure from Ireland. A sudden call of the House, and some unexpected ministerial changes, require Lord Callonby's immediate presence in town ; and probably before this reaches you we shall be on the road. Lord Kilkee, who left us yesterday, was much distressed at not having seen you, — he desired me to say you shall hear from him from Leamington. Although writing amid all the haste and bustle of departure, I must not forget the principal part of my commission, nor, ladylike, defer it to a postscript: my lord entreats that you will, if possible, pass a month or two with us in London this season ; and if any difficulty should occur in obtaining leave of absence, to make any use of his name you think fit at the Horse Guards, where he has some influence. Knowing as I do with what kindness you ever accede to the wishes of your friends, I need not say how much gratification this will afford us all ; but, *sans réponse,* we expect you. Believe me to remain, yours very sincerely,

CHARLOTTE CALLONBY.

P. S. — We are quite well, except Lady Jane, who has a slight cold and has been feverish for the last day or two.

Words cannot convey any idea of the torrent of contending emotions under which I perused this letter. The suddenness of the departure, without an opportunity of even a moment's leave-taking, completely unmanned me. What would I not have given to be able to see her once more, ever for an instant; to say "a good-by;" to watch the feeling with which she parted from me, and augur from it either favorably to my heart's dearest hope or darkest despair. As I continued to read on, the kindly tone of the remainder reassured me; and when I came to the invitation to London, which plainly argued a wish on their part to perpetuate the intimacy, I was obliged to read it again and again before I could convince myself of its reality. There it was, however, most distinctly and legibly impressed in her ladyship's fairest calligraphy; and certainly, great as was its consequence to me at the time, it by no means formed the principal part of the communication. The two lines of postscript contained more, far more, food for hopes and fears than did all the rest of the epistle.

Lady Jane was ill, then; slightly, however, — a mere cold; true, but she was feverish. I could not help asking myself what share had I in causing that flushed cheek and anxious eye, and pictured to myself, perhaps with more vividness than reality, a thousand little traits of manner, all proofs strong as holy writ to my sanguine mind that my affection was returned, and that I loved not in vain. Again and again I read over the entire letter; never, truly, did a *nisi prius* lawyer con over a new Act of Parliament with more searching ingenuity to detect its hidden meaning, than I did to unravel through its plain phraseology the secret intention of the writer towards me.

There is an old and not less true adage that what we wish we readily believe, and so with me. I found myself an easy convert to my own hopes and desires, and actually ended by persuading myself — no very hard task — that my Lord Callonby had not only witnessed but approved of my attachment to his beautiful daughter, and for reasons probably known to him, but concealed from me, opined that I was a suitable *parti*, and gave all due encouragement to my suit. The hint about using his lordship's influence at the Horse Guards I resolved to benefit by, — not, however, in obtaining leave of absence, which I hoped to accomplish more easily, but with his good sanction in pushing my promotion when I should claim him as my right-honorable father-in-law: a point on the propriety of which I had now fully satisfied myself. What visions of rising greatness burst upon my mind as I thought on the prospect that opened before me! But here let me do myself the justice to record that amid all my pleasure and exultation, my proudest thought was in the anticipation of possessing one in every way so much my superior, — the very consciousness of which imparted a thrill of fear to my heart that such good fortune was too much even to hope for.

How long I might have luxuriated in such *châteaux en Espagne*, Heaven knows; thick and thronging fancies came abundantly to my mind, and it was with something of the feeling of the porter in the "Arabian Nights" as he surveyed the fragments of his broken ware hurled down in a moment of glorious dreaminess that I turned to look at the squat and unaristocratic figure of Father Malachi as he sat reading his newspaper before the fire. How came I in such company? Methinks the Dean of Windsor or the Bishop of Durham had been a much more seemly associate for one destined as I was for the flood-tide of the world's favor.

My eye at this instant rested upon the date of the letter, which was that of the preceding morning; and immediately a thought struck me that, as the day was a lowering and gloomy one, perhaps they might have deferred their journey, and I at once determined to hasten to Callonby, and if possible see them before their departure.

"Father Brennan," said I at length, "I have just received a letter which compels me to reach Kilrush as soon as possible. Is there any public conveyance in the village?"

"You don't talk of leaving us, surely," said the priest, "and a haunch of mutton for dinner, and Fin says he'll be down, and your friend too, and we'll have poor Beamish in on a sofa!"

"I am sorry to say my business will not admit of delay; but if possible, I shall return to thank you for all your kindness in a day or two, — perhaps to-morrow."

"Oh! then," said Father Brennan, "if it must be so, why you can have Pether, my own pad, and a better you never laid leg over; only give him his own time, and let him keep the 'canter,' and he'll never draw up from morning till night.   And now I'll just go and have him in readiness for you."

After professing my warm acknowledgments to the good father for his kindness, I hastened to take a hurried fare-well of Curzon before going.   I found him sitting up in bed taking his breakfast.   A large strip of black plaster, extend-ing from the corner of one eye across the nose, and terminat-ing near the mouth, denoted the *locale* of a goodly wound; while the blue, purple, and yellow patches into which his face was partitioned out, left you in doubt whether he more resembled the knave of clubs or a new map of the Ordnance Survey.   One hand was wrapped up in a bandage; and alto-gether a more rueful and woe-begone looking figure I have rarely looked upon; and most certainly I am of opinion that the "glorious, pious, and immortal memory" would have brought pleasanter recollections to Daniel O'Connell him-self than it did on that morning to the Adjutant of his Majesty's 4—th.

"Ah! Harry," said he, as I entered, "what Pandemonium is this we've got into?   Did you ever witness such a busi-ness as last night's?"

"Why, truly," said I, "I know of no one to blame but yourself; surely you must have known what a row your infernal song would bring on."

"I don't know now whether I knew it or not; but cer-tainly at the moment I should have preferred anything to the confounded cross-examination I was under, and was glad to end it by any *coup d'état*.   One wretch was perse-cuting me about green crops, and another about the feeding of bullocks, — about either of which I knew as much as a bear does of a ballet."

"Well, truly, you caused a diversion at some expense to your countenance, for I never beheld anything —"

"Stop there," said he; "you surely have not seen the doctor, — he beats me hollow; they have scarcely left so much hair on his head as would do for an Indian's scalp-lock; and, of a verity, his aspect is awful this morning.

He has just been here, and, by the by, has told me all about your affair with Beamish. It appears that somehow you met him at dinner and gave a very flourishing account of a relative of his who, you informed him, was not only selected for some very dashing service, but actually the personal friend of Picton; and after the family having blazed the matter all over Cork, and given a great entertainment in honor of their kinsman, it turns out that on the glorious 18th he ran away to Brussels faster than even the French to Charleroi, — for which act, however, there was no aspersion ever cast upon his courage, that quality being defended at the expense of his honesty; in a word, he was the paymaster of his company, and had what Theodore Hook calls an 'affection of his chest' that required change of air. Looking only to the running away part of the matter, I unluckily expressed some regret that he did not belong to the North Cork, and I remarked the doctor did not seem to relish the allusion, and *as I* only now remember it was *his* regiment, I suppose I'm in for more mischief."

I had no time to enjoy Curzon's dilemma, and had barely informed him of my intended departure, when a voice from without the room proclaimed that "Pether" was ready; and having commissioned the Adjutant to say the "proper" to Mr. Beamish and the doctor, I hurried away, and after a hearty shake of the hand from Father Brennan, and a faithful promise to return soon, I mounted and set off.

Peter's pace was of all others the one least likely to disturb the lucubrations of a castle-builder like myself. Without any admonition from whip or spur, he maintained a steady and constant canter, which, I am free to confess, was more agreeable to sit than it was graceful to behold; for his head being much lower than his tail, he every moment appeared in the attitude of a diver about to plunge into the water, and more than once I had misgivings that I should consult my safety better if I sat with my face to the tail, — however, what will not habit accomplish? Before I had gone a mile or two, I was so lost in my own reveries and reflections that I knew nothing of my mode of progression, and had only thoughts and feelings for the destiny that awaited me. Sometimes I would fancy myself seated in the House of Commons (on the ministerial benches, of course), while some leading oppositionist was pronouncing a glowing panegyric upon the eloquent and statesmanlike speech of the gallant colonel, — myself; then I thought I was making arrangements for setting out for my new appointment, — and Sancho Panza never coveted the government of an island more than I did, though only a West Indian one; and lastly, I saw myself the chosen diplomat on a difficult mission, and was actually engaged in the easy and agreeable occupation of out-manœuvring Talleyrand and Pozzi di Borgo, when Peter suddenly drew up at the door of a small cabin and convinced me that I was still a mortal man and a lieutenant in his Majesty's 4—th. Before I had time afforded me even to guess at the reason of this sudden halt, an old man emerged from the cabin, which I saw now was a road-side ale-house, and presented Peter with a bucket of meal and water, — a species of "refresher" that he evidently was accustomed to at this place, whether bestrode by a priest or an ambassador. Before me lay a long, straggling street of cabins, irregularly thrown, as if riddled over the ground: this I was informed was Kilkee. While my good steed, therefore, was enjoying his potation, I dismounted, to stretch my legs and look about me; and scarcely had I done so when I found half the population of the village assembled round Peter, whose claims to notoriety, I now learned, depended neither upon his owner's fame, nor even my temporary possession of him. Peter, in fact, had been a racer once, — when, the Wandering Jew might perhaps have told, had he ever visited Clare; for not the oldest inhabitant knew the date of his triumphs on the turf, though they were undisputed traditions, and never did any man appear bold enough to call them in question. Whether it was from his patriarchal character, or that he was the only race-horse ever known in his county, I cannot say, but of a truth the Grand Lama could scarcely be a greater object of reverence in Thibet than was Peter in Kilkee.

"Musha, Peter, but it's well y' 'r looking ! " cried one.

"Ah, thin, maybe ye an't fat on the ribs ! " cried another.

"An' cockin' his tail like a coult," said a third.

I am very certain, if I might venture to judge from the faces about, that had the favorite for the St. Leger passed through Kilkee at that moment, comparisons very little to his favor had been drawn from the assemblage around me. With some difficulty I was permitted to reach my much-admired steed, and with a cheer which was sustained and caught up by every denizen of the village as I passed through, I rode on my way, not a little amused at my equivocal popularity.

Being desirous to lose no time, I diverged from the straight road which leads to Kilrush, and took a cross bridle-path to Callonby, — this, I afterwards discovered, was a *détour* of a mile or two; and it was already sunset when I reached the entrance to the park. I entered the avenue; and now my impatience became extreme, for although Peter continued to move at the same uniform pace, I could not persuade myself that he was not foundering at every step, and was quite sure we were scarcely advancing. At last I reached the wooden bridge and ascended the steep slope, — the spot where I had first met her on whom my every thought now rested. I turned the angle of the clump of beech-trees from whence the first view of the house is caught. I perceived, to my inexpressible delight, that gleams of light shot from many of the windows, and could trace their passing from one to the other. I now drew rein, and with a heart relieved from a load of anxiety, pulled up my good steed, and began to think of the position in which a few brief seconds would place me. I reached the small flower-garden, sacred by a thousand endearing recollections. Oh! of how very little account are the many words of passing kindness and moments of light-hearted pleasure, when spoken or felt, compared to the memory of them when hallowed by time or distance!

"The place, the hour, the sunshine and the shade," all reminded me of the happy past, and all brought vividly before me every portion of that dream of happiness in which I was so utterly, so completely steeped, — every thought of the hopelessness of my passion was lost in the intensity of it, and I did not, in the ardor of my loving, stop to think of its possible success.

It was strange enough that the extreme impatience, the hurried anxiety, I had felt and suffered from while riding up the avenue, had now fled entirely, and in its place I felt nothing but a diffident distrust of myself and a vague sense of awkwardness about intruding thus unexpectedly upon the family while engaged in all the cares and preparations for a speedy departure. The hall-door lay, as usual, wide open; the hall itself was strewn and littered with trunks, imperials, and packing-cases, and the hundred *et ceteras* of travelling baggage. I hesitated a moment whether I should not ring, but at last resolved to enter unannounced, and presuming upon my intimacy, see what effect my sudden appearance would have on Lady Jane, whose feelings towards me would be thus most unequivocally tested. I passed along the wide corridor, entered the music-room: it was still. I walked then to the door of the drawing-room: I paused, I drew a full breath; my hand trembled slightly as I turned the lock; I entered. The room was empty, but the blazing fire upon the hearth, the large arm-chairs drawn round, the scattered books upon the small tables, all told that it had been inhabited a very short time before. "Ah!" thought I, looking at my watch, "they are at dinner;" and I began at once to devise a hundred different plans to account for my late absence and present visit. I knew that a few minutes would probably bring them into the drawing-room, and I felt flurried and heated as the time drew near. At last I heard voices without. I started from the examination of a pencil drawing, partly finished, but the artist of which I could not be deceived in. I listened, — the sounds drew near; I could not distinguish who were the speakers. The door-lock turned, and I rose to make my well-conned but half-forgotten speech, and oh, confounded disappointment! Mrs. Herbert, the housekeeper, entered. She started, not expecting to see me, and immediately said, —

"Oh! Mr. Lorrequer, then you've missed them?"

"Missed them!" said I; "how — when — where?"

"Did you not get a note from my lord?"

"No; when was it written?"

"Oh, dear me, that is so very unfortunate! Why, sir, my lord sent off a servant this morning to Kilrush in Lord Kilkee's tilbury to request you would meet them all in Ennis this evening, where they had intended to stop for to-night; and they waited here till near four o'clock to-day. But when the servant came back with the intelligence that you were from home, and not expected to return soon, they were obliged to set out, and are not going to make any delay now till they reach London. The last direction, however, my lord gave was to forward her ladyship's letter to you as soon as possible."

What I thought, said, or felt, might be a good subject of confession to Father Malachi, for I fear it may be recorded among my sins, as I doubt not that the agony I suffered vented itself in no measured form of speech or conduct; but I have nothing to confess here on the subject, being so totally overwhelmed as not to know what I did or said. My first gleam of reason elicited itself by asking, —

"Is there, then, no chance of their stopping in Ennis to-night?" As I put the question, my mind reverted to Peter and his eternal canter.

"Oh, dear, no, sir! The horses are ordered to take them, since Tuesday; and they only thought of staying in Ennis if you came time enough to meet them, — and they will be so sorry."

"Do you think so, Mrs. Herbert? Do you indeed think so?" said I, in a most insinuating tone.

"I am perfectly sure of it, sir."

"Oh, Mrs. Herbert, you are too kind to think so! But perhaps — that is — may be, Mrs. Herbert, she said something — "

"Who, sir?"

"Lady Callonby, I mean. Did her ladyship leave any message for me about her plants? Or did she remember — "

Mrs. Herbert kept looking at me all the time, with her great wide gray eyes, while I kept stammering and blushing like a schoolboy.

"No, sir, her ladyship said nothing, sir; but Lady Jane — "

"Yes; well, what of Lady Jane, my dear Mrs. Herbert?"

"Oh, sir! But you look pale, — would not you like to have a little wine and water, or perhaps — "

"No, thank you, nothing whatever; I am just a little fatigued. But you were mentioning — "

"Yes, sir; I was saying that Lady Jane was mighty particular about a small plant: she ordered it to be left in her dressing-room. Though Collins told her to have some of the handsome ones of the green-house, she would have nothing but this; and if you were only to hear half the directions she gave about keeping it watered, and taking off dead leaves, you 'd think her heart was set on it."

Mrs. Herbert would have had no cause to prescribe for my paleness had she only looked at me this time; fortunately, however, she was engaged, housekeeper-like, in bustling among books, papers, etc., which she had come in for the purpose of arranging and packing up, — she being left behind to bring up the rear and the heavy baggage.

Very few moments' consideration were sufficient to show me that pursuit was hopeless. Whatever might have been Peter's performance in the reign of "Queen Anne," he had now become, like the goose so pathetically described by my friend Lover, rather "stiff in his limbs;" and the odds were fearfully against his overtaking four horses starting fresh every ten miles, not to mention their being some hours in advance already. Having declined all Mrs. Herbert's many kind offers anent food and rest, I took a last lingering look at the beautiful picture which still held its place in the room lately mine, and hurried from a place so full of recollections; and notwithstanding the many reasons I had for self-gratulation, every object around and about filled me with sorrow and regret for hours that had passed, never, never to return.

It was very late when I reached my old quarters at Kilrush. Mrs. Healy, fortunately, was in bed asleep, — fortunately, I say; for had she selected that occasion to vent her indignation for my long absence, I greatly fear that, in my then temper, I should have exhibited but little of that Job-like endurance for which I was once esteemed. I entered my little mean-looking parlor, with its three chairs and lame table; and as I flung myself upon the wretched substitute for a sofa, and thought . upon the varied events which a few weeks had brought about, it required the aid of her ladyship's letter, which I had open before me, to assure me I was not dreaming.

The entire of that night I could not sleep; my destiny seemed upon its balance; and whether the scale inclined to this side or that, good or evil fortune seemed to betide me. How many were my plans and resolutions, and how often abandoned, — again to be pondered over, and once more given up! The gray dawn of the morning was already breaking, and found me still doubting and uncertain. At last the die was thrown; I determined at once to apply for leave to my commanding officer (which he could, if he pleased, give me, without any application to the Horse Guards), set out for Elton, tell Sir Guy my whole adventure, and endeavor, by a more moving love-story than ever graced even the Minerva Press, to induce him to make some settlement on me and use his influence with Lord Callonby in my behalf; this done, set out for London, and then — and then — what then? Then for the "Morning Post," — "orange-flowers;" "happy couple;" "Lord Callonby's seat in Hampshire," etc.

"You wished to be called at five, sir," said Stubbes.

"Yes; is it five o'clock?"

"No, sir; but I heard you call out something about ' four horses,' and I thought you might be hurried, so I came in a little earlier."

"Quite right, Stubbes. Let me have my breakfast as soon as possible, and see that chestnut horse I brought here last night, fed."

"And now for it," said I.   After writing a hurried note to Curzon, requesting him to take command of my party at Kilrush till he heard from me, and sending my kind re-membrance to my three friends, I despatched the epistle by my servant on Peter, while I hastened to secure a place in the mail for Ennis, on the box-seat of which let my kind reader suppose me seated, as, wrapping my box-coat around me, I lit my cigar and turned my eyes towards Limerick.

CHAPTER VIII.

CONGRATULATIONS. — SICK LEAVE. — HOW TO PASS THE
BOARD.

I HAD scarcely seated myself to breakfast at Swinburn's Hotel in Limerick, when the waiter presented me with a letter. As my first glance at the address showed it to be in Colonel Carden's handwriting, I felt not a little alarmed for the consequences of the rash step I had taken in leaving my detachment; and while quickly thronging fancies of arrest and court-martial flitted before me, I summoned resolution at last to break the seal, and read as follows: —

MY DEAR LORREQUER, —

"'Dear Lorrequer!' dear me," thought I, —."cool, certainly, from one I have ever regarded as an open enemy."

MY DEAR LORREQUER,— I have just accidentally heard of your arrival here, and hasten to inform you that as it may not be impossible your reasons for so abruptly leaving your detachment are known to me, I shall not visit your breach of discipline very heavily. My old and worthy friend Lord Callonby, who passed through here yesterday, has so warmly interested himself in your behalf that I feel disposed to do all in my power to serve you, independent of my desire to do so on your own account. Come over here, then, as soon as possible, and let us talk over your plans together.

Believe me, most truly yours,

HENRY CARDEN.

BARRACKS, 10 o'clock.

However mysterious and difficult to unravel have been some of the circumstances narrated in these "Confessions," I do not scruple to avow that the preceding letter was to *me* by far the most inexplicable piece of fortune I had hitherto met with. That Lord Callonby should have con-

verted one whom I believed an implacable foe into a most
obliging friend, was intelligible enough, seeing that his
lordship had through life been the patron of the Colonel;
but why he had so done, and what communications he could
possibly have made with regard to me, that Colonel Carden
should speak of "my plans" and proffer assistance in them,
was a perfect riddle, and the only solution one so ridiculously flattering that I dared not think of it. I read and
re-read the note; misplaced the stops; canvassed every expression; did all to detect a meaning different from the
obvious one, fearful of a self-deception where so much was
at stake. Yet there it stood forth, a plain, straightforward
proffer of services for some object evidently known to the
writer; and my only conclusion from all was this, that "my
Lord Callonby was the gem of his order, and had a most
remarkable talent for selecting a son-in-law."

I fell into a deep revery upon my past life and the prospects which I now felt were opening before me. Nothing
seemed extravagant to hopes so well founded, to expectations so brilliant; and in my mind's eye I beheld myself
one moment leading my young and beautiful bride through
the crowded salons of Devonshire House, and at the next
I was contemplating the excellence and perfection of my
stud arrangements at Melton, — for I resolved not to give
up hunting. While in this pleasurable exercise of my
fancy I was removing from before me some of the breakfast equipage, or as I then believed it, breaking the trees
into better groups upon my lawn, I was once more brought
to the world and its dull reality by the following passage,
which my eye fell upon in the newspaper before me: "We
understand that the 4—th are daily expecting the route for
Cork, from whence they are to sail, early in the ensuing
month, for Halifax, to relieve the 88th." While it did not
take a moment's consideration to show me that though the
regiment there mentioned was the one I belonged to, I could
have no possible interest in the announcement, — it never
coming into my calculation that *I* should submit to such
expatriation; yet it gave me a salutary warning that there

was no time to be lost in making my application for leave, which once obtained, I should have ample time to manage an exchange into another corps. The wonderful revolution a few days had effected in all my tastes and desires did not escape me at this moment. But a week or two before, and I should have regarded an order for foreign service as anything rather than unpleasant; now, the thought was insupportable. Then, there would have been some charm to me in the very novelty of the *locale* and the indulgence of that vagrant spirit I have ever possessed, — for, like Justice Woodcock, "I certainly should have been a vagabond if Providence had not made me a justice of the peace;" now, I could not even contemplate the thing as possible, and would actually have refused the command of a regiment if the condition of its acceptance were to sail for the colonies.

Besides, I tried — and how ingenious is self-deception — I tried to find arguments in support of my determination totally different from the reasons which governed me. I affected to fear climate and to dread the effect of the tropics upon my health. "It may do very well," thought I, "for men totally destitute of better prospects, with neither talent, influence, nor powerful connection, to roast their cheeks at Sierra Leone, or suck a sugar-cane at St. Lucia. But that you, Harry Lorrequer, should waste your sweetness upon planters' daughters, — that have only to be known to have the world at your feet! The thing is absurd, and not to be thought of! Yes," said I, half aloud, "we read in the army list that Major A. is appointed to the 50th, and Captain B. to the 12th; but how much more near the truth would it be to say, 'That his Majesty, in consideration of the distinguished services of the one, has been graciously pleased to appoint him to ——, a case of blue and collapsed cholera, in India; and also for the bravery and gallant conduct of the other, in his late affair with the "How-dow-dallah Indians," has promoted him to the ——, yellow fever now devastating and desolating Jamaica'?" How far my zeal for the service might have carried me on this point I know not, for I was speedily aroused from my musings by the loud tramp of feet upon the stairs, and the sound of many well-known voices of my brother officers, who were coming to visit me.

"So, Harry, my boy," said the fat Major, as he entered, "is it true we are not to have the pleasure of your company to Jamaica this time?"

"He prefers a pale face, it seems, to a black one; and certainly, with thirty thousand in the same scale, the taste is excusable."

"But. Lorrequer," said a third, "we heard that you had canvassed the county in the Callonby interest. Why, man, where do you mean to pull up?"

"As for me," lisped a large-eyed, white-haired ensign of three months' standing, "I think it devilish hard old Carden did n't send *me* down there too, for I hear there are two girls in the family, eh, Lorrequer?"

Having, with all that peculiar bashfulness such occasions are sure to elicit, disclaimed the happiness my friends so clearly ascribed to me, I yet pretty plainly let it be understood that the more brilliant they supposed my present prospects to be, the more near were they to estimate them justly. One thing certainly gratified me throughout. All seemed rejoiced at my good fortune, and even the old Scotch paymaster made no more caustic remark than that he "wad na wonder if the chiel's black whiskers wad get him made governor of Stirling Castle before he 'd dee."

Should any of my most patient listeners to these my humble "Confessions" wonder, either here or elsewhere, upon what very slight foundations I built these my *châteaux en Espagne*, I have only one answer, that from my boyhood I have had a taste for florid architecture, and would rather have put up with any inconvenience of ground than not build at all.

As it was growing late, I hurriedly bade adieu to my friends and hastened to Colonel Carden's quarters, where I found him waiting for me in company with my old friend Fitzgerald. our regimental surgeon. Our first greetings over, the Colonel drew me aside into a window, and said that from certain expressions Lord Callonby had made use of, certain hints he had dropped, he was perfectly aware of the delicate position in which I stood with respect to his lordship's family. "In fact, my dear Lorrequer," he continued, "without wishing in the least to obtrude myself upon your confidence, I must yet be permitted to say you are the luckiest fellow in Europe, and I most sincerely congratulate you on the prospect before you."

"But, my dear Colonel, I assure you —"

"Well, well, there, — not a word more; don't blush now. I know there is always a kind of secrecy thought necessary on these occasions, for the sake of other parties; so let us pass to your plans. From what I have collected, you have not proposed formally. But, of course, you desire a leave. You 'll not quit the army, I trust, — no necessity for that; such influence as yours can always appoint you to an unattached commission."

"Once more let me protest, sir, that though for certain reasons most desirous to obtain a leave of absence, I have not the most remote — "

"That 's right, quite right; I am sincerely gratified to hear you say so, and so will be Lord Callonby, — for he likes the service."

And thus was my last effort at a disclaimer cut short by the loquacious little Colonel, who regarded my unfinished sentence as a concurrence with his own opinion.

"*Allah il Allah*," thought I, "it is my Lord Callonby's own plot; and his friend Colonel Carden aids and abets him."

"Now, Lorrequer," resumed the Colonel, "let us proceed. You have, of course, heard that we are ordered abroad, — mere newspaper report for the present; nevertheless, it is extremely difficult, almost impossible, without a sick certificate, to obtain a leave sufficiently long for your purpose." And here he smirked and I blushed, *selon les règles.*

"A sick certificate," said I, in some surprise.

"The only thing for you," said Fitzgerald, taking a long

pinch of snuff; "and I grieve to say you have a most villanous look of good health about you."

"I must acknowledge I have seldom felt better."

"So much the worse, so much the worse," said Fitzgerald, despondingly. "Is there no family complaint, no respectable heirloom of infirmity you can lay claim to from your kindred?"

"None that I know of, unless a very active performance on the several occasions of breakfast, dinner, and supper, with a tendency towards port and an inclination to sleep ten in every twenty-four hours, be a sign of sickness. These symptoms I have known many of the family suffer for years without the slightest alleviation, though, strange as it may appear, they occasionally had medical advice."

Fitz took no notice of my sneer at the faculty, but proceeded to strike my chest several times with his finger-tips. "Try a short cough, now," said he. "Ah, that will never do! Do you ever flush, — before dinner, I mean?"

"Occasionally, when I meet with a luncheon."

"I'm fairly puzzled," said poor Fitz, throwing himself into a chair. "Gout is a very good thing; but then, you see, you are only a sub, and it is clearly against the Articles of War to have it before being a field-officer at least. Apoplexy is the best I can do for you; and, to say the truth, any one who witnesses your performance at mess may put faith in the likelihood of it. Do you think you could get up a fit for the medical board?" said Fitz, gravely.

"Why, if absolutely indispensable," said I, "and with good instruction, — something this way, eh, is it not?"

"Nothing of the kind; you are quite wrong."

"Is there not always a little laughing and crying?" said I.

"Oh, no, no; take the cue from the paymaster any evening after mess, and you'll make no mistake, — very florid about the cheeks; rather a lazy look in one eye, the other closed up entirely; snore a little from time to time, and don't be too much disposed to talk."

"And you think I may pass muster in this way?"

"Indeed you may, if old Camie, the inspector, happen to be (what he is not often) in a good humor. But I confess I'd rather you were really ill, for we've passed a great number of counterfeits latterly, and we may be all pulled up ere long."

"Not the less grateful for your kindness," said I; "but still I'd rather matters stood as they do."

Having at length obtained a very formidable statement of my "case" from the doctor, and a strong letter from the Colonel deploring the temporary loss of so promising a young officer, I committed myself and my portmanteau to the inside of his Majesty's mail, and started for Dublin with as light a heart and high spirits as were consistent with so much delicacy of health and the directions of my doctor.

CHAPTER IX.

I SHALL not stop now to narrate the particulars of my visit
to the worthies of the medical board, the rather as some of
my "Confessions" to come have reference to Dublin and
many of those that dwell therein. I shall therefore content myself here with stating that without any difficulty I
obtained a six months' leave, and having received much
advice and more sympathy from many members of that
body, took a respectful leave of them and adjourned to
Bilton's, where I had ordered dinner and (as I was advised
to live low) a bottle of Sneyd's claret. My hours in Dublin
were numbered; at eight o'clock on the evening of my
arrival I hastened to the Pigeon House pier to take my
berth in the packet for Liverpool. And here, gentle reader,
let me implore you, if you have bowels of compassion, to
commiserate the condition of a sorry mortal like myself. In the days of which I now speak, steam-packets
were not, — men knew not then of the pleasure of going to
a comfortable bed in Kingstown harbor, and waking on the
morning after in the Clarence dock at Liverpool, with only
the addition of a little sharper appetite for breakfast before
they set out on an excursion of forty miles per hour
through the air.

In the time I have now to commemorate, the intercourse
between the two countries was maintained by *two* sailing
vessels of small tonnage and still scantier accommodation.
Of the one now in question I well recollect the name, —
she was called the "Alert;" and certainly a more unfortunate misnomer could scarcely be conceived. Well, there

was no choice; so I took my place upon the crowded deck of the little craft, and in a drizzling shower of chilly rain, and amid more noise, confusion, and bustle than would prelude the launch of a line-of-battle ship, we "sidled," goose-fashion, from the shore, and began our voyage towards England.

It is not my intention, in the present stage of my "Confessions," to delay on the road towards an event which influenced so powerfully and so permanently my after-life; yet I cannot refrain from chronicling a slight incident which occurred on board the packet, and which, I have no doubt, may be remembered by some of those who throw their eyes on these pages.

One of my fellow-passengers was a gentleman holding a high official appointment in the viceregal court, either comptroller of the household, master of the horse, or something else equally magnificent; however, whatever the nature of the situation, one thing is certain, — one possessed of more courtly manners and more polished address cannot be conceived; to which he added all the attractions of a very handsome person and a most prepossessing countenance. The only thing the most scrupulous critic could possibly detect as faulty in his whole air and bearing was a certain ultra refinement and fastidiousness, which in a man of acknowledged family and connections was somewhat unaccountable, and certainly unnecessary. The fastidiousness I speak of extended to everything round and about him. He never ate of the wrong dish nor spoke to the wrong man in his life; and that very consciousness gave him a kind of horror of chance acquaintances which made him shrink within himself from persons in every respect his equals. Those who knew Sir Stewart Moore will know I do not exaggerate in either my praise or censure ; and to those who have not had that pleasure, I have only to say theirs was the loss, and they must take my word for the facts.

The very antithesis to the person just mentioned was another passenger then on board. She — for even in sex they were different — she was a short, squat, red-faced, vulgar-looking woman of about fifty, possessed of a most garrulous tendency, and talking indiscriminately with every one about her, careless what reception her addresses met with, and quite indifferent to the many rebuffs she momentarily encountered. To me, by what impulse driven, Heaven knows, this amorphous piece of womanhood seemed determined to attach herself. Whether in the smoky and almost impenetrable recesses of the cabin, or braving the cold and penetrating rain upon deck, it mattered not, she was ever at my side, and not only martyring me by the insufferable annoyance of her vulgar loquacity, but actually, from the appearance of acquaintanceship such constant association gave rise to, frightening any one else from conversing with me, and rendering me, ere many hours, a perfect pariah among the passengers. By no one were we — for, alas! we had become Siamese — so thoroughly dreaded as by the refined baronet I have mentioned; he appeared to shrink from our very approach, and avoided us as though we had the plagues of Egypt about us. I saw this, I felt it deeply, and as deeply and resolutely I vowed to be revenged; and the time was not long distant in affording me the opportunity.

The interesting Mrs. Mulrooney — for such was my fair companion called — was on the present occasion making her *début* on what she was pleased to call the "says;" she was proceeding to the Liverpool market as proprietor and supercargo over some legion of swine that occupied the hold of the vessel, and whose mellifluous tones were occasionally heard in all parts of the ship. Having informed me on these, together with some circumstances of her birth and parentage, she proceeded to narrate some of the cautions given by her friends as to her safety when making such a long voyage, and also to detail some of the antiseptics to that dread scourge, sea-sickness, in the fear and terror of which she had come on board, and seemed every hour to be increasing in alarm about.

"Do you think then, sir, that pork is no good agin the

sickness? Mickey — that's my husband, sir, — says it's the only thing in life for it, av it's toasted."

"Not the least use, I assure you."

"Nor sperits and wather?"

"Worse and worse, ma'am."

"Oh, thin, maybe oaten mail tay would do? It's a beautiful thing for the stomick, anyhow."

"Rank poison on the present occasion, believe me."

"Oh, thin, blessed Mary, what *am* I to do? What is to become of me?"

"Go down at once to your berth, ma'am; lie still and without speaking till we come in sight of land; or" — and here a bright thought seized me — "if you really feel very ill, call for that man there with the fur collar on his coat, — he can give you the only thing I ever knew of any efficacy. He's the steward, ma'am, — Stewart Moore. But you must be on your guard too, as you are a stranger, for he's a conceited fellow, and has saved a trifle, and sets up for a *half* gentleman; so don't be surprised at his manner, — though, after all, you may find him very different; some people, I've heard, think him extremely civil."

"And he has a cure, ye say?"

"The only one I ever heard of, — it is a little cordial of which you take I don't know how much every ten or fifteen minutes."

"And the naygur does n't let the saycret out, bad manners to him?"

"No, ma'am; he has refused every offer on the subject."

"May I be so bowld as to ax his name again?"

"Stewart Moore, ma'am. Moore is the name, but people always call him Stewart Moore; just say that in a loud, clear voice, and you'll soon have him."

With the most profuse protestations of gratitude and promises of pork *à discrétion* if ever I sojourned at Ballinasloe, my fair friend proceeded to follow my advice and descended to the cabin.

Some hours after, I also betook myself to my rest, from which, however, towards midnight, I was awoke by the heavy working and pitching of the little vessel as she labored in a rough sea. As I looked forth from my narrow crib, a more woe-begone picture can scarcely be imagined than that before me. Here and there through the gloomy cabin lay the victims of the fell malady, in every stage of suffering and in every attitude of misery. Their cries and lamentings mingled with the creaking of the bulkheads and the jarring twang of the dirty lamp, whose irregular swing told plainly how oscillatory was our present motion. I turned from the unpleasant sight, and was about again to address myself to slumber with what success I might, when I started at the sound of a voice in the very berth next to me, whose tones, once heard, there was no forgetting. The words ran, as nearly as I can recollect, thus: —

"Oh, thin, bad luck to ye for pigs that ever brought me into the like of this! Oh, Lord, there it is again!" And here a slight interruption to eloquence took place, during which I was enabled to reflect upon the author of the complaint, who, I need not say, was Mrs. Mulrooney.

"I think a little tay would settle my stomick, if I only could get it; but what's the use of talking in this horrid place? They never mind me no more than if I was a pig. Steward, steward! Oh, thin, it's wishing you well I am for a steward! Steward, I say!" and this she really did say, with an energy of voice and manner that startled more than one sleeper. "Oh, you're coming at last, steward!"

"Ma'am," said a little dapper and dirty personage in a blue jacket, with a greasy napkin negligently thrown over one arm *ex officio*, "ma'am, did you call?"

"Call! — is it call? No; but I'm roaring for you this half-hour. Come here. Have you any of the cordial dhrops agin the sickness? You know what I mean."

"Is it brandy, ma'am?"

"No, it isn't brandy."

"We have got gin, ma'am, and bottled porter, — cider, ma'am, if you like."

"Agh, no! sure I want the dhrops agin the sickness."

"Don't know, indeed, ma'am."

"Ah, you stupid creature! Maybe you 're not the real steward. What 's your name?"

"Smith, ma'am."

"Ah, I thought so! Go away, man, go away."

This injunction, given in a *diminuendo* cadence, was quickly obeyed, and all was silence for a moment or two. Once more was I dropping asleep when the same voice as before burst out with, —

"Am I to die here like a haythen, and nobody to come near me? Steward! steward! steward Moore, I say!"

"Who calls *me?*" said a deep, sonorous voice from the opposite side of the cabin, while at the same instant a tall, green-silk nightcap, surmounting a very aristocratic-looking forehead, appeared between the curtains of the opposite berth.

"Steward Moore!" said the lady again, with her eyes straining in the direction of the door by which she expected him to enter.

"This is most strange," muttered the baronet, half aloud. "Why, madam, you are calling *me?*"

"And if I am," said Mrs. Mulrooney, "and if ye heerd me, have ye no manners to answer your name, eh? Are ye Steward Moore?"

"Upon my life, ma'am, I thought so last night when I came on board. But you really have contrived to make me doubt my own identity."

"And is it there ye 're lying on the broad of yer back, and me as sick as a dog fornent ye?"

"I concede, ma'am, the fact; the position is a most irksome one on every account."

"Then why don't ye come over to me?" And this Mrs. Mulrooney said with a voice of something like tenderness, — wishing at all hazards to conciliate so important a functionary.

"Why, really, you *are* the most incomprehensible person I ever met."

"I'm what?" said Mrs. Mulrooney, her blood rushing to her face and temples as she spoke, — for the same reason that her fair townswoman is reported to have borne with stoical fortitude every harsh epithet of the language, until it occurred to her opponent to tell her that "the divil a bit better she was nor a pronoun;" so Mrs, Mulrooney, taking *omne ignotum pro horribile*, became perfectly beside herself at the unlucky phrase. "I'm what? Repate it, av ye dare,

and I'll tear yer eyes out! Ye dirty bla—guard, to be lying there at yer ease under the blankets, grinning at me. What's your thrade — answer me that — av it is n't to wait on the ladies, eh?"

"Oh! the woman must be mad," said Sir Stewart.

"The devil a taste mad, my dear, I'm only sick. Now just come over to me like a decent creature, and give me the dhrop of comfort ye have. Come, avick."

"Go over to you?"

"Ay, and why not? Or, if it's so lazy ye are, why then I'll thry and cross over to *your* side."

These words being accompanied by a certain indication of change of residence on the part of Mrs. Mulrooney, Sir Stewart perceived there was no time to lose; and springing from his berth, he rushed half-dressed through the cabin and up the companion-ladder, just as Mrs. Mulrooney had protruded a pair of enormous legs from her couch, and hung for a moment pendulous before she dropped upon the floor and followed him to the deck. A tremendous shout of laughter from the sailors and deck-passengers prevented my hearing the dialogue which ensued; nor do I yet know how Mrs. Mulrooney learned her mistake. Certain it is, she no more appeared amongst the passengers in the cabin, and Sir Stewart's manner the following morning at break-fast amply satisfied me that I had had my revenge.

CHAPTER X.

No sooner in Liverpool, than I hastened to take my place in the earliest conveyance for London. At that time the Umpire coach was the perfection of fast travelling; and seated behind the box, enveloped in a sufficiency of broadcloth, I turned my face towards town with as much anxiety and as ardent expectations as most of those about me. All went on in the regular monotonous routine of such matters until we reached Northampton, passing down the steep street of which town, the near wheel-horse stumbled and fell; the coach, after a tremendous roll to one side, toppled over on the other, and with a tremendous crash and sudden shock, sent all the outsides, myself among the number, flying through the air like sea-gulls. As for me, after describing a very respectable parabola, my angle of incidence landed me in a bonnet-maker's shop, having passed through a large plate-glass window and destroyed more leghorns and dunstables than a year's pay would recompense. I have but slight recollection of the details of that occasion until I found myself lying in a very spacious bed at the George Inn, having been bled in both arms, and discovering, by the multitude of bandages in which I was enveloped, that at least some of my bones were broken by the fall. That such fate had befallen my collar-bone and three of my ribs, I soon learned; and was horror-struck at hearing from the surgeon who attended me that four or five weeks would be the very earliest period I could bear removal with safety. Here then at once there was a large deduction from my six months' leave, not to think of the misery that awaited me for such a time, confined to my bed in an inn without books, friends, or acquaintances. How-eve-, even this could be remedied by patience, and summoning up all I could command, I "bided my time;" but not before I had completed a term of two months' imprisonment, and had become, from actual starvation, something very like a living transparency.

No sooner, however, did I feel myself once more on the road, than my spirits rose, and I felt myself as full of high hope and buoyant expectancy as ever. It was late at night when I arrived in London. I drove to a quiet hotel in the West End, and the following morning proceeded to Portman Square, bursting with impatience to see my friends the Callonbys and recount all my adventures, — for as I was too ill to write from Northampton, and did not wish to intrust to a stranger the office of communicating with them, I judged that they must be exceedingly uneasy on my account, and pictured to myself the thousand emotions my appearance, so indicative of illness, would give rise to, and could scarcely avoid running, in my impatience to be once more among them. How Lady Jane would meet me, I thought of over again and again; whether the same cautious reserve awaited me, or whether her family's approval would have wrought a change in her reception of me, I burned to ascertain. As my thoughts ran on in this way, I found myself at the door, but was much alarmed to perceive that the closed window-shutters and dismantled look of the house proclaimed them from home. I rang the bell, and soon learned from a servant, whose face I had not seen before, that the family had gone to Paris about a month before, with the intention of spending the winter there. I need not say how grievously this piece of intelligence disappointed me, and for a minute or two I could not collect my thoughts. At last the servant said, —

"If you have anything very particular, sir, that my lord's lawyer can do, I can give you his address."

"No, thank you, nothing;" at the same time I muttered to myself, "I 'll have some occupation for him. though, ere long. The family were all quite well, did n't you say?"

"Yes, sir, perfectly well. My lord had only a slight cold."

"Ah, yes! And their address is Meurice? Very well."

So saying, I turned from the door, and with slower steps than I had come, returned to my hotel.

My immediate resolve was to set out for Paris; my second was to visit my uncle, Sir Guy Lorrequer, first, and having explained to him the nature of my position and the advantageous prospects before me, endeavor to induce him to make some settlement on Lady Jane, in the event of my obtaining her family's consent to our marriage. This, from his liking great people much, and laying great stress upon the advantages of connection, I looked upon as a matter of no great difficulty; so that although my hopes of happiness were delayed in their fulfilment, I believed they were only to be the more securely realized. The same day I set out for Elton, and by ten o'clock at night reached my uncle's house. I found the old gentleman just as I had left him three years before, — complaining a little of gout in the left foot; praising his old specific, port wine; abusing his servants for robbing him; and drinking the Duke of Wellington's health every night after supper, — which meal I had much pleasure in surprising him at on my arrival, not having eaten since my departure from London.

"Well, Harry," said my uncle, when the servants had left the room and we drew over the spider-table to the fire to discuss our wine with comfort, "what good wind has blown you down to me, my boy? For it's odd enough, five minutes before I heard the wheels on the gravel, I was just wishing some good fellow would join me at the grouse — and you see I have had my wish! The old story, I suppose, 'out of cash.' Would not come down here for nothing, eh? Come, lad, tell truth, — is it not so?"

"Why, not exactly, sir; but I really had rather at present talk about you than about my own matters, which we can chat over to-morrow. How do you get on, sir, with the Scotch steward?"

"He's a rogue, sir, — a cheat, a scoundrel; but it is the

same with them all. And your cousin, Harry, — your cousin, that I have reared from his infancy to be my heir [pleasant topic for me!], — he cares no more for me than the rest of them, and would never come near me if it were not that, like yourself, he was hard run for money, and wanted to wheedle me out of a hundred or two."

"But you forget, sir, I told you I have not come with such an object."

"We 'll see that, we 'll see that in the morning," replied he, with an incredulous shake of the head.

"But Guy, sir, what has Guy done?"

"What has he not done? No sooner did he join that popinjay set of fellows, the —th Hussars, than he turned out what he calls a four-in-hand drag, which dragged nine hundred pounds out of my pocket. Then he has got a yacht at Cowes, a grouse mountain in Scotland, and has actually given Tattersall an unlimited order to purchase the Wreckington pack of harriers, which he intends to keep for the use of the corps. In a word, there is not an amusement of that villanous regiment, not a flask of champagne drunk at their mess, I don't bear my share in the cost of, — all through the kind offices of your worthy cousin, Guy Lorrequer."

This was an exceedingly pleasant *exposé* for me to hear of my cousin indulged in every excess of foolish extravagance by his rich uncle, while I, the son of an elder brother, who unfortunately called me by his own name, Harry, remained the sub in a marching regiment, with not three hundred pounds a year above my pay, and whom any extravagance, if such had been proved against me, would have deprived of even that small allowance. My uncle, however, did not notice the chagrin with which I heard his narrative, but continued to detail various instances of wild and reckless expense the future possessor of his ample property had already launched into.

Anxious to say something, without well knowing what, I hinted that probably my good cousin would reform some of these days, and marry.

"Marry!" said my uncle; "yes, that I believe is the best thing we can do with him; and I hope now the matter is in good train, — so the latest accounts say, at least."

"Ah, indeed!" said I, endeavoring to take an interest where I really felt none, for my cousin and I had never been very intimate friends, and the difference in our fortunes had not, at least to my thinking, been compensated by any advances which he, under the circumstances, might have made to me.

"Why, Harry, did you not hear of it?" said my uncle.

"No, not a word, sir."

"Very strange; indeed, — a great match, Harry; a very great match indeed."

"Some rich banker's daughter," thought I. "What will he say when he hears of *my* fortune?"

"A very fine young woman too, I understand, — quite the *belle* of London, — and a splendid property left by an aunt."

I was bursting to tell him of *my* affair, and that he had another nephew to whom, if common justice were rendered, his fortune was as certainly made for life.

"Guy's business happened this way," continued my uncle, who was quite engrossed by the thought of his favorite's success. "The father of the young lady met him in Ireland, or Scotland, or some such place, where he was with his regiment, was greatly struck with his manner and address, found him out to be my nephew, asked him to his house, and, in fact, almost threw this lovely girl at his head before they were two months acquainted."

"As nearly as possible my own adventure," thought I, laughing to myself.

"But you have not told me who they are, sir," said I, dying to have *his* story finished, and to begin *mine*.

"I 'm coming to that, I 'm coming to that. Guy came down here, but did not tell me one word of his having ever met the family, but begged of me to give him an introduction to them, as they were in Paris, where he was going on a short leave; and the first thing I heard of the matter was

by a letter from the papa demanding from me if Guy was
to be my heir, and asking 'how far his attentions in *his*
family met with my approval.'"

"Then how did you know, sir, that they were previously
known to each other?"

"The family lawyer told me, who heard it all talked
over."

"And why, then, did Guy get the letter of introduction
from you, when he was already acquainted with them?"

"I am sure I cannot tell, except that you know he always
does everything unlike every one else; and, to be sure, the
letter seems to have excited some amusement. I must show
you his answer to my first note to know how all was going
on, — for I felt very anxious about matters, — when I heard
from some person who had met them that Guy was ever-
lastingly in the house, and that Lord Callonby could not
live without him."

"Lord who, sir?" said I, in a voice that made the old
man upset his glass and spring from his chair in horror.

"What the devil is the matter with the boy? What
makes you so pale?"

"Whose name did you say at that moment, sir?" said I,
with a slowness of speech that cost me agony.

"Lord Callonby, my old schoolfellow and fag at Eton."

"And the lady's name, sir?" said I, in scarcely an audible whisper.

"I'm sure I forget her name; but here's the letter from
Guy, and I think he mentions her name in the postscript."

I snatched rudely the half-opened letter from the old
man, as he was vainly endeavoring to detect the place he
wanted, and read as follows: —

"My adored Jane is all your fondest wishes for my happiness
could picture, and longs to see her dear uncle, as she already calls
you on every occasion."

I read no more; my eyes swam, the paper, the candles,
everything before me was misty and confused; and although
I heard my uncle's voice still going on, I knew nothing of
what he said.

For some time my mind could not take in the full extent of the base treachery I had met with, and I sat speechless and stupefied. By degrees my faculties became clearer, and with one glance I read the whole business, from my first meeting with them at Kilrush to the present moment. I saw that in their attentions to me they thought they were winning the heir of Elton, the future proprietor of fifteen thousand per annum. From this tangled web of heartless intrigue I turned my thoughts to Lady Jane herself. How had she betrayed me? for certainly she had not only received, but encouraged my addresses, — and so soon too! To think that at the very moment when my own precipitate haste to see her had involved me in a nearly fatal accident, she was actually receiving the attentions of another! Oh, it was too, too bad!

But enough; even now I can scarcely dwell upon the memory of that moment, when the hopes and dreams of many a long day and night were destined to be thus rudely blighted. I seized the first opportunity of bidding my uncle good-night; and having promised him to reveal all my plans on the morrow, hurried to my room.

My plans — alas, I had none! That one fatal paragraph had scattered them to the winds; and I threw myself upon my bed, wretched and almost heart-broken.

I have once before in these "Confessions" claimed to myself the privilege, not inconsistent with a full disclosure of the memorabilia of my life, to pass slightly over those passages, the burden of which was unhappy, and whose memory is still painful. I must now, therefore, claim the "benefit of this act," and beg of the reader to let me pass from this sad portion of my history; and for the full expression of my mingled rage, contempt, disappointment, and sorrow, let me beg of him to receive instead what a learned pope once gave as his apology for not reading a rather polysyllabic word in a Latin letter, — "As for this," said he, looking at the phrase in question, "suppose it said." So say I. And now, *en route.*

CHAPTER XI.

It was a cold, raw evening in February as I sat in the
coffee-room of the Old Plough, in Cheltenham, *Lucullus c.
Lucullo,* — no companion save my half-finished decanter of
port. I had drawn my chair to the corner of the ample
fireplace, and in a half-dreamy state was reviewing the
incidents of my early life, like most men who, however young, have still to lament talents misapplied, opportunities neglected, profitless labor, and disastrous idleness.
The dreary aspect of the large and ill-lighted room, the
close-curtained boxes, the unsocial look of every thing and
body about, suited the habit of my soul, and I was on the
verge of becoming excessively sentimental; the unbroken
silence, where several people were present, had also its
effect upon me, and I felt oppressed and dejected. So sat
I for an hour; the clock over the mantel ticked sharply on,
the old man in the brown surtout had turned in his chair,
and now snored louder, the gentleman who read the
"Times" had got the "Chronicle," and I thought I saw
him nodding over the advertisements. The father who,
with a raw son of about nineteen, had dined at six, sat still
and motionless opposite his offspring, and only breaking
the silence around by the grating of the decanter as he
posted it across the table. The only thing denoting active
existence was a little shrivelled man, who, with spectacles
on his forehead and hotel slippers on his feet, rapidly
walked up and down, occasionally stopping at his table to
sip a little weak-looking negus, which was his moderate
potation for two hours. I have been particular in chroni-

cling these few and apparently trivial circumstances, for by what mere trifles are our greatest and most important movements induced! Had the near wheeler of the Umpire been only safe on his forelegs and — But let me continue. The gloom and melancholy which beset me, momentarily increased. But three months before, and my prospects presented everything that was fairest and brightest, — now all the future was dark and dismal. Then, my best friends could scarcely avoid envy at my fortune, — now, my reverses might almost excite compassion even in an enemy. It was singular enough — and I should not like to acknowledge it, were not these "Confessions" in their very nature intended to disclose the very penetralia of my heart — but singular it certainly was — and so I have always felt it since, when reflecting on it — that although much and warmly attached to Lady Jane Callonby, and feeling most acutely what I must call her abandonment of me, yet the most constantly recurring idea of my mind on the subject was, What will the mess say?   What will they think at headquarters? The raillery, the jesting, the half-concealed allusion, the tone of assumed compassion, which all awaited me, as each of my comrades took up his line of behaving towards me, was, after all, the most difficult thing to be borne, and I absolutely dreaded to join my regiment more thoroughly than did ever schoolboy to return to his labor on the expiration of his holidays. I had framed to myself all manner of ways of avoiding this dread event. Sometimes I meditated an exchange into an African corps; sometimes to leave the army altogether. However I turned the affair over in my mind, innumerable difficulties presented themselves; and I was at last reduced to that stand-still point in which, after continual vacillation, one only waits for the slightest impulse of persuasion from another to adopt any, no matter what, suggestion. In this enviable frame of mind I sat sipping my wine and watching the clock for that hour at which, with a safe conscience, I might retire to my bed, when the waiter roused me by demanding if my name was Mr. Lorrequer, for that a gentleman having seen my card in the bar, had been making inquiry for the owner of it all through the hotel.

"Yes," said I, "such is my name; but I am not acquainted with any one here, that I can remember."

"The gentleman has only arrived an hour since by the London mail, sir, and here he is."

At this moment a tall, dashing-looking, half-swaggering fellow, in a very sufficient envelope of box-coats, entered the coffee-room, and unwinding a shawl from his throat, showed me the honest and manly countenance of my friend Jack Waller, of the —th Dragoons, with whom I had served in the Peninsula.

Five minutes sufficed for Jack to tell me that he was come down on a bold speculation at this unnseasonable time for Cheltenham; that he was quite sure his fortune was about to be made in a few weeks at farthest; and — which seemed nearly as engrossing a topic — that he was perfectly famished, and desired a hot supper *de suite*.

Jack, having despatched this agreeable meal with a traveller's appetite, proceeded to unfold his plans to me as follows: —

There resided *somewhere* near Cheltenham, in what direction he did not absolutely know, an old East India colonel who had returned from a long career of successful staff duties and government contracts with the moderate fortune of two hundred thousand. He possessed, in addition, a son and a daughter: the former, being a rake and a gambler, he had long since consigned to his own devices; and to the latter he had avowed his intention of leaving all his wealth. That she was beautiful as an angel, highly accomplished, gifted, agreeable, and all that, Jack, who had never seen her, was firmly convinced; that she was also bent resolutely on marrying him, or any other gentleman whose claims were principally the want of money, he was quite ready to swear to, — and, in fact, so assured did he feel that "the whole affair was feasible" (I use his own expression) that he had managed a two months' leave, and was come down express to see, make love to, and carry her off at once.

"But," said I, with difficulty interrupting him, "how long have you known her father?"

"Known him? I never saw him."

"Well, that certainly is cool. And how do you propose making his acquaintance? Do you intend to make him a *particeps criminis* in the elopement of his own daughter, for a consideration to be hereafter paid out of his own money?"

"Now, Harry, you 've touched upon the point in which, you must confess, my genius always stood unrivalled. Acknowledge, if you are not dead to gratitude, acknowledge how often should you have gone supperless to bed in our bivouacs in the Peninsula, had it not been for the ingenuity of your humble servant; avow that if mutton was to be had and beef to be purloined within a circuit of twenty miles round, our mess certainly kept no fast-days. I need not remind you of the cold morning on the retreat from Burgos, when the inexorable Lake brought five men to the halberds for stealing turkeys, that at the same moment I was engaged in devising an ox-tail soup from a heifer brought to our tent in jack-boots the evening before, to escape detection by her foot-tracks."

"True, Jack, I never questioned your Spartan talent; but this affair, time considered, does appear rather difficult."

"And if it were not, should I have ever engaged in it? No, no, Harry. I put all proper value upon the pretty girl, with her two hundred thousand pounds pin-money; but I honestly own to you, the intrigue, the scheme, has as great charm for me as any part of the transaction."

"Well, Jack, now for the plan, then!"

"The plan?—oh, the plan! Why, I have several; but since I have seen you, and talked the matter over with you, I have begun to think of a new mode of opening the trenches."

"Why, I don't see how I can possibly have admitted a single new ray of light upon the affair."

"There you are quite wrong. Just hear me out, without interruption, and I 'll explain. I 'll first discover the *locale* of this worthy Colonel, — 'Hydrabad Cottage' he calls it; good, eh? Then I shall proceed to make a tour of the immediate vicinity, and either be taken dangerously ill in his grounds, within ten yards of the hall-door, or be thrown from my gig at the gate of his avenue and fracture my skull, — I don't much care which. Well, then, as I learn the old gentleman is the most kind, hospitable fellow in the world, he 'll admit me at once, his daughter will tend my sick couch, nurse, read to me. Glorious fun, Harry! I 'll make fierce love to her. And now, the only point to be decided is whether, having partaken of the Colonel's hospitality so freely, I ought to carry her off or marry her with papa's consent. You see there is much to be said for either line of proceeding."

"I certainly agree with you there; but since you seem to see your way so clearly up to that point, why, I should advise you leaving that an ' open question,' as the ministers say when they are hard pressed for an opinion."

"Well, Harry, I consent; it shall remain so. Now for *your* part, for I have now come to that."

"*Mine!*" said I, in amazement; "why, how can I possibly have any character assigned me in the drama?"

"I 'll tell you, Harry, — you shall come with me in the gig in the capacity of my valet."

"Your what?" said I, horror-struck at his impudence.

"Come, no nonsense, Harry; you 'll have a glorious time of it, — shall choose as becoming a livery as you like; and you 'll have the whole female world below stairs d*y*ing for you. And all I ask for such an opportunity vouchsafed to you is to puff *me*, your master, in every possible shape and form, and represent me as the finest and most liberal fellow in the world, rolling in wealth, and only striving to get rid of it."

The unparalleled effrontery of Master Jack in assigning to me such an office absolutely left me unable to reply to him; while he continued to expatiate upon the great field for exertion thus open to us both. At last it occurred to me to benefit by an anecdote of a something similar arrangement, of capturing, not a young lady, but a fortified town, by retorting Jack's proposition.

"Come," said I, "I agree, with one only difference, — I 'll be the master, and you the man on this occasion."

To my utter confusion, and without a second's consideration, Waller grasped my hand, and cried, "Done!" Of course I laughed heartily at the utter absurdity of the whole scheme, and rallied my friend on his prospects of Botany Bay for such an exploit, never contemplating in the most remote degree the commission of such extravagance.

Upon this, Jack, to use the expressive French phrase, *prit la parole;* touching, with a master-like delicacy, on my late defeat among the Callonbys (which up to this instant I believed him in ignorance of), he expatiated upon the prospect of my repairing that misfortune and obtaining a fortune considerably larger. He cautiously abstained from mentioning the personal charms of the young lady, supposing, from my lachrymose look, that my heart had not yet recovered the shock of Lady Jane's perfidy, and rather preferred to dwell upon the escape such a marriage would open to me from the mockery of the mess-table, the jesting of my brother officers, and the life-long raillery of the service, wherever the story reached.

The fatal facility of my disposition, so often and so frankly chronicled in these "Confessions;" the openness to be led whither any one might take the trouble to conduct me; the easy indifference to assume any character which might be pressed upon me by chance, accident, or design, assisted by my share of three flasks of champagne, — induced me first to listen, then to attend to, soon after to suggest, and finally, absolutely to concur in and agree to a proposal which, at any other moment, I must have regarded as downright insanity. As the clock struck two, I had just affixed my name to an agreement; for Jack Waller had so much of method in his madness that, fearful of my retracting in the morning, he had committed the whole to writing, which, as a specimen of Jack's legal talents, I copy from the original document, now in my possession.

THE PLOUGH, CHELTENHAM,
Tuesday night or morning, two o'clock — be the same more or less.

I, Harry Lorrequer, sub in his Majesty's — th Regiment of Foot, on the one part, and I, John Waller, commonly called Jack Waller, of the —th Light Dragoons, on the other, hereby promise and agree, each for himself, and not one for the other, to the following conditions which are hereafter subjoined, to wit, I the aforesaid Jack Waller is to serve, obey, and humbly follow the afore-mentioned Harry Lorrequer for the space of one month of four weeks, conducting himself in all respects, modes, ways, manners as his, the aforesaid, Lorrequer's own man, skip, valet, or flunkey, duly praising, puffing, and lauding the aforesaid Lorrequer, and in every way facilitating his success to the hand and fortune of —

"Shall we put in her name, Harry, here?" said Jack.

"I think not; we'll fill it up in pencil; that looks very knowing."

At the end of which period, if successful in his suit, the aforesaid Harry Lorrequer is to render to the aforesaid Waller the sum of ten thousand pounds three and a half per cent, with a faithful discharge in writing for his services, as may be.   If, on the other hand, and which Heaven forbid! the aforesaid Lorrequer fail in obtaining the hand of ——, that he will evacuate the territory within twelve hours, and repairing to a convenient spot selected by the aforesaid Waller, then and there duly invest himself with a livery chosen by the aforesaid Waller—

"You know, each man uses his choice in this particular," said Jack.

—and for the space of four calendar weeks be unto the aforesaid Waller as his skip, or valet, receiving, in the event of success, the like compensation as aforesaid, each promising strictly to maintain the terms of this agreement, and binding, by a solemn pledge, to divest himself of every right appertaining to his former condition for the space of time there mentioned.

We signed and sealed it formally, and finished another flask to its perfect ratification. This done, and after a hearty shake-hands, we parted and retired for the night.

The first thing I saw on waking the following morning was Jack Waller standing beside my bed, evidently in excellent spirits with himself and all the world.

"Harry, my boy, I have done it gloriously," said he. "I only remembered on parting with you last night that one of the most marked features in our old Colonel's character is a certain vague idea he has somewhere picked up that he has been at some very remote period of his history a most distinguished officer. This notion, it appears, haunts his mind, and he absolutely believes he has been in every engagement from the Seven Years' War down to the battle of Waterloo. You cannot mention a siege he did not lay down the first parallel for, nor a storming party where he did not lead the forlorn hope; and there is not a regiment in the service, from those that formed the fighting brigade of Picton down to the London train-bands, with which, to use his own phrase, he has not fought and bled. This mania of heroism is droll enough when one considers that the sphere of his action was necessarily so limited; but yet *we* have every reason to be thankful for the peculiarity, as you'll say when I inform you that this morning I despatched a hasty messenger to his villa with a most polite note, setting forth that ' as Mr. Lorrequer ' — ay, Harry, all above board; there is nothing like it — ' as Mr. Lorrequer, of the —th, was collecting for publication such materials as might serve to commemorate the distinguished achievements of British officers who have at any time been in command, he most respectfully requests an interview with Colonel Kamworth, whose distinguished services on many gallant occasions have called forth the unqualified approval of his Majesty's Government. Mr. Lorrequer's stay is necessarily limited to a few days, as he proceeds from this to visit Lord Anglesey, and therefore would humbly suggest as early a meeting as may suit Colonel K.'s conveneince.' What think you now? Is this a master-stroke, or not?"

"Why, certainly, we are in for it now," said I, drawing a deep sigh. "But, Jack, what is all this? Why, you're in livery already!"

I now for the first time perceived that Waller was arrayed in a very decorous suit of dark gray, with cord shorts and boots, and looked a very knowing style of servant for the side of a tilbury.

"You like it, do you? Well, I should have preferred something a little more showy myself; but as you chose this last night, I of course gave way; and, after all, I believe you're right, — it certainly is neat."

"Did I choose it last night? I have not the slightest recollection of it."

"Yes, you were most particular about the length of the waistcoat and the height of the cockade, and you see I have followed your orders tolerably close; and now adieu to sweet equality for the season, and I am your most obedient servant for four weeks, — see that you make the most of it!"

While we were talking, the waiter entered with a note addressed to me, which I rightly conjectured could only come from Colonel Kamworth. It ran thus: —

Colonel Kamworth feels highly flattered by the polite attention of Mr. Lorrequer, and will esteem it a particular favor if Mr. L. can afford him the few days his stay in this part of the country will permit, by spending them at Hydrabad Cottage. Any information as to Colonel Kamworth's services in the four quarters of the globe, he need not say, is entirely at Mr. L.'s disposal.

Colonel K. dines at six precisely.

When Waller had read the note through, he tossed his hat up in the air, and with something little short of an Indian whoop, shouted out, —

"The game is won already! Harry, my man, give me the check for the ten thousand; she is your own this minute."

Without participating entirely in Waller's exceeding delight, I could not help feeling a growing interest in the part I was advertised to perform, and began my rehearsal with more spirit than I thought I should have been able to command.

The same evening, at the same hour as that in which on the preceding night I sat alone and comfortless by the coffee-room fire, I was seated opposite a very pompous, respectable-looking old man, with a large, stiff queue of white hair, who pressed me repeatedly to fill my glass and pass the decanter. The room was a small library, with handsomely fitted shelves. There were but four chairs, but each would have made at least three of any modern one; the curtains, of deep crimson cloth, effectually secured the room from draught, and the cheerful wood fire blazing on the hearth, which was the only light in the apartment, gave a most inviting look of comfort and snugness to every-thing. "This," thought I, "is all excellent, and however the adventure ends, this is certainly pleasant, and I never tasted better madeira."

"And so, Mr. Lorrequer, you heard of my affair at Cantantrabad, when I took the Rajah prisoner?"

"Yes," said I; "the Governor-General mentioned the gallant business the very last time I dined at Government House."

"Ah! did he? Kind of him, though! Well, sir, I received two lacs of rupees on the morning after, and a promise of ten more if I would permit him to escape; but no, I refused flatly."

"Is it possible! And what did you do with the two lacs? Sent them back, of course —"

"No, that I did n't; the wretches know nothing of the use of money. No, no; I have them this moment in good Government security. I believe I never mentioned to you the storming of Java. Fill yourself another glass, and I 'll describe it all to you, for it will be of infinite conse-quence that a true narrative of this meets the public eye, — they really are quite ignorant of it. Here, now, is Fort Cornelius, and there is the moat; the sugar-basin is the citadel, and the tongs is the first trench; the decanter will represent the tall tower towards the southwest angle, and here, the wine-glass, — this is me. Well, it was a little after ten at night that I got the order from the general in command to march upon this plate of figs, which was an open space before Fort Cornelius, and to take up my posi-tion in front of the fort, and with four pieces of field artillery — these walnuts here — to be ready to open my fire at a moment's warning upon the sou'west tower — But, my dear sir, you have moved the tower; I thought you were drinking madeira. As I said before, — to open my fire upon the sou'west tower, or, if necessary, to protect the sugar-tongs, which I explained to you was the trench. Just at the same time the besieged were making preparations for a sortie to occupy this dish of almonds and raisins, — the high ground to the left of my position. Put another log on the fire, if you please, sir; for I cannot see myself. I thought I was up near the figs, and I find myself down near the half-moon —"

"It is past nine," said a servant, entering the room; "shall I take the carriage for Miss Kamworth, sir?"

This being the first time the name of the young lady was mentioned since my arrival, I felt somewhat anxious to hear more of her; in which laudable desire I was not, however, to be gratified, for the Colonel, feeling considerably annoyed by the interruption, dismissed the servant by saying, —

"What do you mean, sirrah, by coming in at this moment? Don't you see I am preparing for the attack on the half-moon? Mr. Lorrequer, I beg your pardon for one moment; this fellow has completely put me out, — and besides, I perceive you have eaten the flying artillery; and, in fact, my dear sir, I shall be obliged to lay down the position again."

With this praiseworthy interest the Colonel proceeded to arrange the *matériel* of our dessert in battle array, when the door was suddenly thrown open, and a very handsome girl, in a most becoming *demi-toilette*, sprang into the room, and either not noticing or not caring that a stranger was present, threw herself into the old gentleman's arms with a degree of *empressement* exceedingly vexatious for any third and unoccupied party to witness.

"Mary, my dear," said the Colonel, completely forgetting Java and Fort Cornelius at once, "you don't perceive I have a gentleman to introduce to you, — Mr. Lorrequer, my

daughter, Miss Kamworth." Here the young lady curt-
seyed somewhat stiffly, and I bowed reverently; and we
all resumed places. I now found out that Miss Kamworth
had been spending the preceding four or five days at a
friend's in the neighborhood, and had preferred coming
home somewhat unexpectedly to waiting for her own
carriage.

My "Confessions," if recorded *verbatim* from the notes
of that four weeks' sojourn, would only increase the already
too prolix and uninteresting details of this chapter of my
life; I need only say that without falling in love with Mary
Kamworth, I felt prodigiously disposed thereto. She was
extremely pretty, had a foot and ankle to swear by, the
most silvery toned voice I almost ever heard, and a certain
witchery and archness of manner that by its very tantaliz-
ing uncertainty continually provoked attention, and by
suggesting a difficulty in the road to success, imparted a
more than common zest in the pursuit. She was a little,
a very little, blue, — rather a dabbler in the "ologies" than
a real disciple. Yet she made collections of minerals and
brown beetles and cryptogamias and various other homœopathic doses of the creation, infinitesimally small in their
subdivision, in none of which I felt any interest, save in
the excuse they gave for accompanying her in her pony-
phaeton. This was, however, a rare pleasure, since every
morning for at least three or four hours I was obliged to
sit opposite the Colonel, engaged in the compilation of that
narrative of his deeds which was to eclipse the career
of Napoleon, and leave Wellington's laurels but a very
faded lustre in comparison. In this agreeable occupation
did I pass the greater part of my day, listening to the
insufferable prolixity of the most prolix of colonels, and at
times, notwithstanding the propinquity of relationship
which awaited us, almost regretting that he was not
blown up in any of the numerous explosions his memoir
abounded with. I may here mention that while my literary labor was thus progressing, the young lady continued
her avocations as before, — not, indeed, with me for her

companion, but Waller; for Colonel Kamworth, "having remarked the steadiness and propriety of *my* man, felt no scruple in sending him out to drive Miss Kamworth;" particularly as I gave him a most excellent character for every virtue under heaven.

I must hasten on. The last evening of my four weeks was drawing to a close. Colonel Kamworth had pressed me to prolong my visit, and I only waited for Waller's return from Cheltenham, whither I had sent him for my letters, to make arrangements with him to absolve me from my ridiculous bond and accept the invitation. We were sitting round the library fire, the Colonel, as usual, narrating his early deeds and hair-breadth 'scapes. Mary, embroidering an indescribable something, which every evening made its appearance, but seemed never to advance, was rather in better spirits than usual, at the same time her manner was nervous and uncertain; and I could perceive, by her frequent absence of mind, that her thoughts were not as much occupied by the siege of Java as her worthy father believed them. Without laying any stress upon the circumstance, I must yet avow that Waller's not having returned from Cheltenham gave me some uneasiness, and I more than once had recourse to the bell to demand if "my servant had come back yet." At each of these times I well remember the peculiar expression of Mary's look, the half embarrassment, half drollery, with which she listened to the question and heard the answer in the negative. Supper at length made its appearance, and I asked the servant who waited if my man had brought me any letters, varying my inquiry to conceal my anxiety; and again I heard he had not returned. Resolving now to propose in all form for Miss Kamworth the next morning, and by referring the Colonel to my uncle Sir Guy, smooth, as far as I could, all difficulties, I wished them good-night and retired, — not, however, before the Colonel had warned me that they were to have an excursion to some place in the neighborhood the next day, and begging that I might be in the breakfast-room at nine, as they were to assemble there from all parts, and start early on the expedition. I was in a sound sleep the following morning, when a gentle tap at the door awoke me; at the same time I recognized the voice of the Colonel's servant saying, "Mr. Lorrequer, breakfast is waiting, sir."

I sprang up at once, and replying, "Very well, I shall come down," proceeded to dress in all haste; but to my horror I could not discern a vestige of my clothes. Nothing remained of the habiliments I possessed only the day be-fore, — even my portmanteau had disappeared. After a most diligent search, I discovered on a chair in a corner of the room a small bundle tied up in a handkerchief, on open-ing which, I perceived a new suit of livery of the most gaudy and showy description, — the vest and breeches of yellow plush, with light-blue binding and lace, of which color was also the coat, which had a standing collar and huge cuffs, deeply ornamented with worked button-holes and large buttons. As I turned the things over, without even a guess of what they could mean, for I was scarcely well awake, I perceived a small slip of paper fastened to the coat-sleeve, upon which, in Waller's handwriting, the following few words were written: —

The livery, I hope, will fit you, as I am rather particular about how you 'll look. Get quietly down to the stable-yard, and drive the tilbury into Cheltenham, where wait for further orders from your kind master,

JOHN WALLER.

The horrible villany of this wild scamp actually paralyzed me. That I should put on such ridiculous trumpery was out of the question; yet what was to be done? I rang the bell violently. "Where are my clothes, Thomas?"

"Don't know, sir; I was out all the morning, sir, and never seed them."

"There, Thomas, be smart now, and send them up, will you?"

Thomas disappeared, and speedily returned to say that my clothes could not be found anywhere, no one knew any-thing of them, and begged me to come down, as Miss Kam-worth desired him to say that they were still waiting, and she begged Mr. Lorrequer would not make an elaborate toilet, as they were going on a country excursion. An elaborate toilet! I wish to Heaven she saw my costume! No, I'll never do it.

"Thomas, you must tell the ladies, and the Colonel too, that I feel very ill; I am not able to leave my bed; I am subject to attacks, — very violent attacks in my head, and must always be left quiet and alone, — perfectly alone, mind me, Thomas, for a day at least."

Thomas departed; and as I lay distracted in my bed, I heard from the breakfast-room the loud laughter of many persons evidently enjoying some excellent joke. Could it be me they were laughing at? The thought was horrible!

"Colonel Kamworth wishes to know if you'd like the doctor, sir?" said Thomas, evidently suppressing a most inveterate fit of laughing, as he again appeared at the door.

"No, certainly not," said I, in a voice of thunder. "What the devil are you grinning at?"

"You may as well come, my man, — you're found out; they all know it now," said the fellow, with an odious grin.

I jumped out of the bed and hurled the boot-jack at him with all my strength, but had only the satisfaction to hear him go downstairs chuckling at his escape; and as he reached the parlor, the increase of mirth and the loudness of the laughter told me that he was not the only one who was merry at my expense. Anything was preferable to this. Downstairs I resolved to go at once. But how? A blanket, I thought, would not be a bad thing, and particularly as I had said I was ill. I could at least get as far as Colonel Kamworth's dressing-room and explain to him the whole affair; but then, if I was detected *en route!* which I was almost sure to be, with so many people parading about the house. No, that would never do. There was but one alternative, and dreadful, shocking as it was, I could not avoid it; and with a heavy heart, and as much indignation at Waller for what I could not but consider a most scurvy trick, I donned the yellow inexpressibles; next came the

vest, and last the coat, with its broad flaps and lace excrescences, fifty times more absurd and merry-andrew than any
stage servant who makes off with his table and two chairs
amid the hisses and gibes of an upper gallery.

If my costume leaned towards the ridiculous, I resolved
that my air and bearing should be more than usually austere
and haughty; and with something of the stride of John
Kemble in Coriolanus, I was leaving my bedroom, when
I accidentally caught a view of myself in the glass, —and
so mortified, so shocked was I that I sank into a chair and
almost abandoned my resolution to go on; the very gesture
I had assumed for my vindication only increased the ridicule of my appearance, and the strange quaintness of the
costume totally obliterated every trace of any characteristic
of the wearer, so infernally cunning was its contrivance.
I don't think that the most saturnine martyr of gout and
dyspepsia could survey me without laughing. With a bold
effort I flung open my door, hurried down the stairs, and
reached the hall. The first person I met was a kind of
pantry-boy, — a beast only lately emancipated from the
plough, and destined, after a dozen years' training as a
servant, again to be turned back to his old employ for incapacity; he grinned horribly for a minute as I passed, and
then, in a half-whisper, said, —

"Maester, I advise ye run for it; they 're a-waiting for
ye with the constables in the justice's room."

I gave him a look of contemptuous superiority, at which
he grinned the more, and passed on.

Without stopping to consider where I was going, I
opened the door of the breakfast-parlor and found myself
at one plunge in a room full of people. My first impulse
was to retreat again; but so shocked was I at the very first
thing that met my sight that I was perfectly powerless to
do anything. Among a considerable number of people who
stood in small groups round the breakfast-table, I discerned
Jack Waller, habited in a very accurate black frock and
dark trousers, supporting upon his arm — shall I confess?
— no less a person than Mary Kamworth, who leaned on

him with the familiarity of an old acquaintance and chatted gayly with him. The buzz of conversation which filled the apartment when I entered ceased for a second of deep silence; and then followed a peal of laughter so long and so vociferous that in my momentary anger I prayed some one might burst a blood-vessel and frighten the rest. I put on a look of indescribable indignation, and cast a glance of what I intended should be most withering scorn on the assembly; but alas! my infernal harlequin costume ruined the effect, and confound me if they did not laugh the louder! I turned from one to the other with the air of a man who marks out victims for his future wrath, but with no better success; at last, amid the continued mirth of the party, I made my way towards where Waller stood, absolutely suffocated with laughter, and scarcely able to stand without support.

"Waller," said I, in a voice half tremulous with rage and shame together, "Waller, if this rascally trick be yours, rest assured no former term of intimacy between us shall —"

Before I could conclude the sentence, a bustle at the door of the room called every attention in that direction; I turned and beheld Colonel Kamworth, followed by a strong *posse comitatus* of constables, tipstaffs, etc., armed to the teeth, and evidently prepared for vigorous battle. Before I was able to point out my woes to my kind host, he burst out, —

"So you scoundrel, you impostor, you infernal young villain! Pretending to be a gentleman, you get admission into a man's house and dine at his table, when your proper place had been behind his chair! How far he might have gone, Heaven can tell if that excellent young gentleman, his master, had not traced him here this morning; but you 'll pay dearly for it, you young rascal, that you shall."

"Colonel Kamworth," said I, drawing myself proudly up (and, I confess, exciting new bursts of laughter), "Colonel Kamworth, for the expressions you have just applied to me a heavy reckoning awaits you, — not, however, before an-

other individual now present shall atone for the insult he
has dared to pass upon me."

Colonel Kamworth's passion at this declaration knew no
bounds; he cursed and swore absolutely like a madman,
and vowed that transportation for life would be a mild sentence for such an iniquity.

Waller at length, wiping the tears of laughter from his
eyes, interposed between the Colonel and his victim, and
begged that I might be forgiven. "For indeed, my dear
sir," said he, "the poor fellow is of rather respectable
parentage, and such is his taste for good society that he 'd
run any risk to be among his betters, although, as in the
present case, the exposure brings a rather heavy retribution. However, let me deal with him. Come, Henry,"
said he, with an air of insufferable superiority. "take my
tilbury into town, and wait for me at the George; I shall
endeavor to make your peace with my excellent friend

Colonel Kamworth, and the best mode you can contribute
to that object is to let us have no more of your society."

I cannot attempt to picture my rage at these words;
however, escape from this diabolical predicament was my
only present object, and I rushed from the room, and
springing into the tilbury at the door, drove down the
avenue at the rate of fifteen miles per hour, amid the
united cheers, groans, and yells of the whole servants'
hall, who seemed to enjoy my "detection" more even than
their betters. Meditating vengeance, sharp, short, and
decisive, on Waller, the Colonel, and every one else in
the infernal conspiracy against me, — for I utterly forgot
every vestige of our agreement in the surprise by which I
was taken, — I reached Cheltenham. Unfortunately, I had
no friend there to whose management I could commit the
bearing of a message, and was obliged, as soon as I could
procure suitable costume, to hasten up to Coventry, where
the —th Dragoons were then quartered. I lost no time in
selecting an adviser and taking the necessary steps to bring
Master Waller to a reckoning; and on the third morning
we again reached Cheltenham, I thirsting for vengeance
and bursting still with anger. Not so, my friend, however who never could discuss the affair with common
gravity, and even ventured every now and then on a sly
allusion to my yellow shorts. As we passed the last toll-
bar, a travelling carriage came whirling by, with four
horses, at a tremendous pace; and as the morning was
frosty, and the sun scarcely risen, the whole team were
smoking and steaming so as to be half invisible. We
both remarked on the precipitancy of the party; for as our
own pace was considerable, the two vehicles passed like
lightning. We had scarcely dressed and ordered breakfast,
when a more than usual bustle in the yard called us to the
window; the waiter, who came in at the same instant, told
us that four horses were ordered out to pursue a young lady
who had eloped that morning with an officer.

"Ah! our friend in the green travelling-chariot, I 'll be
bound," said my companion; but as neither of us knew

that part of the country, and I was too engrossed by my own thoughts, I never inquired farther. As the chaise in chase drove round to the door, I looked to see what the pursuer was like; and as he issued from the inn, recognized my *ci-devant* host, Colonel Kamworth. I need not say my vengeance was sated at once, — *he* had lost his daughter, and *Waller* was on the road to be married. Apologies and explanations came in due time for all my injuries and sufferings; and I confess the part which pleased me most was that I saw no more of Jack for a considerable period after. He started for the Continent, where he has lived ever since on a small allowance granted by his father-in-law, and never paying me the stipulated sum, as I had clearly broken the compact.

So much for my second attempt at matrimony. One would suppose that such experience should be deemed sufficient to show that my talent did not lie in that way. And here I must rest for the present, with the additional confession that so strong was the memory of that vile adventure that I refused a lucrative appointment under Lord Anglesey's Government when I discovered that his livery included "yellow plush breeches:" to have such *souvenirs* flitting around and about me, at dinner and elsewhere, would have left me without a pleasure in existence.

CHAPTER XII.

DEAR, dirty Dublin, *Io te saluto!* How many excellent
things might be said of thee if, unfortunately, it did not
happen that the theme is an old one, and has been much
better *sung* than it can ever now be *said*. With thus much
of apology for no more lengthened panegyric, let me beg of
my reader, if he be conversant with that most moving melody, the "Groves of Blarney," to hum the following lines,
which I heard shortly after my landing, and which well
express my own feelings for the "loved spot:" —

> "Oh! Dublin, sure, there is no doubtin',
>   Beats every city upon the *say ;*
> 'T is there you 'll see O'Connell spouting,
>   And Lady Morgan making *tay.*
> And 't is the capital of the greatest nation,
>   With finest peasantry on a fruitful sod,
> Fighting like devils for conciliation,
>   And hating each other for the love of God."

Once more, then, I found myself in the "most car-driv-
ingest city," *en route* to join on the expiration of my leave.
Since my departure, my regiment had been ordered to Kilkenny, that sweet city so famed in song for its "fire without smoke," but which, were its character in any way to be
derived from its past or present representative, might certainly with more propriety reverse the epithet, and read
"smoke without fire." My last communication from head-
quarters was full of nothing but gay doings. Balls, dinners,
déjeûners, and, more than all, private theatricals, seemed
to occupy the entire attention of every man of the gallant
—th. I was earnestly entreated to come, without waiting

for the end of my leave; that several of my old "parts were kept open for me;" and that, in fact, the "boys of Kilkenny" were on tiptoe in expectation of my arrival, as though his Majesty's mail were to convey a Kean or a Kemble. I shuddered a little as I read this, and recollected "my last appearance on any stage," little anticipating, at the moment, that my next was to be nearly as productive of the ludicrous, as time and my "Confessions" will show. One circumstance, however, gave me considerable pleasure. It was this: I took it for granted that in the varied and agreeable occupations which so pleasurable a career opened, my adventures in love would escape notice, and that I should avoid the merciless raillery my two failures, in six months, might reasonably be supposed to call forth. I therefore wrote a hurried note to Curzon, setting forth the great interest all their proceedings had for me, and assuring him that my stay in town should be as short as possible, for that I longed once more to "strut the monarch of the boards," and concluded with a sly paragraph, artfully intended to act as a *paratonnerre* to the gibes and jests which I dreaded, by endeavoring to make light of my matrimonial speculations. The postscript ran somewhat thus, —

Glorious fun have I had since we met; but were it not that my good angel stood by me, I should write these hurried lines with a wife at my elbow. But luck, that never yet deserted, is still faithful to your old friend　　　　　　　　H. LORREQUER.

My reader may suppose — for he is sufficiently behind the scenes with me — with what feeings I penned these words; yet anything was better than the attack I looked forward to: and I should rather have changed into the Cape Rifle Corps, or any other army of martyrs, than meet my mess with all the ridicule my late proceedings exposed me to. Having disburdened my conscience of this dread, I finished my breakfast and set out on a stroll through the town.

I believe it is Coleridge who somewhere says that to transmit the first bright and early impressions of our youth, fresh and uninjured, to a remote period of life, constitutes one of the loftiest prerogatives of genius. If this be true, — and I am not disposed to dispute it, — what a gifted people must be the worthy inhabitants of Dublin; for I scruple not to affirm that of all cities of which we have any record in history, sacred or profane, there is not one so little likely to disturb the tranquil current of such reminiscences. "As it was of old, so it is now," enjoying a delightful permanency in all its habits and customs which no changes elsewhere disturb or affect; and in this respect I defy O'Connell and all the tail to refuse it the epithet of "Conservative."

Had the excellent Rip Van Winkle, instead of seeking his repose upon the cold and barren acclivities of the Kaatskills, — as we are veritably informed by Irving, — but betaken himself to a comfortable bed at Morrisson's or the Bilton, not only would he have enjoyed a more agreeable siesta, but, what the event showed of more consequence, the pleasing satisfaction of not being disconcerted by novelty on his awakening. It is possible that the waiter who brought him the water to shave — for Rip's beard, we are told, had grown uncommonly long — might exhibit a little of that wear and tear to which humanity is liable from time; but had he questioned him as to the ruling topics, the popular amusements of the day, he would have heard, as he might have done twenty years before, that there was a meeting to convert Jews at the Rotunda; another to rob parsons at the Corn Exchange; that the Viceroy was dining with the Corporation and congratulating them on the prosperity of Ireland, while the inhabitants were regaled with a procession of the "broad ribbon weavers," who had not weaved, Heaven knows when! This, with an occasional letter from Mr. O'Connell, and now and then a duel in the "Phaynix," constituted the current pastimes of the city. Such, at least, were they in *my* day; and though far from the dear *locale*, an odd, flitting glance at the newspapers induces me to believe that matters are not much changed since.

I rambled through the streets for some hours, revolving such thoughts as pressed upon me involuntarily by all I saw. The same little gray homunculus that filled my "Prince's mixture" years before, stood behind the counter at Lundy Foot's, weighing out rappee and high toast just as I last saw him. The fat college porter, that I used to mistake in my schoolboy days for the Provost, God forgive me! was there as fat and as ruddy as heretofore and wore his Roman costume of helmet and plush breeches with an air as classic. The state trumpeter at the Castle — another object of my youthful veneration, poor "old God save the King," as we used to call him — walked the streets as of old, — his cheeks, indeed, a little more lanky and tendinous; but then there had been many viceregal changes, and the "one sole melody his heart delighted in" had been more frequently called into requisition as he marched in solemn state with the other antique gentlemen in tabards. As I walked along, each moment some familiar and early association being suggested by the objects around, I felt my arm suddenly seized. I turned hastily round, and beheld a very old companion in many a hard-fought field and merry bivouac, Tom O'Flaherty, of the 8th. Poor Tom was sadly changed since we last met, which was at a ball in Madrid. He was then one of the best-looking fellows of his stamp I ever met, tall and athletic, with the easy bearing of a man of the world, and a certain jauntiness that I have never seen but in Irishmen who have mixed much in society.

There was also a certain peculiar devil-may-care recklessness about the self-satisfied swagger of his gait, and the free-and-easy glance of his sharp black eye, united with a temper that nothing could ruffle, and a courage nothing could daunt. With such qualities as these, he had been the prime favorite of his mess, to which he never came without some droll story to relate, or some choice expedient for future amusement. Such had Tom once been, — now he was much altered; and though the quiet twinkle of his dark eye showed that the spirit of fun within was not "dead, but only sleeping," to myself, who knew something of his history, it seemed almost cruel to awaken him to anything which might bring him back to the memory of bygone days. A momentary glance showed me that he was no longer what he had been, and that the unfortunate charge in his condition, the loss of all his earliest and oldest associates, and his blighted prospects, had nearly broken a heart that never deserted a friend nor quailed before an enemy. Poor O'Flaherty was no longer the delight of the circle he once adorned; the wit that "set the table in a roar" was all but departed, — he had been dismissed the service. The story is a brief one.

In the retreat from Burgos, the —th Light Dragoons, after a fatiguing day's march, halted at the wretched village of Cabeñas. It had been deserted by the inhabitants the day before, who, on leaving, had set it on fire; and the blackened walls and fallen roof-trees were nearly all that now remained to show where the little hamlet had once stood.

Amid a downpour of rain that had fallen for several hours, drenched to the skin, cold, weary, and nearly starving, the gallant 8th reached this melancholy spot at nightfall, with little better prospect of protection from the storm than the barren heath through which their road led might afford them. Among the many who muttered curses, not loud, but deep, on the wretched termination to their day's suffering, there was one who kept up his usual good spirits, and not only seemed himself nearly regardless of the privations and miseries about him, but actually succeeded in making the others who rode alongside as perfectly forgetful of their annoyances and troubles as was possible under such circumstances. Good stories, joking allusions to the more discontented ones of the party, ridiculous plans for the night's encampment, followed each other so rapidly that the weariness of the way was forgotten; and while some were cursing their hard fate that ever betrayed them into such misfortunes, the little group round O'Flaherty were almost convulsed with laughter at the wit and drollery of one over whom, if the circumstances had any influence, they seemed only to heighten his passion for amusement. In the early part of the morning he had captured a turkey, which hung gracefully from his holster on one side, while a small goat-skin of Valencia wine balanced it on the other. These good things were destined to form a feast that evening, to which he had invited four others, — that being, according to his most liberal calculation, the greatest number to whom he could afford a reasonable supply of wine.

When the halt was made, it took some time to arrange the dispositions for the night; and it was nearly midnight before all the regiment had got their billets and were housed, even with such scanty accommodation as the place afforded. Tom's guests had not yet arrived, and he himself was busily engaged in roasting the turkey before a large fire, on which stood a capacious vessel of spiced wine, when the party appeared. A very cursory "reconnoissance" through the house — one of the only ones untouched in the village — showed that from the late rain it would be impossible to think of sleeping in the lower story, which already showed signs of being flooded; they therefore proceeded in a body upstairs, — and what was their delight to find a most comfortable room, neatly furnished with chairs and a table, but above all, a large old-fashioned bed, an object of such luxury as only an old campaigner can duly appreciate. The curtains were closely tucked in all round, and in their fleeting and hurried glance, they felt no inclination to disturb them, and rather proceeded to draw up the table before the hearth to which they speedily removed the fire from below; and ere many minutes, with that activity which a bivouac life invariably teaches, their supper smoked before them, and five happier fellows did not sit down that night within a large circuit around. Tom was unusually great; stores of drollery, unlocked before, poured from him unceasingly, and what with his high spirits to excite them, and the reaction inevitable after a hard day's severe march, the party soon lost the little reason that usually sufficed to guide them, and became as pleasantly tipsy as can well be conceived. However,

all good things must have an end, and so had the wine-
skin. Tom had placed it affectionately under his arm like
a bagpipe, and failed, with even a most energetic squeeze,
to extract a drop. There was now nothing for it but to go
to rest, — and, indeed, it seemed the most prudent thing
for the party.

The bed became accordingly a subject of grave deliberation; for as it could only hold two, and the party were five,
there seemed some difficulty in submitting their chances to
lot, which all agreed was the fairest way. While this was
under discussion, one of the party had approached the con-
tested prize, and drawing aside the curtains, proceeded to
jump in, when what was his astonishment to discover that
it was already occupied! The exclamation of surprise he
gave forth soon brought the others to his side, and to their
horror, drunk as they were, they found that the body before
them was that of a dead man arrayed in all the ghastly
pomp of a corpse. A little nearer inspection showed that
he had been a priest, — probably the *padre* of the village;
on his head he had a small velvet skull-cap embroidered
with a cross, and his body was swathed in a vestment such
as priests usually wear at the mass; in his hand he held a
large wax taper, which appeared to have burnt only half
down, and probably been extinguished by the current of air
on opening the door. After the first brief shock which
this sudden apparition had caused, the party recovered as
much of their senses as the wine had left them, and proceeded to discuss what was to be done under the circumstances; for not one of them ever contemplated giving up
a bed to a dead priest while five living men slept on the
ground. After much altercation, O'Flaherty, who had
hitherto listened without speaking, interrupted the contending parties, saying. "Stop, lads, I have it!"

"Come," said one of them, "let us hear Tom's proposal."

"Oh!" said he, with difficulty steadying himself while
he spoke, "we'll put him to bed with old Ridgeway, the
quartermaster!"

The roar of loud laughter that followed Tom's device was

renewed again and again, till not a man could speak from absolute fatigue. There was not a dissentient voice. Old Ridgeway was hated in the corps, and a better way of disposing of the priest and paying off the quartermaster could not be thought of.

Very little time sufficed for their preparations; and if they had been brought up under a certain well-known duke, they could not have exhibited a greater taste for a "black job." The door of the room was quickly taken from its hinges, and the priest placed upon it at full length; a moment more sufficed to lift the door upon their shoulders, and, preceded by Tom, who lit a candle in honor of being, as he said, "chief mourner," they took their way through the camp towards Ridgeway's quarters. When they reached the hut where their victim lay, Tom ordered a halt, and proceeded stealthily into the house to "reconnoitre." The old quartermaster he found stretched on his sheepskin before a large fire, the remnants of an ample supper strewed about him, and two empty bottles standing on the hearth; his deep snoring showed that all was safe, and that no fears of his awaking need disturb them. His shako and sword lay near him, but his sabretasche was under his head. Tom carefully withdrew the two former, and hastening to his friends without, proceeded to decorate the priest with them. expressing, at the same time, considerable regret that he feared it might wake Ridgeway if he were to put the velvet skull-cap on him for a nightcap.

Noiselessly and stealthily they now entered, and proceeded to put down their burden, which, after a moment's discussion, they agreed to place between the quartermaster and the fire, of which hitherto he had reaped ample benefit. This done, they quietly retreated, and hurried back to their quarters, unable to speak with laughter at the success of their plot and their anticipation of Ridgeway's rage on awakening in the morning.

It was in the dim twilight of a hazy morning that the bugler of the 8th aroused the sleeping soldiers from their miserable couches, which, wretched as they were, they nevertheless rose from reluctantly, so wearied and fatigued had they been by the preceding day's march. Net one among the number felt so indisposed to stir as the worthy quartermaster; his peculiar avocations had demanded a more than usual exertion on his part, and in the posture he had lain down at night he rested till morning, without stirring a limb. Twice the reveille had rung through the little encampment, and twice the quartermaster had essayed to open his eyes, but in vain; at last he made a tremendous effort, and sat bolt upright on the floor, hoping that the sudden effort might sufficiently arouse him. Slowly his eyes opened, and the first thing they beheld was the figure of the dead priest with a light cavalry helmet on his head, seated before him. Ridgeway, who was a good Catholic, trembled in every joint, — it might be a ghost, it might be a warning; he knew not what to think. He imagined the lips moved; and so overcome with terror was he at last that he absolutely shouted like a maniac, and never ceased till the hut was filled with officers and men, who, hearing the uproar, ran to his aid. The surprise of the poor quartermaster at the apparition was scarcely greater than that of the beholders. No one was able to afford any explanation of the circumstance, though all were assured that it must have been done in jest. The door upon which the priest had been conveyed afforded the clew, — they had forgotten to restore it to its place. Accordingly, the different billets were examined, and at last O'Flaherty was discovered in a most commodious bed, in a large room without a door, still fast asleep, and alone; how and when he had parted from his companions he never could precisely explain, though he has since confessed it was part of his scheme to lead them astray in the village, and then retire to the bed, which he had determined to appropriate to his sole use.

Old Ridgeway's rage knew no bounds; he absolutely foamed with passion, and in proportion as he was laughed at his choler rose higher. Had this been the only result, it had been well for poor Tom; but unfortunately the affair got to be rumored through the country. The inhabitants of the village learned the indignity with which the *padre* had been treated; they addressed a memorial to Lord Wellington. Inquiry was immediately instituted; O'Flaherty was tried by court-martial, and found guilty. Nothing short of the heaviest punishment that could be inflicted under the circumstances would satisfy the Spaniards, and at that precise period it was part of our policy to conciliate their esteem by every means in our power. The commander-in-chief resolved to make what he called an "example," and poor O'Flaherty — the life and soul of his regiment, the darling of his mess — was broke, and pronounced incapable of ever serving his Majesty again. Such was the event upon which my poor friend's fortune in life seemed to hinge. He returned to Ireland, if not entirely broken-hearted, so altered that his best friends scarcely knew him. His "occupation was gone;" the mess had been his home; his brother officers were to him in place of relatives; and he had lost all. His after-life was spent in rambling from one watering-place to another, — more with the air of one who seeks to consume than enjoy his time; and with such a change in appearance as the alteration in his fortune had effected, he now stood before me, but altogether so different a man that but for the well-known tones of a voice that had often convulsed me with laughter, I should scarcely have recognized him.

"Lorrequer, my old friend, I never thought of seeing you here. This is indeed a piece of good luck."

"Why, Tom, you surely knew that the 4—th were in Ireland, did n't you?"

"To be sure. I dined with them only a few days ago; but they told me you were off to Paris to marry something superlatively beautiful and most enormously rich, — the daughter of a duke, if I remember right; but *certes*, they said your fortune was made, and I need not tell you there was not a man among them better pleased than I was to hear it."

"Oh! they said so, did they? Droll dogs, — always

quizzing; I wonder you did not perceive the hoax, eh? Very good, was it not?" This I poured out in short, broken sentences, blushing like scarlet, and fidgeting like a schoolgirl with downright nervousness.

"A hoax! Devilish well done too," said Tom; "for old Carden believed the whole story, and told me that he had obtained a six mouths' leave for you to make your *cour*, and, moreover, said that he had got a letter from the nobleman, Lord— Confound his name!"

"Lord Grey, is it?" said I, with a sly look at Tom.

"No, my dear friend," said he, dryly, "it was not Lord Grey. But to continue: he had got a letter from him, dated from Paris, stating his surprise that you had never joined them there, according to promise, and that they knew your cousin Guy, and a great deal of other matter I can't remember. So what does all this mean? Did you hoax the noble lord as well as the Horse Guards, Harry?"

This was indeed a piece of news for me; I stammered out some ridiculous explanation, and promised a fuller detail. Could it be that I had done the Callonbys injustice, and that they never intended to break off my attentions to Lady Jane, —that she was still faithful, and that of all concerned, I alone had been to blame? Oh! how I hoped this might be the case; heavily as my conscience might accuse, I longed ardently to forgive and deal mercifully with myself. Tom continued to talk about indifferent matters, as these thoughts flitted through my mind; perceiving at last that I did not attend, he stopped suddenly, and said, —

"Harry, I see clearly that something has gone wrong, and perhaps I can guess at the mode too. But however, you can do nothing about it now; come and dine with me to-day, and we'll discuss the affair together after dinner; or if you prefer a 'distraction,' as we used to say in Dunkerque, why then I'll arrange something fashionable for your evening's amusement. Come, what say you to hearing Father Keogh preach? or would you like a supper at the Carlingford? or perhaps you prefer a· *soirée chez*

Miladi? For all of these Dublin affords, — all three good in their way, and very intellectual."

"Well, Tom, I 'm yours. But I should prefer your dining with *me*, — I am at Bilton's; we 'll have our cutlet quite alone, and — "

"And be heartily sick of each other, you were going to add. No, no, Harry, you must dine with *me;* I have some remarkably *nice* people to present you to. Six is the hour, — sharp six, — number —, Molesworth Street, Mrs. Clanfrizzle's. Easily find it, — large fanlight over the door, huge lamp in the hall, and a strong odor of mutton broth for thirty yards on each side of the premises. And as good luck will have it, I see old Daly, the counsellor, as they call him, — he 's the very man to get to meet you; you always liked a character, eh? "

Saying this, O'Flaherty disengaged himself from my arm and hurried across the street towards a portly, middle-aged looking gentleman with the reddest face I ever beheld. After a brief but very animated colloquy, Tom returned and informed me that all was right; he had secured Daly.

"And who is Daly? " said I, inquiringly, for I was rather interested in hearing what peculiar qualification as a diner-out the counsellor might lay claim to, many of Tom's *friends* being as remarkable for being the quizzed as the quizzers.

"Daly," said he, "is the brother of a most distinguished member of the Irish Bar, of which he himself is also a follower, — bearing, however, no other resemblance to the clever man than the name; for as assuredly as the reputation of the one is inseparably linked with success, so unerringly is the other's coupled with failure. And strange to say, the stupid man is fairly convinced that his brother owes all his advancement to him, and that to his disinterested kindness the other is indebted for his present exalted station. Thus it is through life; there seems ever to accompany dulness a sustaining power of vanity that, like a life-buoy, keeps a mass afloat whose weight unassisted would sink into obscurity. Do you know that my friend

Denis, there, imagines himself the first man that ever enlightened Sir Robert Peel as to Irish affairs? — and upon my word, his reputation on this head stands incontestably higher than on most others."

"You surely cannot mean that Sir Robert Peel ever consulted with, much less relied upon, the statements of such a person as you describe your friend Denis to be?"

"He did both; and if he was a little puzzled by the information, the only disgrace attaches to a government that sends men to rule over us unacquainted with our habits of thinking, and utterly ignorant of the language — ay, I repeat it. But come, you shall judge for yourself; the story is a short one, and fortunately so, for I must hasten home to give timely notice of your coming to dine with me. When Sir Robert Peel, then Mr. Peel, came over here as secretary to Ireland, a very distinguished political leader of the day invited a party to meet him at dinner, consisting of men of different political leanings, among whom were, as may be supposed, many members of the Irish Bar. The elder Daly was too remarkable a person to be omitted, but as the two brothers resided together, there was a difficulty about getting him; however, he must be had, and the only alternative that presented itself was adopted, — both were invited. When the party descended to the dining-room, by one of those unfortunate accidents which, as the proverb informs us, occasionally take place in the best regulated establishments, the wrong Mr. Daly got placed beside Mr. Peel, — which post of honor had been destined by the host for the more agreeable and talented brother. There was now no help for it; and with a heart somewhat nervous for the consequences of the proximity, the worthy entertainer sat down to do the honors as best he might. He was consoled during dinner by observing that the devotion bestowed by honest Denis on the viands before him effectually absorbed his faculties, and thereby threw the entire of Mr. Peel's conversation towards the gentleman on his other flank. This happiness was, like most others, destined to be a brief one. As the dessert made its appearance, Mr. Peel began to listen with some attention to the conversation of the persons opposite, with one of whom he was struck most forcibly; so happy a power of illustration, so vivid a fancy, such logical precision in argument as he evinced, perfectly charmed and surprised him. Anxious to learn the name of so gifted an individual, he turned towards his hitherto silent neighbor, and demanded who he was.

"' Who is he, is it?' said Denis, hesitatingly, as if he half doubted such extent of ignorance as not to know the person alluded to.

"Mr. Peel bowed in acquiescence.

"' That's Bushe!' said Denis, giving at the same time the same sound to the vowel u as it obtains when occurring in the word ' rush.'

"' I beg pardon,' said Mr. Peel, ' I did not hear.'

"' Bushe!' replied Denis, with considerable energy of tone.

"' Oh, yes! I know,' said the secretary, — ' Mr. Bushe, a very distinguished member of your Bar, I have heard.'

"' Faith, you may say that!' said Denis, tossing off his wine at what he esteemed a very trite observation.

"' Pray,' said Mr. Peel, again returning to the charge, though certainly feeling not a little surprised at the singular laconicism of his informant, no less than the mellifluous tones of an accent then perfectly new to him, ' pray, may I ask, what is the peculiar character of Mr. Bushe's eloquence, — I mean, of course, in his professional capacity?'

"' Eh!' said Denis, ' I don't comprehend you exactly.'

"' I mean,' said Mr. Peel, ' in one word, what's his forte?'

"' His forte?'

"' I mean what his peculiar gift consists in — '

"' Oh, I perceave; I have ye now, — the juries!'

"' Ah! addressing a jury.'

"' Ay, the juries.'

"' Can you oblige me by giving me an idea of the manner in which he obtains such signal success in this difficult branch of eloquence?'

"'I'll tell ye,' said Denis, leisurely finishing his glass, and smacking his lips, with the air of a man girding up his loins for a mighty effort, 'I'll tell ye. Well, ye see, the way he has is this, — here Mr. Peel's expectation rose to the highest degree of interest, — 'the way he has is this, — *he first butthers them up, and then slithers them down!* That's all; devil a more of a secret there's in it.'"

How much reason Denis had to boast of imparting early information to the new secretary I leave my English readers to guess; my Irish ones I may trust to do him ample justice.

My friend now left me to my own devices to while away the hours till time to dress for dinner. Heaven help the gentleman so left in Dublin, say I. It is, perhaps, the only city of its size in the world where there is no lounge, no promenade. Very little experience of it will convince you that it abounds in pretty women, and has its fair share of agreeable men; but where are they in the morning? I wish Sir Dick Lauder, instead of speculating where salmon pass the Christmas holidays, would apply his most inquiring mind to such a question as this. True it is, however, they are not to be found. The squares are deserted, the streets are very nearly so, and all that is left to the luckless wanderer in search of the beautiful is to ogle the beauties of Dame Street, who are shopkeepers in Grafton Street, or the beauties of Grafton Street, who are shopkeepers in Dame Street. But, confound it, how cranky I am getting! I must be tremendously hungry. True, it's past six. So now for my suit of sable, and then to dinner.

CHAPTER XIII.

Punctual to my appointment with O'Flaherty, I found myself, a very few minutes after six o'clock, at Mrs. Clanfrizzle's door. My very authoritative summons at the bell was answered by the appearance of a young, pale-faced invalid in a suit of livery, the taste of which bore a very unpleasant resemblance to the one I so lately figured in. It was with considerable difficulty I persuaded this functionary to permit my carrying my hat with me to the drawing-room, — a species of caution on my part, as he esteemed it, savoring much of distrust. This point, however, I carried, and followed him up a very ill-lighted stair to the drawing-room. Here I was announced by some faint resemblance to my real name, but sufficiently near to bring my friend Tom at once to meet me, who immediately congratulated me on my fortune in coming off so well, for that the person who preceded me, Mr. Jones Blennerhasset, had been just announced as Mr. Blatherhashit, — a change the gentleman himself was not disposed to adopt. "But come along. Harry; while we are waiting for Daly, let me make you known to some of our party. This, you must know, is a boarding-house, and always has some capital fun, — queerest people you ever met. I have only one hint: cut every man, woman, and child of them, if you meet them hereafter; I do it myself, though I have lived here these six months." Pleasant people, thought I, these must be, with whom such a line is advisable, much less practicable.

"Mrs. Clanfrizzle, my friend Mr. Lorrequer; thinks he 'll stay the summer in town. Mrs. Clan, should like him to be one of us." The latter was said *sotto voce*, and was a practice he continued to adopt in presenting me to his several friends through the room.

"Miss Riley," — a horrid old fright in a bird of paradise plume and corked eyebrows, gibbeted in gilt chains and pearl ornaments, and looking, as the grisettes say, *superbe en chrysolithe,* — "Miss Riley, Captain Lorrequer, — a friend I have long desired to present to you. Fifteen thousand a year and a baronetcy, if he has sixpence," — *sotto* again. "Surgeon M'Culloch, — he likes the title," said Tom, in a whisper, — "Surgeon, Captain Lorrequer. By the by, lest I forget it, he wishes to speak to you in the morning about his health; he is stopping at Sandymount for the baths, — you could go out there, eh?" The tall thing in green spectacles bowed, and acknowledged Tom's kindness by a knowing touch of the elbow. In this way he made the tour of the room for about ten minutes, during which brief space I was, according to the kind arrangements of O'Flaherty, booked as a resident in the boarding-house, a lover to at least five elderly and three young ladies, a patient, a client, a second in a duel to a clerk in the Post-office, and had also volunteered (through him always) to convey, by all of his Majesty's mails, as many parcels, packets, band-boxes, and bird-cages as would have comfortably filled one of Pickford's vans. All this he told me was requisite to my being well received, though no one thought much of any breach of compact subsequently, except Mrs. Clan herself. The ladies had, alas! been often treated vilely before; the doctor had never had a patient; and as for the belligerent knight of the dead office, he'd rather have died than fought any day.

The last person to whom my friend deemed it necessary to introduce me was a Mr. Garret Cudmore, from the Reeks on Kerry, lately matriculated to all the honors of freshman-ship in the Dublin University. This latter was a low-sized, dark-browed man, with round shoulders and particularly long arms, the disposal of which seemed sadly to distress him. He possessed the most perfect brogue I ever listened to; but it was difficult to get him to speak, for on coming up to town some weeks before, he had been placed by some intelligent friend at Mrs. Clanfrizzle's establishment, with the express direction to mark and thoroughly digest as much as he could of the habits and customs of the circle about him, which he was rightly informed was the very focus of good-breeding and *haut ton,* but on no account, unless driven thereto by the pressure of sickness or the wants of nature, to trust himself with speech, which, in his then unformed state, he was assured would inevitably ruin him among his fastidiously cultivated associates.

To the letter and the spirit of the despatch he had received, the worthy Garret acted rigidly; and his voice was scarcely ever known to transgress the narrow limits prescribed by his friends. In more respects than one was this a good resolve; for so completely had he identified himself with college habits, things, and phrases, that whenever he conversed, he became little short of unintelligible to the vulgar, — a difficulty not lessened by his peculiar pronunciation.

My round of presentation was just completed, when the pale figure in light-blue livery announced Counsellor Daly and dinner; for both came fortunately together. Taking the post of honor, Miss Riley's arm, I followed Tom, who I soon perceived ruled the whole concern, as he led the way with another ancient vestal in black satin and bugles. The long procession wound its snake-like length down the narrow stair and into the dining-room, where at last we all got seated. And here let me briefly vindicate the motives of my friend. Should any unkind person be found to impute to his selection of a residence any base and grovelling passion for "gourmandise," that day's experience should be an eternal vindication of him. The soup — alas! that I should so far prostitute the word, for the black broth of Sparta was mock-turtle in comparison — retired to make way for a mass of beef, whose tenderness I did not question, for it sank beneath the knife of the carver like a feather-bed, — the skill of Saladin himself would have failed to divide it; the fish was a most rebellious pike, and nearly killed every loyal subject at table; and then down the sides were various dishes of chickens with azure bosoms, and hams with hides like a rhinoceros; covered "decoys" of decomposed vegetable matter called spinach and cabbage; potatoes arrayed in small masses and browned, resembling those ingenious architectural structures of mud children raise in the highways and call dirt-pies. Such were the chief constituents of the "feed;" and such, I am bound to confess, waxed beautifully less under the vigorous onslaught of the party.

The conversation soon became both loud and general. That happy familiarity which I had long believed to be the exclusive prerogative of a military mess, where constant daily association sustains the interest of the veriest trifles, I here found in a perfection I had not anticipated, — with this striking difference, that there was no absurd deference to any existing code of etiquette in the conduct of the party generally, each person quizzing his neighbor in the most free-and-easy style imaginable, and all, evidently from long habit and conventional usage, seeming to enjoy the practice exceedingly. Thus, droll allusions, good stories, and smart repartees fell thick as hail and twice as harmless, which, anywhere else that I had ever heard of, would assuredly have called for more explanations, and perhaps gunpowder, in the morning than usually are deemed agreeable. Here, however, they knew better; and though the lawyer quizzed the doctor for never having another patient than the house-dog, all of whose arteries he had tied in the course of the winter for practice, and the doctor retorted as heavily by showing that the lawyer's practice had been other than beneficial to those for whom he was concerned, his *one* client being found guilty mainly through his ingenious defence of him, — yet they never showed any, the slightest irritation; on the contrary, such little playful *badinage* ever led to some friendly passages of taking wine together, or in arrangements for a party to the "Dargle" or "Dunleary." And thus went on the entire party, the young ladies dart-ing an occasional slight at their elders, who certainly

returned the fire often with advantage; all uniting now
and then, however, in one common cause, — an attack of the
whole line upon Mrs. Clanfrizzle herself for the beef or the
mutton or the fish or the poultry, each of which was sure to
find some sturdy defamer ready and willing to give evidence
in dispraise. Yet even these — and I thought them rather
dangerous sallies — led to no more violent results than dignified replies from the worthy hostess upon the goodness of
her fare and the evident satisfaction it afforded while being
eaten, if the appetites of the party were a test. While this
was at its height, Tom stooped behind my chair and whispered gently, —

"This is good, is n't it, eh? — life in a boarding-house;
quite new to you. But they are civilized now, compared
to what you will find them in the drawing-room. When
short whist for fivepenny points sets in, then Greek meets
Greek, and we 'll have it."

During all this *mêlée* tournament, I perceived that the
worthy "jib," as he would be called in the parlance of Trinity, Mr. Cudmore, remained perfectly silent and apparently
terrified. The noise, the din of voices, and the laughing
so completely addled him that he was like one in a very
horrid dream. The attention with which I had observed
him having been remarked by my friend O'Flaherty, he
informed me that the scholar, as he was called there, was
then under a kind of cloud, — an adventure which occurred
only two nights before being too fresh in his memory to
permit him enjoying himself even to the limited extent it
had been his wont to do. As illustrative, not only of Mr.
Cudmore, but the life I have been speaking of, I may as
well relate it.

Soon after Mr. Cudmore's enlistment under the banners
of the Clanfrizzle, he had sought and found an asylum in
the drawing-room of the establishment, which promised,
from its geographical relations, to expose him less to the
molestations of conversation than most other parts of the
room. This was a small recess beside the fireplace, not
uncommon in old-fashioned houses, and which, from its

incapacity to hold more than one, secured to the worthy recluse the privacy he longed for; and here, among super-annuated hearth-brushes, an old hand-screen, an asthmatic bellows, and a kettle-holder, sat the timid youth, "alone, but in a crowd." Not all the seductions of loo, limited to threepence, nor even that most appropriately designated game, beggar-my-neighbor, could withdraw him from his blest retreat. Like his countryman, Saint Kevin, — my friend Petrie has ascertained that the saint was a native of Tralee, — he fled from the temptations of the world and the blandishments of the fair; but alas! like the saint him-self, the —

> "poor 'jib' little knew
> All that wily sex can do; "

for while he hugged himself in the security of his fortress, the web of his destiny was weaving. So true is it, as he himself used, no less pathetically than poetically, to express it, "Misfortune will find you out if ye were hid in a tay-chest."

It happened that in Mrs. Clanfrizzle's establishment the *enfant bleu* already mentioned was the only individual of his sex retained; and without for a moment disparaging the ability or attentions of this gifted person, yet it may reasonably be credited that in waiting on a party of twenty-five or thirty persons at dinner, all of whom he had ad-mitted as porter and announced as *maître d'hôtel*, with the subsequent detail of his duties in the drawing-room, Peter, — Blue Peter, his boarding-house sobriquet, — not enjoying the bird-like privilege of "being in two places at once," gave one rather the impression of a person of hasty and fidgety habits, for which nervous tendency the treatment he underwent was certainly injudicious, — it being the invariable custom for each guest to put his services in requisition, perfectly irrespective of all other claims upon him, from whatsoever quarter coming; and then at the pre-cise moment that the luckless valet was snuffing the candles, he was abused by one for not bringing coal; by another for having carried off his teacup, sent on an expedition for sugar; by a third for having left the door open, which he had never been near; and so on to the end of the chapter.

It chanced that a few evenings previous to my appearance at the house, this indefatigable Caleb was ministering as usual to the various and discrepant wants of the large party assembled in the drawing-room. With his wonted alacrity, he had withdrawn from their obscure retreat against the wall sundry little tables, destined for the players at whist, or "spoil five,"—the popular game of the establishment. With a dexterity that savored much of a stage education, he had arranged the candles, the cards, the counters; he had poked the fire, settled the stool for Miss Riley's august feet, and was busily engaged in changing five shillings into small silver for a desperate victim of loo, when Mrs. Clanfrizzle's third, and, as it appeared, last time of asking for the kettle smote upon his ear. His loyalty would have induced him at once to desert everything on such an occasion; but the other party engaged held him fast, saying, —

"Never mind *her*, Peter; you have sixpence more to give me."

Poor Peter rummaged one pocket, then another, discovering at last threepence in copper and some farthings, with which he seemed endeavoring to make a composition with his creditor for twelve shillings in the pound; when, Mrs. Clan's patience finally becoming exhausted, she turned towards Mr. Cudmore, the only unemployed person she could perceive, and with her blandest smile said, —

"Mr. Cudmore, may I take the liberty of requesting you would hand me the kettle beside you?"

Now, though the kettle aforesaid was, as the hostess very properly observed, beside him, yet the fact that in complying with the demand it was necessary for the bashful youth to leave the recess he occupied, and, with the kettle, proceed to walk half across the room, there to perform certain manual operations requiring skill and presence of mind before a large and crowded assembly, was horror to the mind of the poor jib, and he would nearly as soon have acceded to a desire to dance a hornpipe, if such had been

suggested as the wish of the company. However, there was nothing for it, and summoning up all his nerve, knitting his brows, clenching his teeth like one prepared to "do or die," he seized the hissing caldron and strode through the room like the personified genius of steam, — very much to the alarm of all the old ladies in the vicinity, whose tasteful drapery benefited but little from his progress. Yet he felt but little of all this; he had brought up his courage to the sticking place, and he was absolutely half unconscious of the whole scene before him. Nor was it till some kind mediator had seized his arm, while another drew him back by the skirts of the coat, that he desisted from the deluge of hot water with which, having filled the tea-pot, he proceeded to swamp everything else upon the tray, in his unfortunate abstraction. Mrs. Claufrizzle screamed; the old ladies accompanied her; the young ones tittered; the men laughed; and in a word, poor Cudmore, perfectly unconscious of anything extraordinary, felt himself the admired of all admirers, — very little, it is true, to his own satisfaction. After some few minutes' exposure to these signs of mirth, he succeeded in depositing the source of his griefs within the fender, and once more retired to his sanctuary, having registered a vow which, should I speak it, would forfeit his every claim to gallantry forever.

Whether, in the vow aforesaid, Mr. Cudmore had only been engaged in that species of tessellation which furnishes the pavement so celebrated in the lower regions, I know not; but true it is that he retired that night to his chamber very much discomfited at his *début* in the great world, and half disposed to believe that Nature had intended him for neither a Brummell nor a D'Orsay. While he was ruminating on such matters, he was joined by O'Flaherty, with whom he had been always more intimate than any other inmate of the house, Tom's tact having entirely concealed what the manners of the others too plainly evinced, — a perfect appreciation of the student's oddity and singularity. After some few observations on general matters, O'Flaherty began, with a tone of some seriousness, to express towards Cudmore the warm interest he had ever taken in him since his first coming among them, his great anxiety for his welfare, and his firm resolve that no chance or casual inattention to mere ceremonial observances on his part should ever be seized on by the other guests as a ground for detraction or an excuse for ridicule of him.

"Rely upon it, my dear boy," said he, "I have watched over you like a parent; and having partly foreseen that something like this affair of to-night would take place sooner or later —"

"What affair?" said Cudmore, his eyes staring half out of his head.

"The business of the kettle."

"Kett—el. The kettle! What of that?" said Cudmore.

"What of it? Why, if *you* don't feel it, I am sure it is not *my* duty to remind you; only —"

"Feel it, oh, yes! I saw them laughing because I spilled the water over old Mrs. Jones, or something of that sort."

"No, no, my dear young friend, they were not laughing at *that*, — their mirth had another object."

"What the devil was it at, then?"

"You don't know, don't you?"

"No, I really do not."

"Nor can't guess, eh?"

"Confound me if I can."

"Well, 1 see, Mr. Cudmore, you are really too innocent for these people. But come; it shall never be said that youth and inexperience ever suffered from the unworthy ridicule and cold sarcasm of the base world while Tom O'Flaherty stood by a spectator. Sir," said Tom, striking his hand with energy on the table, and darting a look of fiery indignation from his eye, "sir, you were this night trepanned, — yes, sir, vilely, shamefully trepanned — I repeat the expression — into the performance of a menial office, — an office so degrading, so offensive, so unbecoming the rank, the station, and the habits of gentlemen, my very blood recoils when I only think of the indignity."

The expression of increasing wonder and surprise depicted in Mr. Cudmore's face at these words, my friend Phiz might convey, — I cannot venture to describe it; suffice it to say that even O'Flaherty himself found it difficult to avoid a burst of laughter as he looked at him and resumed, —

"Witnessing, as I did, the entire occurrence, feeling deeply for the inexperience which the heartless worldlings had dared to trample upon, I resolved to stand by you, and here I am come for that purpose."

"Well, but what in the devil's name have I done all this time?"

"What! are you still ignorant? Is it possible? Did you not hand the kettle from the fireplace, and fill the teapot? Answer me that."

"I did," said Cudmore, with a voice already becoming tremulous.

' Is that the duty of a gentleman? Answer me that."

A dead pause stood in place of a reply, while Tom proceeded, —

"Did you ever hear any one ask me, or Counsellor Daly, or Mr. Fogarty, or any other person to do so? Answer me that."

"No, never," muttered Cudmore, with a sinking spirit.

"Well, then, why, may I ask, were *you* selected for that office, that, by your own confession, no one else would stoop to perform? I 'll tell you, — because, from your youth and inexperience, your innocence was deemed a fit victim to the heartless sneers of a cold and unfeeling world." And here Tom broke forth into a very beautiful apostrophe, beginning, "Oh, virtue!" — this I am unfortunately unable to present to my readers, and must only assure them that it was a very faithful imitation of the well-known one delivered by Burke in the case of Warren Hastings, — and concluding with an exhortation to Cudmore to wipe out the stain of his wounded honor by repelling with indignation the slightest future attempt at such an insult.

This done, O'Flaherty retired, leaving Cudmore to dig

among Greek roots and chew over the cud of his misfortune.
Punctual to the time and place, that same evening beheld
the injured Cudmore resume his wonted corner, pretty
much with the feeling with which a forlorn hope stands,
match in hand, to ignite the train destined to explode with
ruin to thousands, — himself, perhaps, among the number.
There he sat, with a brain as burning and a heart as excited
as though, instead of sipping his bohea beside a sea-coal
fire, he was that instant trembling beneath the frown of
Dr. Elrington for the blunders in his Latin theme, — and
what terror to the mind of a "jib" can equal that one?

As luck would have it, this was a company night in the
boarding-house. Various young ladies, in long blue sashes
and very broad ribbon sandals, paraded the rooms, chatting gayly with very distinguished-looking young gentlemen with gold brooches and party-colored inside waistcoats;
sundry elderly ladies sat at card-tables, discussing the "lost
honor by an odd trick they played," with heads as large as
those of Jack or Jill in the pantomime; spruce clerks in
public offices (whose vocation the expansive tendency of
the right ear, from long pen-carrying, betokened) discussed
fashion "and the musical glasses" to some very over-
dressed married ladies who preferred flirting to five-and-
ten. The tea-table, over which the amiable hostess
presided, had also its standing votaries, — mostly grave
parliamentary-looking gentlemen, with powdered heads
and very long-waisted black coats, among whom the Sir
Oracle was a functionary of his Majesty's High Court of
Chancery, though, I have reason to believe, not Lord Manners. Meanwhile, in all parts of the room might be seen
Blue Peter distributing tea, coffee, and biscuit, and occasionally interchanging a joke with the dwellers in the
house. While all these pleasing occupations proceeded,
the hour of Cudmore's trial was approaching. The teapot,
which had stood the attack of fourteen cups without flinch-
ing, at last began to fail, and discovered to the prying eyes
of Mrs. Clanfrizzle nothing but an olive-colored deposit of
soft matter closely analogous in appearance and chemical

property to the residuary precipitate in a drained fish-pond; she put down the lid with a gentle sigh, and turning towards the fire, bestowed one of her very blandest and most captivating looks on Mr. Cudmore, saying as plainly as looks could say, "Cudmore, you're wanting." Whether the youth did, or did not, understand, I am unable to record; I can only say the appeal was made without acknowledgment. Mrs. Clanfrizzle again essayed, and by a little masonic movement of her hand to the teapot, and a sly glance at the hob, intimated her wish, — still hopelessly. At last there was nothing for it but speaking; and she donned her very softest voice and most persuasive tone, saying, "Mr. Cudmore, I am really very troublesome; will you permit me to ask you — "

"Is it for the kettle, ma'am?" said Cudmore, with a voice that startled the whole room, disconcerting three whist-parties, and so absorbing the attention of the people at loo that the pool disappeared without any one being able to account for the circumstance, — "is it for the kettle, ma'am?"

"If you will be so *very* kind," lisped the hostess.

"Well, then, upon my conscience, you *are* impudent," said Cudmore, with his face crimsoned to the ears, and his eyes flashing fire.

"Why, Mr. Cudmore," began the lady, "why, really, this is so strange! Why, sir, what *can* you mean?"

"Just *that*," said the imperturbable jib, who, now his courage was up, dared everything.

"But, sir, you must surely have misunderstood me. I only asked for the kettle, Mr. Cudmore."

"The devil a more," said Cud, with a sneer.

"Well, then, of course — "

"Well, then, I'll tell you, of coorse," said he repeating her words, "the sorrow taste of the kettle I'll give you. Call your own skip, — Blue Pether there; damn me if I'll be your skip any longer!"

For the uninitiated, I have only to add that "skip" is the Trinity College appellation for servant, which was there-

fore employed by Mr. Cudmore on this occasion as expressing more contemptuously his sense of the degradation of
the office attempted to be put upon him. Having already
informed my reader on some particulars of the company, I
leave him to suppose how Mr. Cudmore's speech was received. Whist itself was at an end for that evening, and
nothing but laughter, long, loud, and reiterated, burst from
every corner of the room for hours after.

As I have so far travelled out of the record of my own
peculiar Confessions as to give a leaf from what might one
day form the matter of Mr. Cudmore's, I must now make
the only *amende* in my power, by honestly narrating that
short as my visit was to the classic precincts of this agreeable establishment, I did not escape without exciting my
share of ridicule, though I certainly had not the worst of
the joke, and may therefore with better grace tell the story,
which, happily for my readers, is a short one. A custom
prevailed in Mrs. Clanfrizzle's household which, from my
unhappy ignorance of boarding-houses, I am unable to pred-
icate if it belong to the genera at large or this one specimen
in particular; however, it is a sufficently curious fact, even
though thereby hang no tale for my stating it here. The
decanters on the dinner-table were never labelled with their
more appropriate designation of contents, whether claret,
sherry, or port, but with the names of their respective
owners, it being a matter of much less consequence that any
individual at table should mix his wine by pouring "port
upon madeira," than commit the truly legal offence of ap-
propriating to his own use and benefit, even by mistake, his
neighbor's bottle. However well the system may work
among the regular members of the "domestic circle," —
and I am assured that it does succeed extremely, — to the
newly arrived guest or uninitiated visitor the affair is per-
plexing, and leads occasionally to awkward results.

It so chanced, from my friend O'Flaherty's habitual
position at the foot of the table, and my post of honor near
the head, that on the first day of my appearing there, the
distance between us not only precluded close intercourse,

but any of those gentle hints as to habits and customs a new arrival looks for at the hands of his better-informed friend. The only mode of recognition, to prove that we belonged to each other, being by that excellent and truly English custom of drinking wine together, Tom seized the first idle moment from his avocation as carver to say, —

"Lorrequer, a glass of wine with you."

Having, of course, acceded, he again asked, —

"What wine do you drink?" intending thereby, as I afterwards learned, to send me from his end of the table what wine I selected. Not conceiving the object of the inquiry, and having hitherto, without hesitation, helped myself from the decanter which bore some faint resemblance to sherry, I immediately turned for correct information to the bottle itself, upon whose slender neck was ticketed the usual slip of paper. My endeavors to decipher the writing occupied time sufficient again to make O'Flaherty ask, —

"Well, Harry, I'm waiting for you. Will you have claret?"

"No, I thank you," I replied, having by this revealed the inscription, — "no, I thank you; I'll just stick to my old friend here, Bob M'Grotty," — for thus I rendered familiarly the name of Rt. M'Grotty on the decanter, and which I, in my ignorance, believed to be the boarding-house sobriquet for bad sherry. That Mr. M'Grotty himself little relished my familiarity with either his name or property I had a very decisive proof, for, turning round upon his chair, and surveying my person from head to foot with a look of fiery wrath, he thundered out in very broad Scotch, —

"And by my saul, my freend, ye may just as weel finish it noo, for deil a glass o' his ain wine did Bob M'Grotty, as ye ca' him, swallow this day."

The convulsion of laughter into which my blunder and the Scotchman's passion threw the whole board lasted till the cloth was withdrawn and the ladies had retired to the drawing-room, the only individual at table not relishing

the mistake being the injured proprietor of the bottle, who
was too proud to accept reparation from my friend's decanter, and would scarcely condescend to open his lips during
the evening; notwithstanding which display of honest indignation, we contrived to become exceedingly merry and
jocose, most of the party communicating little episodes of
their life, in which, it is true, they frequently figured in
situations that nothing but their native and natural candor
would venture to avow. One story I was considerably
amused at; it was told by the counsellor, Mr. Daly, in
illustration of the difficulty of rising at the Bar, and which,
as showing his own mode of obviating the delay that young
professional men submit to from hard necessity, as well as
in evidence of his strictly legal turn, I shall certainly
recount one of these days for the edification of the Junior
Bar.

CHAPTER XIV.

On the morning after my visit to the boarding-house I received a few hurried lines from Curzon, informing me that no time was to be lost in joining the regiment, that a grand fancy ball was about to be given by the officers of the "Dwarf" frigate, then stationed off Dunmore, who, when inviting the 4—th, specially put in a demand for my well-known services, to make it go off, and concluding with an extract from the "Kilkenny Moderator," which ran thus: "An intimation has just reached us, from a quarter on which we can place the fullest reliance, that the celebrated amateur performer, Mr. Lorrequer, may shortly be expected among us. From the many accounts we have received of this highly gifted gentleman's powers, we anticipate a great treat to the lovers of the drama," etc. "So you see, my dear Hal," continued Curzon, "thy vocation calls thee; therefore come, and come quickly. Provide thyself with a black satin costume slashed with light-blue, point-lace collar and ruffles, a Spanish hat looped in front, and, if possible, a long rapier with a flat hilt. Carden is not here, so you may show your face under any color with perfect impunity."

This clever epistle "from the side-scenes" sufficed to show that the gallant 4—th had gone clean theatrical mad; and although from my "last appearance on any stage" it might be supposed I should feel no peculiar desire to repeat the experiment, yet the opportunity of joining during Colonel Carden's absence was too tempting to resist, and I at once made up my mind to set out, and without a moment's delay hurried across the street to the coach-office to book myself an inside in the mail of that night. Fortunately, no difficulty existed in my procuring the seat, for the way-bill was a perfect blank, and I found myself the only person who had as yet announced himself a passenger. On returning to my hotel I found O'Flaherty waiting for me. He was greatly distressed on hearing my determination to leave town, explained how he had been catering for my amusement for the week to come, — that a picnic to the Dargle was arranged in a committee of the whole house, and a boating-party, with a dinner at the Pigeon House, was then under consideration. Resisting, however, such extreme temptations, I mentioned the necessity of my at once proceeding to headquarters, and all other reasons for my preciptancy failing, concluded with that really knock-down argument, "I have taken my place." This, I need scarcely add, finished the matter, — at least, *I* have never known it fail in such cases. Tell your friends that your wife is hourly expecting to be confined; your favorite child is in the measles; your best friend waiting your aid in an awkward scrape; your one vote only wanting to turn the scale in an election, — tell them, I say, each or all of these, or a hundred more like them, and from any one you so speak to, the answer is, "Pooh, pooh, my dear fellow! never fear, don't fuss yourself, take it easy, — to-morrow will do just as well." If on the other hand, however, you reject such flimsy excuses, and simply say, "I'm booked in the mail," the opposition at once falls to the ground, and your quondam antagonist, who was ready to quarrel with you, is at once prepared to assist in packing your portmanteau.

Having soon satisfied my friend Tom that resistance was in vain, I promised to eat an early dinner with him at Morrisson's, and spent the better part of the morning in putting down a few notes of my "Confessions" as well as the particulars of Mr. Daly's story, which, I believe, I half or wholly promised my readers at the conclusion of my last chapter, but which I must defer to a more suitable opportunity, when mentioning the next occasion of my meeting him on the southern circuit.

My dispositions were speedily made. I was fortunate in securing the exact dress my friend's letter alluded to among the stray costumes of Fishamble Street; and rich in the possession of the only "properties" it had been my lot to acquire, I despatched my treasure to the coach-office and hastened to Morrisson's, it being by this time nearly five o'clock. There, true to time, I found O'Flaherty deep in the perusal of the bill, along which figured the *novel* expedients for dining I had been in the habit of reading in every Dublin hotel since my boyhood, — "mock-turtle, mutton gravy, roast beef and potatoes; shoulder of mutton and potatoes! ducks and peas, potatoes! ham and chicken, cutlet, steak, and potatoes! apple-tart and cheese." With a slight *cadenza* of a sigh over the distant glories of Véry, or still better the "Frères," we sat down to a very patriarchal repast, and what may be always had *par excellence* in Dublin, — a bottle of Sneyd's claret.

Poor Tom's spirits were rather below their usual pitch; and although he made many efforts to rally and appear gay, he could not accomplish it. However, we chatted away over old times and old friends, and forgetting all else but the topics we talked of, the timepiece over the chimney first apprised me that two whole hours had gone by, and that it was now seven o'clock, — the very hour the coach was to start. I started up at once, and notwithstanding all Tom's representations of the impossibility of my being in time, had despatched waiters in different directions for a jarvey, more than ever determined upon going, — so often is it that when real reasons for our conduct are wanting, any casual or chance opposition confirms us in an intention which before was but wavering. Seeing me so resolved, Tom at length gave way, and advised my pursuing the mail, which must be now gone at least ten minutes, and which, with smart driving, I should probably overtake before getting free of the city, as they have usually many delays in so doing. I at once ordered out the "yellow post-chaise," and before many minutes had elapsed, what with imprecation and bribery, I started in pursuit of his Majesty's Cork and Kilkenny mail-coach, then patiently waiting in the court-yard of the Post-office.

"Which way now, yer honor?" said a shrill voice from the dark, — for such the night had already become, and threatened, with a few heavy drops of straight rain, the fall of a tremendous shower.

"The Naas road," said I; "and harkye, my fine fellow, if you overtake the coach in half an hour, I'll double your fare."

"Be gorra, I'll do my endayvor," said the youth; at the same instant dashing in both spurs, we rattled down Nassau Street at a very respectable pace for harriers. Street after street we passed, and at last I perceived we had got clear of the city, and were leaving the long line of lamp-lights behind us. The night was now pitch dark; I could not see anything whatever. The quick clattering of the wheels, the sharp crack of the postilion's whip, or the still sharper tone of his "gee-hup," showed me that we were going at a tremendous pace, had I not even had the experience afforded by the frequent visits my head paid to the roof of the chaise, so often as we bounded over a stone or splashed through a hollow. Dark and gloomy as it was, I constantly let down the window, and with half my body protruded, endeavored to catch a glimpse of the "Chase;" but nothing could I see. The rain now fell in actual torrents, and a more miserable night it is impossible to conceive.

After about an hour so spent, we at last came to a check, so sudden and unexpected on my part that I was nearly precipitated, harlequin fashion, through the front window. Perceiving that we no longer moved, and suspecting that some part of our tackle had given way, I let down the sash, and cried out, "Well, now, my lad, anything wrong?" My question was, however, unheard; and although, amid the steam arising from the wet and smoking horses, I could perceive several figures indistinctly moving about, I could not distinguish what they were doing, nor what they said. A laugh I certainly did hear, and heartily cursed the unfeeling wretch, as I supposed him to be, who was enjoying himself at my disappointment. I again endeavored to find out what had happened, and called out still louder than before.

"We are at Ra'coole, your honor," said the boy, approaching the door of the chaise, "and she 's only beat us by hafe a mile."

"Who the devil is she? " said I.

"The mail, your honor, is always a female in Ireland."

"Then why do you stop now? You 're not going to feed, I suppose? "

"Of coorse not, your honor, — it 's little feeding troubles these bastes, anyhow; but they tell me the road is so heavy we 'll never take the chaise over the next stage without leaders."

"Without leaders! " said I. "Pooh! my good fellow, no humbugging, — four horses for a light post-chaise and no lugagge. Come, get up, and no nonsense."

At this moment a man approached the window with a lantern in his hand, and so strongly represented the dreadful state of the roads from the late rains, the length of the stage, the frequency of accidents latterly from under-horsing, etc., that I yielded a reluctant assent, and ordered out the leaders, comforting myself the while that considering the inside fare of the coach I made such efforts to overtake was under a pound, and that time was no object to me, I was certainly paying somewhat dearly for my character for resolution.

At last we got under way once more and set off, cheered by a tremendous shout from at least a dozen persons, doubtless denizens of that interesting locality, amid which I once again heard the laugh that had so much annoyed me already. The rain was falling if possible more heavily than before, and had evidently set in for the entire night. Throwing myself back into a corner of the "leathern convenience," I gave myself up to the full enjoyment of the Rochefoucauld maxim that there is always a pleasure felt in the misfortunes of even our best friends, and certainly experienced no small comfort in my distress by contrasting my present

position with that of my two friends in the saddle as they
sweltered on through mud and mire, rain and storm. On
we went, splashing, bumping, rocking, and jolting, till I
began at last to have serious thoughts of abdicating the seat
and betaking myself to the bottom of the chaise, for safety
and protection. Mile after mile succeeded; and as after
many a short and fitful slumber, which my dreams gave an
apparent length to, I awoke only to find myself still in
pursuit, the time seemed so enormously protracted that I
began to fancy my whole life was to be passed in the
dark, in chase of the Kilkenny mail, as we read in the true
history of the Flying Dutchman, who for his sins of impatience, like mine, spent centuries vainly endeavoring to
double the Cape; or the Indian mariner in Moore's beautiful ballad, of whom we are told, as —

> " Many a day to night gave way,
>   And many a morn succeeded,
>   Yet still his flight, by day and night,
>   That restless mariner speeded."

This might have been all very well in the tropics, with a
smart craft and doubtless plenty of sea store; but in a
chaise, at night, and on the Naas road, I humbly suggest
I had all the worst of the parallel.

At last the altered sound of the wheels gave notice of
our approach to a town, and after about twenty minutes'
rattling over the pavement we entered what I supposed,
correctly, to be Naas. Here I had long since determined
my pursuit should cease. I had done enough, and more
than enough, to vindicate my fame against any charge of
irresolution as to leaving Dublin, and was bethinking me
of the various modes of prosecuting my journey on the morrow, when we drew up suddenly at the door of the Swan.
The arrival of a chaise and four at a small country town
inn suggests to the various officials therein anything rather
than the traveller in pursuit of the mail, and so the moment
I arrived I was assailed with innumerable proffers of horses,
supper, bed, and so on. My anxious query was thrice repeated in vain, "When did the coach pass?"

"The mail?" replied the landlord at length. "Is it the down-mail?"

Not understanding the technical, I answered, "Of course not the Down, — the Kilkenny and Cork mail."

"From Dublin, sir?"

"Yes, from Dublin."

"Not arrived yet, sir, nor will it for three-quarters of an hour. They never leave Dublin till a quarter-past seven, — that is, in fact, half-past; and their time here is twenty minutes to eleven."

"Why, you stupid son of a boot-top, we have been posting on all night like the devil, and all this time the coach has been ten miles behind us!"

"Well, we've cotch them, anyhow," said the urchin as he disengaged himself from his wet saddle and stood upon the ground; "and it is not my fault that the coach is not before us."

With a satisfactory anathema upon all innkeepers, waiters, ostlers, and post-boys, with a codicil including coach-proprietors, I followed the smirking landlord into a well-lighted room with a blazing fire, when, having ordered supper, I soon regained my equanimity.

My rasher and poached eggs, all Naas could afford me, were speedily despatched, and as my last glass from my one pint of sherry was poured out, the long-expected coach drew up. A minute after, the coachman entered to take his dram, followed by the guard. A more lamentable spectacle of condensed moisture cannot be conceived: the rain fell from the entire circumference of his broad-brimmed hat, like the ever-flowing drop from the edge of an antique fountain; his drab coat had become of a deep orange hue, while his huge figure loomed still larger as he stood amid a nebula of damp that would have made an atmosphere for the Georgium Sidus.

"Going on to-night, sir?" said he, addressing me. "Severe weather, and no chance of its clearing, — but of course you're inside."

"Why, there is very little doubt of that," said I. "Are you nearly full inside?"

"Only one, sir, but he seems a real queer chap; made fifty inquiries at the office if he could not have the whole inside to himself, and when he heard that one place had been taken, — yours, I believe, sir, — he seemed like a scalded bear."

"You don't know his name, then?"

"No, sir, he never gave a name at the office, and his only luggage is two brown-paper parcels, without any ticket, and he has them inside, — indeed, he never lets them from him, even for a second."

Here the guard's horn, announcing all ready, interrupted our colloquy and prevented my learning anything further of my fellow-traveller, whom, however, I at once set down in my own mind for some confounded old churl that made himself comfortable everywhere, without ever thinking of any one else's convenience.

As I passed from the inn door to the coach, I once more congratulated myself that I was about to be housed from the terrific storm of wind and rain that railed without.

"Here 's the step, sir," said the guard; "get in, sir, — two minutes late already."

"I beg your pardon, sir," said I, as I half fell over the legs of my unseen companion; "may I request leave to pass you?"   While he made way for me for this purpose, I perceived that he stooped down towards the guard and said something, who, from his answer, had evidently been questioned as to who I was.

"And how did he get here, if he took his place in Dublin?" asked the unknown.

"Came half an hour since, sir, in a chaise and four," said the guard, as he banged the door behind him and closed the interview.

Whatever might have been the reasons for my fellow-traveller's anxiety about my name and occupation I knew not, yet could not help feeling gratified at thinking that, as I had not given my name at the coach-office, I was as great a puzzle to him as he to me.

"A severe night, sir," said I, endeavoring to break ground in conversation.

"Mighty severe," briefly and half-crustily replied the unknown, with a richness of brogue that might have stood for a certificate of baptism in Cork or its vicinity.

"And a bad road too, sir," said I, remembering my lately accomplished stage.

"That's the reason I always go armed," said the unknown, clinking at the same moment something like the barrel of a pistol.

Wondering somewhat at his readiness to mistake my meaning, I felt disposed to drop any further effort to draw him out, and was about to address myself to sleep as comfortably as I could.

"I'll just trouble ye to lean off that little parcel there, sir," said he, as he displaced from its position beneath my elbow one of the paper packages the guard had already alluded to.

In complying with this rather gruff demand, one of my pocket-pistols, which I carried in my breast pocket, fell out upon his knee; upon which he immediately started, and asked hurriedly, "And are you armed too?"

"Why, yes," said I, laughingly; "men of my trade seldom go without something of this kind."

"Be gorra! I was just thinking that same," said the traveller, with a half sigh to himself.

Why he should or should not have thought so, I never troubled myself to canvass, and was once more settling myself in my corner, when I was startled by a very melancholy groan, which seemed to come from the bottom of my companion's heart.

"Are you ill, sir?" said I, in a voice of some anxiety.

"You may say that," replied he, "if you knew who you were talking to, although maybe you've heard enough of me, though you never saw me till now."

"Without having that pleasure even yet," said I, "it would grieve me to think you should be ill in the coach."

"Maybe it might," briefly replied the unknown, with a species of meaning in his words I could not then understand. "Did ye never hear tell of Barney Doyle?" said he.

"Not to my recollection."

"Then I 'm Barney," said he, "that 's in all the news-papers in the metropolis.   I 'm seventeen weeks in Jervis Street Hospital, and four in the Lunatic, and the devil a better after all.   You must be a stranger, I 'm thinking, or you 'd know me now."

"Why, I do confess I 've only been a few hours in Ire-land for the last six months."

"Ay, that 's the reason; I knew you would not be fond of travelling with me, if you knew who it was."

"Why, really," said I, beginning at the moment to fathom some of the hints of my companion, "I did not anticipate the pleasure of meeting you."

"It 's pleasure ye call it; then there 's no accountin' for tastes, as Dr. Colles said when he saw me bite Cusack Rooney's thumb off!"

"Bite a man's thumb off!" said I, in horror.

"Ay," said he, with a kind of fiendish animation, "in one chop.   I wish you 'd seen how I scattered the consulta-tion; begad! they did n't wait to ax for a fee."

"Upon my soul, a very pleasant vicinity," thought I. "And may I ask, sir," said I, in a very mild and soothing tone of voice, "may I ask the reason for this singular pro-pensity of yours?"

"There it is now, my dear," said he, laying his hand upon my knee familiarly; "that 's just the very thing they can't make out.   Colles says it 's all the ceribellum, ye see, that 's inflamed and combusted, and some of the others think it 's the spine, and more the muscles; but my real impression is, the devil a bit they know about it at all."

"And have they no name for the malady?" said I.

"Oh! sure enough they have a name for it."

"And, may I ask —"

"Why, I think you 'd better not, because, ye see, maybe I might be throublesome to ye in the night, — though I 'll not if I can help it; and it might be uncomfortable to you to be here if I was to get one of the fits."

"One of the fits! Why, it's not possible, sir," said I, "you would travel in a public conveyance in the state you mention, — your friends surely would not permit it!"

"Why, if they *knew*, perhaps," slyly responded the interesting invalid, — "if they *knew*, they might not exactly like it; but, ye see, I escaped only last night, and there'll be a fine hubbub in the morning when they find I'm off. Though I'm thinking Rooney's barking away by this time."

"Rooney barking! Why what does that mean?"

"They always bark for a day or two after they're bit, if the infection comes first from the dog."

"You are surely not speaking of hydrophobia," said I, my hair actually bristling with horror and consternation.

"Ain't I?" replied he. "Maybe you've guessed it, though."

"And have you the malady on you at present?" said I, trembling for the answer.

"This is the ninth day since I took to biting," said he, gravely, perfectly unconscious, as it appeared, of the terror such information was calculated to convey.

"And with such a propensity, sir, do you think yourself warranted in travelling in a public coach, exposing others — "

"You'd better not raise your voice that way," quietly responded he. "If I'm roused, it'll be worse for ye, that's all."

"Well, but," said I, moderating my zeal, "is it exactly prudent, in your present delicate state, to undertake a journey?"

"Ah!" said he, with a sigh, "I've been longing to see the fox-hounds throw off near Kilkenny; these three weeks I've been thinking of nothing else. But I'm not sure how my nerves will stand the cry; I might be troublesome."

"Upon my soul," thought I, "I shall not select that morning for my *début* in the field."

"I hope, sir, there's no river or watercourse on this road, — anything else I can, I hope, control myself against; but water — running water particularly — makes me troublesome."

Well knowing what he meant by the latter phrase, I felt the cold perspiration settling on my forehead as I remembered that we must be within about ten or twelve miles of Leighlin Bridge, where we should have to pass a very wide river. I strictly concealed this fact from him, however, and gave him to understand that there was not a well, brook, or rivulet for forty miles on either side of us. He now sank into a kind of moody silence, broken occasionally by a low muttering noise, as if speaking to himself. What this might portend I knew not, but thought it better, under all circumstances, not to disturb him. How comfortable my present condition was, I need scarcely remark, sitting *vis-à-vis* to a lunatic with a pair of pistols in his possession, who had already avowed his consciousness of his tendency to do mischief and his inability to master it, — all this in the dark, and in the narrow limits of a mail-coach, where there was scarcely room for defence, and no possibility of escape. How heartily I wished myself back in the coffee-room at Morrisson's with my poor friend Tom! The infernal chaise, that I cursed a hundred times, would have been an "exchange" better than into the Life Guards, — ay, even the outside of the coach, if I could only reach it, would, under present circumstances, be a glorious alternative to my existing misfortune. What were rain and storm, thunder and lightning, compared with the chances that awaited me here? Wet through I should inevitably be; but then I had not yet contracted the horror of moisture my friend opposite labored under. "Ha! what is that? Is it possible he can be asleep, — is it really a snore? Heaven grant that little snort be not what the medical people call a premonitory symptom; if so, he'll be in upon me now, in no time. Ah! there it is again, — he must be asleep, surely; now then is my time, or never." With these words muttered to myself, and a heart throbbing almost audibly at the risk of his awakening, I slowly let down the window of the coach, and stretching forth my hand, turned the handle cautiously and slowly; I next disengaged my legs; and by a long continuous effort of creeping — which I had learned perfectly once, when practising to go as a boa-constrictor to a fancy ball — I withrew myself from the seat and reached the step, when I muttered something very like a thanksgiving to Providence for my rescue. With little difficulty I now climbed up beside the guard, whose astonishment at my appearance was indeed considerable. That any man should prefer the out to the inside of a coach in such a night, was rather remarkable; but that the person so doing should be totally unprovided with a box-coat or other similar protection, argued something so strange that I doubt not, if he were to decide upon the applicability of the statute of lunacy to a traveller in the mail, the palm would certainly have been awarded to me, and not to my late companion. Well, on we rolled, and heavily as the rain poured down, so relieved did I feel at my change of position that I soon fell fast asleep, and never woke till the coach was driving up Patrick Street. Whatever solace to my feelings reaching the outside of the coach might have been attended with at night, the pleasure I experienced on awakening was really not unalloyed. More dead than alive, I sat a mass of wet clothes, like nothing under heaven except it be that morsel of black and spongy wet cotton at the bottom of a schoolboy's ink-bottle, saturated with rain and the black dye of my coat. My hat, too, had contributed its share of coloring matter, and several long black streaks coursed down my "wrinkled front," giving me very much the air of an Indian warrior who had got the first priming of his war-paint. I certainly must have been a rueful object, were I only to judge from the faces of the waiters as they gazed on me when the coach drew up at Rice and Walsh's Hotel. Cold, wet, and weary as I was, my curiosity to learn more of my late agreeable companion was strong as ever within me, — perhaps stronger, from the sacrifices his acquaintance had exacted from me. Before, however, I had disengaged myself from the pile of trunks and carpet-bags I had surrounded myself with, he had got out of the coach, and all I could catch a glimpse of was the back of a little short man in a kind of gray upper coat, and long galligaskins on his legs. He carried his two bundles under his arm, and stepped nimbly up the steps of the hotel, without ever turning his head to either side.

"Don't fancy you shall escape me *now*, my good friend," I cried out, as I sprang from the roof to the ground with one jump, and hurried after the great unknown into the coffee-room. By the time I reached it he had approached the fire, on the table near which having deposited the mysterious paper parcels, he was now busily engaged in divesting himself of his great-coat; his face was still turned from me, so that I had time to appear employed in divesting myself of my wet drapery before he perceived me. At last the coat was unbuttoned, the gaiters followed, and throwing them carelessly on a chair, he tucked up the skirts of his coat, and spreading himself comfortably, *à l'anglaise*, before the fire, displayed to my wondering and stupefied gaze the pleasant features of Dr. Finucane.

"Why, Dr., Dr. Finucane," cried I, "is this possible? Were you then really the inside in the mail last night?"

"Devil a doubt of it, Mr. Lorrequer; and may I make bould to ask were you the outside?"

"Then what, may I beg to know, did you mean by your damned story about Barney Doyle, and the hydrophobia, and Cusack Rooney's thumb, eh?"

"Oh, by the Lord!" said Finucane, "this will be the death of me. And it was *you* that I drove outside in all the rain last night! Oh, it will kill Father Malachi outright with laughing when I tell him." And he burst out into a fit of merriment that nearly induced me to break his head with the poker.

"Am I to understand, then, Mr. Finucane, that this practical joke of yours was contrived for *my* benefit, and for the purpose of holding *me* up to the ridicule of your confounded acquaintances?"

"Nothing of the kind, upon my conscience," said Fin,

drying his eyes, and endeavoring to look sorry and sentimental. "If I had only the least suspicion in life that it was you, upon my oath I 'd not have had the hydrophobia at all, and to tell you the truth, you were not the only one frightened, — you alarmed me devilishly too."

"I alarmed you! Why, how can that be?"

"Why, the real affair is this. I was bringing these two packages of notes down to my cousin Callaghan's bank in Cork, — fifteen thousand pounds, devil a less; and when you came into the coach at Naas, after driving there with your four horses, I thought it was all up with me. The guard just whispered in my ear that he saw you look at the priming of your pistols before getting in; and faith, I said four Paters and a Hail Mary before you 'd count five. Well, when you got seated, the thought came into my mind that maybe, highwayman as you were, you would not like dying a natural death, more particularly if you were an Irishman; and so I trumped up that long story about the hydrophobia, and the gentleman's thumb, and devil knows what besides; and while I was telling it, the cold perspiration was running down my head and face, for every time you stirred I said to myself, 'Now, he 'll do it.' Two or three times, do you know, I was going to offer you ten shillings in the pound, and spare my life; and once, God forgive me, I thought it would not be a bad plan to shoot you ' by mistake,' do you perceive?"

"Why, upon my soul, I 'm very much obliged to you for your excessively kind intentions; but really I feel you have done quite enough for me on the present occasion. But come now, Doctor, I must get to bed, and before I go, promise me two things, — to dine with us to-day at the mess, and not to mention a syllable of what occurred last night: it tells, believe me, very badly for both. So keep the secret, for if these confounded fellows of ours ever get hold of it, I may sell out and quit the army; I 'll never hear the end of it!"

"Never fear, my boy; trust me. I 'll dine with you, and you 're as safe as a church-mouse for anything I 'll tell them; so now you 'd better change your clothes, for I 'm thinking it rained last night."

Muttering some very dubious blessings upon the learned Fin, I left the room infinitely more chagrined and chopfallen at the discovery I had made than at all the misery and exposure the trick had consigned me to. "However," thought I, "if the doctor keep his word, all goes well, — the whole affair is between us both solely; but should it not be so, I may shoot half the mess before the other half would give up quizzing me." Revolving such pleasant thoughts, I betook myself to bed, and, what with mulled port and a blazing fire, became once more conscious of being a warm-blooded animal, and fell sound asleep, to dream of doctors, strait-waistcoats, shaved heads, and all the pleasing associations my late companion's narrative so readily suggested.

CHAPTER XV.

At six o'clock I had the pleasure of presenting the worthy Dr. Finucane to our mess, taking at the same time an opportunity, unobserved by him, to inform three or four of my brother officers that my friend was really a character, abounding in native drollery, and richer in good stories than even the generality of his countrymen.

Nothing could possibly go on better than the early part of the evening. Fin, true to his promise, never once alluded to what I could plainly perceive was ever uppermost in his mind; and what with his fund of humor, quaintness of expression, and quickness at reply, garnished throughout by his most mellifluous brogue, the true "Bocca Corkana," kept us from one roar of laughter to another. It was just at the moment in which his spirits seemed at their highest that I had the misfortune to call upon him for a story which his cousin, Father Malachi, had alluded to on the ever-memorable evening at his house, and which I had a great desire to hear from Fin's own lips. He seemed disposed to escape telling it, and upon my continuing to press my request, dryly remarked, —

"You forget, surely, my dear Mr. Lorrequer, the weak condition I 'm in; and these gentlemen here, they don't know what a severe illness I 've been laboring under lately, or they would not pass the decanter so freely down this quarter."

I had barely time to throw a mingled look of entreaty and menace across the table when half a dozen others, rightly judging from the doctor's tone and serio-comic expression that his malady had many more symptoms of fun than suffering about it, called out together, —

"Oh, Doctor, by all means tell us the nature of your late attack; pray relate it."

"With Mr. Lorrequer's permission, I'm your slave, gentlemen," said Fin, finishing off his glass.

"Oh! as for me," I cried, "Dr. Finucane has my full permission to detail whatever he pleases to think a fit subject for your amusement."

"Come, then, Doctor, Harry has no objection, you see; so out with it, and we are all prepared to sympathize with your woes and misfortunes, whatever they be."

"Well, I am sure, I never could think of mentioning it without his leave; but now that he sees no objection — Eh, do you, though? If so, then, don't be winking and making faces at me, but say the word, and devil a syllable of it I'll tell to man or mortal."

The latter part of this delectable speech was addressed to me across the table, in a species of stage whisper, in reply to some telegraphic signals I had been throwing him, to induce him to turn the conversation into another channel.

"Then that's enough," continued he, *sotto voce;* "I see you'd rather I'd not tell it."

"Tell it and be d——d," said I, wearied by the incorrigible pertinacity with which the villain assailed me. My most unexpected energy threw the whole table into a roar, at the conclusion of which Fin began his narrative of the mail-coach adventure.

I need not tell my reader who has followed me throughout in these my "Confessions" that such a story lost nothing of its absurdity when intrusted to the doctor's powers of narration. He dwelt with a poet's feeling upon the description of his own sufferings, and my sincere condolence and commiseration; he touched with the utmost delicacy upon the distant hints by which he broke the news to me; but when he came to describe my open and undisguised terror, and my secret and precipitate retreat to the roof of the coach, there was not a man at the table that was not convulsed with laughter, and — shall I acknowledge it? — even I myself was unable to withstand the effect, and joined in the general chorus against myself.

"Well," said the remorseless wretch as he finished his story, "if ye have n't the hard hearts to laugh at such a melancholy subject! Maybe, however, you 're not so cruel after all; here 's a toast for you: ' A speedy recovery to Cusack Rooney.' " This was drunk, amid renewed peals, with all the honors, and I had abundant time before the uproar was over to wish every man of them hanged. It was to no purpose that I endeavored to turn the tables by describing Fin's terror at my supposed resemblance to a highwayman, — his story had the precedence, and I met nothing during my recital but sly allusions to mad dogs, muzzles, and doctors; and contemptible puns were let off on every side at my expense.

"It 's little shame I take to myself for the mistake, any-how," said Fin: "for putting the darkness of the night out of the question, I 'm not so sure I would not have ugly suspicions of you by daylight."

"And besides, Doctor," added I, "it would not be your first blunder in the dark."

"True for you, Mr. Lorrequer," said he, good-humoredly; "and now that I have told them your story, I don't care if they hear mine, — though, maybe, some of ye have heard it already; it 's pretty well known in the North Cork."

We all gave our disclaimers on this point, and having ordered in a fresh cooper of port, disposed ourselves in our most easy attitudes while the doctor proceeded as follows:

"It was in the hard winter of the year '99 that we were quartered in Maynooth, — as many said, for our sins; for a more stupid place, the Lord be merciful to it! never were men condemned to. The people at the college were much better off than we; they had whatever was to be got in the country, and never were disturbed by mounting guard or night patrols. Many of the professors were good fellows, that liked grog fully as well as Greek, and understood short whist and five-and-ten quite as intimately as they knew the Vulgate or the Confessions of Saint Augustine. They made no ostentatious display of their pious zeal, but whenever they were not fasting or praying or something of that kind, they were always pleasant and agreeable, and, to do them justice, never refused, by any chance, an invitation to dinner, — no matter at what inconvenience. Well, even this solace to our affliction was soon lost by an unfortunate mistake of that Orange rogue of the world, Major Jones, that gave a wrong pass one night, — Mr. Lorrequer knows the story" (here he alluded to an adventure detailed in an early chapter of my "Confessions"); "and from that day forward we never saw the pleasant faces of the Abbé d'Array or the Professor of the Humanities at the mess. Well, the only thing I could do was just to take an opportunity to drop in at the college in the evening, where we had a quiet rubber of whist and a little social and intellectual conversation, with maybe an oyster and a glass of punch, just to season the thing, before we separated, all done discreetly and quietly; no shouting, or even singing, for the ' superior ' had a prejudice about profane songs. Well, one of those nights — it was about the first week in February — I was detained by stress of weather from eleven o'clock, when we usually bade good-night, to past twelve, and then to one o'clock, waiting for a dry moment to get home to the barracks, — a good mile and a half off. Every time old Father Mahony went to look at the weather he came back, saying, ' It 's worse it 's getting; such a night of rain, glory be to God, never was seen.' So there was no good in going out to be drenched to the skin, and I sat quietly waiting, taking between times a little punch, just not to seem impatient nor distress their rev'rences. At last it struck two, and I thought, ' Well, the decanter is empty now, and I think, if I mean to walk, I 've taken enough for the present; ' so wishing them all manner of happiness and pleasant dreams, I stumbled my way downstairs and set out on my journey. I was always in the habit of taking a short cut on my way home across the ' Gurt na brocha,' the priest's meadows, as they call them, — it saved nearly half a mile; although on the present occasion it exposed one wofully to the rain, for there was nothing to shelter under the entire way, not even a tree. Well, out I set in a half trot, for I stayed so late I was pressed for time; besides, I felt it easier to run than to walk, — I 'm sure I can't tell why; maybe the drop of drink I took got into my head. Well, I was just jogging on across the common, the rain beating hard in my face, and my clothes pasted to me with the wet; notwithstanding I was singing to myself a verse of an old song to lighten the road, when I heard suddenly a noise near me like a man sneezing. I stopped and listened, — in fact, it was impossible to see your hand, the night was so dark; but I could hear nothing. The thought then came over me, maybe it 's something ' not good,' for there were very ugly stories going about what the priests used to do formerly in these meadows; and bones were often found in different parts of them. Just as I was thinking this, another voice came nearer than the last; it might be only a sneeze after all, but in real earnest it was mighty like a groan. ' The Lord be about us!' I said to myself; ' what 's this? Have ye the pass?' I cried out. ' Have ye the pass? or what brings ye walking here, *in nomine Patri?* ' for I was so confused whether it was a sperit or not, I was going to address him in Latin, — there 's nothing equal to the dead languages to lay a ghost, everybody knows. Faith, the moment I said these words, he gave another groan, deeper and more melancholy like than before. 'If it 's uneasy ye are,' says I, ' for any neglect of your friends,' for I thought he might be in purgatory longer than he thought convenient, ' tell me what you wish, and go home peaceably out of the rain; for this weather can do no good to living or dead. Go home,' said I; ' and if it 's masses ye 'd like, I 'll give you a day's pay myself, rather than you should fret yourself this way.' The words were not well out of my mouth when he came so near me that the sigh he gave went right through both my ears. ' The Lord be merciful to me!' said I, trembling. ' Amen!' says he, in a husky voice. The moment he said that, my mind was relieved,

for I knew it was not a sperit, and I began to laugh heartily
at my mistake. ' And who are ye at all,' said I, ' that 's
roving about at this hour of the night?　Ye can't be
Father Luke, for I left him asleep on the carpet before I
quitted the college; and faith, my friend, if you had n't the
taste for divarsion, ye would not be out now.'　He coughed
then so hard that I could not make out well what he said,
but just perceived that he had lost his way on the common,
and was a little disguised in liquor.　' It 's a good man's
case,' said I, ' to take a little too much, though it 's what I
don't ever do myself; so take a hold of my hand, and I 'll
see you safe.'　I stretched out my hand, and got him, not
by the arm, as I hoped, but by the hair of the head, for he
was all dripping with wet, and had lost his hat.　' Well,
you 'll not be better of this night's excursion,' thought I,
' if ye are liable to the rheumatism.　And now, whereabouts
do you live, my friend? for I 'll see you safe before I leave
you.'　What he said then I never could clearly make out,
for the wind and rain were both beating so hard against my
face that I could not hear a word; however, I was able just
to perceive that he was very much disguised in drink, and
spoke rather thick.　' Well, never mind,' said I, ' it 's not
a time of day for much conversation; so come along, and
I 'll see you safe to the guard-house, if you can't remember
your own place of abode in the meanwhile.'　It was just
at the moment I said this that I first discovered he was not
a gentleman.　Well, now, you 'd never guess how I did it;
and, faith, I always thought it a very 'cute thing of me,
and both of us in the dark."

"Well, I really confess it must have been a very difficult
thing, under the circumstances; pray how did you contrive?" said the Major.

"Just guess how."

"By the tone of his voice, perhaps, and his accent," said
Curzon.

"Devil a bit; for he spoke remarkably well, considering
how far gone he was in liquor."

"Well, probably by the touch of his hand, — no bad
test."

"No, you're wrong again, for it was by the hair I had a hold of him for fear of falling; for he was always stooping down. Well, you'd never guess it, — it was just by the touch of his foot."

"His foot! Why, how did that give you any information?"

"There it is now, — that's just what only an Irishman would ever have made anything out of; for while he was stumbling about, he happened to tread upon my toes, and never since I was born did I feel anything like the weight of him. 'Well,' said I, 'the loss of your hat may give you a cold, my friend, but upon my conscience you are in no danger of wet feet with such a pair of strong brogues as you have on you.' Well, he laughed at that till I thought he'd split his sides, and in good truth I could not help joining in the fun, although my foot was smarting like mad; and so we jogged along through the rain, enjoying the joke just as if we were sitting by a good fire, with a jorum of punch between us. I am sure I can't tell you how often we fell that night; but my clothes the next morning were absolutely covered with mud, and my hat crushed in two, — for he was so confoundedly drunk it was impossible to keep him up, and he always kept boring along with his head down, so that my heart was almost broke in keeping him upon his legs. I'm sure I never had a more fatiguing march in the whole Peninsula than that blessed mile and a half; but every misfortune has an end at last, and it was four o'clock striking by the college clock as we reached the barracks. After knocking a couple of times and giving the countersign, the sentry opened the small wicket, and my heart actually leaped with joy that I had done with my friend; so I just called out the sergeant of the guard and said, 'Will you put that poor fellow on the guard-bed till morning? for I found him on the common, and he could neither find his way home nor tell me where ho lived.' 'And where is he?' said the sergeant. 'He's outside the gate there,' said I, 'wet to the skin, and shaking as if he had the ague.' 'And is this him?' said the sergeant, as we went outside. 'It is,' said I; 'maybe you know him.' 'Maybe I 've a guess,' said he, bursting into a fit of laughing that I thought he 'd choke with. 'Well, Sergeant,' said I, 'I always took you for a humane man; but if that 's the way you treat a fellow-creature in distress —' 'A fellow-creature!' said he, laughing louder than before. 'Ay, a fellow-creature,' said I, — for the sergeant was an Orangeman, — 'and if he differs from you in matters of religion, sure he 's your fellow-creature still.' 'Troth, Doctor, I think there 's another trifling difference betune us,' said he. 'Damn your politics,' said I; 'never let them interfere with true humanity.' Was n't I right, Major? 'Take good care of him, and here 's half-a-crown for ye.' So, saying these words, I steered along by the barrack wall, and after a little groping about, got upstairs to my quarters, when, thanks to a naturally good constitution and regular habits of life, I soon fell fast asleep."

When the doctor had said thus much, he pushed his chair slightly from the table, and taking off his wine, looked about him with the composure of a man who has brought his tale to a termination.

"Well, but, Doctor," said the Major, "you are surely not done. You have not yet told us who your interesting friend turned out to be."

"That 's the very thing, then, I 'm not able to do."

"But of course," said another, "your story does not end there."

"And where the devil would you have it end?" replied he. "Did n't I bring my hero home, and go asleep afterwards myself; and then, with virtue rewarded, how could I finish it better?"

"Oh! of course; but still you have not accounted for a principal character in the narrative," said I.

"Exactly so," said Curzon. "We were all expecting some splendid catastrophe in the morning, — that your companion turned out to be the Duke of Leinster at least, or perhaps a rebel general with an immense price upon his head."

"Neither the one nor the other," said Fin, dryly.

"And do you mean to say there never was any clew to the discovery of him?"

"The entire affair is wrapped in mystery to this hour," said he. "There was a joke about it, to be sure, among the officers, but the North Cork never wanted something to laugh at."

"And what was the joke?" said several voices together.

"Just a complaint from ould Mickey Oulahan, the post-master, to the Colonel in the morning that some of the officers took away his blind mare off the common, and that the letters were late in consequence."

"And so, Doctor," called out seven or eight, "your friend turned out to be —"

"Upon my conscience they said so, and that rascal the sergeant would take his oath of it; but my own impression I 'll never disclose to the hour of my death."

CHAPTER XVI.

Our *séance* at the mess that night was a late one, for after we had discussed some coopers of claret, there was a very general public feeling in favor of a broiled bone and some devilled kidneys, followed by a very ample bowl of bishop, over which simple condiments we talked "green-room" till near the break of day.

From having been so long away from the corps I had much to learn of their doings and intentions to do, and heard with much pleasure that they possessed an exceedingly handsome theatre, well stocked with scenery, dresses, and decorations, that they were at the pinnacle of public estimation from what they had already accomplished, and calculated on the result of my appearance to crown them with honor. I had, indeed, very little choice left me in the matter; for not only had they booked me for a particular part, but bills were already in circulation, and sundry little three-cornered notes enveloping them were sent to the *élite* of the surrounding country, setting forth that "on Friday evening the committee of the garrison theatricals, intending to perform a dress rehearsal of 'The Family Party,' request the pleasure of Mr. —— and Mrs. ——'s company on the occasion. Mr. Lorrequer will undertake the part of Captain Beaugarde. Supper at twelve. An answer will oblige."

The sight of one of these pleasant little epistles, of which the foregoing is a true copy, was presented to me as a great favor that evening, it having been agreed upon that I was to know nothing of their high and mighty resolves till the following morning. It was to little purpose that I assured them all, collectively and individually, that of Captain

Beaugarde I absolutely knew nothing; had never read the piece, nor even seen it performed. I felt, too, that my last appearance in character in a "Family Party" was anything but successful; and I trembled lest, in the discussion of the subject, some confounded allusion to my adventure at Cheltenham might come out. Happily they seemed all ignorant of this; and fearing to bring conversation in any way to the matter of my late travels, I fell in with their humor, and agreed that if it were possible in the limited time allowed me to manage it, — I had but four days, — I should undertake the character. My concurrence failed to give the full satisfaction I expected, and they so habitually did what they pleased with me that, like all men so disposed, I never got the credit for concession which a man more niggardly of his services may always command.

"To be sure you will do it, Harry," said the Major; "why not? I could learn the thing myself in a couple of hours, as for that."

Now, be it known that the aforesaid Major was so incorrigibly slow of study and dull of comprehension that he had been successively degraded at our theatrical board from the delivering of a stage message to the office of check-taker.

"He's so devilish good in the love-scene," said the junior ensign, with the white eyebrows. "I say, Curzon, you'll be confoundedly jealous though, for he is to play with Fanny."

" I rather think not," said Curzon. who was a little tipsy.

"Oh, yes," said Frazer. "Hepton is right. Lorrequer has Fanny for his *première;* and, upon my soul, I should feel tempted to take the part myself upon the same terms, — though I verily believe I should forget I was acting, and make fierce love to her on the stage."

"And who may *la charmante* Fanny be?" said I, with something of the air of the Dey of Algiers in my tone.

"Let Curzon tell him," said several voices together; "he is the only man to do justice to such perfection."

"Quiz away, my merry men," said Curzon. "All I know is that you are a confoundedly envious set of fellows; and

if so lovely a girl had thrown her eyes on one amongst
you —"

"Hip! hip! hurrah!" said old Fitzgerald, "Curzon is a
gone man. He 'll be off to the palace for a license some
fine morning, or I know nothing of such matters."

"Well, but," said I, "if matters are really as you all say,
why does not Curzon take the part you destine for me?"

"We dare not trust him," said the Major; "Lord bless
you, when the call-boy would sing out for Captain Beaugarde in the second act, we 'd find that he had levanted
with our best slashed trousers and a bird-of-paradise feather
in his cap."

"Well," thought I, "this is better at least than I anticipated; for if nothing else offers, I shall have rare fun teas-
ing my friend Charley," — for it was evident that he had
been caught by the lady in question.

"And so you 'll stay with us? Give me your hand, —
you are a real trump." These words, which proceeded
from a voice at the lower end of the table, were addressed
to my friend Finucane.

"I 'll stay with ye, upon my conscience," said Fin; "ye
have a most seductive way about ye, and a very superior
taste in milk punch."

"But, Doctor," said I, "you must not be a drone in the
hive; what will you do for us? You should be a capital
Sir Lucius O'Trigger, if we could get up 'The Rivals.'"

"My forte is the drum, — the big drum; put me among
what the Greeks call the *mousikoi*, and I 'll astonish ye."

It was at once agreed that Fin should follow the bent of
his genius; and after some other arrangements for the rest
of the party, we separated for the night, having previously
toasted the "Fanny," to which Curzon attempted to reply,
but sank, overpowered by punch and feelings, and looked
unutterable things, without the power to frame a sentence.

During the time which intervened between the dinner
and the night appointed for our rehearsal I had more business upon my hands than a Chancellor of the Exchequer
the week of the budget being produced. The whole man-

agement of every department fell, as usual, to my share, and all those who, previously to my arrival, had contributed their quota of labor, did nothing whatever now but lounge about the stage, or sit half the day in the orchestra, listening to some confounded story of Finucane's, who contrived to have an everlasting mob of actors, scene-painters, fiddlers, and call-boys always about him, who from their uproarious mirth and repeated shouts of merriment nearly drove me distracted, as I stood almost alone and unassisted in the whole management. Of *la belle* Fanny, all I learned was that she was a professional actress of very considerable talent and extremely pretty; that Curzon had fallen desperately in love with her the only night she had appeared on the boards there; and that, to avoid his absurd persecution of her, she had determined not to come into town until the morning of the rehearsal, she being at that time on a visit to the house of a country gentleman in the neighborhood. Here was a new difficulty I had to contend with, — to go through my part alone was out of the question to making it effective; and I felt so worried and harassed that I often fairly resolved on taking the wings of the mail and flying away to the uttermost parts of the South of Ireland till all was still and tranquil again. By degrees, however, I got matters into better train; and by getting over our rehearsal early before Fin appeared, as he usually slept somewhat later after his night at mess, I managed to have things in something like order, — he and his confounded drum, which, whenever he was not story-telling, he was sure to be practising on, being, in fact, the greatest difficulties opposed to my managerial functions. One property he possessed, so totally at variance with all habits of order that it completely baffled me. So numerous were his narratives that no occasion could possibly arise, no chance expression be let fall on the stage, but Fin had something he deemed *à propos*, and which, *sans façon*, he at once related for the benefit of all whom it might concern, — that was usually the entire *corps dramatique*, who eagerly turned from stage directions and groupings to laugh at his ridiculous jests. 1 shall give an instance of this habit of interruption, and let the unhappy wight who has filled such an office as mine pity my woes.

I was standing one morning on the stage, drilling my corps as usual. One most refractory spirit, to whom but a few words were intrusted, and who bungled even those, I was endeavoring to train into something like his part.

"Come, now, Elsmore, try it again, — just so. Yes, come forward in this manner, — take her hand tenderly; press it to your lips; retreat towards the flat; and then, bowing deferentially, — thus, — say 'Good night, good night!' That's very simple, eh? Well, now, that's all you have to do, and that brings you over here; so you make your exit at once."

"Exactly so, Mr. Elsmore; always contrive to be near the door under such circumstances. That was the way with my poor friend Curran. Poor Philpot, when he dined with the Guild of Merchant Tailors they gave him a gold box with their arms upon it, — a goose proper with needles saltier-wise, or something of that kind, — and they made him free of their 'ancient and loyal corporation' and gave him a very grand dinner. Well, Curran was mighty pleas-ant and agreeable, and kept them laughing all night, till the moment he rose to go away, and then he told them that he never spent so happy an evening and all that. 'But, gentlemen,' said he, 'business has its calls; I must tear myself away. So wishing you now' — there were just eigh-teen of them — 'wishing you now every happiness and prosperity, permit me to take my leave' — and here he stole near the door — 'to take my leave, and bid you *both* good night.'"

With a running fire of such stories, it may be sup-posed how difficult was my task in getting anything done upon the stage.

Well, at last the long-expected Friday arrived, and I rose in the morning with all that peculiar *tourbillon* of spirits that a man feels when he is half pleased and whole fright-ened with the labor before him. I had scarcely accom-

plished dressing when a servant tapped at my door and
begged to know if I could spare a few moments to speak to
Miss Ersler, who was in the drawing-room. I replied, of
course, in the affirmative, and rightly conjecturing that my
fair friend must be the lovely Fanny already alluded to,
followed the servant downstairs.

"Mr. Lorrequer," said the servant; and closing the door
behind me, left me in sole possession of the lady.

"Will you do me the favor to sit here, Mr Lorrequer?"
said one of the sweetest voices in the world as she made
room for me on the sofa beside her. "I am particularly
short-sighted; so pray sit near me, as I really cannot talk
to any one I don't see."

I blundered out some platitude of a compliment to her
eyes, — the fullest and most lovely blue that ever man
gazed into, — at which she smiled as if pleased, and continued: "Now, Mr. Lorrequer, I have really been longing
for your coming, for your friends of the 4—th are doubtless
very dashing, spirited young gentlemen, perfectly versed in
war's alarms; but pardon me if I say that a more wretched
company of strolling wretches never graced a barn. Now,
come, don't be angry, but let me proceed. Like all amateur people, they have the happy knack, in distributing the
characters, to put every man in his most unsuitable position; and then that poor dear thing, Curzon, — I hope
he s not a friend of yours, — by some dire fatality always
plays the lovers' parts, ha! ha! ha! True, I assure you,
so that if you had not been announced as coming this week,
I should have left them and gone off to Bath."

Here she rose and adjusted her brown ringlets at the
glass, giving me ample time to admire one of the most perfect figures I ever beheld. She was most becomingly
dressed, and betrayed a foot and ankle which for symmetry
and "smallness" might have challenged the Rue Rivoli
itself to match it.

My first thought was poor Curzon; my second, happy
and thrice fortunate Harry Lorrequer! There was no time,
however, for indulgence in such very pardonable gratula-

tion; so I at once proceeded, *pour faire l'aimable*, to pro-
fess my utter inability to do justice to her undoubted
talents, but slyly added that in the love-making part of the
matter she should never be able to discover that I was not
in earnest. We chatted then gayly for upwards of an hour,
until the arrival of her friend's carriage was announced,
when tendering me most graciously her hand, she smiled
benignly, and saying, "*Au revoir, donc,*" drove off.

As I stood upon the steps of the hotel, viewing her "out
of the visible horizon," I was joined by Curzon, who evidently, from his self-satisfied air and jaunty gait, little
knew how he stood in the fair Fanny's estimation.

"Very pretty, very pretty indeed; deeper and deeper
still," cried he, alluding to my most courteous salutation
as the carriage rounded the corner and its lovely occupant
kissed her hand once more. "I say, Harry, my friend, you
don't think that was meant for you, I should hope?"

"What! the kiss of the hand? Yes, faith, but I do."

"Well, certainly, that is good! Why, man, she just saw
me coming up that instant. She and I, — we understand
each other; never mind, don't be cross, — no fault of yours,
you know."

"Ah! so she is taken with you," said I, "eh, Charley?"

"Why, I believe that. I may confess to *you* the real
state of matters. She was devilishly struck with me the
first time we rehearsed together. We soon got up a little
flirtation; but the other night, when I played Mirabel to
her, it finished the affair. She was quite nervous, and
could scarcely go through with her part. I saw it, and
upon my soul I am sorry for it; she's a prodigiously fine
girl, — such lips and such teeth. Egad! I was delighted
when you came ; for, you see, I was in a manner obliged
to take one line of character, and I saw pretty plainly
where it must end. And you know with you it's quite
different; she'll laugh and chat and all that sort of thing,
but she'll not be carried away by her feelings. You understand me."

"Oh! perfectly; it's quite different, as you observed."

If I had not been supported internally during this short dialogue by the recently expressed opinion of the dear Fanny herself upon my *friend* Curzon's merits, I think I should have been tempted to take the liberty of wringing his neck off. However, the affair was much better as it stood, as I had only to wait a little with proper patience, and I had no fears but that my friend Charley would become the hero of a very pretty episode for the mess.

"So I suppose you must feel considerably bored by this kind of thing," I said, endeavoring to draw him out.

"Why, I do," replied he, "and I do not. The girl is very pretty. The place is dull in the morning, and altogether it helps to fill up time."

"Well," said I, "you are always fortunate, Curzon. You have ever your share of what floating luck the world affords."

' It is not exactly all luck, my dear friend; for, as I shall explain to you — "

"Not now," replied I, "for I have not yet breakfasted." So saying, I turned into the coffee-room, leaving the worthy Adjutant to revel in his fancied conquest and pity such unfortunates as myself.

After an early dinner at the club-house I hastened down to the theatre, where numerous preparations for the night were going forward. The green-room was devoted to the office of a supper-room, to which the audience had been invited. The dressing-rooms were many of them filled with the viands destined for the entertainment, where, among the wooden fowls and "impracticable" flagons, were to be seen very imposing pasties and flasks of champagne littered together in most admirable disorder. The confusion naturally incidental to all private theatricals was tenfold increased by the circumstances of our projected supper. Cooks and scene-shifters, fiddlers and waiters, were most inextricably mingled; and as in all similar cases, the least important functionaries took the greatest airs upon them, and appropriated without hesitation whatever came to their hands. Thus, the cook would not have scrupled to light a fire with the violoncello of the orchestra; and I actually caught one of the "marmitons" making a "soufflé" in a brass helmet I had once worn when astonishing the world as Coriolanus!

Six o'clock struck. "In another short hour and we begin," thought I, with a sinking heart, as I looked upon the littered stage crowded with hosts of fellows that had nothing to do there. Figaro himself never wished for ubiquity more than I did as I hastened from place to place, entreating, cursing, begging, scolding, execrating, and imploring by turns. To mend the matter, the devils in the orchestra had begun to tune their instruments, and I had to bawl like a boatswain of a man-of-war to be heard by the person beside me.

As seven o'clock struck I peeped through the small aperture in the curtain, and saw, to my satisfaction, — mingled, I confess, with fear, — that the house was nearly filled, the lower tier of boxes entirely so. There were a great many ladies, handsomely dressed, chatting gayly with their chaperons, and I recognized some of my acquaintances on every side; in fact, there was scarcely a family of rank in the county that had not at least some member of it present. As the orchestra struck up the overture to "Don Giovanni," I retired from my place to inspect the arrangements behind.

Before the performance of "The Family Party" we were to have a little one-act piece called "A Day in Madrid," written by myself; the principal characters being expressly composed for "Miss Ersler and Mr. Lorrequer."

The story of this trifle it is not necessary to allude to, — indeed, if it were, I should scarcely have patience to do so, so connected is my recollection of it with the distressing incident which followed.

In the first scene of the piece, the curtain, rising, displays *la belle* Fanny sitting at her embroidery in the midst of a beautiful garden surrounded with statues, fountains, etc.; at the back is seen a pavilion, in the ancient Moorish style of architecture, over which hang the branches of some large and shady trees. She comes forward expressing her impatience at the delay of her lover, whose absence she tortures herself to account for by a hundred different suppositions; and after a very sufficient *exposé* of her feelings, and some little explanatory details of her private history, conveying a very clear intimation of her own amiability and her guardian's cruelty, she proceeds, after the fashion of other young ladies similarly situated, to give utterance to her feelings by a song. After, therefore, a suitable prelude from the orchestra, for which, considering the impassioned state of her mind, she waits patiently, she comes forward and begins a melody, —

"Oh! why is he far from the heart that adores him ?"

in which, for two verses, she proceeds with sundry *sol feggi* to account for the circumstances and show her own disbelief of the explanation in a very satisfactory manner. Meanwhile, for I must not expose my reader to an anxiety on my account similar to what the dear Fanny here labored under, I was making the necessary preparations for flying to her presence and clasping her to my heart, — that is to say, I had already gummed on a pair of mustachios, had corked and arched a ferocious pair of eyebrows, which, with my rouged cheeks, gave me a look half Whiskerando, half Grimaldi; these operations were performed, from the stress of circumstances, sufficiently near the object of my affections to afford me the pleasing satisfaction of hearing from her own sweet lips her solicitude about me, — in a word, all the dressing-rooms but two being filled with hampers of provisions, glass, china, and crockery, from absolute necessity I had no other spot where I could attire myself unseen, except in the identical pavilion already alluded to. Here, however, I was quite secure, and had abundant time also; for I was not to appear till scene the second, when I was to come forward in full Spanish costume, "every inch a hidalgo." Meantime, Fanny had been singing, "Oh! why is he far," etc. At the conclusion of the last verse, just as she repeats the words "Why, why, why," in a very distracted and melting cadence, a voice behind startles her; she turns and beholds her guardian, — so, at least, runs the course of events in the real drama; that it should follow thus now, however, *Diis aliter visum,* for just as she came to the very moving apostrophe alluded to, and called out, "Why comes he not?" a gruff voice from behind answered in a strong Cork brogue, "Ah! would ye have him come in a state of nature?" At the instant a loud whistle ran through the house, and the pavilion scene slowly drew up, discovering me, Harry Lorrequer, seated on a small stool before a cracked looking-glass, my only habiliments, as I am an honest man, being a pair of long white-silk stockings and a very richly embroidered shirt with point-lace collar. The shouts of laughter are yet in my ears; the loud roar of inextinguishable mirth which, after the first brief pause of astonishment gave way, shook the entire building. My recollection may well have been confused at such a moment of unutterable shame and misery; yet I clearly remember seeing Fanny, the sweet Fanny herself, fall into an arm-chair nearly suffocated with convulsions of laughter. I cannot go on; what I did I know not. I suppose my exit was additionally ludicrous, for a new *éclat de rire* followed me out. I rushed out of the theatre, and wrapping only my cloak round me, ran without stopping to the barracks. But I must cease; these are woes too sacred for even "Confessions" like mine, so let me close the curtain of my room and my chapter together, and say adieu for a season.

CHAPTER XVII.

It might have been about six weeks after the events
detailed in my last chapter had occurred that Curzon broke
suddenly into my room one morning before I had risen, and
throwing a precautionary glance around, as if to assure
himself that we were alone, seized my hand with a most
unusual earnestness, and steadfastly looking at me, said:

"Harry Lorrequer, will you stand by me?"

So sudden and unexpected was his appearance at the
moment that I really felt but half awake, and kept puz-
zling myself for an explanation of the scene, rather than
thinking of a reply to his question; perceiving which, and
auguring but badly from my silence, he continued, —

"Am I, then, really deceived in what I believed to be an
old and tried friend?"

"Why, what the devil's the matter?" I cried out. "If
you are in a scrape, why of course you know I'm your man;
but still, it's only fair to let one know something of the
matter in the mean while."

"In a scrape!" said he, with a long-drawn sigh intended
to beat the whole Minerva Press in its romantic cadence.

"Well, but get on a bit," said I, rather impatiently;
"who is the fellow you've got the row with? Not one of
ours, I trust?"

"Ah, my dear Hal," said he, in the same melting tone
as before, "how your imagination does run upon rows and
broils and duelling *reneontres!*" (he, the speaker, be it
known to the reader, was the fire-eater of the regiment.)
"As if life had nothing better to offer than the excitement
of a challenge or the mock heroism of a meeting."

As he made a dead pause here, after which he showed no
disposition to continue, I merely added, —

"Well, at this rate of proceeding we shall get at the matter in hand on our way out to Corfu, for I hear we are the next regiment for the Mediterranean."

The observation seemed to have some effect in rousing him from his lethargy, and he added, —

"If you only knew the nature of the attachment, and how completely all my future hopes are concerned upon the issue —"

"Ho!" said I; "so it's a money affair, is it? And is it old Watson has issued the writ? I'll bet a hundred on it."

"Well, upon my soul, Lorrequer," said he, jumping from his chair, and speaking with more energy than he had before evinced, "you are, without exception, the most worldly-minded, cold-blooded fellow I ever met. What have I said that could have led you to suppose I had either a duel or a law-suit upon my hands this morning? Learn once and for all, man, that I am in love, — desperately and over head and ears in love."

"*E poi?*" said I, coolly.

"And intend to marry immediately."

"Oh! very well," said I; "the fighting and debt will come later, that's all. But to return, — now for the lady."

"Come, you must make a guess."

"Why, then, I really must confess my utter inability; for your attentions have been so generally and impartially distributed since our arrival here that it may be any fair one, from your venerable partner at whist last evening to Mrs. Henderson, the pastrycook, inclusive, for whose macaroni and cherry-brandy your feelings have been as warm as they are constant."

"Come, no more quizzing, Hal. You surely must have remarked that lovely girl I waltzed with at Power's ball on Tuesday last."

"Lovely girl! Why, in all seriousness, you don't mean the small woman with the tow wig?"

"No, I do *not* mean any such thing, but a beautiful creature, with the brightest locks in Christendom, — the very light brown waving ringlets Domenichino loved to paint, and a foot — Did you see her foot?"

"No; that was rather difficult, for she kept continually bobbing up and down, like a boy's cork-float in a fishpond."

"Stop there. I shall not permit this any longer; I came not here to listen to —"

"But, Curzon, my boy, you're not angry?"

"Yes, sir, I am angry."

"Why, surely, you have not been serious all this time?"

"And why not, pray?"

"Oh! I don't exactly know, — that is, faith, I scarcely thought you were in earnest, for if I did, of course I should honestly have confessed to you that the lady in question struck me as one of the handsomest persons I ever met."

"You think so really, Hal?"

"Certainly I do; and the opinion is not mine alone, — she is, in fact, universally admired."

"Come, Harry, excuse my bad temper; I ought to have known you better. Give me your hand, old boy, and wish me joy; for, with your aiding and abetting, she is mine to-morrow morning."

I wrung his hand heartily, congratulating myself, meanwhile, how happily I had got out of my scrape; as I now, for the first time, perceived that Curzon was actually in earnest.

"So you will stand by me, Hal?" said he.

"Of course. Only show me how, and I'm perfectly at your service. Anything, from riding postilion on the leaders to officiating as bridesmaid, and I am your man. And if you are in want of such a functionary, I shall stand *in loco parentis* to the lady, and give her away with as much *onction* and tenderness as though I had as many marriageable daughters as King Priam himself. It is with me in marriage as in duelling, — I'll be anything rather than a principal; and I have long since disapproved of either method as a means of ' obtaining satisfaction.'"

"Ah! Harry, I shall not be discouraged by your sneers; you've been rather unlucky, I'm aware. But now to return. Your office on this occasion is an exceedingly simple one; and yet that which I could only confide to one as much my friend as yourself. You must carry my dearest Louisa off."

"Carry her off! Where? when? how?"

"All that I have already arranged, as you shall hear."

"Yes. But first of all please to explain why, if going to run away with the lady, you don't accompany her yourself."

"Ah! I knew you would say that, — I could have laid a wager you'd ask that question; for it is just that very explanation will show all the native delicacy and feminine propriety of my darling Loo. And first I must tell you that old Sir Alfred Jonson, her father, has some confounded prejudice against the army, and never would consent to her marriage with a red-coat; so that, his consent being out of the question, our only resource is an elopement. Louisa consents to this, but only upon one condition, and this she insists upon so firmly — I had almost said obstinately — that, notwithstanding all my arguments and representations, and even entreaties against it, she remains inflexible; so that I have at length yielded, and she is to have her own way."

"Well, and what is the condition she lays such stress upon?"

"Simply this, that we are never to travel a mile together until I obtain my right to do so by making her my wife. She has got some trumpery notions in her head that any slight transgression over the bounds of delicacy made by women before marriage is ever after remembered by the husband to their disadvantage, and she is therefore resolved not to sacrifice her principle even at such a crisis as the present."

"All very proper, I have no doubt; but still, pray explain what I confess appears somewhat strange to me at present. How does so very delicately minded a person reconcile herself to travelling with a perfect stranger under such circumstances?"

"That I can explain perfectly to you. You must know

that when my darling Loo consented to take this step,
which I induced her to do with the greatest difficulty, she
made the proviso I have just mentioned; I at once showed
her that I had no maiden aunt or married sister to confide
her to at such a moment, and what was to be done? She
immediately replied, ' Have you no elderly brother officer,
whose years and discretion will put the transaction in such
a light as to silence the slanderous tongues of the world?
For with such a man I am quite ready and willing to trust
myself.' You see I was hard pushed there. What could
I do? Whom could I select? Old Hayes, the paymaster,
is always tipsy; Jones is five and forty, — but still, if he
found out there was thirty thousand pounds in the case,
egad! I 'm not so sure I 'd have found my betrothed at the
end of the stage. You were my only hope; I knew I could
rely upon you, — you would carry on the whole affair with
tact and discretion. And as to age, your stage experience
would enable you, with a little assistance from costume, to
pass muster, — besides that, I have always represented you
as the very Methuselah of the corps; and in the gray dawn
of an autumnal morning — with maiden bashfulness assisting — the scrutiny is not likely to be a close one. So now,
your consent is alone wanting to complete the arrangements which, before this time to-morrow, shall have made
me the happiest of mortals."

Having expressed in fitting terms my full sense of
obligation for the delicate flattery with which he pictured
me as "Old Lorrequer" to the lady, I begged a more
detailed account of his plan, which I shall shorten for my
reader's sake, by the following brief *exposé*.

A post-chaise and four was to be in waiting at five o'clock
in the morning to convey me to Sir Alfred Jonson's residence, about twelve miles distant. There I was to be met
by a lady at the gate-lodge, who was subsequently to accompany me to a small village on the Nore, where an old
college friend of Curzon's happened to reside as parson,
and by whom the treaty was to be concluded.

This was all simple and clear enough, the only condition

necessary to insure success being punctuality, particularly
on the lady's part.   As to mine, I readily promised my best
aid and warmest efforts in my friend's behalf.

"There is only one thing more," said Curzon.   "Louisa's
younger brother is a devilish hot-headed, wild sort of a fellow, and it would be as well, just for precaution's sake, to
have your pistols along with you, if, by any chance, he
should make out what was going forward, — not but that
you know, if anything serious was to take place, I should
be the person to take all that upon my hands."

"Oh! of course, I understand," said I.   Meanwhile 1
could not help running over in my mind the pleasant possi-
bilities such an adventure presented, heartily wishing that
Curzon had been content to marry by banns, or any other
of the legitimate modes in use, without risking his friend's
bones.   The other *pros* and *cons* of the matter, with full
and accurate directions as to the road to be taken on obtaining possession of the lady, being all arranged, we parted,
I to settle my costume and appearance for my first performance in an old man's part, and Curzon to obtain a short
leave for a few days from the commanding officer of the
regiment.

When we again met, which was at the mess-table, it was
not without evidence on either side of that peculiar consciousness which persons feel who have, or think they
have, some secret in common which the world wots not of.
Curzon's unusually quick and excited manner would at once
have struck any close observer as indicating the eve of some
important step, no less than continual allusions to whatever
was going on, by sly and equivocal jokes and ambiguous
jests.   Happily, however, on the present occasion, the
party were otherwise occupied than watching him, being
most profoundly and learnedly engaged in discussing medicine and matters medical with all the acute and accurate
knowledge which characterizes such discussions among the
non-medical public.

The present conversation originated from some mention
our senior surgeon, Fitzgerald, had just made of a consul-

tation which he was invited to attend on the next morning at the distance of twenty miles, and which necessitated him to start at a most uncomfortably early hour. While he continued to deplore the hard fate of such men as himself, so eagerly sought after by the world that their own hours were eternally broken in upon by external claims, the juniors were not sparing of their mirth on the occasion at the expense of the worthy doctor, who, in plain truth, had never been disturbed by a request like the present within any one's memory. Some asserted that the whole thing was a puff got up by Fitz himself, who was only going to have a day's partridge-shooting; others hinting that it was a blind to escape the vigilance of Mrs. Fitzgerald — a well-known virago in the regiment — while Fitz enjoyed himself; and a third party, pretending to sympathize with the doctor, suggested that a hundred pounds would be the least he could possibly be offered for such services as his on so grave an occasion.

"No, no, only fifty," said Fitz, gravely.

"Fifty! Why, you tremendous old humbug, you don't mean to say you 'll make fifty pounds before we are out of our beds in the morning?" cried one.

"I 'll take your bet on it," said the doctor, who had in this instance reason to suppose his fee would be a large one.

During this discussion the claret had been pushed round rather freely; and fully bent as I was upon the adventure before me, I had taken my share of it as a preparation. I thought of the amazing prize I was about to be instrumental in securing for my friend, — for the lady had really thirty thousand pounds, — and I could not conceal my triumph at such a prospect of success in comparison with the meaner object of ambition. They all seemed to envy poor Fitzgerald. I struggled with my secret for some time; but my pride and the claret together got the better of me, and I called out, "Fifty pounds on it, then, that before ten to-morrow morning I 'll make a better hit of it than you, and the mess shall decide between us afterwards as to the winner. And if you will," said I, seeing some reluctance on Fitz's part to take the wager, and getting emboldened in consequence, "let the judgment be pronounced over a couple of dozen of champagne, paid by the loser."

This was a *coup d'état* on *my* part, for I knew at once there were so many parties to benefit by the bet, terminate which way it might, there could be no possibility of evading it. My device succeeded, and poor Fitzgerald, fairly badgered into a wager, the terms of which he could not in the least comprehend, was obliged to sign the conditions inserted in the Adjutant's note-book, his greatest hope in so doing being in the quantity of wine he had seen me drink during the evening. As for myself, the bet was no sooner made than I began to think upon the very little chance I had of winning it; for even supposing my success perfect in the department allotted to me, it might with great reason be doubted what peculiar benefit I myself derived as a counterbalance to the fee of the doctor. For this, my only trust lay in the justice of a decision which I conjectured would lean more towards the goodness of a practical joke than the equity of the transaction. The party at mess soon after separated, and I wished my friend good-night for the last time before meeting him as a bridegroom.

I arranged everything in order for my start. My pistol-case I placed conspicuously before me, to avoid being forgotten in the haste of departure; and having ordered my servant to sit up all night in the guard-room until he heard the carriage at the barrack-gate, threw myself on my bed, but not to sleep. The adventure I was about to engage in suggested to my mind a thousand associations, into which many of the scenes I have already narrated entered. I thought how frequently I had myself been on the verge of that state which Curzon was about to try, and how it always happened that when nearest to success failure had intervened. From my very schoolboy days, my love adventures had the same unfortunate abruptness in their issue; and there seemed to be something very like a fatality in the invariable unsuccess of my efforts at marriage. I feared, too, that my friend Curzon had placed himself in very unfortunate hands, if augury were to be relied upon. "Something will surely happen," thought I, "from my confounded ill luck, and all will be blown up." Wearied at last with thinking, I fell into a sound sleep for about three quarters of an hour, at the end of which I was awoke by my servant informing me that a chaise and four was drawn up at the end of the barrack lane.

"Why surely they are too early, Stubbes? It's only four o'clock."

"Yes, sir; but they say that the road for eight miles is very bad, and they must go it almost at a walk."

"That is certainly pleasant," thought I; "but I'm in for it now, so can't help it."

In a few minutes I was up and dressed, and so perfectly transformed by the addition of a brown scratch-wig and large green spectacles and a deep-flapped waistcoat that my servant, on re-entering my room, could not recognize me. I followed him now across the barrack-yard; as with my pistol-case under one arm, and a lantern in his hand, he proceeded to the barrack-gate.

As I passed beneath the Adjutant's window I saw a light; the sash was quickly thrown open, and Curzon appeared.

"Is that you, Harry?"

"Yes; when do you start?"

"In about two hours. I've only eight miles to go; you have upwards of twelve, and no time to lose. Success attend you, my boy! We'll meet soon."

"Here's the carriage, sir; this way."

"Well, my lads, you know the road, I suppose?"

"Every inch of it, your honor's glory, — we're always coming in for doctors and 'pothecaries; they're never a week without them."

I was soon seated, the door clapped to, the words "all right" given, and away we went.

Little as I had slept during the night, my mind was too much occupied with the adventure I was engaged in to permit any thoughts of sleep now, so that I had abundant opportunity afforded me of pondering over all the bearings of the case with much more of deliberation and caution than I had yet bestowed upon it. One thing was certain, whether success did or did not attend our undertaking, the risk was mine and mine only; and if by any accident the affair should be already known to the family, I stood a very fair chance of being shot by one of the sons, or stoned to death by the tenantry, while my excellent friend Curzon should be eating his breakfast with his reverend friend, and only interrupting himself in his fourth muffin to wonder "what could keep them." And besides, for minor miseries will, like the blue devils in "Don Giovanni," thrust up their heads among their better-grown brethren, my fifty-pound bet looked rather blue; for even under the most favorable light considered, however Curzon might be esteemed a gainer, it might well be doubted how far I had succeeded better than the doctor when producing his fee in evidence. Well, well, I'm in for it now; but it certainly is strange all these very awkward circumstances never struck me so forcibly before. And, after all, it was not quite fair of Curzon to put any man forward in such a transaction, — the more so as such a representation might be made of it at the Horse Guards as to stop a man's promotion, or seriously affect his prospects for life; and I at last began to convince myself that many a man so placed would carry the lady off himself, and leave the Adjutant to settle the affair with the family. For two mortal hours did I conjure up every possible disagreeable contingency that might arise. My being mulcted of my fifty, and laughed at by the mess, seemed inevitable, even were I fortunate enough to escape a duel with the fire-eating brother. Meanwhile a thick, misty rain continued to fall, adding so much to the darkness of the early hour that I could see little of the country about me, and knew nothing of where I was.

Troubles are like laudanum, a small dose only excites, a strong one sets you to sleep, — not a very comfortable sleep, mayhap, but still it is sleep, and often very sound sleep; so it now happened with me. I had pondered over, weighed, and considered all the *pros*, *cons*, turnings, and windings of this awkward predicament, till I had fairly convinced myself that I was on the high road to a confounded scrape; and then, having established that fact to my entire satisfaction, I fell comfortably back in the chaise and sank into a most profound slumber.

If to any of my readers I may appear here to have taken a very despondent view of this whole affair, let him only call to mind my invariable ill luck in such matters, and how always it had been my lot to see myself on the fair road to success only up to that point at which it is certain; besides — But why explain? These are my "Confessions." I may not alter what are matters of fact, and my reader must only take me with all the imperfections of wrong motives and headlong impulses upon my head, or abandon me at once.

Meanwhile the chaise rolled along, and the road being better and the pace faster, my sleep became more easy; thus about an hour and a half after I had fallen asleep passed rapidly over, when the sharp turning of an angle disturbed me from my leaning position, and I awoke. I started up and rubbed my eyes; several seconds elapsed before I could think where I was or whither going. Consciousness at last came, and I perceived that we were driving up a thickly-planted avenue. Why, confound it, they can't have mistaken it, thought I, or are we really going up to the house, instead of waiting at the lodge? I at once lowered the sash, and stretching out my head, cried out, "Do you know what ye are about, lads, — is this all right?" but unfortunately, amid the rattling of the gravel and the clatter of the horses, my words were unheard; and thinking I was addressing a request to go faster, the villains cracked their whips, and breaking into a full gallop, before five minutes flew over, they drew up with a jerk at the foot of a long portico to a large and spacious cut-stone mansion. When I rallied from the sudden check, which had nearly thrown me through the window, I gave myself up for lost; here I was, *vis-à-vis* the very hall-door of the man whose

daughter I was about to elope with, — whether so placed by
the awkwardness and blundering of the wretches who drove
me, or delivered up by their treachery, it mattered not, my
fate seemed certain; before I had time to determine upon
any line of acting in this confounded dilemma, the door was
jerked open by a servant in sombre livery, who, protruding
his head and shoulders into the chaise, looked at me steadily for a moment and said, "Ah! then, Doctor, darlin',
but ye 're welcome." With the speed with which sometimes
the bar of an air long since heard, or the passing glance of
an old familiar face can call up the memory of our very earliest childood bright and vivid before us, did that one single
phrase explain the entire mystery of my present position,
and I saw in one rapid glance that I had got into the chaise
intended for Dr. Fitzgerald, and was absolutely, at that
moment, before the hall-door of the patient. My first impulse was an honest one to avow the mistake and retrace
my steps, taking my chance to settle with Curzon, whose
matrimonial scheme I foresaw was doomed to the untimely
fate of all those I had ever been concerned in. My next
thought — how seldom is the adage true which says that
"second thoughts are best!"— was upon my luckless wager;
for even supposing that Fitzgerald should follow me in the
other chaise, yet, as I had the start of him, if I could only
pass muster for half an hour, I might secure the fee and
evacuate the territory. Besides that, there was a great
chance of Fitz's having gone on *my* errand, while I was
journeying on *his*, in which case I should be safe from
interruption. Meanwhile, Heaven only could tell what his
interference in poor Curzon's business might not involve.
These serious reflections took about ten seconds to pass
through my mind as the grave-looking old servant proceeded to encumber himself with my cloak and my pistol-
case, remarking as he lifted the latter, "And may the Lord
grant ye won't want the instruments this time, Doctor, for
they say he is better this morning." Heartily wishing
amen to the benevolent prayer of the honest domestic for
more reasons than one, I descended leisurely, as I conjec-

tured a doctor ought to do, from the chaise, and with a solemn pace and grave demeanor followed him into the house.

In the small parlor to which I was ushered sat two gentlemen somewhat advanced in years, who I rightly supposed were my medical *confrères*. One of these was a tall, pale, ascetic-looking man, with gray hair and retreating forehead, slow in speech and lugubrious in demeanor. The other, his antithesis, was a short, rosy-cheeked, apoplectic-looking subject, with a laugh like a suffocating wheeze, and a paunch like an alderman, his quick, restless eye and full nether lip denoting more of the *bon vivant* than the abstemious disciple of Æsculapius. A moment's glance satisfied me that if I had only these to deal with, I was safe, for I saw that they were of the stamp of country practitioner, — half-physician, half-apothecary, — who rarely come in contact with the higher orders of their art, and then only to be dictated to, obey, and grumble.

"Doctor, may I beg to intrude myself, Mr. Phipps, on your notice? Dr. Phipps, or Mr., it's all one; but I have only a license in pharmacy, though they call me doctor. Surgeon Riley, sir, a very respectable practitioner," said he, waving his hand towards his rubicund *confrère*.

I at once expressed the great happiness it afforded me to meet such highly informed and justly celebrated gentlemen; and fearing every moment the arrival of the real Simon Pure should cover me with shame and disgrace, begged they would afford me, as soon as possible, some history of the case we were convened for. They accordingly proceeded to expound, in a species of duet, some curious particulars of an old gentleman who had the evil fortune to have them for his doctors, and who labored under some swelling of the neck which they differed as to the treatment of, and in consequence of which the aid of a third party (myself, Heaven bless the mark!) was requested.

As I could by no means divest myself of the fear of Fitz's arrival, I pleaded the multiplicity of my professional engagements as a reason for at once seeing the patient;

upon which I was conducted upstairs by my two brethren, and introduced to a half-lighted chamber. In a large easy-chair sat a florid-looking old man, with a face in which pain and habitual ill-temper had combined to absorb every expression.

"This is the doctor of the regiment, sir, that you desired to see," said my tall coadjutor.

"Oh! then, very well; good-morning, sir. I suppose you will find out something new the matter, for them two there have been doing so every day this two months."

"I trust, sir," I replied stiffly, "that with the assistance of my learned friends much may be done for you. Ha! hem! so this is the malady. Turn your head a little to that side." Here an awful groan escaped the sick man, for I, it appears, had made considerable impression upon rather a delicate part, — not unintentionally, I must confess; for as I remembered Hoyle's maxim at whist, "when in doubt play a trump," so I thought it might be true in physic, when posed by a difficulty, to do a bold thing also. "Does that hurt you, sir?" said I, in a soothing and affectionate tone of voice.

"Like the devil," growled the patient.

"And here?" said I.

"Oh! oh! I can't bear it any longer."

"Oh! I perceive," said I, "the thing is just as I expected." Here I raised my eyebrows, and looked indescribably wise at my *confrères*.

"No aneurism, Doctor," said the tall one.

"Certainly not."

"Maybe," said the short man, "maybe it's a stay-at-home-with-us tumor after all," — so at least he appeared to pronounce a confounded technical, which I afterwards learned was "steatomatous." Conceiving that my rosy friend was disposed to jeer at me, I gave him a terrific frown and resumed, "This must not be touched."

"So you won't operate upon it," said the patient.

"I would not take a thousand pounds to do so," I replied. "Now, if you please, gentlemen," said I, making a step

towards the door, as if to withdraw for consultation; upon which they accompanied me downstairs to the breakfast-room. As it was the only time in my life I had performed in this character, I had some doubts as to the propriety of indulging a very hearty breakfast appetite, not knowing if it were unprofessional to eat; but from this doubt my learned friends speedily relieved me, by the entire devotion which they bestowed for about twenty minutes upon ham, rolls, eggs, and cutlets, barely interrupting these important occupations by sly allusions to the old gentleman's malady and his chance of recovery.

"Well, Doctor," said the pale one, as at length he rested from his labors, "what are we to do?"

"Ay," said the other, "there's the question."

"Go on," said I, "go on as before; I can't advise you better." Now, this was a deep stroke of mine, for up to the present moment I did not know what treatment they were practising; but it looked a shrewd thing to guess it, and it certainly was civil to approve of it.

"So you think that will be best?"

"I am certain that I know nothing better," I answered.

"Well, I 'm sure, sir, we have every reason to be gratified for the very candid manner in which you have treated us. Sir, I 'm your most obedient servant," said the fat one.

"Gentlemen, both your good healths and professional success also." Here I swallowed a glass of brandy, thinking all the while there were worse things than the practice of physic.

"I hope you are not going?" said one, as my chaise drew up at the door.

"Business calls me," said I, "and I can't help it."

"Could not you manage to see our friend here again in a day or two?" said the rosy one.

"I fear it will be impossible," replied I; "besides, I have a notion he may not desire it."

"I have been commissioned to hand you this," said the tall doctor, with a half sigh, as he put a check into my hand.

I bowed slightly, and stuffed the crumpled paper with a half-careless air into my waistcoat pocket; and wishing them both every species of happiness and success, shook hands four times with each, and drove off, never believing myself safe till I saw the gate-lodge behind me, and felt myself flying on the road to Kilkenny at about twelve miles Irish an hour.

CHAPTER XVIII.

It was past two o'clock when I reached the town. On entering the barrack-yard I perceived a large group of officers chatting together, and every moment breaking into immoderate fits of laughter. I went over and immediately learned the source of their mirth, which was this. No sooner had it been known that Fitzgerald was about to go to a distance on a professional call than a couple of young officers laid their heads together and wrote an anonymous note to Mrs. Fitz, who was the very dragon of jealousy, informing her that her husband had feigned the whole history of the patient and consultation as an excuse for absenting himself on an excursion of gallantry, and that if she wished to satisfy herself of the truth of the statement she had only to follow him in the morning and detect his entire scheme; the object of these amiable friends being to give poor Mrs. Fitz a twenty miles' jaunt, and confront her with her injured husband at the end of it.

Having a mind actively alive to suspicions of this nature, the worthy woman made all her arrangements for a start; and scarcely was the chaise-and-four, with her husband, out of the town than she was on the track of it, with a heart bursting with jealousy, and vowing vengeance to the knife against all concerned in this scheme to wrong her.

So far the plan of her persecutors had perfectly succeeded; they saw her depart on a trip of, as they supposed, twenty miles, and their whole notions of the practical joke were limited to the *éclaircissement* that must ensue at the end. Little, however, were they aware how much more near the suspected crime was the position of the poor doctor to turn out; for as, by one blunder, I had taken his chaise, so he, without any inquiry whatever, had got into the one intended for me, and never awoke from a most refreshing slumber till shaken by the shoulder by the postilion, who whispered in his ear, "Here we are, sir; this is the gate."

"But why stop at the gate? Drive up the avenue, my boy."

"His honor told me, sir, not for the world to go farther than the lodge, nor to make as much noise as a mouse."

"Ah! very true. He may be very irritable, poor man! Well, stop here, and I'll get out."

Just as the doctor had reached the ground, a very smart-looking soubrette tripped up and said to him, —

"Beg pardon, sir, but you are the gentleman from the barrack, sir?"

"Yes, my dear," said Fitz, with a knowing look at the pretty face of the damsel; "what can I do for you?"

"Why, sir, my mistress is here in the shrubbery; but she is so nervous and so frightened, I don't know she'll go through it."

"Ah! she's frightened, poor thing, is she? Oh! she must keep up her spirits; while there's life there's hope."

"Sir?"

"I say, my darling, she must not give way. I'll speak to her a little. Is not *he* rather advanced in life?"

"Oh, Lord, no, sir! Only two and thirty, my mistress tells me."

"Two and thirty! Why, I thought he was above sixty."

"Above sixty! Law, sir, you have a bright fancy! This is the gentleman, ma'am. Now, sir, I'll just slip aside for a moment and let you talk to her."

"I am grieved, ma'am, that I have not the happiness to make your acquaintance under happier circumstances."

"I must confess, sir, though I am ashamed —"

"Never be ashamed, ma'am; your grief, although I trust causeless, does you infinite honor. — Upon my soul, she is rather pretty," said the doctor to himself here.

"Well, sir, as I have the most perfect confidence in you, from all I have heard of you, I trust you will not think me abrupt in saying that any longer delay here is dangerous."

"Dangerous! Is he in so critical a state as that, then?"

"Critical a state, sir, why, what do you mean?"

"I mean, ma'am, do you think, then, it must be done to-day?"

"Of course I do, sir; and I shall never leave the spot without your assuring me of it."

"Oh! in that case make your mind easy; I have the instruments in the chaise."

"The instruments in the chaise! Really, sir, if you are not jesting, — I trust you don't think this is a fitting time for such, — I entreat of you to speak more plainly and intelligibly."

"Jesting, ma'am! I'm incapable of jesting at such a moment."

"Ma'am, ma'am! I see one of the rangers, ma'am, at a distance; so don't lose a moment, but get into the chaise at once."

"Well, sir, let us away; for I have now gone too far to retract."

"Help my mistress into the chaise, sir. Lord! what a man it is."

A moment more saw the poor doctor seated beside the young lady, while the postilions plied whip and spur with their best energy, and the road flew beneath them. Meanwhile the delay caused by this short dialogue enabled Mrs. Fitz's slower conveyance to come up with the pursuit, and her chaise had just turned the angle of the road as she caught a glimpse of a muslin dress stepping into the carriage with her husband.

There are no words capable of conveying the faintest idea of the feelings that agitated Mrs. Fitz at this moment. The fullest confirmation to her worst fears was before her eyes, — just at the very instant when a doubt was beginning to cross over her mind that it might have been merely a hoax that was practised on her, and that the worthy doctor was innocent and blameless. As for the poor doctor himself, there seemed little chance of his being enlightened as to the real state of matters; for from the moment the young lady had taken her place in the chaise, she had buried her face in her hands and sobbed continually. Meanwhile he concluded that they were approaching the house by some back entrance to avoid noise and confusion, and waited with due patience for the journey's end.

As, however, her grief continued unabated, Fitz at length began to think of the many little consolatory acts he had successfully practised in his professional career, and was just insinuating some very tender speech on the score of resignation, with his head inclined towards the weeping lady beside him, when the chaise of Mrs. Fitz came up alongside, and the postilions having yielded to the call to halt, drew suddenly up, displaying to the enraged wife the *tableau* we have mentioned.

"So, wretch!" she screamed rather than spoke, "I have detected you at last."

"Lord bless me! Why, it is my wife."

"Yes, villain! your injured, much-wronged wife! And you, madam, may I ask what have you to say for thus eloping with a married man?"

"Shame! My dear Jemima," said Fitz, "how can you possibly permit your foolish jealousy so far to blind your reason? Don't you see I am going upon a professional call?"

"Oh! you are, are you? Quite professional, I'll be bound!"

"Oh, sir, oh, madam, I beseech you, save me from the anger of my relatives and the disgrace of exposure! Pray take me back at once."

"Why, Heavens! ma'am, what do *you* mean? You are not gone mad, as well as my wife!"

"Really, Mr. Fitz," said Mrs. F., "this is carrying the

joke too far. Take your unfortunate victim — as I suppose she is such — home to her parents, and prepare to accompany me to the barrack; and if there be law and justice in — "

"Well! may the Lord in his mercy preserve my senses, or you will both drive me clean mad."

"Oh, dear! oh, dear!" sobbed the young lady, while Mrs Fitzgerald continued to upbraid at the top of her voice, heedless of the disclaimers and protestations of innocence poured out with the eloquence of despair by the poor doctor. Matters were in this state when a man dressed in a fustian jacket, like a groom, drove up to the side of the road in a tax-cart; he immediately got down, and tearing open the door of the doctor's chaise, lifted out the young lady and deposited her safely in his own conveyance, merely adding, —

"I say, master, you're in luck this morning that Mr. William took the lower road; for if *he* had come up with you instead of me, he'd blow the roof off your skull, that's all."

While these highly satisfactory words were being addressed to poor Fitz, Mrs. Fitzgerald had removed from her carriage to that of her husband, — perhaps preferring four horses to two; or perhaps she had still more unexplained views of the transaction, which might as well be told on the road homeward.

Whatever might have been the nature of Mrs. F.'s dissertation, nothing is known. The chaise containing these turtle-doves arrived late at night at Kilkenny, and Fitz was installed safely in his quarters before any one knew of his having come back. The following morning he was reported ill, and for three weeks he was but once seen, and at that time only at his window, with a flannel nightcap on his head, looking particularly pale, and rather dark under one eye.

As for Curzon, the last thing known of him that luckless morning was his hiring a post-chaise for the Royal Oak, from whence he posted to Dublin, and hastened on to England.　In a few days we learned that the Adjutant had exchanged into a regiment in Canada; and to this hour there are not three men in the 4—th who know the real secret of that morning's misadventures.

CHAPTER XIX.

DETACHMENT DUTY. — AN ASSIZE TOWN.

As there appeared to be but little prospect of poor
Fitzgerald ever requiring any explanation from me as to
the events of that morning, for he feared to venture from
his room lest he might be recognized and prosecuted for
abduction, I thought it better to keep my own secret also;
and it was therefore with a feeling of anything but regret
that I received an order, which under other circumstances
would have rendered me miserable, to march on detachment
duty. To any one at all conversant with the life we lead
in the army, I need not say how unpleasant such a change
usually is. To surrender your capital mess with all its
well-appointed equipments, your jovial brother officers,
your West India Madeira, your cool Lafitte, your daily,
hourly, and half-hourly flirtations with the whole female
population, — never a deficient one in a garrison town, —
not to speak of your matches at trotting, coursing, and
pigeon-shooting, and a hundred other delectable modes of
getting over the ground through life till it please your
ungrateful country and the Horse Guards to make you a
major-general, — to surrender all these, I say, for the noise,
dust, and damp disagreeables of a country inn, with bacon
to eat, whiskey to drink, and the priest or the constabulary
chief to get drunk with (I speak of Ireland here), and your
only affair *par amours* being the occasional ogling of the
apothecary's daughter opposite as often as she visits the
shop in the exciting occupation of measuring out garden
seeds and senna. These are, indeed, the exchanges, with
a difference, for which there is no compensation; and for
my own part, I never went upon such duty that I did not
exclaim with the honest Irishman when the mail went over

him, "O Lord! what is this for?" firmly believing that in the earthly purgatory of such duties I was reaping the heavy retribution attendant on past offences.

Besides, from being rather a crack man in my corps, I thought it somewhat hard that my turn for such duty should come round about twice as often as that of my brother officers. But so it is; I never knew a fellow a little smarter than his neighbors that was not pounced upon by his colonel for a victim. Now, however, I looked at these matters in a very different light. To leave head-quarters was to escape being questioned; while there was scarcely any post to which I could be sent where something strange or adventurous might not turn up and serve me to erase the memory of the past and turn the attention of my companions in any quarter rather than towards myself.

My orders on the present occasion were to march to Clonmel, from whence I was to proceed a short distance to the house of a magistrate upon whose information, trans-mitted to the Chief Secretary, the present assistance of a military party had been obtained; and not without every appearance of reason. The assizes of the town were about to be held, and many capital offences stood for trial in the calendar; and as it was strongly rumored that in the event of certain convictions being obtained, a rescue would be attempted, a general attack upon the town seemed a too natural consequence; and if so, the house of so obnoxious a person as him I have alluded to would be equally certain of being assailed. Such, at least, is too frequently the history of such scenes. Beginning with no one definite object, — sometimes a slight one, — more ample views and wider conceptions of mischief follow, and what has begun in a drunken riot, a casual *rencontre*, may terminate in the slaughter of a family or the burning of a village. The finest peasantry — God bless them! — are a quick people, and readier at taking a hint than most others, and have, withal, a natural taste for fighting that no acquired habits of other nations can pretend to vie with.

As the worthy person to whose house I was now about to

proceed was, and, if I am rightly informed, is, rather a remarkable character in the local history of Irish politics, I may as well say a few words concerning him. Mr. Joseph Larkins, Esq., — for so he signed himself, — had only been lately elevated to the bench of magistrates. He was originally one of that large but intelligent class called in Ireland "small farmers," remarkable chiefly for a considerable tact in driving hard bargains, a great skill in wethers, a rather national dislike to pay all species of imposts, whether partaking of the nature of tax, tithe, grand jury cess, or anything of that nature whatsoever. So very accountable — I had almost said (for I have been long quartered in Ireland) so very laudable — a propensity excited but little of surprise or astonishment in his neighbors, the majority of whom entertained very similar views, — none, however, possessing anything like the able and lawyer-like ability of the worthy Larkins for the successful evasion of these inroads upon the liberty of the subject. Such, in fact, was his talent, and so great his success in this respect, that he had established what, if it did not actually amount to a statute of exemption in law, served equally well in reality; and for several years he enjoyed a perfect immunity on the subject of money-paying in general. His "little houldin'," as he unostentatiously called some five hundred acres of bog, mountain, and sheep-walk, lay in a remote part of the county; the roads were nearly impassable for several miles in that direction; land was of little value; the agent was a timid man with a large family; of three tithe-proctors who had penetrated into the forbidden territory, two labored under a dyspepsia for life, not being able to digest parchment and sealing-wax, for they usually dined on their own writs, and the third gave five pounds out of his pocket to a large, fresh-looking man, with brown whiskers and beard, that concealed him two nights in a hayloft to escape the vengeance of the people, — which act of philanthropy should never be forgotten, if some ill-natured people were not bold enough to say that the kind individual in question was no other man than Larkins himself.

However this may be, true it is that this was the last attempt made to bring within the responsibilities of the law so refractory a subject; and so powerful is habit that although he was to be met with at every market and cattle-fair in the county, an arrest of his person was no more contemplated than if he enjoyed the privilege of parliament to go at large without danger.

When the country became disturbed, and nightly meetings of the peasantry were constantly held, followed by outrages against life and property to the most frightful extent, the usual resources of the law were employed una-vailingly. It was in vain to offer high rewards; approvers could not be found; and so perfectly organized were the secret associations that few beyond the very ringleaders knew anything of consequence to communicate. Special commissions were sent down from Dublin, additional police force, detachments of military; long correspondences took place between the magistracy and the government. But all in vain, the disturbances continued, and at last to such a height had they risen that the country was put under martial law; and even this was ultimately found perfectly insufficient to repel what now daily threatened to become an open rebellion rather than mere agrarian disturbance. It was at this precise moment, when all resources seemed to be fast exhausting themselves, that certain information reached the Castle of the most important nature. The individual who obtained and transmitted it had perilled his life in so doing; but the result was a great one, — no less than the capital conviction and execution of seven of the most influential amongst the disaffected peasantry. Confidence was at once shaken in the secrecy of their associates; distrust and suspicion followed. Many of the boldest sank beneath the fear of betrayal, and themselves became evidence for the Crown; and in five months a county abounding in midnight meetings and blazing with insurrectionary fires became almost the most tranquil in its province. It may well be believed that he who rendered this important service on this trying emergency could not be passed over, and the name of J. Larkins soon after appeared in the "Gazette" as one of his Majesty's justices of the peace for the county, — pretty much in the same spirit in which a country gentleman converts the greatest poacher in his neighborhood by making him his game-keeper.

In person he was a large and powerfully built man, considerably above six feet in height, and possessing great activity, combined with powers of enduring fatigue almost incredible. With an eye like a hawk and a heart that never knew fear, he was the person of all others calculated to strike terror into the minds of the country people. The reckless daring with which he threw himself into danger, the almost impetuous quickness with which he followed up a scent whenever information reached him of an important character, had their full effect upon a people who, long accustomed to the slowness and the uncertainty of the law, were almost paralyzed at beholding detection and punishment follow on crime as certainly as the thunder-crash follows the lightning.

His great instrument for this purpose was the obtaining information from sworn members of the secret societies, and whose names never appeared in the course of a trial or a prosecution until the measure of their iniquity was completed, when they usually received a couple of hundred pounds blood-money, as it was called, with which they took themselves away to America or Australia, — their lives being only secured while they remained by the shelter afforded them in the magistrate's own house. And so it happened that constantly there numbered from ten to twelve of these wretches, inmates of his family, each of whom had the burden of participation in one murder at least, waiting for an opportunity to leave the country unnoticed and unwatched.

Such a frightful and unnatural state of things can hardly be conceived; and yet, shocking as it was, it was a relief to that which led to it. I have dwelt, perhaps, too long upon this painful subject; but let my reader now accompany me

a little farther, and the scene shall be changed. Does he
see that long, low white house, with a tall, steep roof, per-
forated with innumerable narrow windows? There are a
few straggling beech-trees upon a low, bleak-looking field
before the house, which is called by courtesy the lawn; a
pig or two, some geese, and a tethered goat are here and
there musing over the state of Ireland; while some rosy,
curly-headed, noisy, and bare-legged urchins are gambolling
before the door. This is the dwelling of the worshipful
justice, to which myself and my party were now approaching with that degree of activity which attends on most
marches of twenty miles under the oppressive closeness of
a day in autumn. Fatigued and tired as I was, yet I could
not enter the little enclosure before the house without stopping for a moment to admire the view before me. It was
a large tract of rich country, undulating on every side, and
teeming with corn-fields in all the yellow gold of ripeness;
here and there, almost hid by small clumps of ash and
alder, were scattered some cottages, from which the blue
smoke rose in a curling column into the calm evening sky.
All was graceful and beautifully tranquil, and you might
have selected the picture as emblematic of that happiness
and repose we so constantly associate with our ideas of the
country; and yet before that sun had even set which now
gilded the landscape, its glories would be replaced by the
lurid glare of nightly incendiarism and — But here, fortunately for my reader, and perhaps myself, I am interrupted in my meditations by a rich, mellifluous accent,
saying, in the true Doric of the South, —

"Mr. Lorrequer, you 're welcome to Curryglass, sir!
You 've had a hot day for your march. Maybe you 'd take
a taste of sherry before dinner? Well, then, we 'll not wait
for Molowny, but order it up at once."

So saying, I was ushered into a long, low drawing-room,
in which were collected together about a dozen men, to
whom I was specially and severally presented, and among
whom I was happy to find my boarding-house acquaintance,
Mr. Daly, who, with the others, had arrived that same day

for the assizes, and who were all members of the legal profession, either barristers, attorneys, or clerks of the peace.

The hungry aspect of the guests, no less than the speed with which dinner made its appearance after my arrival, showed me that my coming was only waited for to complete the party, the Mr. Molowny before alluded to being unanimously voted present. The meal itself had but slight pretensions to elegance, — there were no delicacies of Parisian taste, no triumphs of French cookery; but in their place stood a lordly fish of some five and twenty pounds weight, a massive sirloin, with all the usual armament of fowls, ham, pigeon-pie, beefsteak, etc., lying in rather a promiscuous order along either side of the table. The party were evidently disposed to be satisfied, and I acknowedge I did not prove an exception to the learned individuals about me, either in my relish for the good things, or my appetite to enjoy them. *Dulce est desipere in loco,* says some one, — by which I suppose is meant that a rather slang company is occasionally good fun. Whether from my taste for the "humanities" or not, I am unable to say, but certainly in my then humor I should not have exchanged my position for one of much greater pretensions to elegance and *ton.* There was first a general onslaught upon the viands, crashing of plates, jingling of knives, mingling with requests for "more beef," "the hard side of the salmon," or "another slice of ham." Then came a dropping fire of drinking wine, which quickly increased, the decanters of sherry for about ten minutes resting upon the table about as long as Taglioni touches this mortal earth in one of her flying movements. Acquaintances were quickly formed between the members of the Bar and myself, and I found that my momentary popularity was likely to terminate in my downfall; for as each introduction was followed by a bumper of strong sherry, I did not expect to last till the end of the feast. The cloth at length disappeared, and I was just thanking Providence for the respite from hob-nobbing which I imagined was to follow, when a huge square decanter of whiskey appeared, flanked by an enormous jug of boiling water, and renewed preparations for drinking upon a large scale seriously commenced. It was just at this moment that I for the first time perceived the rather remarkable figure who had waited upon us at dinner, and who, while I chronicle so many things of little import, deserves a slight mention. IIe was a little old man of about fifty-five or sixty years, wearing upon his head a barrister's wig, and habited in clothes which originally had been the costume of a very large and bulky person, and which, consequently, added much to the drollery of his appearance. He had been for forty years the servant of Judge Vandeleur, and had entered his present service rather in the light of a preceptor than a menial, invariably dictating to the worthy justice upon every occasion of etiquette or propriety by a reference to what "the judge himself" did, which always sufficed to carry the day in Nicholas's favor, opposition to so correct a standard never being thought of by the justice.

"That's Billy Crow's own whiskey, the ' *small still,*' " said Nicholas, placing the decanter upon the table; "make much of it, for there is n't such dew in the county."

With this commendation upon the liquor, Nicholas departed, and we proceeded to fill our glasses.

I cannot venture — perhaps it is so much the better that I cannot — to give any idea of the conversation which at once broke out, as if the barriers that restrained it had at length given way. But law-talk in all its plenitude followed; and for two hours I heard of nothing but writs, detainers, declarations, traverses in prox, and alibis, with sundry hints for *qui tam processes*, interspersed, occasionally, with sly jokes about packing juries and confounding witnesses, among which figured the usual number of good things attributed to the Chief-Baron O'Grady and the other sayers of smart sayings at the Bar.

"Ah!" said Mr. Daly, drawing a deep sigh at the same instant, "the Bar is sadly fallen off since I was called in the year '76. There was not a leader in one of the circuits at that time that could n't puzzle any jury that ever sat in a box; and as for driving through an Act of Parliament, it was, as Sancho Panza says, cakes and gingerbread to them. And then there is one special talent lost forever to the present generation, — just like stained glass, and illuminated manuscripts, and slow poisons, and the like, that were all known years ago, — I mean the beautiful art of addressing the judge before the jury, and not letting them know you were quizzing them, if ye like to do that same. Poor Peter Purcell for that — rest his ashes! — he could cheat the devil himself if he had need, — and maybe he has had before now. Peter is sixteen years dead last November."

"And what was Peter's peculiar tact in that respect, Mr. Daly?" said I.

"Oh! then, I might try for hours to explain it to you in vain; but I'll just give you an instance that'll show you better than all my dissertations on the subject, and I was present myself when it happened, more by token it was the first time I ever met him on circuit.

"I suppose there is scarcely any one here now, except myself, that remembers the great cause of Mills *versus* Mulcahy, a Widow, and Others, that was tried in Ennis in the year '82. It's no matter if there is not. Perhaps it may be more agreeable for me, for I can tell my story in my own way, and not be interrupted. Well, that was called 'the old record,' for they tried it seventeen times. I believe, on my conscience, it killed old Jones, who was in the Common Pleas; he used to say, if he put it for trial on the day of judgment, one of the parties would be sure to lodge an appeal. Be that as it may, the Millses engaged Peter special, and brought him down with a great retainer, in a chaise-and-four, flags flying, and favors in the postilion's hats, and a fiddler on the roof, playing the 'Hare in the Corn.' The inn was illuminated the same evening, and Peter made a speech from the windows upon the liberty of the Press and religious freedom all over the globe, and there was n't a man in the mob did n't cheer him, — which was the more civil because few of them knew a word of English, and the others thought he was a play-actor. But it all went off well, nevertheless, for Peter was a clever fellow;

and although he liked money well, he liked popularity more, and he never went anywhere ' special ' that he had n't a public meeting of some kind or other, either to abolish rents, or suppress parsons, or some such popular and beneficial scheme, which always made him a great favorite with the people and got him plenty of clients. But I am wandering from the record. Purcell came down, as I said before, special for Mills; and when he looked over his brief, and thought of the case, he determined to have it tried by a gentleman jury, for although he was a great man* with the mob, he liked the country gentlemen better in the jury-box, for he was always coming out with quotations from the classics, which, whether the grand jury understood or not, they always applauded very much. Well, when he came into court that morning you may guess his surprise and mortification to find that the same jury that had tried a common ejectment case were still in the box, and waiting, by the chief-justice's direction, to try Mills *versus* Mulcahy, the great case of the assizes.

"I hear they were a set of common clod-hopping wretches, with frieze coats and brogues, that no man could get round at all, for they were as cunning as foxes, and could tell blarney from good sense rather better than people with better coats on them.

"Now, the moment that Mr. Purcell came into the court, after bowing politely to the judge, he looked up to the box; and when he saw the dirty faces of the dealers in pork and potatoes, and the unshaven chins of the small farmers, his heart fell within him, and he knew in a minute how little they 'd care for the classics if he quoted Cæsar's Commentaries itself for them, ignorant creatures as they were.

"Well, the cause was called, and up gets Peter, and he began to ' express,' as he always called it himself, ' the great distress his client and himself would labor under if the patient and most intelligent jury then on the panel should come to the consideration of so very tedious a case as this promised to be, after their already most fatiguing exertions; ' he commented upon their absence from their wives and families, their farms neglected, their crops hazarded, and in about fifteen minutes he showed them they were, if not speedily released and sent home, worse treated and harder used than many of the prisoners condemned to three months' imprisonment; and actually so far worked upon the feelings of the chief himself that he turned to the foreman of the jury and said that although it was a great deviation from his habitual practice, if at this pressing season their prospects were involved to the extent the learned counsel had pictured, why then he would so far bend his practice on this occasion, and they should be dismissed. Now, Peter, I must confess, here showed the most culpable ignorance in not knowing that a set of country fellows, put up in a jury box, would rather let every blade of corn rot in the ground than give up what they always supposed so very respectable an appointment; for they invariably imagine in these cases that they are something very like my lord the judge, 'barrin' the ermine;' besides that on the present occasion Peter's argument in their favor decided them upon staying, for they now felt like martyrs, and firmly believed that they were putting the chief-justice under an obligation to them for life.

"When, therefore, they heard the question of the court, it did not take a moment's time for the whole body to rise *en masse*, and bowing to the judge, call out, 'We'll stay, my lord, and try every mother's son of them for you, — ay, if it lasted till Christmas.'

"'I am sure, my lord,' said Peter, collecting himself for an effort, 'I cannot sufficiently express my gratitude for the great sacrifice these gifted and highly intelligent gentlemen are making in my client's behalf; for being persons who have great interests in the country at stake, their conduct on the present occasion is the more praiseworthy; and I am certain they fully appreciate, as does your lordship, the difficulty of the case before us, when documents will be submitted requiring a certain degree of acquaintance with such testimonials sufficiently to comprehend. Many of the title-deeds, as your lordship is aware, being obtained under old abbey charters, are in the learned languages; and we all know how home to our hearts and bosoms comes the beautiful line of the Greek poet, "Vacuus viator cantabit ante latronem." ' The sound of the quotation roused the chief-justice, who had been in some measure inattentive to the preceding part of the learned counsel's address, and he called out rather sharply, ' Greek! Mr. Purcell, — why, I must have mistaken. Will you repeat the passage? '

" ' With pleasure, my lord. I was just observing to your lordship and the jury, with the eloquent poet Hergesius, "Vacuus viator cantabit ante latronem." '

" ' Greek, did you call it? '

" ' Yes, my lord, of *course* I did. '

" ' Why, Mr. Purcell, you are quoting Latin to me. And what do you mean by talking of the learned Hergesius and Greek all this time? The line is Juvenal's.'

" ' My lord, with much submission to your lordship, and every deference to your great attainments and very superior talents, let me still assure you that I am quoting Greek, and that your lordship is in error.'

" ' Mr. Purcell, I have only to remark that if you are desirous to make a jest of the court, you had better be cautious, I say, sir; ' and here the judge waxed exceeding wroth. ' I say the line is Latin, — Latin, sir; Juvenal's Latin, sir, — every schoolboy knows it.'

" ' Of course, my lord,' said Peter, with great humility, ' I bow myself to the decision of your lordship; the line is, therefore, Latin. Yet I may be permitted to hint that were your lordship disposed to submit this question, as you are shortly about to do another and a similar one, to those clear-sighted and intelligent gentlemen there, I am satisfied, my lord, it would be Greek to every man of them.'

"The look, the voice, and the peculiar emphasis with which Peter gave these words were perfectly successful. The acute judge anticipated the wish of the counsel, the jury were dismissed, and Peter proceeded to his case before those he knew better how to deal with, and with whom the result was more certain to be as he wished it."

To this anecdote of the counsellor succeeded many others, of which, as the whiskey was potent and the hour late, my memory is not over retentive; the party did not break up till near four o'clock, and even then our *séance* only concluded because some one gravely remarked that as we should be all actively engaged on the morrow, early hours were advisable.

CHAPTER XX.

I HAD not been above a week in my new quarters when my servant presented me, among my letters one morning, with a packet which, with considerable pains, I at length recognized to be directed to me. The entire envelope was covered with writing in various hands, among which I detected something which bore a faint resemblance to my name; but the address which followed was perfectly un-readable, not only to me, as it appeared, but also to the "experts" of the different post-offices, for it had been fol-lowed by sundry directions to try various places beginning with T, which seemed to be the letter commencing the "great unknown locality," — thus I read, "Try Tralee," "Try Tyrone," "Try Tanderagee," etc. I wonder that they did n't add, "Try Teheran;" and I suppose they would at last, rather than abandon the pursuit.

"But, Stubbes," said I, as I conned over the various addresses on this incomprehensible cover, "are you sure this is for me?"

"The postmaster, sir, desired me to ask if you 'd have it, for he has offered it to every one down in these parts lately; the waterguard officers will take it at 8*d*., sir, if you won't, but I begged you might have the refusal."

"Oh! very well; I am happy to find matters are managed so impartially in the post-office here. Nothing like a pub-lic auction for making matters find their true level. Tell the postmaster, then, I 'll keep the letter, and the rather, as it happens, by good luck, to be intended for me."

"And now for the interior," said I, as I broke the seal and read: —

Paris, Rue Castiglione.

My dear Mr. Lorrequer, — As her ladyship and my son have in vain essayed to get anything from you in the shape of reply to their letters, it has devolved upon me to try my fortune, which, were I to augur from the legibility of my writing, may not, I should fear, prove more successful than the [what can the word be ?— "the —the" — why, it can't be "damnable," surely ? — no, it is "amiable," I see] — than the amiable epistle of my lady. I cannot, however permit myself to leave this without apprising you that we are about to start for Baden, where we purpose remaining a month or two. Your cousin Guy, who has been staying for some time with us, has been obliged to set out for Geneva, but hopes to join in some weeks hence. He is a great favorite with us all, but has not effaced the memory of our older friend, yourself. Could you not find means to come over and see us, if only a flying visit ? Rotterdam is the route, and a few days would bring you to our quarters. Hoping that you may feel so disposed, I have enclosed herewith a letter to the Horse Guards, which I trust may facilitate your obtaining leave of absence. I know of no other mode of making your peace with the ladies, who are too highly incensed at your desertion to send one civil postscript to this letter, and Kilkee and myself are absolutely exhausted in our defence of you.

Believe me, yours truly,

Callonby.

Had I received an official notification of my being appointed paymaster to the forces or chaplain to Chelsea Hospital, I believe I should have received the information with less surprise than I perused this letter. That after the long interval which had elapsed, during which I had considered myself totally forgotten by this family, I should now receive a letter, — and such a letter too, quite in the vein of our former intimacy and good feeling, inviting me to their house, and again professing their willingness that I should be on the terms of our old familiarity, — was little short of wonderful to me. I read, too, — with what pleasure! — that slight mention of my cousin whom I had so long regarded as my successful rival, but who I began now to hope had not been preferred to me. Perhaps it was not yet too late to think that all was not hopeless. It appeared, too, that several letters had been written which had never

reached me; so, while I accused them of neglect and forget-
fulness, I was really more amenable to the charge myself;
for from the moment I had heard of my cousin Guy's having been domesticated amongst them, and the rumors of his
marriage had reached me, I suffered my absurd jealousy to
blind my reason, and never wrote another line after. I
ought to have known how *bavard* Guy always was; that he
never met with the most commonplace attentions anywhere
that he did not immediately write home about settlements
and pin-money, and portions for younger children, and all
that sort of nonsense. Now I saw it all plainly; and ten
thousand times quicker than my hopes were extinguished
they were again kindled, and I could not refrain from
regarding Lady Jane as a mirror of constancy, and myself
the most fortunate man in Europe. My old castle-building
propensities came back upon me in an instant, and I pictured myself with Lady Jane as my companion wandering
among the beautiful scenery of the Neckar beneath the
lofty ruins of Heidelberg, or skimming the placid surface
of the Rhine, while "mellowed by distance" came the rich
chorus of a student's melody filling the air with its flood of
song. How delightful I thought to be reading the lyrics
of Uhland or Bürger with one so capable of appreciating
them, with all the hallowed associations of the "Vaterland"
about us! "Yes," said I aloud, repeating the well-known
line of a German *Lied :* —

"Bekränzt mit Laub, den lieben vollen Becher."

"Upon my conscience," said Mr. Daly, who had for some
time past been in silent admiration of my stage-struck
appearance, — "upon my conscience, Mr. Lorrequer, I had
no conception you knew Irish."

The mighty talisman of the counsellor's voice brought
me back in a moment to a consciousness of where I was
then standing, and the still more unfortunate fact that I
was only a subaltern in his Majesty's 4—th.

"Why, my dear counsellor, that was German I was
quoting, not Irish."

"With all my heart," said Mr. Daly, breaking the top off
his third egg, — "with all my heart; I'd rather you'd talk
it than me. Much conversation in that tongue, I'm thinking, would be mighty apt to loosen one's teeth."

"Not at all; it is the most beautiful language in Europe,
and the most musical too. Why, even for your own peculiar taste in such matters, where can you find any language
so rich in Bacchanalian songs as German?"

"I'd rather hear the ' Cruiskeen Lawn,' or the ' Jug of
Punch,' as my old friend Pat Samson could sing them, than
a score of your High-Dutch jawbreakers."

"Shame upon ye, Mr. Daly! And for pathos, for true
feeling, where is there anything equal to Schiller's
ballads?"

"I don't think I've ever heard any of his; but if you
will talk of ballads," said the counsellor, "give me old
Mosey M'Garry's. What's finer than" — and here he
began, with a most nasal twang and dolorous emphasis,
to sing, —

> " 'And I stepped up unto her,
> An' I made a congee,
> And I axed her her pardon
> For the making so free.'

"And then the next verse she says, —

> " 'Are you goin' to undo me,
> In this desert alone?' —

There's a shake there."

"For Heaven's sake," I cried, "stop! When I spoke of
ballads, I never meant such infernal stuff as that."

"I'll not give up my knowledge of ballads to any man
breathing," said Mr. Daly; "and with God's blessing, I'll
sing you one this evening, after dinner, that will give you
a cramp in the stomach."

An animated discussion upon lyrical poetry was here
interrupted by a summons from our host to set out for the
town. My party were, by the desire of the magistracy, to
be in readiness near the court-house in the event of any

serious disturbance, which there existed but too much reason to apprehend, from the highly excited state of feeling
on the subject of the approaching trials. The soliers were,
under the guidance of Mr. Larkins, safely ensconced in a
tan-yard; and I myself having consigned them for the present to a non-commissioned officer, was left at perfect liberty
to dispose of my time and person as it might please me.

While these arrangements were taking place, I had
entirely lost sight of Mr. Daly, under whose guidance
and protection I trusted to obtain a place within the bar
to hear the trials; so that I was now perfectly alone, for
my host's numerous avocations entirely precluded any
thought of my putting myself under his care.

My first object was to reach the court-house, and there
could be little difficulty in finding it, for the throng of
persons in the street were all eagerly bending their way
thither. I accordingly followed with the stream, and soon
found myself among an enormous multitude of frieze-coated
and red-cloaked people of both sexes in a large open square
which formed the market-place, one side of which was
flanked by the court-house, — for as such I immediately
recognized a massive-looking gray stone building, — in
which the numerous windows, all open and filled with
people, exhaled a continued steam from the crowded atmosphere within. To approach it was perfectly impossible;
for the square was packed so closely that as the people
approached by the various streets they were obliged to
stand in the avenues leading to it, and regard what was
going on from a distance. Of this large multitude I soon
became one, hoping that at length some fortunate opportunity might enable me to obtain admission through some of
my legal acquaintances.

That the fate of those who were then upon their trial
for their lives absorbed the entire feelings of those without, a momentary glance at the hundreds of anxious and
careworn faces in the crowd would completely satisfy.
Motionless and silent they stood; they felt no fatigue, no
want of food or refreshment; their interest was one and

und.vided, — all their hopes and fears were centred in the events then passing at a short distance from them, but to which their ignorance imparted an additional and more painful excitement; the only information of how matters were going on being by an occasional word, sometimes a mere gesture, frcm some one stationed in the windows to a friend in the crowd.

When the contemplation of this singularly impressive scene was beginning to weary from the irksomeness of my position, I thought of retiring, but soon discovered hcw impossible was such a step. The crowd had blocked up so completely all the avenues of approach that even had I succeeded in getting from the market-place, it would be only to remain firmly impacted among the mob in the street.

It now also occurred to me that although I had been assured by Larkins no call could possibly be made upon my services or those of my party till after the trial, yet were that to conclude at any moment, I should be perfectly unable to gain the place where I had stationed them, and the most serious consequences might ensue from the absence of their officer if the men were required to act.

From the time this thought took possession of me, I became excessively uncomfortable. Every expression of the people that denoted the progress of the trial only alarmed me for the conclusion, which I supposed might not be distant, and I began, with all my ingenuity, to attempt my retreat, which, after half an hour's severe struggle, I completely abandoned, finding myself scarcely ten yards from where I started.

At length the counsel for the Crown, who had been speaking to evidence, ceased; and an indistinct murmur was heard through the court-house, which was soon repressed by the voice of the crier calling "Silence!" All now seemed still and silent as the grave; yet, on listening attentively for some time, you could catch the low tones of a voice speaking, as it appeared, with great deliberation and slowness. This was the judge addressing the jury. In a short time this also ceased; and for about half an hour the silence was perfectly unbroken, and both within and without there reigned one intense and aching sense of anxiety that absorbed every feeling, and imparted to every face an expression of almost agonizing uncertainty. It was, indeed, a moment well calculated to excite such emotions. The jury had retired to deliberate upon their verdict. At length a door was heard to open, and the footsteps of the jury, as they resumed their places, sounded through the court, and were heard by those without. How heavily upon many a stout heart those footsteps fell! They had taken their seats; then came another pause, after which the monotonous tones of the clerk of the court were heard, addressing the jury for their verdict. As the foreman rises, every ear is bent, every eye strained, every heart-string vibrates. His lips move, but he is not heard; he is desired by the judge to speak louder; there is another pause; he appears to labor for a few seconds with a mighty effort, and at last pronounces the words, "Guilty, my lord; all guilty!"

I have heard the wild war-whoop of the Red Indian as in his own pine-forest he has unexpectedly come upon the track of his foe, and the almost extinguished hope of vengeance has been kindled again in his cruel heart; I have listened to the scarcely less savage hurrah of a storming party as they have surmounted the crumbling ruins of a breach and devoted to fire and sword, with that one yell, all who await them; and once in my life it has been my fortune to hear the last yell of defiance from a pirate crew as they sank beneath the raking fire of a frigate rather than surrender, and went down with a cheer of defiance that rose even above the red artillery that destroyed but could not subdue them, — but never, in any or all of these awful moments, did my heart vibrate to such sounds as rent the air when the fatal "Guilty" was heard by those within, and repeated to those without. It was not grief, it was not despair, neither was it the cry of sharp and irrepressible anguish from a suddenly blighted hope; but it was the long pent-up and carefully concealed burst of feeling which called aloud for vengeance, — red and reeking revenge upon all who had been instrumental in the sentence then delivered. It ceased, and I looked towards the court-house, expecting that an immediate and desperate attack upon the building and those whom it contained would at once take place. But nothing of the kind ensued; the mob were already beginning to disperse, and before I recovered perfectly from the excitement of these few and terrible moments, the square was nearly empty, and I almost felt as if the wild and frantic denunciation that still rang through my ears had been conjured up by a heated and fevered imagination.

When I again met our party at the dinner-table, I could not help feeling surprised on perceiving how little they sympathized in my feeling for the events of the day, which indeed they only alluded to in a professional point of view, — criticising the speeches of the counsel on both sides, and the character of the different witnesses who were examined.

"Well," said Mr. Daly, addressing our host, "you never could have had a conviction to-day if it was n't for Mike. He 's the best evidence I ever heard. I 'd like to know very much how you ever got so clever a fellow completely in your clutches."

"By a mere accident, and very simply," replied the justice. "It was upon one of our most crowded fair-days, half the county was in town, when the information arrived that the Walshes were murdered the night before at the cross-roads above Telenamuck Mills. The news reached me as I was signing some tithe-warrants, one of which was against Mickey. I sent for him into the office, knowing that as he was in the secret of all the evil doings, I might as well pretend to do him a service and offer to stop the warrant out of kindness, as it were. Well, one way or another, he was kept waiting several hours while I was engaged in writing, and all the country people, as they passed the window, could look in and see Mickey Sheehan standing before me while I was employed busily writing

letters.   It was just at this time that a mounted policeman
rode in with the account of the murder, upon which I immediately issued a warrant to arrest the two MacNeills and
Owen Shirley upon suspicion.   I thought I saw Mike turn
pale as I said the names over to the sergeant of police, and
I at once determined to turn it to account; so I immediately
began talking to Mickey about his own affairs, breaking off,
every now and then, to give some directions about the men
to be captured.   The crowd outside was increasing every
instant, and you need not have looked at their faces twice
to perceive that they had regarded Mickey as an approver;
and the same night that saw the MacNeills in custody,
witnessed the burning of Sheehan's house and haggart, and
he only escaped by a miracle over to Curryglass, where,
once under my protection, with the imputation upon his
character of having turned king's evidence, I had little
trouble in persuading him that he might as well benefit by
the report as enjoy the name without the gain.   He soon
complied, and the convictions of this day are partly the
result."

When the applause which greeted this clever stroke of
our host had subsided, I inquired what results might, in
all likelihood, follow the proceedings of which I had that
day been a witness.

"Nothing will be done immediately," replied the justice,
"because we have a large force of police and military about
us; but let either, or unhappily both, be withdrawn, and
the cry you heard given in the market-place to-day will be
the death-wail for more than one of those who are well and
hearty at this moment."

The train of thought inevitably forced upon me by all I
had been a spectator of during the day but little disposed
me to be a partaker in the mirth and conviviality which,
as usual, formed the staple of the assize dinners of Mr.
Larkins; and I accordingly took an early opportunity to
quit the company and retire for the night.

CHAPTER XXI.

On the third day of my residence at Curryglass arrived my friend Mortimer to replace me, bringing my leave from the colonel and a most handsome letter, in which he again glanced at the prospect before me in the Callonby family, and hinted at my destination, which I had not alluded to, adding that if I made the pretence of study in Germany the reason for my application at the Horse Guards, I should be almost certain to obtain a six months' leave. With what spirits I ordered Stubbes to pack up my portmanteau and secure our places in the Dublin mail for that night, while I myself hurried to take leave of my kind entertainer and his guests, as well as to recommend to their favor and attention my excellent friend Mortimer! He, being a jovial fellow, not at all in love, was a happy exchange for me, since despite Daly's capital stories, I had spent the last two days in watching the high road for my successor's arrival.

Once more, then, I bade adieu to Curryglass and its hospitable owner, whose labors for "justice to Ireland" I shall long remember, and depositing myself in the bowels of his Majesty's mail, gave way to the full current of my hopes and imaginings, which at last ended in a sound and refreshing sleep, from which I only awoke as we drew up at the door of the Hibernian, in Dawson Street.

Even at that early hour there was considerable bustle and activity of preparation, which I was at some loss to account for till informed by the waiter that there were upwards of three hundred strangers in the house, it being the day of his Majesty's expected arrival on his visit to Ireland, and a very considerable section of the county of Galway being at that moment, with their wives and families, installed for the occasion in this their favorite hotel.

Although I had been reading of this approaching event every day for the last three months, I could not help feeling surprised at the intense appearance of excitement it occasioned, and in the few minutes' conversation I held with the waiter, learned the total impossibility of procuring a lodging anywhere, and that I could not have a bed, even were I to offer five guineas for it. Having, therefore, no inclination for sleep, even upon easier terms, I ordered my breakfast to be ready at ten, and set out upon a stroll through the town. I could not help, in my short ramble through the streets, perceiving how admirably adapted were the worthy Dublinites for all the honors that awaited them. Garlands of flowers, transparencies, flags, and the other insignia of rejoicing were everywhere in preparation, and at the end of Sackville Street a considerable erection, very much resembling an impromptu gallows, was being built, for the purpose, as I afterwards learned, of giving the worshipful the lord mayor the opportunity of opening the city gates to royalty, — creating the obstacle where none existed being a very ingenious conceit, and considerably Irish into the bargain. I could not help feeling some desire to witness how all should go off, to use the theatrical phrase; but in my anxiety to get on to the Continent, I at once abandoned every thought of delay. When I returned to the coffee-room of my hotel, I found it crowded to excess; every little table, originally destined for the accommodation of one, having at least two, and sometimes three occupants. In my hurried glance round the room to decide where I should place myself, I was considerably struck with the appearance of a stout elderly gentleman with red whiskers and a high, bald forehead; he had, although the day was an oppressively hot one, three waistcoats on, and by the brown York tan of his long-topped boots evinced a very considerable contempt either for weather or fashion; in the quick glance of his sharp gray eye I read that he listened half doubtingly to the narrative of his companion, whose back was turned towards me, but who appeared, from the occasional words which reached me, to be giving a rather marvellous and melodramatic version of the expected pleasures of the capital. There was something in the tone of the speaker's voice that I thought I recognized; I accordingly drew near, and what was my surprise to discover my friend Tom O'Flaherty. After our first salutation was over, Tom presented me to his friend Mr. Burke, of somewhere, who, he continued to inform me, in a stage whisper, was a "regular quiz," and never in Dublin in his life before.

"And so you say, sir, that his Majesty cannot enter without the permission of the lord mayor?"

"And the aldermen too," replied Tom. "It is an old feudal ceremony. When his Majesty comes up to the gate, he demands admission, and the lord mayor refuses, because he would be thus surrendering his great prerogative of head of the city; then the aldermen get about him and cajole him, and by degrees he's won over by the promise of being knighted, and the king gains the day and enters."

"Upon my conscience, a mighty ridiculous ceremony it is, after all," said Mr. Burke, "and very like a bargain for sheep in Ballinasloe fair, when the buyer and seller appear to be going to fight, till a mutual friend settles the bargain between them."

At this moment Mr. Burke suddenly sprang from his chair, which was nearest the window, to look out; I accordingly followed his example, and beheld a rather ludicrous procession, if such it could be called, consisting of so few persons. The principal individual in the group was a florid, fat, happy-looking gentleman of about fifty, with a profusion of nearly white whiskers which met at his chin, mounted upon a sleek charger, whose half-ambling, half-prancing pace had evidently been acquired by long habit of going in procession; this august figure was habited in a scarlet coat and cocked-hat having "tags" and all the other appanage of a general officer; he also wore tight buckskin breeches and high jack-boots, like those of the Horse

Guards. As he looked from side to side, with a self-satisfied, contented air, he appeared quite insensible of the *cortège* which followed and preceded him, — the latter consisting of some score of half-ragged boys, yelling and shouting with all their might, and the former being a kind of instalment in hand of the Dublin Militia Band, and who, in numbers and equipment, closely resembled the "army" which accompanies the first appearance of Bombastes, the only difference, that these I speak of did not play the "Rogue's March," which might have perhaps appeared personal.

As this goodly procession advanced, Mr. Burke's eyes became riveted upon it; it was the first wonder he had yet beheld, and he devoured it.

"May I ask, sir," said he, at length, "who that is?"

"Who that is?" said Tom, surveying him leisurely as he spoke, "why surely, sir, you must be jesting, or you would not ask such a question! I trust, indeed, every one knows who he is, — eh, Harry?" said he, looking at me for a confirmation of what he said, and to which, of course, I assented by a look.

"Well, but, my dear Mr. O'Flaherty, you forget how ignorant I am of everything here — "

"Ah, true!" said Tom, interrupting; "I forget you never saw him before."

"And who is he, sir?"

"Why, that's the Duke of Wellington, sir!"

"Lord have mercy upon me! is it?" said Mr. Burke, as he upset the table and all its breakfast equipage, and rushed through the coffee-room like one possessed. Before I could half recover from the fit of laughing this event threw me into, I heard him, as he ran full speed down Dawson Street, waving his hat, and shouting at the top of his lungs, "God bless your Grace! Long life to your Grace! Hurrah for the hero of Waterloo! the great captain of the age!" etc., which I grieve to say, for the ingratitude of the individual lauded, seemed not to afford him half the pleasure and none of the amusement it did the mob, who re-echoed the shouts

and cheering till he was hid within the precincts of the
Mansion House.

"And now," said Tom to me, "finish your breakfast as
fast as possible; for when Burke comes back, he will be
boring me to dine with him, or some such thing, as a kind
of acknowledgment of his gratitude for showing him the
duke. Do you know, he has seen more wonders through
my poor instrumentality within the last three days in
Dublin than a six months' trip to the Continent would
show most men. I have made him believe that Burke
Bethel is Lord Brougham, and I am about to bring him to
a *soirée* at *Miladi's*, whom he supposes to be the Marchio-
ness of Conyngham. *A propos* to the dear ' Blew,' let me
tell you of a ' good hit ' I was witness to a few nights since.
You know, perhaps, old Sir Charles Giesecke, eh?"

"I have seen him once, I think, — the professor of
mineralogy."

"Well, poor old Sir Charles, one of the most modest and
retiring men in existence, was standing the. other night
among the mob. in one of the drawing-rooms, while a
waltzing-party were figuring away, at which, with that
fondness for *la danse* that characterizes every German of
any age, he was looking with much interest, when my lady
came tripping up, and the following short dialogue ensued
within my ear-shot: —

"'*Ah! mon cher Sir Charles, ravie de vous voir.* But
why are you not dancing?'

"'*Ah! Miladi, je ne puis pas, — c'est-à-dire, ich kann es
nicht;* I am too old; *ich bin —*'

"' Oh, you horrid man! I understand you perfectly.
You hate ladies; that is the real reason. You do, — you
know you do.'

"'*Ah, Miladi, gnädige Frau, glauben Sie mich;* I do
loave de ladies; I do adore de sex. Do you know, *Miladi,*
when I was in Greenland I did keep four womans.'

"'Oh, shocking, horrid, vile Sir Charles! How could
you tell *me* such a story? I shall die of it!'

"'*Ah, mein Gott, Miladi, Sie irren sich; vous vous*

trompez. You are quite in mistake; it was only to *row my boat!*'

"I leave you to guess how my lady's taste for the broad-side of the story, and poor Sir Charles's vindication of himself, in regard to his estimation of *le beau sexe*, amused all who heard it; as for me, I had to leave the room, half-choked with suppressed laughter. And now let us bolt, for I see Burke coming; and, upon my soul, I am tired of telling him lies, and must rest on my oars for a few hours at least."

"But where is the necessity for so doing?" said I. "Surely where there is so much of novelty as a large city presents to a visitor for the first time there is little occasion to draw upon imagination for your facts."

"Ah, my dear Harry, how little do you know of life! There is a kind of man whose appetite for the marvellous is such that he must be crammed with miracles, or he dies of inanition; and you might as well attempt to feed a tiger upon *pâté de foie gras* as satisfy him by mere naked, unvarnished truth. I'll just give you an easy illustration: you saw his delight this morning when the 'duke' rode past; well, I'll tell you the converse of that proposition now. The night before last, having nothing better to do, we went to the theatre; the piece was 'La Pérouse,' which they have been playing here for the last two months to crowded houses, to exhibit some North American Indians whom some theatrical speculator brought over 'special,' in all the horrors of fur, wampum, and yellow ochre. Finding the 'spectacle' rather uninteresting, I leaned back in my box and fell into a doze. Meanwhile, my inquiring friend Mr. Burke, who felt naturally anxious, as he always does, to get *au fond* of matters, left his place to obtain information about the piece, the audience, and, above all, the authenticity of the Indians, who certainly astonished him considerably.

"Now it so happened that about a fortnight previously some violent passion to return home to their own country had seized these interesting individuals, and they felt the

most irresistible longing to abandon the savage and unnatural condiments of roast beef and Guinness's porter and
resume their ancient and more civilized habits of life. In
fact like the old African lady mentioned by the missionary
at the Cape, they felt they could die happy if they 'could
only once more have a roast child for supper;' and as such
luxuries are dear in this country, stay another week they
would not, whatever the consequences might be. The
manager reasoned, begged, implored, and threatened by
turns, all would not do, so they were determined; and all
that the unfortunate proprietor could accomplish was to
make a purchase of their properties in fur, belts, bows,
arrows, and feathers, and get them away quietly without
the public being the wiser. The piece was too profitable a
one to abandon, so he looked about anxiously to supply the
deficiency in his *corps dramatique*. For several days nothing presented itself to his thoughts, and the public were
becoming more clamorous for the repetition of a drama
which had greatly delighted them. What was to be done?
In a mood of doubt and uncertainty the wretched manager
was taking his accustomed walk upon the lighthouse pier
while a number of unfortunate country fellows, bare-legged
and lanky, with hay ropes fastening their old gray coats
around them, were standing beside a packet, about to take
their departure for England for the harvest. Their uncouth
appearance, their wild looks, their violent gestures, and,
above all, their strange and guttural language, — for they
were all speaking Irish, — attracted the attention of the
manager; the effect, to his professional eye, was good.
The thought struck him at once: here were the very fellows he wanted. It was scarcely necessary to alter anything about them; they were ready made to his hand, and
in many respects better savages than their prototypes.
Through the mediation of some whiskey, the appropriate
liquor in all treaties of this nature, a bargain was readily
struck, and in two hours more these 'forty thieves' were
rehearsing upon the classic boards of our theatre, and once
more 'La Pérouse,' in all the glory of red capital letters,

shone forth in the morning advertisements. The run of
the piece continued unabated; the Indians were the rage;
nothing else was thought or spoken of in Dublin, and
already the benefit of Ashewaballagh Ho was announced,
— who, by the by, was a little fellow from Martin's estate
in Connemara, and one of the drollest dogs I ever heard of.
Well, it so happened that it was upon one of their nights
of performing that I found myself, with Mr. Burke, a spectator of their proceedings; I had fallen into an easy slumber, when a dreadful row in the box lobby roused me from
my dream, and the loud cry of ' Turn him out! ' ' Pitch
him over! ' ' Beat his brains out! ' and other humane pro-
posals of the like nature, effectually restored me to consciousness. I rushed out of the box into the lobby, and
there, to my astonishment, in the midst of a considerable
crowd, beheld my friend Mr. Burke belaboring the box-
keeper with all his might with a cotton umbrella of rather
unpleasant proportions, accompanying each blow with an
exclamation of ' Well, are they Connaught-men now, you
rascal, eh? Are they all west of Athlone, tell me that,
now? I wonder what's preventing me beating the soul
out of ye.' After obtaining a short cessation of hostilities,
and restoring poor Sharkey to his legs, much more dead
than alive from pure fright, I learned at last the *teterrima
causa belli*. Mr. Burke, it seems, had entered into conversation with Sharkey, the box-keeper, as to all the particulars of the theatre and the present piece, but especially as
to the real and authentic history of the Indians, whose language he remarked in many respects to resemble Irish.
Poor Sharkey, whose benefit night was approaching,
thought he might secure a friend for life by imparting
to him an important state secret; and when, therefore,
pressed rather closely as to the ' savages' whereabout,'
resolved to try a bold stroke and trust his unknown inter-
rogator. ' And so you don't really know where they come
from, nor can't guess?' ' Maybe, Peru,' said Mr. Burke,
innocently. ' Try again, sir,' said Sharkey, with a knowing grin. ' Is it Behring's Straits?' said Mr. Burke.

'What do you think of Galway, sir?' said Sharkey, with a leer intended to cement a friendship for life. The words were no sooner out of his lips than Burke, who immediately took them as a piece of direct insolence to himself and his country, felled him to the earth, and was in the act of continuing the discipline when I arrived on the field of battle."

CHAPTER XXII.

"And you must really leave us so soon!" said Tom, as we issued forth into the street. "Why, I was just planning a whole week's adventure for you. Town is so full of all kinds of idle people, I think I could manage to make your time pass pleasantly enough."

"Of that," I replied, "I have little doubt; but, for the reasons I have just mentioned, it is absolutely necessary that I should not lose a moment; and after arranging a few things here, I shall start to-morrow by the earliest packet, and hasten up to London at once."

"By Jupiter," said Tom, "how lucky! I just remember something which comes admirably *à propos*. You are going to Paris, — is it not so?"

"Yes, direct to Paris."

"Nothing could be better. There is a particularly nice person, a great friend of mine, Mrs. Bingham, waiting for several days in hopes of a chaperon to take care of herself and daughter — a lovely girl, only nineteen, you wretch — to London, *en route* to the Continent; the mamma a delightful woman and a widow, with a very satisfactory jointure, — you understand, — but the daughter a regular, downright beauty and a ward in Chancery, with how many thousand pounds I am afraid to trust myself to say. You must know, then, they are the Binghams of — Upon my soul, I forget where, but highly respectable."

"I regret I have not the pleasure of their acquaintance, and the more because I shall not be able to make it now."

"As why?" said Tom, gravely.

"Because, in the first place, I am so confoundedly pressed for time that I could not possibly delay under any contingency that might arise; and your fair friends are, doubtless, not so eagerly determined upon travelling night and day till they reach Paris. Secondly, to speak candidly, with my present hopes and fears weighing upon my mind, I should not be the most agreeable travelling companion to two ladies with such pretensions as you speak of; and thirdly — ”

“ Confound your thirdly! I suppose we shall have sixteenthly, like a Presbyterian minister’s sermon, if I let you go on. Why, they ’ll not delay you one hour. Mrs. Bingham, man, cares as little for the road as yourself; and as for your *petits soins*, I suppose if you get the fair ladies through the Custom House and see them safe in a London hotel, it is all that will be required at your hands.”

“ Notwithstanding all you say, I see the downright impossibility of my taking such a charge at this moment, when my own affairs require all the little attention I can bestow, and when, were I once involved with your fair friends, it might be completely out of my power to prosecute my own plans.”

As I said this, we reached the door of a handsome-looking house in Kildare Street, upon which Tom left my arm, and informing me that he desired to drop a card, knocked loudly.

“ Is Mrs. Bingham at home? ” said he, as the servant opened the door.

“ No, sir, she ’s out in the carriage.”

“ Well, you see, Harry, your ill-luck befriends you; for I was resolved on presenting you to my friends and leaving the rest to its merits.”

“ I can safely assure you that I should not have gone upstairs,” said I. “ Little as I know of myself, there is one point of my character I have never been deceived in, — the fatal facility by which every new incident or adventure can turn me from following up my best-matured and longest-digested plans; and as I feel this weakness and cannot correct it, the next best thing I can do is to fly the causes.”

“ Upon my soul,” said Tom, “ you have become quite a

philosopher since we met. There is an old adage which says, 'No king is ever thoroughly gracious if he has not passed a year or two in dethronement;' so I believe your regular lady-killer — yourself, for instance — becomes a very quiet animal for being occasionally jilted. But now, as you have some commissions to do, pray get done with them as fast as possible, and let us meet at dinner. Where do you dine to-day?"

"Why, upon that point I am at your service completely."

"Well, then, I have got a plan which I think will suit you. You said you wished to go by Holyhead, for fear of delay; so we 'll drive down at six o'clock to Skinner's, and dine with him on board the packet at Howth. Bring your luggage with you, and it will save you a vast deal of fuss and trouble in the morning."

Nothing could be better management for me than this, so I accordingly promised acquiescence; and having appointed a rendezvous for six o'clock, bade O'Flaherty good-by, inwardly rejoicing that my plans were so far forwarded, and that I was not to be embarrassed with either Mrs. Bingham or her daughter, for whose acquaintance or society I had no peculiar ambition.

My commissions, though not very numerous, occupied the few hours which remained, and it was already a few minutes past six o'clock when I took my stand under the piazza of the Post-office to wait for O'Flaherty. I had not long to do so, for immediately after I had reached the spot he arrived in an open barouche and four posters, with three other young men to whom he severally introduced me, but whose names I have totally forgotten; I only remember that two of the party were military men then quartered in town.

When I had taken my seat, I could not help whispering to Tom that although his friend Skinner might be *bon* for a visitation for two at his dinner, yet as we were now so strong a party, it might be as well to dine at the hotel.

"Oh!" said he, "I have arranged all that; I have sent him a special messenger two hours since, and so make your mird easy, — we shall not be disappointed, nor he short-taken."

Cur drive, although a long one, passed quickly over, and before we had reached our destination I had become tolerably intimate with all the party, who were evidently picked men, selected by O'Flaherty for a pleasant evening.

We drove along the pier to the wharf where the steamer lay, and were received at once by Tom's friend with all the warm welcome and hospitality of a sailor, united with the address and polish of a very finished gentleman. As we descended the companion-ladder to the cabin, my mind became speedily divested of any fears I might have indulged in as to the want of preparation of our entertainer. The table was covered with handsome plate and cut glass, while the side-tables glittered with a magnificent dessert, and two large wine-coolers presented an array of champagne necks shining with their leaden cravats that would have tempted an anchorite.

I remember very little else of that evening than the *coup d'œil* I have mentioned. Besides, were my memory more retentive, I might scruple to trespass farther on my reader's patience by the detail of those pleasures which, like love-letters, however agreeable to the parties immediately concerned, are very unedifying to all others. I do remember, certainly, that good stories and capital songs succeeded each other with a rapidity only to be equalled by the popping of corks, and have also a very vague and indistinct recollection of a dance round the table, — evidently to finish a chorus, but which, it appears, finished me too, for I saw no more that night.

How many have commemorated the waking sensations of their fellow-men after a night's debauch! Yet at the same time, I am not aware of any one having perfectly conveyed even a passing likeness to the mingled throng of sensations which crowd one's brain on such an occasion. The doubt of what has passed, by degrees yielding to the half-consciousness of the truth; the feeling of shame inseparable, except to the habitually hard-goer, from the events thus dimly pictured; the racking headache and intense thirst, with the horror of the potation recently indulged in; the recurring sense of the fun or drollery of a story or an incident which provokes us again to laugh, despite the jarring of our brain from the shaking, — all this, and more, most men have felt; and happy are they when their waking thoughts are limited to such, at times like these. The matter becomes considerably worse when the following morning calls for some considerable exertion for which, even in your best and calmest moments, you barely find yourself equal.

It is truly unpleasant, on rubbing your eyes and opening your ears, to discover that the great bell is ringing the half-hour before your quarterly examination at college, while Locke, Lloyd, and Lucian are dancing a reel through your brain little short of madness; scarcely less agreeable is it to learn that your friend Captain Wildfire is at the door in his cab, to accompany you to the Phœnix, to stand within twelve paces of a cool gentleman who has been sitting with his arm in cold water for the last half-hour, that he may pick you out "artist-like." There are, besides these, innumerable situations in which our preparations of the night would appear as none of the wisest; but I prefer going at once to my own, which, although considerably inferior in difficulty, was not without its own *désagréments*.

When I awoke, therefore, on board the "Firefly" the morning after our dinner-party, I was perfectly unable, by any mental process within my reach, to discover where I was. On shipboard I felt I must be, — the narrow berth, the gilded and panelled cabin which met my eye through my half-open curtains, and that peculiar swelling motion inseparable from a vessel in the water, all satisfied me of this fact. I looked about me, but could see no one to give me the least idea of my position. Could it be that we were on our way out to Corfu, and that I had been ill for some time past?

But this cabin had little resemblance to a transport. Perhaps it might be a frigate, — I knew not. Then, again, were we sailing, or at anchor? for the ship was nearly motionless. At this instant a tremendous noise like thunder crashed through my head, and for a moment I expected we had exploded and would be all blown up; but an instant after, I discovered it must be the escape of the steam, and that I was on board a packet-ship. Here, then, was some clew to my situation, and one which would probably have elicited all in due season; but just at this moment a voice on deck saved me from any further calculations. Two persons were conversing, whose voices were not altogether unknown to me, but why, I knew not.

"Then, Captain, I suppose you consider this as an excellent passage?"

"Yes, of course I do," replied the captain; "it's only five hours since we left Howth, and now, you see, we are nearly in. If we have this run of the tide, we shall reach the Head before twelve o'clock."

"Ha, ha!" said I to myself; "now I begin to learn something. So we have crossed the Channel while I was sleeping, — not the least agreeable thing for a man to hear who suffers martyrdom from sea-sickness. But let me listen again."

"And that large mountain there, is that Snowdon?"

"No, you cannot see Snowdon, there is too much mist about it; that mountain is Capel Curig! And there, that bold bluff to the eastward, that is Penmaenmawr."

"Come, there is no time to be lost," thought I; so springing out of my berth, accoutred as I was, in merely trousers and slippers, with a red handkerchief fastened, nightcap fashion, round my head, I took my way through the cabin.

My first thought on getting upon my legs was, how tremendously the vessel pitched, which I had not remarked while in my berth, but now I could scarce keep myself from falling at every step. I was just about to call the steward when I again heard the voices on deck.

"You have but few passengers this trip?"

"I think only yourself and a Captain Lorrequer," replied

the captain, — "who, by the by, is losing all this fine coast, which is certainly a great pity."

"He shall not do so much longer," thought I; "for as I find that there are no other passengers, I'll make my toilet on deck, and enjoy the view besides." With this determination I ascended slowly and cautiously the companion-ladder, and stepped out upon the deck; but scarcely had I done so when a roar of the loudest laughter made me turn my head towards the poop, and there, to my horror of horrors, I beheld Tom O'Flaherty seated between two ladies, whose most vociferous mirth I soon perceived was elicited at my expense.

All the party of the preceding night were also there, and as I turned from their grinning faces to the land, I saw, to my shame and confusion, that we were still lying beside the pier at Howth; while the bandboxes, trunks, and imperials of new arrivals were incessantly pouring in, as travelling carriages kept driving up to the place of embarkation. I stood perfectly astounded and bewildered. Shame for my ridiculous costume would have made me fly at any other time; but there I remained to be laughed at patiently, while that villain O'Flaherty, leading me passively forward, introduced me to his friends: "Mrs. Bingham, Mr. Lorrequer; Mr. Lorrequer, Miss Bingham. Don't be prepossessed against him, ladies, for when not in love and properly dressed, he is a marvellously well-looking young gentleman; and as — "

What the remainder of the sentence might be, I knew not; for I rushed down into the cabin, and locking the door, never opened it till I could perceive from the stern windows that we were really off on our way to England, and recognized once more the laughing face of O'Flaherty, who, as he waved his hat to his friends from the pier, reminded them that "they were under the care and protection of his friend Lorrequer, who, he trusted, would condescend to increase his wearing apparel under the circumstances."

CHAPTER XXIII.

When I did at last venture upon deck, it was with a costume studiously accurate, and as much of manner as I could possibly muster to endeavor at once to erase the unfortunate impression of my first appearance; this, however, was not destined to be a perfectly successful manœuvre, and I was obliged, after a few minutes, to join the laugh, which I found could not be repressed, at my expense. One good result certainly followed from all this, — I became almost immediately on intimate terms with Mrs. Bingham and her daughter, and much of the awkwardness in my position as their chaperon, which, *bon gré, mal gré*, I was destined to be, was at once got over. Mrs. Bingham herself was of that style of widow which comes under the "fat, fair, and forty" category, with a never-ceasing flow of high, almost boisterous spirits, an excellent temper, good health, and a well-stocked purse. Life to her was like a game of her favorite "speculation." When she *believed* the "company honest," and *knew* her cards trumps, she was tolerably easy for the result. She liked Kingstown; she liked whist; she liked the military; she liked "the Junior Bar," of which she knew a good number; she had a well-furnished house in Kildare Street and a well-cushioned pew in St. Anne's; she was a favorite at the Castle, and Dr. Labatt "knew her constitution." Why, with all these advantages, she should ever have thought of leaving the "happy valley" of her native city, it was somewhat hard to guess. Was it that thoughts of matrimony, which the Continent held out more prospect for, had invaded the fair widow's heart? Was it that the altered condition to which politics had greatly reduced Dublin had effected this change of opinion?

Or was it like that indescribable longing for the unknown something which we read **of** in the pathetic history of the fair lady celebrated, I believe, by Petrarch? But I quote from memory, —

> " Mrs. Gill is very ill;
>   Nothing can improve her
> But to see the Tuileries
> And waddle through the Louvre."

None of these, I believe, however good and valid reasons in themselves, were the moving powers upon the present occasion; the all-sufficient one being that Mrs. Bingham had a daughter. Now, Miss Bingham was Dublin too, — but Dublin of a later edition, and a finer, more hot-pressed copy than her mamma. She had been educated at Mrs. Somebody's seminary in Mountjoy Square, had been taught to dance by Montague, and had learned French from a Swiss governess, with a number of similar advantages, — a very pretty figure, dark eyes, long eyelashes and a dimple, and last, but of course least, the deserved reputation of a large fortune. She had made a most successful *début* in the Dublin world, where she was much admired and flattered, and which soon suggested to her quick mind, as it has often done in similar cases to a young provincial *débutante*, not to waste her attractions upon the minor theatres, but at once to appear upon the "great boards," — so far evidencing a higher flight of imagination and enterprise than is usually found among the class of her early associates, who may be characterized as that school of young ladies who admire "The Corsair" and Kingstown, and say, "Ah, don't!"

She possessed much more common-sense than her mamma, and promised, under proper advantages, to become speedily quite sufficiently acquainted with the world and its habitudes. In the mean while, I perceived that she ran a very considerable risk of being carried off by some mustachioed Pole, with a name like a sneeze, who might pretend to enjoy access to the fashionable circles of the Continent.

Very little study of my two friends enabled me to see thus much, and very little "usage" sufficed to render me speedily intimate with both; the easy good-nature of the mamma, who had a very methodistical appreciation of what the "connection" call "creature comforts," amused me much, and opened one ready path to her good graces by the opportunity afforded of getting up a luncheon of veal cutlets and London porter, of which I partook, — not a little to the evident loss of the fair daughter's esteem.

While, therefore, I made the tour of the steward's cell in search of Harvey's sauce, I brushed up my memory of "The Corsair" and "Childe Harold," and alternately discussed Stilton and Southey, Shelley and lobsters, Haynes Bayley and ham.

The day happened to be particularly calm and delightful, so that we never left the deck, and the six hours which brought us from land to land quickly passed over in this manner; and ere we reached "the Head," I had become the warm friend and legal adviser of the mother; and with the daughter I was installed as chief confidant of all her griefs and sorrows, both of which appointments cost me a solemn promise to take care of them till their arrival in Paris, where they had many friends and acquaintances awaiting them. Here, then, as usual, was the fatal facility with which I gave myself up to any one who took the trouble to influence me! One thing, nevertheless, I was determined on, — to let no circumstance defer my arrival at Paris a day later than was possible; therefore, though my office as chaperon might engage me on the road, it should not interfere with the object before me. Had my mind not been so completely engaged with my own immediate prospects, when hope, suddenly and unexpectedly revived, had become so tinged with fears and doubts as to be almost torture, I must have been much amused with my present position, as I found myself seated with my two fair friends, rolling along through Wales in their comfortable travelling carriage, giving all the orders at the different hotels, seeing after the luggage, and acting *en maître* in every respect.

The good widow enjoyed particularly the difficulty which
my precise position with regard to her and her daughter
threw the different innkeepers on the road into, sometimes
supposing me to be her husband, sometimes her son, and
once her son-in-law, — which very alarming conjecture
brought a crimson tinge to the fair daughter's cheek; an
expression, which, in my ignorance, I thought looked very
like an inclination to faint in my arms.

At length we reached London; and having been there
safely installed at Mivart's, I sallied forth to present my
letter to the Horse Guards and obtain our passport for the
Continent.

"Number 9, Poland Street, sir," said the waiter, as I
inquired the address of the French consul. Having discovered that my interview with the commander-in-chief was
appointed for four o'clock, I determined to lose no time,

but make every possible arrangement for leaving London in the morning.

A cab quietly conveyed me to the door of the consul, around which stood several other vehicles of every shape and fashion, while in the doorway were to be seen numbers of people, thronging and pressing, like the opera-pit on a full night. Into the midst of this assemblage I soon thrust myself, and borne upon the current, at length reached a small back parlor filled also with people. A door opening into another small room in the front showed a similar mob there, with the addition of a small elderly man in a bag-wig and spectacles, very much begrimed with snuff, and speaking in a very choleric tone to the various applicants for passports, who, totally ignorant of French, insisted upon interlarding their demands with an occasional stray phrase, making a kind of tessellated pavement of tongues which would have shamed Babel. Nearest to the table at which the functionary sat stood a mustachioed gentleman in a blue frock and white trousers, a white hat jauntily set upon one side of his head, and primrose gloves. He cast a momentary glance of a very undervaluing import upon the crowd around him, and then, turning to the consul, said in a very soprano tone, —

"*Passe-port, monsieur!*"

"*Que voulez-vous que je fasse?*" replied the old Frenchman, gruffly.

"*Je suis — j'ai —* that is, *donnez-moi passe-port.*"

"Where do you go?" replied the consul.

"*Calai.*"

"*Comment, diable!* Speak Inglis, an' I understan' you as besser. Your name?"

"Lorraine Snaggs, *gentilhomme.*"

"What age have you, — how old?"

"Twenty-two."

"*C'est ça,*" said the old consul, flinging the passport across the table with the air of a man who thoroughly comprehended the applicant's pretension to the designation of *gentilhomme anglais.*

As I followed the worthy representative of Seven Dials with my eye, another person had neared the table. She was a rather pretty young woman, with blue eyes and brown hair braided quietly on her forehead, and wearing a plain close bonnet of a very coquettish appearance.

"Will you be seated, mamselle?" said the polite old Frenchman, who had hitherto been more like a bear than a human being. "*Où allez-vous donc?* where to, *ma chère?*"

"To Paris, sir."

"By Calais?"

"No, sir; by Boulogne."

"*C'est bon; quel âge avez-vous?* What old, *ma belle?*"

"Nineteen, sir, in June."

"And are you alone quite, eh?"

"No, sir, my little girl."

"Ah! your leetel girl — *c'est fort bien; je m'aperçois.* And your name?"

"Fanny Linwood, sir."

"*C'est fini, ma chère,* — Mademoiselle Fanny Linwood," said the old man, as he wrote down the name.

"Oh, sir, I beg your pardon, but you have put me down 'mademoiselle,' and — and — you see, sir, I have my little girl."

"*Ah! c'est égal, mamselle;* they don't mind these things in France. *Au plaisir de vous voir, adieu!*"

"'They don't mind these things in France!'" said I to myself, repeating the old consul's phrase, which I could not help feeling as a whole chapter on his nation.

My business was soon settled, for I spoke nothing but English, very little knowledge of the world teaching me that when we have any favor, however slight, to ask, it is always good policy to make the demand by propitiating the self-esteem of the granter, — if, happily, there be an opportunity for so doing.

When I returned to Mivart's, I found a written answer to my letter of the morning, stating that his lordship of the Horse Guards was leaving town that afternoon, but would

not delay my departure for the Continent, to visit which a
four months' leave was granted me, with a recommendation
to study at Weimar.

The next day brought us to Dover, in time to stroll about
the cliffs during the evening, when I again talked sentiment
with the daughter till very late. The mamma herself was
too tired to come out, so that we had our walk quite alone.
It is strange enough how quickly this travelling together
has shaken us into intimacy. Isabella says she feels as if I
were her brother, and I begin to think myself she is *not*
exactly like a sister. She has a marvellously pretty foot
and ankle.

The climbing of cliffs is a very dangerous pastime. How
true the French adage, — *C'est plus facile de glisser sur le
gazon que sur la glace.* But still nothing can come of it;
for if Lady Jane be not false, I must consider myself an
engaged man.

"Well, but I hope," said I, rousing myself from a revery
of some minutes, and inadvertently pressing the arm which
leaned upon me, "your mamma will not be alarmed at our
long absence?"

"Oh! not in the least; for she knows I'm with *you.*"

And here I felt a return of the pressure, — perhaps also
inadvertently given, but which, whether or not, effectually
set all my reasonings and calculations astray; and we returned to the hotel silent on both sides.

The appearance of "mamma" beside the hissing tea-urn
brought us both back to ourselves; and after an hour's
chatting we said "Good night," to start on the morrow for
the Continent.

CHAPTER XXIV.

CALAIS.

It was upon a lovely evening in autumn as the Dover steamboat rounded the wooden pier at Calais, amid a fleet of small boats filled with eager and anxious faces, soliciting, in every species of bad English and *patois* French, the attention and patronage of the passengers.

"*Hôtel des Bains, milor.*"

"*Hôtel d'Angleterre,*" said another, in a voice of the most imposing superiority. "*C'est superbe,* — pretty well."

"*Hôtel du Nord, votre Excellence; remise de poste* and delays [query, relays] at all hours."

"*Commissionnaire, miladi,*" sang out a small shrill treble from the midst of a crowded cock-boat, nearly swamped beneath our paddle-wheel.

What a scene of bustle, confusion, and excitement does the deck of a steamer present upon such an occasion! Every one is running hither or thither. *Sauve qui peut* is now the watchword; and friendships that promised a lifelong endurance only half an hour ago, find here a speedy dissolution. The lady who slept all night upon deck enveloped in the folds of your Astrakhan cloak scarcely deigns an acknowledgment of you as she adjusts her ringlets before the looking-glass over the stove in the cabin; the polite gentleman that would have flown for a reticule or a smelling-bottle upon the high seas, won't leave his luggage in the harbor; and the gallantry and devotion that stood the test of half a gale of wind and a wet jacket is not proof when the safety of a carpet-bag or the security of a "Mackintosh" is concerned.

And thus here, as elsewhere, is prosperity the touchstone of good feeling. All the various disguises which have been assumed *per viaggio* are here immediately abandoned, and stripped of the travelling costume of urbanity and courtesy, which they put on for the voyage, they stand forth in all the unblushing front of selfishness and self-interest.

Some tender scenes yet find their place amid the ruins of this chaotic state. Here may be seen a careful mother adjusting innumerable shawls and handkerchiefs round the throat of a sea-green young lady with a cough, — her maid, at the same instant, taking a tender farewell of the steward in the after-cabin.

Here is a very red-faced and hot individual, with punch-colored breeches and gaiters, disputing "one brandy too much" in his bill, and vowing that the company shall hear of it when he returns to England. There, a tall, elderly woman, with a Scotch-gray eye and a sharp cheek-bone, is depositing within her muff various seizable articles, that, until now, had been lying quietly in her trunk. Yonder, that raw-looking young gentleman, with the crumpled frock-coat and loose cravat and sea-sick visage, is asking every one if they think he may land without a passport. You scarcely recognize him for the cigar-smoking dandy of yesterday, that talked as if he had lived half his life on the Continent. While there, a rather pretty girl is looking intently at some object in the blue water beside the rudder post. You are surprised you cannot make it out; but then, she has the advantage of you, for the tall, well-looking man, with the knowing whiskers, is evidently whispering something in her ear.

"Steward, this is not my trunk; mine was a leather —"

"All the ' leathers ' are gone in the first boat, sir."

"Most scandalous way of doing business."

"Trouble you for two-and-sixpence, sir."

"There 's Matilda coughing again," says a thin, shrewish woman, with a kind of triumphant scowl at her better half; "but you *would* have her wear that thin shawl!"

"Whatever may be the fault of the shawl, I fancy no one will reproach her ankles for thinness," murmurs a young guardsman as he peeps up the companion-ladder.

Amid all the Babel of tongues and uproar of voices, the thorough bass of the escape steam keeps up its infernal thunders till the very brain reels; and sick as you have been of the voyage, you half wish yourself once more at sea, if only to have a moment of peace and tranquillity.

Numbers now throng the deck who have never made their appearance before. Pale, jaundiced, and crumpled, they have all the sea-sick look and haggard cheek of the real martyr, — all except one, a stout, swarthy, brown-visaged man, of about forty, with a frame of iron and a voice like the fourth string of a violoncello. You wonder why he should have taken to his bed. Learn, then, that he is his Majesty's courier from the Foreign Office, with despatches to Constantinople, and that as he is not destined to lie down in a bed for the next fourteen days, he is glad even of the narrow resemblance to one he finds in the berth of a steamboat. At length you are on shore, and marched off in a long string, like a gang of convicts, to the Bureau de l'Octroi; and here is begun an examination of the luggage which promises, from its minuteness, to last for the three months you destined to spend in Switzerland. At the end of an hour you discover that the *soi-disant commissionnaire* will transact all this affair for a few francs; and after a tiresome wait in a filthy room, jostled, elbowed, and trampled upon by boors with sabots, you adjourn to your inn and begin to feel that you are not in England.

Our little party had but few of the miseries here recounted to contend with. My *savoir faire*, with all modesty be it spoken, had been long schooled in the art and practice of travelling; and while our less-experienced fellow-travellers were deep in the novel mysteries of cotton stockings and petticoats, most ostentatiously displayed upon every table of the Bureau, we were comfortably seated in the handsome salon of the Hôtel du Nord, looking out upon a pretty grass-plot surrounded with orange-trees, and displaying in the middle a fountain about the size of a walking-stick.

"Now, Mr. Lorrequer," said Mrs. Bingham, as she seated herself by the open window, "never forget how totally dependent we are upon your kind offices. Isabella has discovered already that the French of Mountjoy Square, however intelligible in that neighborhood, and even as far as Mount Street, is Coptic and Sanscrit here; and as for myself, I intend to affect deaf-and-dumbness till I reach Paris, where I hear every one can speak English a little."

"Now, then, to begin my functions," said I, as I rang for the waiter and ran over in my mind rapidly how many invaluable hints for my new position my present trip might afford me, "always provided," as the lawyers say, that Lady Jane Callonby might feel herself tempted to become my travelling companion, in which case — But, confound it, how I am castle-building again! Meanwhile, Mrs. Bingham is looking as hungry and famished as though she would eat the waiter. "Ha! this is the *carte*."

"Now, then, to order supper."

"*Cotelettes d'agneau.*"

"*Mayonnaise de homard.*"

"*Perdreaux rouges aux truffes,* — mark that, *aux truffes.*"

"*Gelée au maraschino.*"

"And the wine, sir," said the waiter, with a look of approval at my selection. "Champagne, — no other wine, sir?"

"No," said I, "champagne only. *Frappé*, of course," I added. And the waiter departed with a bow that would have graced St. James's.

As long as our immaterial and better part shall be doomed to keep company with its fleshly tabernacle, with all its attendant miseries of gout and indigestion, how much of our enjoyment in this world is dependent upon the mere accessory circumstances by which the business of life is carried on and maintained, and to despise which is neither good policy nor sound philosophy. In this conclusion, a somewhat long experience of the life of a traveller has fully established me. And nowhere does it press more forcibly upon the mind than when first arrived in a Continental inn, after leaving the best hotels of England still fresh in your memory. I do not for a moment dispute the very great superiority in comfort of the latter, by which I would be understood to mean all those resemblances to one's own home which an English hotel so eminently possesses, and every other one so markedly wants; but I mean that in contrivances to elevate the spirit, cheer the jaded and tired wayfarer by objects which, however they may appeal to the mere senses, seem, at least, but little sensual, give me a foreign inn. Let me have a large, spacious salon, with its lofty walls and its airy, large-paned windows (I shall not object if the cornices and mouldings be gilded, because such is usually the case); let the sun and heat of a summer's day come tempered through the deep lattices of a well-fitting *jalousie* bearing upon them the rich incense of a fragrant orange-tree in blossom, and the sparkling drops of a neighboring fountain, the gentle plash of which is faintly audible amid the hum of the drone-bee; let such be the *agréments* without; while within, let the more substantial joys of the table await, in such guise as only a French *cuisine* can present them, — give me these, I say, and I shall never sigh for the far-famed and long-deplored comforts of a box in a coffee-room like a pew in a parish church, though certainly not so well cushioned, and fully as dull, with a hot waiter and a cold beefsteak; the only thing higher than your game being your bill, and the only thing less drinkable than your port being the porter.

With such exotic notions, imagine, my dear reader, whether or not I felt happy as I found myself seated between my two fair friends doing the honors of a little supper, and assisting the exhilaration of our champagne by such efforts of wit as, under favorable circumstances like these, are ever successful, and which, being like the foaming liquid which washes them down, to be swallowed without waiting, are ever esteemed good from the excitement that results, and never seriously canvassed for any more sterling merit. Nothing ever makes a man so agreeable as the belief that he is so; and certainly my fair companions appeared to have the most excellent idea of my powers in that respect; and I fancy that I made more *bons mots*, hit

off more epigrams, and invented more choice incidents on
that happy evening than, if now remembered, would suffice
to pay my tailor's bill when collated for "Bentley's Mis-
cellany," and illustrated by Cruikshank. Alas! that, like
the good liquor that seasoned them, both are gone by, and
I am left but to chronicle the memory of the fun in dulness,
and counterfeit the effervescence of the grape-juice by soda-
water. One thing, however, is certain, — we formed a most
agreeable party; and if a feeling of gloom ever momentarily
shot through my mind, it was that evenings like these came
so rarely in this work-a-day world that each such should
be looked on as our last.

If I had not already shown myself up to my reader as a
weathercock of the first water, perhaps I should now hesi-
tate about confessing that I half regretted the short space
during which it should be my privilege to act as the guide
and mentor of my two friends. The impetuous haste which
I before felt necessary to exercise in reaching Paris immediately was now tempered by prudent thoughts about travelling at night, and reflections about sun-stroke by day;
and even moments most devoted to the object of my heart's
aspirations were fettered by the very philosophic idea that
it could never detract from the pleasure of the happiness
that awaited me if I travelled on the primrose path to its
attainment. I argued thus: if Lady Jane be true, if — if,
in a word, I am destined to have any success in the Callonby family, then will a day or two more not risk it. My
present friends I shall, of course, take leave of at Paris,
where their own acquaintances await them; and, on the
other hand, should I be doomed once more to disappointment, I am equally certain I should feel no disposition to
form a new attachment. Thus did I reason, and thus I
believed; and though I was a kind of "consultation opinion" among my friends in "suits of love," I was really then
unaware that at no time is a man so prone to fall in love as
immediately after his being jilted. If common-sense will
teach us not to dance a bolero upon a sprained ankle, so
might it also convey the equally important lesson not to

expose our more vital and inflammatory organ to the fire the day after its being singed.

Reflections like these did not occur to me at this moment; besides that I was "going the pace" with a forty-horse power of agreeability that left me little time for thought, —least of all, of serious thought. So stood matters. I had just filled our tall, slender glasses with the creaming and "sparkling" source of wit and inspiration when the loud crack, crack, crack of a postilion's whip, accompanied by the shaking trot of a heavy team and the roll of wheels, announced a new arrival.

"Here they come!" said I. "Only look at them,— four horses and one postilion, all apparently straggling and straying after their own fancy, but yet going surprisingly straight, notwithstanding. See how they come through that narrow archway,— it might puzzle the best four-in-hand in England to do it better."

"What a handsome young man, if he had not those odious mustachios! Why, Mr. Lorrequer, he knows *you*, —see, he is bowing to you."

"*Me!* Oh! no. Why, surely, it must be! The devil, — it is Kilkee, Lady Jane's brother! I know his temper well. One five minutes' observation of my present intimacy with my fair friends, and adieu to all hopes for me of calling Lord Callonby my father-in-law. There is not, therefore, a moment to lose."

As these thoughts revolved through my mind, the confusion I felt had covered my face with scarlet, and with a species of blundering apology for abruptly leaving them for a moment. I ran downstairs only in time sufficient to anticipate Kilkee's questions as to the number of my apartment, to which he was desirous of proceeding at once. Our first greetings over, Kilkee questioned me as to my route, adding that his now was necessarily an undecided one, for if his family happened not to be at Paris, he should be obliged to seek after them among the German watering-places. "In any case, Lorrequer," said he, "we shall hunt them in couples. I must insist upon your coming along with me."

"Oh! that," said I, "you must not think of. Your carriage is a *coupé*, and I cannot think of crowding you."

"Why, you don't seriously wish to affront me, I hope; for I flatter myself that a more perfect carriage for two people cannot be built. Hobson made it on a plan of my own, and I am exceedingly proud of it, I assure you. Come, — that matter is decided; now for supper. Are there many English here just now? By the by, the ladies I think I saw you standing with on the balcony, who are they?"

"Oh! the ladies; oh! yes, people I came over with —"

"One was pretty, I fancied. Have you supped? Just order something, will you; meanwhile, I shall write a few lines before the post leaves." Saying which, he dashed upstairs after the waiter, and left me to my meditations.

"This begins to be pleasant," thought I, as the door closed, leaving me alone in the salon. In circumstances of such moment I had never felt so nonplussed as now. How to decline Kilkee's invitation, without discovering my intimacy with the Binghams, — and yet I could not, by any possibility, desert them thus abruptly. Such was the dilemma. "I see but one thing for it," said I, gloomily, as I strode through the coffee-room with my head sunk and my hands behind my back; "I see but one thing left, — I must be taken ill to-night, and not be able to leave my bed in the morning: a fever, — a contagious fever; blue and red spots all over me; and be raving wildly before breakfast-time; and if ever any discovery takes place of my intimacy above stairs, I must only establish it as a premonitory symptom of insanity, which seized me in the packet. And now for a doctor that will understand my case and listen to reason, as they would call it in Ireland." With this idea uppermost, I walked out into the court-yard to look for a *commissionnaire* to guide me in my search. Around on every side of me stood the various carriages and vehicles of the hotel and its inmates, to the full as distinctive and peculiar in character as their owners. "Ah! there is Kilkee's," said I, as my eye lighted upon the well-balanced and elegant little carriage which he had been only with justice encomiumizing. "It is certainly perfect; and yet I 'd give a handful of louis d'or if it was like that venerable cabriolet yonder, with the one wheel and no shafts. But, alas! those springs give little hope of a break-down, and that confounded axle will outlive the patentee. But still, can nothing be done, eh? Come, the thought is a good one. I say, *garçon*, who greases the wheels of the carriages here?"

"*C'est moi, monsieur*," said a great oaf in wooden shoes and a blouse.

"Well, then, do you understand these?" said I, touching the patent axle-boxes with my cane.

He shook his head.

"Then who does here?"

"Ah! Michel understands them perfectly."

"Then bring him here," said I.

In a few minutes a little, shrewd old fellow, with a smith's apron, made his appearance and introduced himself as M. Michel. I had not much difficulty in making him master of my plan, which was to detach one of the wheels, as if for the purpose of oiling the axle, and afterwards render it incapable of being replaced, — at least for twenty-four hours.

"This is my idea," said I; "nevertheless, do not be influenced by me. All I ask is, disable the carriage from proceeding to-morrow, and here are three louis d'or at your service."

"*Soyez bien tranquille, monsieur;* milor shall spend to-morrow in Calais if I know anything of my art." Saying which, he set out in search of his tools, while I returned to the salon with my mind relieved, and fully prepared to press the urgency of my reaching Paris without any delay.

"Well, Lorrequer, said Kilkee, as I entered, "here is supper waiting, and I am as hungry as a wolf."

"Oh! I beg pardon, I 've been getting everything in readiness for our start to-morrow morning; for I have not told you how anxious I am to get to Paris before the 8th, — some family business which requires my looking after, compelling me to do so."

"As to that, let your mind be at rest, for I shall travel to-morrow night if you prefer it. Now for the *Volnay*. Why, you are not drinking your wine. What do you say to our paying our respects to the fair ladies above stairs? I am sure the attentions you have practised coming over would permit the liberty."

"Oh. hang it, no! There's neither of them pretty, and I should rather avoid the risk of making a regular acquaintance with them," said I.

"As you like, then; only as you'll not take any wine, let us have a stroll through the town."

After a short ramble through the town, in which Kilkee talked the entire time, but of what I know not, my thoughts being upon my own immediate concerns, we returned to the hotel. As we entered the *porte-cochère* my friend Michel passed me, and as he took off his hat in salutation, gave me one rapid glance of his knowing eye that completely satisfied me that Hobson's pride in my friend's carriage had by that time received quite sufficient provocation to throw him into an apoplexy.

"By the by," said I, "let us see your carriage. I am curious to look at it," and so I was.

"Well, then, come along this way; they have placed it under some of these sheds, which they think coach-houses."

I followed my friend through the court till we arrived near the fatal spot; but before reaching it he caught a glimpse of the mischief, and shouted out a most awful imprecation upon the author of the deed which met his eye. The fore-wheel of the *coupé* had been taken from the axle, and in the difficulty of so doing, from the excellence of the workmanship, two of the spokes were broken, the patent box was a mass of rent metal, and the end of the axle turned downwards like a hoe.

I cannot convey any idea of poor Kilkee's distraction, — and, in reality, my own was little short of it; for the wretch had so far outstripped my orders that I became horrified at the cruel destruction before me. We both, therefore, stormed in the most imposing English and French, first separately, and then together. We offered a reward for the apprehension of the culprit, whom no one appeared to know, — although, as it happened, every one in a large household was aware of the transaction but the proprietor himself. We abused all, innkeeper, waiters, ostlers, and chambermaids, collectively and individually, condemned Calais as a den of iniquity, and branded all Frenchmen as rogues and vagabonds. This seemed to alleviate considerably my friend's grief and excite my thirst, — fortunately, perhaps, for us; for if our eloquence had held out much longer, I am afraid our auditory might have lost their patience, — and, indeed, I am quite certain, if our French had not been in nearly as disjointed a condition as the spokes of the *calèche*, such must have been the case.

"Well, Lorrequer, I suppose, then, we are not destined to be fellow-travellers; for if you must go to-morrow — "

"Alas! it is imperative," said I.

"Then, in any case, let us arrange where we shall meet, for I hope to be in Paris the day after you."

"I'll stop at Meurice's."

"Meurice's be it," said he; "so now good-night till we meet in Paris."

END OF VOL. I.